WHEN HARRY HIT HOLLYWOOD

Mara Goodman-Davies

SOURCEBOOKS LANDMARK™
AN IMPRINT OF SOURCEBOOKS, INC.®
NAPERVILLE, ILLINOIS

Published by Sourcebooks Landmark, an imprint of Sourcebooks, Inc.
P.O. Box 4410, Naperville, Illinois 60567-4410
(630) 961-3900
Fax: (630) 961-2168
www.sourcebooks.com

Library of Congress Cataloging-in-Publication Data

Goodman-Davies, Mara.
  When Harry hit Hollywood / Mara Goodman-Davies.
    p. cm.
  ISBN-13: 978-1-4022-0642-9
  ISBN-10: 1-4022-0642-9
  1. Celebrities--Fiction. 2. Marriages of celebrities--Fiction. 3.
Hollywood (Los Angeles, Calif.)--Fiction. I. Title.

PS3607.O59225W46 2005
813'.6--dc22

Printed and bound in the United States of America.
VP 10 9 8 7 6 5 4 3 2 1

This book is dedicated to Lisa Applebaum Haddad for being a fabulous friend and having a wonderful sense of humor.

This book is also once again dedicated to Gareth Esersky for her constant support and friendship.

chapter one

O h my God, I feel like I've been waiting forever just to see you," Jessica whispered to the blond, Adonis-like young man standing in the massive doorway of her father's East Hampton beachfront mansion. "Thank goodness, you're finally here. I wish you had come to the back door. I didn't want anyone to catch us together." Dusk was just beginning to fall and the rays from the setting sun formed a radiant glow around the young man's stunning physique. "You better come inside before anyone sees you," Jessica muttered under her breath as she quickly ushered him into the grand marble foyer.

"Sssshhh... Follow me," she said, taking the man's hand and guiding him up the elegant, winding staircase, then down the long hallway to her bedroom. They tiptoed carefully, hoping to sneak by the upstairs maid, Jessica's father (who was dozing off with a newspaper in the den), and her new European stepmother (who usually took tea outside on the veranda overlooking the ocean).

When they reached her room, Jessica quietly shut the big oak door behind them and let out a huge sigh of relief. "I don't think anyone saw us," she said as he handed her his

Ralph Lauren white linen blazer, which she promptly hung up in her professionally organized walk-in cedar closet. Jessica hopped up on her big four-poster canopy bed, adjusted her twelve goose-down pillows, sat back, and attempted to get comfortable. She was wearing nothing more than a pink silk La Perla robe with a lacy cream Victoria's Secret nightie underneath. Even at the age of thirty-three, Jessica Ackerman, a beautiful artist who spent most days playing with watercolors in father's garden, unknowingly embodied the ultimate "naughty but nice" girl fantasy, with her baby-doll peaches-and-cream complexion sporting a few new freckles from the East Hampton Indian summer sun, and her auburn cherub curls. The comely, yet very naive Miss Ackerman, who would become Mrs. Harry Raider in just one week, had no idea of the magic spell her unspoiled innocence held over the opposite sex. Nor was she aware of the light, youthful aura she still possessed in spirit as well as appearance. Hence the need for today's secret visitor, a mysterious wizard whose mission for the afternoon was to make Jessica feel young and hot again.

As the young man reached into his hunter green Hermès briefcase and unpacked the various accoutrements that would aid him in making Jessica feel reborn, she couldn't help but admire his perfectly sculpted muscular arms. She wiggled her legs around a little bit to try to hide her apprehensive excitement. Somehow, she always found herself getting sexually excited when she was anxious.

"May I join you?" the young man asked, eyeing the side of the big bed.

"Why not? We might as well get started," Jessica murmured, trying not to let on exactly how scared of this whole thing she really was.

He leaned over and sweetly took her small delicate face in his large hands. "I'm sorry, darling, that I've been so hard to get a hold of. It's just that time of year, you know. Too many people want a piece of me," he said, as he softly ran his fingers around her almond-shaped eyes, perfectly pointy nose, and rosebud lips.

"I know exactly what you mean," Jessica exhaled, twirling her fingers around the soft belt of her robe. "Getting ready for this wedding is making me absolutely insane. Chas has had me running around for months interviewing a million different dress designers, dragging me to flower shows across the country, making me listen to CDs from about five hundred bands, and feeding me endless amounts of wedding cake." Jessica sat up, her big green eyes meeting the young man's sympathetic glance as she moved closer to him. "Who the hell can tell the difference between lemon meringue and lemon chiffon? And who really cares? At this point I'd be just as happy to have a big Twinkie with a candle in the middle of it. I'm mean, it's supposed to be one of the happiest occasions of my life and sometimes I feel like I am just about to explode."

"Sounds rough, sweetie," he said, leaning her back in the bed. "But it's not just any wedding is it? After all, Miss Jessica Ackerman has finally tamed Harry Raider, Beverly Hills' billionaire playboy of the century. That's quite an accomplishment, my dear. I'm sure that many women on both coasts have tried unsuccessfully to pull off such a feat, but only you did it. You should be quite proud of yourself," the young man chuckled. He then tied his wild hair back into a ponytail with a leather barrette he had placed on the nightstand along with the other devilish devices he had previously pulled from his Hermès bag of tricks.

"I wasn't trying to do anything. I just followed my heart," Jessica insisted as she studied her lavender-painted toes. "But somehow, what's supposed to be a celebration of true love has turned into a national event. I just didn't think it would be like this. That's why I'm so glad to be able to finally see you. I'm running myself ragged and I think only someone like you can make me feel relaxed and refreshed again," Jessica said meekly.

"Aw, that's sweet of you to say. But you know, I can only offer you a temporary fix," the young man said, slightly leaning away from Jessica.

"Yes, I know that. Don't worry, I won't get addicted to you," Jessica blushed while letting out a girlish giggle. "Besides, Chas Greer said I shouldn't feel guilty—everybody needs a little something extra from time to time."

"Chas Greer?" he shouted, jumping up. "Chas Greer, personal shopper and style Svengali to all of the Hamptons and Manhattan, knows you're seeing me?" the young man said, quite startled. "My God, he is the biggest gossip queen in town. I thought you didn't want anyone to know. I thought this was our little secret," the young man continued.

"Relax, Chas won't say anything. He's planning my wedding and he is making too much money off the kick-backs to do anything to upset me. Last week, when we were having lunch in my garden, a check for a hundred thousand dollars fell out of his wallet. It was from an event planner at the Pierre Hotel in Manhattan, where I'm having my reception. He tried to pick it up before I could see it, but Cindy, my poodle, grabbed it in her mouth and ran off with it. Chas almost had a heart attack. He was dying of humiliation. Listen, we both know he has to make a living, but let's just say he wouldn't dare step out of line and embarrass me any further," Jessica said reassuringly, patting the young man on the back, as he sat back down on the bed next to her.

"Oh, yes, I know that, but I had no idea that he made this introduction. Maybe he was trying to be discreet for once in his catty life. He has sent me a lot of women in the past, but nobody like you, Jessica. You are one of the most naturally beautiful girls who has ever come my way," the young man said genuinely, moving even closer to Jessica.

"That says a lot, because I know there have been many others before me. But even so, I just knew you'd make me feel special. As long as Harry doesn't find out, I guess I'm okay with this," Jessica said, bravely taking a deep breath.

She was absolutely terrified, but at this point there was no turning back. She was at the stranger's mercy. "Just try to relax and enjoy it, baby... remember, it's supposed to be fun."

"YEEEEEOOOOOW!" Jessica screamed. She was suddenly overcome by a stinging, burning sensation where the young man had stuck a hypodermic needle into the unsuspecting virgin skin between her eyebrows. At that moment, in her final preparation to become the next Mrs. Harry Raider, Beverly Hills wife extraordinaire, Jessica Ackerman had received her first shot of Botox.

Rumor had it that Dr. Mark's "fountain of youth" in a syringe was not the normal FDA-approved stuff that most doctors were using to erase any sign of inconvenient, untimely "maturing" in the salons of Madison Avenue and the billionaire beaches of East Hampton. Apparently, Dr. Mark had tapped into a ring of black-market Botox shots that contained other unidentified and illegal materials designed to amplify its anti-aging effects. Everybody who was anybody in New York high society knew that a session with Dr. Mark, often costing five thousand dollars and upwards, could rejuvenate even the most "seasoned" dowager and make her look like she was ready for the prom. So of course when it was the future Mrs. Harry Raider's turn to step into the public eye on her wedding day, Dr. Mark was summoned to work his magic.

The good doctor continued to stick Jessica in the other areas of her face that displayed tiny laugh lines, hints of crow's-feet, and any other signs of premature aging. Any flaws on what would be one of the most-photographed faces in the high-society papers and gossip columns around the world had to be eradicated before the big day.

Even though Jessica still had youth and beauty on her side, Chas Greer had convinced her that no paparazzo's flashbulb should be allowed to shoot between the lines, so to speak. Unlike the rest of Chas's Hampton-Manhattan coterie of fabulous women, who viewed Botox shots like taking their Rolls Royces in for a tune-up, Jessica Ackerman would never have thought to have a form of poisonous botulism injected into her face just to shave off a few extra years. Unlike everyone else in the world she lived in, she didn't feel the need to do anything to her appearance.

But as sweet as she was, Jessica Ackerman was not a stupid girl. She knew that a wedding of someone as high-profile as Harry Raider was a "social Super Bowl" for the media from New York to LA, and she was the star quarterback. All eyes would be on her performance that momentous evening at New York's Pierre Hotel. Bookies from coast to coast were placing their bets on Jessica's big day. Would she sweep the dance floor with grace or fumble over Harry's shoes? There were plenty of jealous social climbers who would love nothing better than to see Jessica take a dive and fall flat on her face.

But the catty high-society women were the least of Jessica's concerns. She had ignored them all of her life and was good at it by now. The real problem was Harry's deviant Hollywood gang. After the wedding, Jessica and Harry would be moving back to LA, Harry's old stomping ground. Jessica was terrified that living back in his familiar surroundings, engulfed by a crew of wild party boys, would be a recipe for disaster for her newly sober husband.

So even though it was not her nature to care what other people thought of her, this time Jessica wanted to put on a good show. She felt it was her duty to all the people who were counting on her. So when Chas Greer suggested a little pre-game pick-me-up with Dr. Mark, much to his delighted surprise, she did not object.

★★★

"There we go, baby. All finished. Now that wasn't all that bad, was it, sweetie?" Dr. Mark asked as he got up and started to repack his goody bag.

"No, I guess not," Jessica said, still leaning back on her mountain of big poofy pillows. She did feel a slight burning sensation and was slightly short of breath, but she guessed that the stinging was par for the course. The lack of air was probably nothing more than a mild panic attack, or a release of nervous energy.

"Now don't lie too far backwards, or it could drip into those gorgeous green eyes, and we don't want that to happen, do we, sexy girl?" Dr. Mark shamelessly flirted, without even turning around to check on his patient as he searched the closet for his Polo jacket.

"Okay...no problem," Jessica replied, trying to still herself on the bed in an attempt to relax and resume normal breathing. "Is that it? What do I do now?" Jessica asked. She didn't like the fact that Dr. Mark seemed to be in a rush to get to his next appointment.

"Not much, baby. Just chill out for a while. In an hour or two you can return to your normal daily routine, but no gym today and swimming is probably not a great idea. Why not take a bath and watch a little *Oprah After the Show?* I think she has the Hilton sisters and their mother on today,"

Dr. Mark said with the utmost sincerity in his voice.

It thoroughly amazed Jessica that Dr. Mark, just like the personal trainers, masseuses, chefs, hairdressers, and shrinks in the Hamptons, made a strict habit of keeping himself up on the happenings of the hip and trendy. She had half a mind to be insulted, but then relaxed, knowing that Dr. Mark was just trying to appear as if he knew what was going on in what he thought was her world.

Jessica sat up and immediately wanted to see the results. Dazed and confused, she felt as though she must be looking at herself in a distorted funhouse mirror. Soon Jessica realized that the mirror hadn't been changed. The red, swollen, blown up, freaky-looking face actually belonged to her!

"HOLY SHIT, WHAT'S HAPPENING TO ME?" Her forehead seemed unnaturally smooth, yet swollen at the same time. It almost looked like her brows were pushing downward, seeking her eyes. The areas around her nose and mouth were also seriously red and ballooned-up.

"Relax, baby, it's only a little redness and swelling," the doctor laughed. "It's totally to be expected, especially since you are a virgin." He headed for her bedroom door.

"Are you sure I'll be okay?" Jessica touched her face in disbelief and tried to navigate around its freaky, blown-up "newness" with her tiny fingers. "Is my face going to go back to normal? Am I really going to look *good* after this?"

"You're going to look fantastic, kiddo, I promise. What's the matter? Don't you trust Dr. Mark?"

"Of course I trust you. It's just that...I don't...feel so good," Jessica stuttered. She was finding it harder and harder to breathe. *Maybe I just need a little fresh air*, she thought to herself, standing up and stepping her dainty feet into a pair of Stubbs and Wooten house slippers.

"Would you like to join me for a snack or something out by the beach?" Jessica asked the impatient doctor. He glared at her like she had already taken too much of his precious time. Originally she wanted him to come and go unnoticed by anyone else in the Ackerman household, but now she was so afraid of looking like Frankenstein that she wanted the doctor to stay a while. She wanted reassurance that her face would deflate to normal proportions before Harry got back from his bachelor's weekend at his family's estate in Acapulco.

"No thanks, sweetie, I gotta get going. I have three more appointments before driving back to the city for a black-tie dinner. I really have to disappear," Dr. Mark said, swirling his jacket around his shoulders like a magician's cloak.

"Okay, well then I will just see you out," Jessica said, following behind Dr. Mark, who had already bolted from her room and was making his way back down the long, winding staircase.

As she struggled to keep up with the Prada-footed sprinter in front of her, Jessica began to feel woozy and lightheaded. She tried to focus on the back of Dr. Mark's head, and the ponytail that swung back and forth like a pendulum. Now it was becoming one big blond blur. She could see her body moving as she took step by step, but no longer felt her legs. She wanted to scream for help, but couldn't find her voice. As she fell, she reached up and yanked the doctor's hair so hard that he let out a shrill shriek of painful surprise. Dr. Mark's scream was the last sound Jessica heard for a long time.

chapter two

The September sun peered its way through the window of Jessica's private room at Greater Hampton Hospital. She had been in and out of a coma since her date with Dr. Mark four days ago. It was now just three days before her wedding, and no one knew for sure if she would make it to the prestigious Temple Emanu El on Fifth Avenue in time to become Mrs. Harry Raider. Lucky for Jessica, the severe, life-threatening allergic reaction she suffered was finally dissipating. It was now about midday, but to a groggy Jessica it felt like early morning. She was fully conscious for the first time since the ambulance had rushed her to the emergency room.

Jessica looked around her to find her disheveled fiancé asleep and snoring loudly. He was crunched up uncomfortably in a hospital chair and his latest high-tech camera was dangling around his neck. Although she just becoming fully alert, she couldn't help but notice that Harry, a funny, elf-like creature with big frizzy hair and a "forever young" aura about him, was wearing bathing trunks, flip-flops, and a Hawaiian shirt. He certainly didn't look like the tightly wound, obsessively groomed boys she had grown up with in New York. Perhaps this is why she loved him so much. As she looked at him more closely, she could tell that the particles of sand between his unevenly tanned toes were too white and powdery to be from a local Hamptons beach.

Funny the little things you notice about the one you love, Jessica thought to herself.

I wonder why he didn't wash his feet and change clothes before coming home from Acapulco, her fuzzy mind drifted.

It slowly began to dawn on her that she wasn't in her own bed. At once she felt the wires and tubes and took a big whiff of the sterile hospital smell. *What the hell happened?* Jessica wondered.

Oh fuck, the wedding! Did I miss it? Oh my God, I've got to get out of here! Jessica's mind flooded with the most dreadful thoughts all at once. Was she a no-show on the biggest day of her life? Did she embarrass herself, her friends, and her family? Most important, did she devastate Harry? The fact that he was still snoring away at the foot of her hospital bed had to be a good sign, she thought.

Although the sight Harry was somewhat of a comfort, Jessica felt a pressing need to get out immediately. Experiencing a rush of energy, she shot up in bed and tried to tear free from all of the hospital gadgets she was attached to.

Before she could do any damage, Harry snapped awake. "Hey, hey, hold on now, sweetheart, you're not going anywhere," Harry said, climbing onto the hospital bed, putting his arms lovingly around her.

"Great to see you babe. Shit, I thought we almost lost you." Harry spoke loudly, with the enthusiasm of a little boy whose parents had left him with Grandma too long. "You had some kind of funky reaction to that weird shit Doctor Dickhead put into that gorgeous face of yours. Thank heavens your dad called an ambulance and got you to the hospital on time. You know, that moronic medic ran out of the house and took off before help arrived. I'm so glad you made it, baby. I would have missed you so much!" He hugged her fiercely and planted a wet kiss on her parched lips. Jessica listlessly put her arms around her husband, in an effort to return his affections, but she was still too groggy to match his gusto.

"Hey, before you get up, let's get a picture. When the doctors assured me that you were gonna be okay, I told them I wanted to be right here when you woke up so I could catch the whole thing on camera." Ever since he was a kid, Harry had loved taking pictures. He was obsessed with capturing all of life's little moments on film. Perhaps if he had been born into different circumstances, Harry would have been a famous photographer. However, as a rich man's son, Harry never had any motivation to have his passion turn into anything more than a hobby.

"Harry, really, I..." Jessica protested, thinking to herself that this was not her most photogenic moment. She was also so embarrassed that he knew about the Botox, she just wished they could leave the hospital and forget the whole incident. She could explain why she did it in the first place to Harry later when things calmed down, but right now Jessica just wanted to go home quietly.

"Smile honey, say shiiiiiiiiiiiit," Harry said cheerfully as he shot a few fast pictures of Jessica sitting in her hospital gown surrounded by bouquets of "Get Well" flowers, cards, obnoxious Mylar balloons, and teddy bears. Looking around the room, Jessica realized that it was practically wall-to-wall with floral arrangements. *My God, who knows I'm here? Who else knows what I did?* Jessica wondered to herself, as Harry hit the timer on the camera, threw his arms around her, smiled his famous shit-eating grin, and stuck his head right up next to hers for a couples' shot.

Jessica felt a wave of guilt, even though she somewhat enjoyed being welcomed back to life by a playful Harry. "I'm so glad this is all over. I was really scared, babe, with the wedding coming up and everything," Harry whispered in Jessica's ear.

"So, I didn't miss the wedding then," Jessica sighed with relief.

"No way, babe, we still have three days left before I become Mr. Jessica. Don't worry, if you couldn't have come to the Pierre, I would have dragged the rabbi right here to this room. There was no way I wasn't going to marry you. I love you, Jes." Wiping a tear from his devilish eyes, Harry kissed Jessica and tenderly held her close. Nuzzling the man she loved the most, Jessica noticed that he smelled like cocoa butter instead of his customary cologne.

As Jessica realized that she had been passed out for four days, she could tell by Harry's overly energetic demeanor that he arrived the hospital much later than he should have. Jessica interpreted Harry's extreme exuberance as a sign of good old-fashioned Jewish guilt. Something definitely wasn't kosher here and she wanted to know exactly what had gone on. "How long have I been here, Harry?" Jessica asked him point blank.

"Uhm...about four days I think," Harry said, stuttering and lowering his head in shame.

"Harry, what the hell happened in Acapulco? Why didn't you get here sooner? I could have died and you were miles away!" a furious Jessica yelled, pushing him away.

"Honestly, I swear it was not my fault. I had to stay down there because of Chas."

"Chas?" Jessica proclaimed, a little bit confused. "What does he have to do with you coming home to be with me?" Jessica asked, trying to control her anger.

"Everything. When your dad called down to our villa to

tell me what happened, I was out with a bunch of buddies who flew down from LA for my bachelor's weekend. Anyway, Chas answered the phone and convinced your father and my parents that it was better for me to stay away from the hospital until you were ready to go home. I think that they were afraid the whole thing would freak me out and I'd want to call off the wedding," Harry said. Jessica could tell by Harry's soft tone of voice that he was hurt and frustrated that her father, his parents, and Chas had thought so little of his character.

"That's ridiculous," Jessica exclaimed, patting Harry's head, mothering him even though she had just survived a near-fatal medical emergency.

Good thinking, my man Chas. Nice save, Jessica thought secretly. Even though Jessica loved Harry deeply and she knew that he loved her, she couldn't totally disregard the person he had been for most of his life. Before meeting her, Harry didn't know the meaning of the words "commitment" or "responsibility." Jessica was secretly afraid that he would bolt if he was faced with a crisis he couldn't deal with. Jessica also thought that expecting him to handle "too much too soon" could send Harry back over the edge. There was always the fear that he would resort to drugs or booze when the going got tough. So Jessica believed the best thing to do was to ease Harry into mature adulthood and keep him out of harm's way. At least in the beginning of their life together.

"Anyway, when your dad called yesterday and said that you had turned the corner, Chas and my parents came down to the beach where I was hanging out and told me what happened. I was so furious I didn't say a word to anyone. I just went straight to the airport, got on our private plane, and flew straight to Westhampton Beach airport. I will never forgive them, Jessica, for keeping me away from you like that. I know I've been a total fuck-up in the past, but you're gonna be my wife now and things with me are gonna be different," Harry said, once again kissing Jessica sweetly.

"It's nice to know I have a husband I can depend on, Harry. That's a good feeling, especially when I haven't been so perfect myself either," Jessica said, catching a glimpse of herself in the bedside mirror. There were still some signs of what she had done, but over all she was relieved to see that her face had shrunk considerably, back to where she could recognize her old pre-Botox self.

Harry cuddled closer to Jessica. His fingers soon found their way under her hospital gown and he started playing with her breasts.

"Harry, what are you doing?" Jessica blushed. "I don't think you should be doing that in a hospital. It's a public place, you know," Jessica said, removing Harry's hand while fighting back a fit of giggles.

"We've got a private room, babe," Harry insisted as his hands went under her gown again.

"Harry, please, enough!" Jessica objected, only half-heartedly.

"Oh, c'mon, baby, we've done it in much wilder places than this. Remember last summer when we did it under the table in your garden when your ex-husband and your dad were watching TV just inside the house?" Harry said, seductively kissing Jessica's neck and furtively working his way down towards her bosom.

"That was different, Harry," Jessica replied, unable to resist her fiancé's unbridled passion.

"That was so ballsy of you, babe. What about Penny Marks's pool party? Remember how I made you come on the beach chair in front of all of those people? That Hamptons crowd was so caught up in their own agenda for the evening, they didn't even see you creaming on the plastic," Harry said. His breathing was getting heavier as he looked seductively at Jessica.

"That night was exciting," Jessica said, licking her lips and tickling the curly chest hairs just under his neck.

Getting excited by Jessica's touch, Harry unbuttoned his tacky shirt and loosened his still-damp shorts. "So glad I held it together for you. It totally intensifies the pleasure," Harry gushed.

"What do you mean 'held it together for me'?" Jessica blurted out, pushing Harry's hand away. In the heat of the moment, Jessica didn't like what she was hearing from Harry.

"I mean, I'm so glad that I was good in Acapulco," Harry said, having such a good time that he didn't give much thought to what he had just said to his future wife.

"Why wouldn't you have been 'good'?" Jessica said, pushing Harry off her, losing the lusty mood she had just enjoyed with him.

"What? What did I do? I didn't do anything bad down there, I swear!" Harry said, upset and confused. He thought he was doing the right thing by telling Jessica that he was on good behavior during his stag weekend. Harry jumped up off of the bed and began pacing around the room, shrugging his shoulders and neurotically waving his hands up in the air.

"Were you tempted to do something, Harry? I mean, did you even think about cheating on me while you were in Mexico?" Jessica looked him straight in the eye.

"NO! Of course not!" Harry swore, crossing himself up and down.

"Harry, you're Jewish," Jessica reminded him. "You don't have to cross yourself. All right, I believe you. It just sounded like you had to pass up some big temptation for my sake, that's all."

"No, Jessica, it wasn't for you, it was for me," Harry said, digging himself a grave that nobody in that hospital could prevent him from falling into.

"What are you talking about, Harry?" Jessica asked, getting annoyed.

"When my buddies came down from Hollywood, they had this whole wild weekend planned for me—strippers, hookers, skinny-dipping in the ocean. You know, the whole regular stag-party deal," Harry said nonchalantly, as if Jessica was supposed to think this was completely normal and par for the course.

"Anyway, after we left the titty bar, I told my friends that I wasn't interested in sleeping with anyone anymore but my Jessica. So I got in the limo and went home, and they partied the night away."

"You went to a titty bar in Acapulco!" Jessica shouted. "Harry, how could you?" She pushed him off the bed.

"Hey, chill out, babe. I just told you I didn't do a thing. I just watched the show, that's all. And let me tell you something, none of those señoritas had anything on my girl," Harry boasted, hopping back into Jessica's hospital bed and going for her gown again, trying to cop a feel.

Jessica grabbed his hands and looked straight into his eyes. "Were there drugs there, Harry?"

"I'm really sorry about this whole mess. I know how badly you must be freaking out right now. Of course, my buds had some grade-A stuff. These guys always get the best blow and some other trippy treats, but not to worry, I didn't touch a thing. I don't do that anymore. I didn't even have a margarita on the beach. I just wanted to stay clean." Harry was very proud of himself.

"Well, that's good to hear," Jessica said, relieved. Her fiancé had his arms around her and she was once again beginning to feel safe in his embrace.

"Harry, let me ask you something."

"Ask me anything you want, babe. I told you, Saint Harry has a new halo. I got nothing to hide," Harry said, tickling the inside of Jessica's ear, hoping to excite her again. He was one determined man.

"Harry, what are we going to do with these buds of yours when we move to Beverly Hills? They don't sound like the type of people we should be hanging around with."

Harry began tickling Jessica's arm, hoping to distract her, set her mind at ease, and get her in the mood for in having sex.

"Now, wait a minute, honey. These guys may be no angels, but I go way back with them. They're not total dirt-bags, you know. Mike 'My Do' Roman is a pretty awesome race car driver. Todd 'The Kranks' Krane is a chef at the hottest restaurant in town, and Donny Mayberry, 'Time Maaaaaaaay,' is a major finance guy! His company works with all of the big studios. My buddy Bill Ladd is the only hetero makeup artist in Hollywood. At least we think he's straight. Rumor has it Bill is a part-time butt pirate because he wears a little blue eyeliner, mascara, and women's panties from Frederick's of Hollywood. But only when he goes out clubbing. He may be kind of bisexual, though he never hit on any of us. Bill's very popular with the all the actresses too, kind of like Warren Beatty's character in the flick *Shampoo*, only he's into lipstick, not liplocks." Harry grinned mischievously. Unfortunately, Jessica could tell he was really fond of his lifelong brotherhood, a motley crew consisting of a public defecator, a drug dealer, a drunk, and a cross-dresser.

Talking about his friends made Harry grin from ear to ear. Unable to hide her disgust, Jessica slid away from him and started to sink under the hospital bed sheets. She was beginning to reckon that all this and probably much more was eagerly awaiting her and Harry's arrival in his home-town, the hellacious hills of Hollywood. "What about Chas? Isn't he a longtime friend of yours too?" Jessica asked Harry hopelessly. She never thought she would see the day when the devious Chas Greer would seem like a healthy alternative for Harry.

Chas and Harry also went way back and were old child-hood friends. There was real history there and they shared a deep bond, even though neither one of them liked to admit it. They both grew up in Beverly Hills, but had vastly different experiences. Harry was a billionaire's son, while poor Chas was the result of a marriage between the Jewish hostess and the Swedish tennis pro at Pine Valley, LA's toni-est country club. While all the other rich Beverly Hills brats would torture young Chas as he worked for his father as ball boy, Harry often came to his defense and took him under his wing. Even as cynical and jaded as Chas had become today, surely he couldn't forget the years of Harry's kindness. And Harry, Jessica knew, wasn't the type to turn his back on an old friend. Suddenly silent, Jessica's mind started zeroing in on her future.

Chas needs my marriage to Harry to work out almost as much as I do. Not only has he made a fortune planning my wedding, now he stands to make even bigger bucks as my "go-to-for-everything guy." Once I move to Beverly Hills, I will call Chas to ask him to use his LA connections to help set up my house in LA. Too bad I can't move Chas back to LA with us to keep Harry out of trouble. I wonder how much I'd have to pay him to drop his business in New York and be with me full-time. It would be a fortune, but it would be well worth it!

She might be willing to go all out and do the "Hollywood wife thing" if she could count on Chas's "people" to not only set her up but to be Harry's unofficial watch dogs and secret minders, too. Harry started talking again.

"Chas is usually okay. I wouldn't have let him come with us to Acapulco if I didn't think he was cool, but I'm way pissed at him for not telling me about what happened to you. Besides, we're moving back to LA, honey, and I need my buddies there. Chas is staying in New York." Harry smiled. Little did he know that Chas had been paid dearly out of Jessica's wallet to be an undercover chaperone for the extent of the bachelor party. She felt bad about it—it went against her trusting nature to pay someone like Chas to spy on her beloved Harry. But the relationship was still new, and every once in a while her insecurities took over.

How ironic is it that I wound up in the hospital and Harry behaved himself in Acapulco while being surrounded by his hooligans? Jessica thought to herself. Still, she knew that Harry had to get away from his old partners in crime if they were going to have a solid future together.

"Harry, I know these gentlemen have been in your life for a long time, but you're not going to be in their party scene anymore. Are you still going to find them interesting? Do you think you'll still have anything in common with them?" Jessica asked, calmly stroking Harry's untamed mane of salty frizz.

"You don't get it, Jessica. These guys are like my blood brothers. We did a lot more than raise hell in Hollywood. We grew up together. My parents didn't really have time for me. Dad was always busy with work and Mom was doing her charity stuff and hanging out at the club. I was alone with the help most of the time, except when I hung around my boys," Harry said wistfully.

I love when he's being open, honest, and vulnerable. I guess I'm just going to have to overlook all this for now, Jessica thought to herself. *What the future will hold, nobody can predict. All I know is that I am about to marry a man who still is looking for a lot of love.* Jessica's mind wandered off as Harry moved to the end of the bed and began massaging her feet. His rubbing and tickling quietly turned into kissing and caressing. Before long, Harry's tongue found its way to his favorite part of Jessica. Her musky, earthy aroma was a complete turn-on for him as he ravished her womanhood.

Before Jessica came to a climax, once again Harry mounted her and this time there was no stopping him. "Oh shit, Jessica, you feel so good. My body is on fire," Harry exclaimed as he licked and nibbled on Jessica's earlobe. He so enjoyed being inside her that he didn't give a damn if a patient down the hall or a nurse passing by heard his verbal expressions of pure carnal pleasure. "Let me hear you scream my name when I get off. It makes me go wild, " Harry whispered loudly to Jessica, seconds before reaching his point of no return.

"Oh my God, HARRY!" he heard, as he erupted like an exploding volcano deep into Jessica's welcoming cavern of love. "Harry! What are you doing?" he heard a voice say, as he collapsed from sexual exhaustion onto Jessica's petite body, still partially clad in a hospital gown.

chapter three

Unfortunately for Harry, it was not his beautiful, wanton Jessica who screamed his name during his moment of physical nirvana. It was Chas Greer. He stood in the doorway of Jessica's private hospital room, clutching his men's Prada purse, garbed in a Hugo Boss shirt, Calvin Klein khakis, a multi-colored Versace sweater tied perfectly around his shoulders, and classic Gucci loafers on his little feet. His thirty-something bronzed face was perfectly moisturized with a three-hundred-dollar-a-bottle version of cold cream from Chanel, and his naturally Nordic blond hair had recently been enhanced with butter-yellow highlights from a Madison Avenue hairdresser. Heaven forbid Chas should come back from Acapulco looking less than sun-kissed spectacular.

"Harry, you naughty boy," Chas snickered with delight as he sashayed into their love nest, perched himself on a hospital chair, and crossed his legs. Harry and Jessica both scurried to pull the covers over themselves in a weak attempt to mask their passion.

Chas had no problem barging in on Harry and Jessica's private passion and making himself right at home. He felt that now that the almost newlyweds had had their fun, it was time to get down to business. Chas's "business" was getting Jessica out of the hospital and making the final preparations for the wedding. There was no way he was going to let a batch of bad Botox spoil months of hard work. The whole wedding extravaganza was almost as important to Chas's career as it was to Harry and Jessica.

If he's good enough for Jessica Ackerman Raider, he is CERTAINLY good enough for me, were the words that Chas longed to hear come out of the mouths of every blushing billionaire bride-to-be on both coasts. For Chas, it was a reminder to the matrons and patrons of New York and LA high society that the marriage merger of the century would ultimately be a Chas Greer production. From now on, if a filthy-rich man's future wife wanted HER wedding to be as notorious as the Ackerman-Raider affair, she would have no choice but to employee Chas Greer to put the whole thing together.

It was also a rude wake-up call for the many merchants who catered to the rich and famous. If they wanted to keep their fabulous clientele, they better make it worth Chas's while with healthy six-figure kickbacks. He was already secretly adding up the commissions he'd make spending other people's cash.

Of course he knew he'd have to deal with some demanding Bridezillas from time to time, but this was par for the course for Chas. He was used to kowtowing to the moneyed set in order to make a living. One day he dreamed that he'd make enough of his own dough to be treated like the Queen Bee. But that was a long way off. In the back of his mind, he knew that he was only one slight well-heeled step above the rest of the hired help. This was the huge chip on Chas's shoulder, the one he kept neatly covered by his Versace sweater. No matter how small and insignificant he felt in the jaded world of big-buck brides, he would never let any of them know that he was nothing less than fabulousness personified. And Jessica Ackerman, as sweet, down-to-earth, and almost-normal as she was, was no exception to Chas's "not a hair out of place" rule.

"Jessica, I'm glad to see that you are feeling so much better. Nothing like some great nookie to shake you out of an allergic coma," Chas snidely giggled. He smiled sweetly at Jessica, who self-consciously pulled the gown around her now not-so-private parts.

"I can't believe you'd think I'd bolt and leave my Jessica after what happened to her. What do you think, I'm some kind of low-life wuss?" Harry yelled while swiftly jumping off of the bed and shoving his face in Chas's. This was not an easy scolding for Chas to bear.

"Now wait a minute, cowboy, nobody thinks you're anything but a totally stand-up guy. It's just…" Chas stuttered, trying to wiggle out of the potential mine field gracefully.

My goodness, I thought he'd be grateful and appreciative that I spared him such ugliness. I wonder what he would have done if he had arrived to find a hospitalized half-dead wife he couldn't screw back to life, Chas thought as he searched his mind for a good excuse to validate his deception of Harry. *To have Jessica Ackerman angry with me would indeed be a nuisance. However, to have Harry Raider hold a grudge against Chassy would be very dangerous. Who knows what this spoiled brat feels he needs to prove to his new family. I certainly can't let him flex his balls at my expense,* Chas thought, nervously running his fingers through his golden locks of perennial peroxide.

"It's just that I knew for sure that Jessica wouldn't want her minor health issue to ruin your last weekend of freedom. Would you, Jessica?" Chas said, arching an eyebrow triumphantly and looking straight into Jessica's surprised sea-green eyes. Ah yes, he was still the master. Chas knew exactly how to tap into his girls' insecurities to get exactly what he wanted. In just that second it dawned on Chas that the only way out of this situation was to enlist Jessica's help, even if it was unknowingly so.

"No, of course not," Jessica smiled helplessly and nodded, knowing exactly where Chas was going with this. *Oh boy, Chas might turn me into an old ball and chain, even before Harry and I get married, if I don't go along with this. To let Harry feel trapped and burdened will definitely end our life together before it starts.* Jessica slowly stood up for the first time in days and with some effort, went over and massaged Harry's shoulders to calm him down.

"Easy baby, don't move too fast," Harry said, now turning his total attention to his future wife.

"I'm fine, damn it!" Jessica proclaimed strongly, as she swayed a little bit and grabbed the end of the bed for support.

"You see, Harry? Jessica is a big girl. So she had a little souped-up Botox aftershock, so what? I say kudos to her. Bravo, Jessica!" Chas clapped his perfectly manicured hands together and shot Jessica his ultimate look of approval. They both knew that he was really silently applauding her because she was shrewd enough to play his game.

"Still, you should have told me what was going on!" Harry insisted, neither buying into Chas's bullshit nor quite understanding why Jessica seemed to be agreeing with the blond snake in the grass. Chas absolutely did.

"It was the best thing for my recuperation, I think. That's why I feel so much better now," Jessica said, propping herself up against the hospital wall, wanting desperately to project the picture of good health.

"Do you swear to me that this is what you wanted and that you're going to be all right, Jes?" Harry asked, befuddled by the situation.

"Oh, yes, absolutely," Jessica assured him, revealing only half the truth.

"All righty then, Jessica, let's get the doctor and see when we can blow this pop stand!" Harry said, enthused and relieved that somehow everything had worked out for the best, although it didn't really feel that way. Harry Raider was no rocket scientist, but he was an intuitive animal guided by sheer instinct. *I can tell that something is still definitely off with Jessica, but she wants me to believe her so badly that I'm just going to go with it.* Harry put his arms around Jessica and gave her a much-needed reassuring hug.

"Not so quickly, Harry, my boy," Chas butted in, now safely back on firm ground with both Harry and Jessica. "I'm sure they'll want to keep her in just one more day for observation. I called Vera Wang and asked the tailor to meet me at the hospital around one. He can do the final fitting for the dress today," Chas squealed in delight. *How the hell does he think of these things?* Harry wondered, as he helped Jessica back into bed, unable to stay angry with his old friend.

"You are absolutely amazing, Chas. Thank you for taking care of everything when I couldn't. I mean everything!" Jessica winked at the unsinkable Mr. Greer.

"My greatest pleasure," Chas grinned wryly, loving every second of the power play. Once again, he was where he wanted to be—in total control.

☆ ☆ ☆

As predicted, at 1 p.m. sharp, Jessica's tailor was there to do his duty. "Hiro, so good to see you," Chas gushed and fluttered his eyelashes as he sauntered over to the blatantly gay tailor while simultaneously extending his limp wrist. The two overly coiffed effete men exchanged air kisses, hugs, and indiscreet glances.

"Sorry to barge in like this, but the final work must be done!" Hiro turned and said to Jessica.

"That's quite all right, Hiro. Only in the Hamptons would somebody expect to have her wedding dressed altered immediately after coming out of a coma," Harry attempted to joke. While Hiro was fumbling through his bag, the attending doctor came to check on Jessica. Harry was the happiest to see the young medic, hoping he would let Jessica out of there quickly.

"When can she go home, doc?" Harry wanted to know, his arms lovingly wrapped around Jessica.

"Her vitals look good, but just to play it safe, I'm going to ask her to stay the night for some final observation. But if she's okay in the morning, you can take your bride home, sir," replied the doctor with a smile.

"Great!" exclaimed Harry, and planted a big, sloppy kiss on Jessica's cheek

"I'm fine, doctor, really," Jessica said, doing her best to convince him and Harry that she was well on her way to being the perfect bride.

"That's good to know, Jessica, but if you need anything, you just have the nurse call me, okay?"

"Thanks, doc!" Harry said, as the doctor quickly left the room.

"Ugh, did you get a load of the greasy, yellowing gray hair on that guy? Gross! It looks like he's been to some kind of time-warp barber from 1952. You would think a medical professional in the Hamptons' top hospital would dress for life-and-death success," Chas snarked, helping Jessica out of her bed.

"Who cares what he looks like, Chas, as long as he made my Jessica well again," Harry said.

"Now, Harry, I'm going to have to ask you to leave too. You know, it's bad luck for a groom to see his wife in her magic dress. I don't want to put Kainahura on your wedding." Chas's half-Jewish upbringing popped up now and then and he threw in a few choice Yiddish words to help get his point across.

"I can't go back out there now. All the paparazzi are still hanging out on the lawn; they swarmed and pounced on me on the way in. I had to take off, make them think I was leaving, then sneak inside through the janitor's entrance in the back."

"What paparazzi?" Jessica inquired of Chas. "Has someone famous checked into the hospital?" Silence fell over the room. Nobody knew how to tell Jessica what was going on, not even the master of disaster himself, Chas Greer. It was Hiro who innocently dropped the bombshell that, unbeknownst to her, would change Jessica's life forever.

"Oh my gosh, honey, you have been in a coma, haven't you? Don't you know that your story's been the hottest thing to hit the Hamptons since Lizzie Grubman mowed down that nightclub crowd in her Mercedes?" Hiro said to Jessica, disbelievingly.

"What are you talking about, Hiro?" Jessica asked naively, as Harry nervously paced back and forth. Chas, who was now standing behind Jessica, waved his arms like a crazy man, silently signaling Hiro to shut his deadly mouth.

"What's your problem, Chassy?" Hiro whined defiantly. "You can't keep Jessica locked up in this hospital room and in the dark forever," he proclaimed as he reached into his bag and pulled out that morning's *New York Post, New York Daily News,* and the week's editions of *Hamptons Magazine* and *New York Magazine.* As if the local gossip bibles weren't enough, the nation's most scandalous publications including the *Star,* the *Globe,* and the *National Enquirer* were also about to give Jessica the shock of her life. Chas tried to intercept the rag sheets that Hiro was handing to Jessica, but it was too late. Jessica snatched the papers away from Chas's weak grasp.

"Let me see it, Chas. I want to know what the hell is going on."

BILLIONAIRE BOTOX BRIDE ON THE BRINK OF LIFE, screamed the front page of the *New York Post*. **BLACK MARKET BOTOX BOTCH JOB ALMOST BURIES BILLIONAIRE BRIDE ON THE BEACH**, read the headlines of the *New York Daily News*—and just below them was a picture of Dr. Mark Green being hauled off to jail in handcuffs.

SHE'S DYING TO LOOK GOOD ON HER WEDDING DAY; THE DEADLY BEAUTY SECRETS OF THE RICH AND FAMOUS; CUTIE'S IN A COMA FROM COSMETIC CORRUPTION; HOW FAR WOULD YOU GO TO LOOK LIKE THIS HAMPTONS HOTTIE? were some of the other headlines that were scattered across the newspapers, tabloids, and glossy magazines, from New York to Los Angeles and everywhere in between. Jessica was absolutely astonished to see an array of pictures of herself, including photos from her freshman high school yearbook, her first wedding album, her art debut at a Hamptons gallery, and finally the horrible "hidden camera" shots of her being carried into the hospital on a stretcher, totally unconscious, with an oxygen mask covering her delicate features.

"I can't believe this. How do they all know what happened to me?" Jessica said.

"Are you kidding, Jessica? You're in Greater Hampton Hospital. Half the staff here is on the take from the tabloids to get insider information on who checks in here and what goes on behind the hospital doors. I wouldn't be surprised if your doctor himself didn't leak your info. You never know," Chas said.

"But why would anyone care about me? I'm not a celebrity," Jessica stammered, a little confused as she came back down to earth.

"Jessica, my dear, you're the only daughter of one of the richest men on the East Coast and you're marrying into the wealthiest, most prominent family in all of Beverly Hills, Bel Air, Malibu, and Hollywood combined! This type of merger of two great dynasties doesn't happen every day. You're such a grade above the average trailer trash that does a few movies, wins a few golden statue awards, and all of a sudden becomes a Hollywood famous name," Chas ranted and raved, subconsciously swinging his male purse in the air.

"Jessica, you and Harry will be more like American royalty. You could be a Jewish Jackie Bouvier and Jack Kennedy, Grace Kelly and Prince Rainier. You and Harry are the hottest thing to come onto the international power-couple scene in a long time! This is so exciting!" Chas squealed, thrilled to be a part of what he considered to be social history in the making.

"Calm down, Chassy, my man. We're just getting married. It's not like I'm running for president," Harry chuckled, truly amused by his friend's vivid imagination.

"Now, dear Jessica, stop worrying about a little bad press and put on that dress. Hiro doesn't have all day, sweetie, not even for you," Chas grinned. He loved to put his clients in their place. Rich they may be, but in his mind they were all just walking cash machines for him to push around as necessary.

Still in a state of disbelief from the media interest in her ordeal, Jessica went into the bathroom to slip on her wedding dress. She took off her hospital gown and put on her breathtakingly gorgeous ivory, and pearl-laced wedding dress. It was a Vera Wang original, made especially for Jessica

Ackerman, who was a heartbeat away from being Mrs. Harry Raider.

While Hiro made the appropriate alterations, Jessica stood still as a statue, staring out the window at the sea of paparazzi with their cameras in front of the hospital. Some of them were talking on cell phones, others were eating sandwiches and reading the paper, and others were walking around the outside of the hospital questioning people as they walked in and out. *This has to be a one-time freaky thing,* Jessica thought to herself. *They probably just think it's a cool story because it has to do with bad Botox, which is always a hot topic. They couldn't possibly be this interested in just me.*

The next day she was smuggled out of hospital by Harry and Chas, through the hospital's kitchen exit and into an unmarked rented SUV with tinted windows, to Manhattan. To Jessica, this was a surreal experience, one reserved for people like Madonna and Britney Spears. In her mind, all this fuss had nothing to do with her and the way she had always lived, quietly and unbothered. It was then she began to wonder when life would return to normal.

I'm sure after the wedding it will all die down, Jessica reassured herself, guzzling glass after glass of champagne and clutching her white toy poodle, Cindy Brady, as she was checked into her wedding suite at the Pierre Hotel. The staff at the front desk had to call the police because four freelance celebrity photographers and two reporters from the *National Enquirer* were trailing Jessica.

Just one more day, and I can go back to being myself. I'm sure they won't care about me anymore. Just one more day, Jessica thought, as she plopped her purse on the floor, ignored her puppy's manic yelping, and flopped onto the big four-poster bed to fall into a deep, booze-induced sleep. Instead of curling up next to Jessica's head on her big, white, fluffy pillow, like she normally did every night, Cindy quieted down and finally planted herself on the throw rug in front of the hotel-room door. It was as if she was trying to protect her owner and let her relish the last moments of quiet calm before the tsunami-sized social storm of tomorrow's main event. That fortuitous evening, even an animal's intuitive instinct couldn't have predicted what would happen to the new Mrs. Harry Raider.

chapter four

For the evening of the wedding, the Pierre Hotel—one of Manhattan's most elaborate, ornate wedding venues—was to be transformed into an international festival of flowers, in honor of Jessica's garden at her father's East Hampton mansion. The garden was the magical place she and Harry had first made love, and she wanted their "blooming passion" to be the theme of the wedding. Chas thought this was a wonderful idea, since he would earn a fortune in kickbacks for turning the Pierre's main ballroom into nothing less than a bountiful, botanical paradise. And on top of that, it gave his lover Juan the opportunity for his professional debut as a "floral creations" expert. His designs would be seen by the most illustrious audience of A-list guests.

Juan, a drop-dead gorgeous twenty-something Venezuelan man, had been toiling as a junior florist and botanical-themed event planner at Fleur de Fleur, a trendy, up-and-coming flower shop in Greenwich Village. For Juan to bring this mega-bucks, high profile wedding to the company was quite a coup for the young lad. The owners, an aging gay couple named Arthur and Thomas, were very impressed. Not only were they giving Juan an extra commission for bringing in the job, but they were also giving him creative carte blanche and effectively putting him in charge.

Juan would be responsible for everything including the chuppah made out of two thousand red roses, the tremendous centerpieces featuring every exotic flower he could find, the lilies to adorn the aisle, and filling a massive fountain structured completely from flowers that was the first thing that people saw when they entered the ballroom. If Juan did a bang-up job with this wedding of the century, he could write his own ticket as florist to the stars (and those who spend like them).

Naturally, Juan's big break had come from none other than his lover of six months, Chas Greer. For Chas, who had a revolving-door sex life in his past, to be with the same man for such a long time was indeed remarkable. Yet there was something so alluring about this young man, with his soulful dark eyes, long curly eyelashes, and tight little buns, that kept the once perennially fickle Chas Greer coming back for more. Although it killed him to admit it, after the sexy summer they had just spent together in the Hamptons, Chas considered Juan life-partner material.

Juan genuinely seemed to love Chas and didn't care much that neither of them had any money. The notion of true, unconditional love without an ulterior motive didn't yet fit into Chas's mindset so he did whatever he could to promote Juan professionally since he couldn't afford to give him an indulgent life of luxury.

★★★

Minutes before Jessica was expected to walk down the aisle, Juan was in the bridal suite putting the finishing touches on her hair and makeup. Like Chas, Juan had been a male model/hairdresser/makeup artist in his teens, so he was responsible for getting her ready while Chas took care of the last-minute details downstairs. Jessica looked like a living doll as she sat in her wedding dress in front of the full-length baroque mirror with her faithful canine Cindy by her side. She decided to wear her late mother's Cartier diamond tiara, with the necklace and earrings to match. On the upper part of her body alone, Jessica displayed about five million dollars' worth of diamonds, not counting the half-million-dollar diamond engagement ring that Harry Raider had put on her finger.

"My Lord, Jessica, you look absolutely heavenly!" Chas gushed, as he burst into the suite, dashing in his new Armani tux. "The perfect bride for the perfect night," he said, clapping his hands together and gazing triumphantly out the window at the majestic New York City skyline.

"Isn't she just fantastic?" Juan purred in his adorable accented English. "I've never seen anybody as wonderful as Jessica," Juan exulted, putting the finishing touches on Jessica's mascara.

"You guys are so sweet," Jessica said, a little embarrassed. For a girl who normally didn't make a fuss over herself, tonight she reveled in being the beautiful bride. "What's going on downstairs?" Jessica asked Chas excitedly.

"Oh, don't you worry about a thing, Jes. Everything has fallen into place, and everyone who is anyone is here. The cocktail hour is just finishing up and people are beginning to file in and take their seats for the ceremony." Chas smiled and winked, crossing his legs and reclining comfortably on the chaise lounge. "Are you in the mood for a little dish to take your mind off of your big moment?"

"Sure, why not?" Jessica giggled. For the most part she didn't care for Chas's catty gossip, but tonight she was allowing herself indulgences of every kind.

"Well, Goldie Hawn and Kurt Russell came early with

Cher, who is looking incredible in a vintage Bob Mackey gown. I swear I'd love to rip it right off of her back and wear it to party downtown later tonight!" Chas chortled. "Glamour queen Joan Collins is here with that hot baby-faced husband of hers, and so is the invincible Ivana Trump with her infant boyfriend. They were huddling around the caviar ice sculpture whispering with the always done-up Joan Rivers. I swear, they are all starting to look alike. But that's because all they all go to the same tried and true Beverly Hills plastic surgeon. Naturally I had to sit them on the opposite side of the room from The Donald and gorgeous Melania, but even so.... mm, honey, if looks could kill! Sharp daggers were flying like crazy across the room. The tension was so thick you could cut it with a wedding-cake knife. Lucky for me, Harry's buddies Billy Joel, Mick Jagger, and Rod Stewart came in together with their childlike better halves. Don't you know, Sting and David Bowie are the only music legends here tonight who married women near their age? Anyway, the other rock-and-roll cradle-robbers eventually found their way over to the new and improved Trumps, so the older gang of gal pals and their puppy-faced paramours were forced to retreat." Chas laughed wickedly.

"What about Harry's friends?' Jessica asked, somewhat worried.

"Who's that?" Chas mumbled nonchalantly, like they were of absolute no importance to him among the star-studded celebrity crowd.

"You know, the guys with the weird nicknames, My Do, Time May, Todd Kranks, and Bill Lude."

"Bill Ladd, that homo-wannabe-straight-guy-who-do-you-think-you're-kidding loser from LA?" Chas raised an eyebrow disapprovingly.

"Yes, I guess that's him." Jessica frowned.

"I can't understand why Harry still keeps Bill, Mike, Todd, and Donny around," Chas went on. "I would have thought that he'd outgrown that gang of misfits years ago."

Jessica tried not to look nervous. She didn't like the fact that Chas would so openly voice his disgust with Harry's closets friends. *My God, if Chas hates them, they really must be terrible. He grew up with them too,* Jessica thought to herself as she looked down at her specially designed diamond-encrusted Rolex, realizing that show time was drawing near.

"It's bad enough I had to put up with them in Acapulco, and it's more of a shame that they'll be at the wedding," Chas spit in frustration. "Don't worry, I've seated them waaaaay in the back. They'll be secluded in social Siberia, so nobody who matters will notice them. Leave it to those jerks to show up late. Of course I haven't seen any of them yet."

"You haven't?" Jessica said, sounding a bit alarmed.

"No, not yet, but I'm sure they'll come staggering in, all four of them high as kites, as usual." Chas shrugged his shoulders disdainfully.

"What about Harry?" Jessica asked in a small, quiet voice. "Have you seen him?"

For a moment that seemed like an eternity, Chas was dead quiet. *How could it not have occurred to me to check on Harry?* Chas thought to himself, looking away from Jessica while smoothing down his perfectly gelled hair in an attempt to hide his huge oversight.

"I saw Harry a little while ago. He was getting ready in his suite and he looked fantastic," Chas lied through his pearly whites.

"Great, Chas, that makes me feel so much better," Jessica beamed. "I know I can trust Harry to show up, otherwise I wouldn't be marrying him. I guess I just have a case of the last-minute jitters," Jessica said, picking up Cindy and giving her a cuddle.

"For heaven's sake, put the poodle down. She might pee on your dress," Chas chastised and carefully removed Cindy from Jessica's lap. Cindy looked up and growled at the stranger who dared to remove her from her mistress's loving embrace. Chas would have growled right back at the little coiffed beast if he weren't so preoccupied with Harry's whereabouts.

"I'll tell you what, Jessica, you stay here with Juan and finish getting gorgeous. I'll come up and get you right before it's time to make your dramatic entrance. Let me run downstairs and make sure everyone is seated, and I'll be up in a nanosecond," Chas said quickly, anxious to get the hell out of Jessica's suite and over to Harry as fast as possible.

"I really should go downstairs right now. It's about time to begin," Jessica said, worried and heading towards the door herself.

"WAIT!" screamed Chas, almost losing his composure. "Please, Jessica, you don't want anyone to see you before you start walking down the aisle. You know Jewish weddings never start on time. Just give me five seconds to make sure everything is in place, then I'll come right back up and get you. Okay?" Chas squeaked, as if he just inhaled helium.

"Okay, Chas, calm down. Go downstairs and work your magic. I'll wait here until you come get me. But hurry up, I don't want to be late for my own wedding," Jessica joked.

"You're the star of the show, baby cakes," Chas schmoozed and he blew her and Juan a kiss as he bolted out the door.

Harry, Harry, Harry, please tell me you are either in your suite or already at the cocktail party, ready to become a married man, Chas thought to himself as he raced down the hall. He was so scared that Harry might have had last-minute second thoughts that he was too shaky to even wait for the elevator. Chas flew down the exit stairs, jumping two and three at a time, in a panic to reach Harry's floor. When he finally got there, he darted down the hall and banged loudly on the door of Harry's suite.

"Come on, Harry, open up...open the door! Please tell me you're in there!" Chas muttered under his breath. The harder he knocked the quieter the response. The silence of waiting for Harry was excruciating. Chas saw a chambermaid coming towards him. *My savior,* he thought to himself.

"Señora, señora, por favor. Can you let me in the room? Mi amigo is very sick. You have to let me in!" Chas pleaded with the maid in a half-attempt to speak Spanish.

"I'm sorry, sir, I can't let you in there," the English-speaking maid said coldly.

"You have to, it's an emergency!" Chas nearly wept. The maid wouldn't budge and stared coyly at Chas's pockets.

"What, you want me to pay you to let me in there? Are you crazy? I know the manager of this hotel and I ought to have you fired!" Chas screamed. He shot the maid a deadly look of defiance.

"Suit yourself," the maid smiled stubbornly and pushed her cart right past Chas.

"Oh, all right. Here you go," Chas took out a twenty-dollar bill and handed it to the maid. Not impressed by his small financial gesture, she handed it back to him and began to start off down the hall. "Jesus lady, you're a fucking thief," Chas whispered loudly, but he handed her a fifty. Not overly grateful, she took his money and finally opened the door to Harry's suite with her pass key.

Chas desperately looked around the room. He saw a men's garment bag strewn carelessly over an overstuffed chair, one half of a pair of shoes on the air conditioning unit and the other one thrown across the room, under the nightstand. Chas also noticed a stack of porno magazines sitting on top of the television, blatantly resting under a half bottle of Diet Coke. These were visible signs that Harry had been in the room, but unless he was hiding under the bed, he sure wasn't there now. Just as a panic-stricken Chas was about to collapse into a big chair and pop a Valium, Harry Raider appeared from the bathroom, wearing nothing but a tiny towel.

"Hey, jazzy Chassy, ready to watch me become transformed into an honest man?" Harry joked, waving a razor around like a magic wand. His face was covered in shaving foam.

"Oh shit, Harry, it's great to see you," Chas said, putting away the pills and carefully patting away the beads of perfumed sweat on his suntanned brow. "Now, what are you doing still putzing away? You should be downstairs already; it's almost time to begin!" Chas said, once more in control. Chas was so happy not to have lost the groom that he didn't even care that he just paid a maid fifty bucks to see Harry Raider standing half naked.

"I'm just going to wash off, throw on my tux, and I'll be down there in ten seconds flat. Look, I've got my yarmulke on already," Harry pointed, bowing his head towards Chas.

"That's wonderful, Harry. Juan is helping Jessica with some finishing touches. Wait until you see her! You won't believe your eyes. She was always a beautiful girl, but tonight, she's really something special," Chas offered, obligated to give Harry a last vote of confidence, just in case he was experiencing the least bit of doubt.

"That's one of the many reasons I'm marrying her," Harry smiled, and Chas was finally completely assured Harry would make it to the altar.

"I'm going down the main ballroom now to make sure everyone is seated. I'll tell the rabbi we will begin the ceremony in about fifteen minutes, so please don't dawdle. Let's put a move on it, Harry, chop chop!" Chas exclaimed as he snapped his fingers and breezed out of Harry's suite. No matter how lovely Jessica looked, tonight Chas felt like *he* would be the belle of the ball.

True to his word, just minutes after Chas left, Harry was dressed and ready to seal his fate. Wearing a five-thousand-dollar black Armani tux, with his normally wild, frizzy hair gelled firmly into place, Harry Raider was a handsome sight to behold. As he was walking down the hall towards the elevator, he felt someone tap his back. Harry turned around to see who it was and felt a hard knock on the head. Harry fell on the floor, and before he could tell what was going on a pillowcase was thrown over his head. He was bodily carried away toward the service elevator by a few pairs of strong arms. Harry tried to wriggle loose and scream for help, but whoever was holding his head had their big hand covering his mouth. It was totally useless. Harry Raider was being kidnapped just minutes before he was to be married.

★★★

Harry could tell he was being carried out of the hotel and shoved into of some sort of vehicle. When he was safely inside, the car pulled away and began to speed through the streets of Manhattan. As soon as it crossed over the Brooklyn Bridge, the pillowcase was removed. Harry looked around, shocked to discover who his captors were.

"Hey buddy, we thought we'd never get you out of there!" cracked Mike Roman, otherwise known as "My Do." "Motherfucker, was the security tight. I think half of the Israeli army was hired to protect all of those famous folks coming to your wedding. But they were still no match for us!" Even dressed in a formal tuxedo, he was a rough-looking, scraggily sort of man, with a crater face of teenage acne scars and a crooked, uncared-for smile. In the motor home he had driven all the way from LA, Mike now sat next to Harry on a bench seat while triumphantly cracking open a bottle of Dom Perignon to celebrate the successful kidnapping.

On Harry's other side was Todd Krane, a thirty-something washed-out surfer boy with a bandana around tied around his white-blonde head. Todd was pulling a hefty bag of cocaine out of his tuxedo jacket and rolling a few hundred-dollar bills to help him snort it. "Hey, Harry, wait till you try this stuff, man. It's so pure, you won't be able to feel your face for days," Todd said, earnestly spreading some coke on a flat mirror and chopping it with his black American Express card.

"I can't believe you guys have done this to me! This is so fucked up," Harry moaned, holding his head in his hands. He knew he was in deep trouble and couldn't figure how to get out of it. Harry grabbed his stomach and held it like he had been put on a roller coaster against his will. Any moment now he was sure that he was going to throw up as the car carrying his favorite bunch of hooligans sped forward.

"Hiya, Harry!" yelled Donny Mayberry from the driver's seat of the RV. Chubby, clubby Donny, stuffed into a Ralph Lauren tuxedo, was an overgrown floppy-preppy schoolboy of a man. Like Harry, Donny was the official misfit of his old guard "Holmby Hills" WASPy family. Yet, unlike Harry, Donny actually managed to hold down a job as a portfolio manager in his family's prestigious investment bank in downtown LA. Harry Raider had never worked a day in his pathetic life.

"Aren't you glad that we got you out of there in time? You could have married that girl and screwed up everything," Donny chuckled as he drove like a wild man through the streets of Brooklyn, looking for an entrance to the expressway.

"I wanted...I mean I want to marry Jessica, Donny," Harry said making his way up to the front of the motor home. "This is not funny. You guys have to turn this thing around and take me back to the Pierre right now."

"No way, Raider. There is no way we are going to let you make the biggest mistake of your life. We were going to talk you out of it in Acapulco, but you ran out of there so fast, we didn't have time. That's when we decided it was time for more drastic measures. If you would have married that girl tonight, you would have been happy for about five minutes. Then once all that lovey-dovey crap wore off, you would have been stuck with her, man. It probably would have cost you a fortune to get out of it, not to mention really pissing off your parents," Mike said, moving over to Todd to snort a line of his coke and swig some champagne from the bottle.

"And you think pulling a runner at the last minute is going to make my parents *happy?*" Harry demanded, as he paced back and forth the length of the luxury van.

"Of course not, buddy, but they'll get over the initial shock. You've been pulling moves like that all of your life. I'm sure they're used to it by now. Remember your Bar Mitzvah, dude? I believe you were losing your first nut in Vegas when Sam and Irma Raider and four hundred and fifty of their nearest and dearest were waiting for you to read from the Torah in temple," Todd said, rubbing some excess cocaine on his gums and grabbing the champagne bottle out of Mike's hand. "There's really no way your parents expect you to show up for this one, man. They probably just wanted an excuse to have a big, fancy party. Irma lives for that shit."

"No, you guys are all wrong. This was...I mean *is*...the real thing. I love Jessica, and I want to be there. I want to marry her! I know what I'm doing! Please, you gotta believe me and take me back to the city before it's too late," Harry begged his buddies, who were getting too high to listen or care. "Sure, dude, you tell me you want to marry that girl and have to stick you dick in the same place every night, for the rest of your life, after this. Oh, Mr. Ladly…Señor Raider is ready to be put to the test," Mike teased, as he got up and knocked on the back bedroom door.

All of a sudden Bill Ladd appeared. He was a lithe, lanky "Ziggy Stardust" freak, with ghostly pale skin and icy-blue and maroon-magenta streaks in his jet-black bone-straight goth hair. Bill wore a white tuxedo with a rose corsage in his lapel and a black silk scarf tied around his neck. He had a face full of makeup, with sparkling multicolored eye shadow, red blush to accentuate his sunken cheekbones, purple eyeliner, and long false eyelashes. Even though his attire was borderline drag queen, Bill was feeling very much a man that night. Two scantily clad strippers with mammoth silicone breasts, a light-skinned redhead and an exotic brunette, flanked him. "Hi, Harry," Ladly purred. "Meet Ruby Scorch and Marrakech Gold. My ladies are this evening's entertainment. They'll be more fun than that stuffy band you had playing at the Pierre!"

Bill clapped his hands and on cue the strippers went to work. Ruby Scorch pushed Harry down on the couch and seductively rubbed his neck and shoulders while Marrakech Gold gave him a lap dance. *Oh shit, I can't do this now. I've got to get back to my wedding, before the next party someone gives me is my funeral,* Harry thought. Pushing the girls off, he headed back up to driver Donny.

"Sit back and relax, Raider," Donny said, shoving Harry back with one hand. "Why don't you stop whining like a big baby. Go back there and enjoy the show."

Harry turned around to see the two strippers starting to

provocatively fondle each other on the floor of the motor home. Bill unzipped his pants and joined them while Mike and Todd did more lines of coke and egged the threesome on, cheering wildly.

That's it, I'm gone before I'm a goner, Harry thought. When Donny was forced to stop at a red light, Harry fumbled with the lock on the RV's door and managed to push it open. Just as Donny was about to step on the gas, Harry pushed the door open and leaped out.

"Hey, where you going, jerk-off? We went to a lot of trouble to save your ass, Harry," Donny screamed after him. Harry disappeared from Donny's sight, hiding in a small, dirty alley between two industrial buildings.

"Aw shit, screw him. If he wants to suffer the rest of his time on the earth, let him. I'm driving back to LA," Donny groused and turned the RV around, leaving Brooklyn behind as he headed west.

★ ★ ★

With the motor home now out of sight, Harry walked onto the main street, totally disheveled and sweating like a pig. Dazed, he realized he had no idea where he was and didn't have a clue how to get back to the city. He looked across the East River and gazed at the Manhattan skyline. Somewhere in that concrete jungle were a devastated Jessica and a room full of very angry people.

Maybe it's too late now to go back to the Pierre and try to fix this horrible situation. Perhaps I better look for a pay phone and try to reach the guys to come back, pick me up, and take me back to LA with them. Jessica will never believe what happened and will probably never forgive me. Maybe I should just give up. Harry was terrified of confrontations and this was one mega-sized mess. He wandered the streets, which seemed unnaturally empty for a place that was just across the water from Manhattan. Harry found a bench by the river and sat down to think. A few seats down was an older homeless couple, sharing a pretzel and affectionately wiping the mustard off of each other's mouths.

Isn't that something? They seem to have nothing but each other, yet they seem so content. I just walked away from booze, grade A drugs, and two hot girls, and I'm totally miserable right now. Asshole, what am I doing here? I gotta get back to the Pierre and make it right, no matter what happens. Harry's soul screamed at him to grab his last chance at finding true love and long-term happiness.

"Excuse me, I don't mean to interrupt," Harry said, pulling out his Hermès silk handkerchief and handing it to the homeless man to use to remove more mustard from his wife's face.

"Can you tell me where I am, sir?" Harry asked.

"DUMBO!" the old man grunted, taking Harry's hanky, not knowing or caring how expensive it was.

"Yeah, I know, I'm a dumbo. I must look like a total putz right now, but if you could just tell me where I am and how to get back to the city, I'd be very grateful," Harry pleaded.

The old couple laughed out loud. "No, son, you're in DUMBO. Down, Under the Manhattan and Brooklyn Bridge. It used to be empty warehouses in my day, but now...fuggeddaboutit... it's a very trendy area of Brooklyn. You have to be rich to live here, unless you live with us." The old woman smiled sweetly and pointed out a group of cardboard boxes and old blankets, haphazardly put together to make some sort of a shelter. Harry was speechless. His heart went out to these people, but he had no idea how to deal with them. He was out of his element and all alone.

"Take the subway by the bridge. It will take you right into midtown in about fifteen minutes," the old man said to Harry, sensing his urgency. He pointed Harry in the right direction and gave him a pat on the back.

"Thank you, thank you so much, sir," Harry said hopefully. He reached into his tuxedo jacket pocket for his wallet to give the homeless couple some money. And then he realized that he had left everything in the hotel room except a handful of change. Harry instead took off his fifty-thousand-dollar gold and diamond Piaget watch and handed it to the old man, who studied the jewelry carefully before he slipped it on his wife's wrist. She didn't seem too impressed with the gift and handed it back to her husband.

"Mind if we sell it and move to Miami? The winters are getting tough here." The old man winked at Harry and smiled a toothless grin.

"Do whatever you want. Wear it or hock it in good health." Harry waved goodbye and sprinted towards the subway entrance, hoping to be back where he belonged in time to save the day. He had left his cell phone in his hotel room when he was going down to his wedding, not thinking he would need it on the most important night of his life. There was no way to let anyone know where he was, so he just to do his best and get back to the Pierre as soon as he could.

Not being a New Yorker and having never ridden the subway in his life, Harry darted down the stairs. He didn't have any money to buy a token but luckily he was only five foot five and could easily sneak under the turnstile when the attendant was busy reading the *Times*. Once by the tracks, Harry blindly jumped on the first train that appeared. It never occurred to him that he could get on the wrong train. He just assumed that all trains would go to Manhattan. He was dead wrong.

chapter five

Four hours, seven trains, two round trips out to Queens and then to the South Shore of Long Island later, Harry Raider eventually found his way back to the island of Manhattan. He tried several times to call the Pierre, but there was no answer at Jessica's suite and he could never seem to get anyone on the phone who could help him. Harry prayed that someone gave Jessica one of the many messages he left.

When Harry finally arrived in the lobby of the Pierre, he was too pissed off and frustrated to be afraid anymore. He burst into the main ballroom to find the chuppah being dismantled, the elaborate wedding decorations taken down, chairs and tables folded and put away, and a clean-up crew vacuuming the massive event space. In a quiet corner, sitting around the last standing table were Harry's distraught parents, Sam and Irma Raider, with Jessica's shaken father Jerry Ackerman and his regal wife, an Eva Gabor look-alike countess from Monaco named Martine Chantal Christine Marie de Bourbon, de Luxembourg de Two Sicilies. Her Brooklyn-born billionaire husband lovingly called her "Countess Marty."

The aging but elegant group of seventy-something bil-
lionaires was sitting with Rabbi Isaac Harmon, who had
flown in from the prestigious Wilshire Boulevard Temple in
Los Angeles to perform the ceremony. Instead, he was faced
with the unpleasant task of comforting the family in the
wake of Harry's disappearance. Unfortunately for the seasoned rabbi, this was not the first time he had to provide a
shoulder to kvetch on for the Raider clan. He was the same
rabbi who, almost forty years ago, insisted that Sam maintain
a sense of humor when Harry peed all over his newly rich
father's first Saville Row suit during the circumcision ritual.

Rabbi Harmon was also there at Harry's no-show Bar
Mitzvah from hell, and flew with Sam on his private plane
to collect Harry from Caesar's Palace. Throughout the
years Sam Raider's generous donations to the temple had
built a new wing for worship and a beautiful hall for Jewish community events. Therefore, Rabbi Harmon, like most
of the others in the Jewish world of Beverly Hills, would do
anything to curry Sam Raider's favor. So, this time when he
boarded the Queen Irma Two, the Raider's new Gulf
Stream jet, Rabbi Harmon wanted to have faith that Harry
would make everybody happy, break the glass, and become
Jessica's husband. Luckily he had secretly prepared a con-
dolence sermon for the Raider and Ackerman families, just
in case Harry pulled one of his usual antics.

Rabbi Harmon was smack in the middle of his "what's
meant to be will be, with God's help" speech when Harry
marched up to the table. Even with his willful determination and adrenaline pumping nonstop, Harry felt his stomach drop like he was on a roller coaster at an amusement
park. He was so nervous he thought he might pass out.

"Harry, you son of a bitch bastard," yelled his father,
popping up from his chair. His aging, raspy voice had suddenly the strength and seriousness of a young man. "I ought

to push over this table and smack the crap out of you, you good for nothing piece of shit!" Sam kept screaming.

"Sammy, watch your language and please calm down. You'll give yourself a heart attack," the rabbi said, taking Sam's hand and sitting him down again.

"I'm sorry, Rabbi, I don't mean to curse, but this lousy excuse of a son of mine has made me too angry. I want to take this knife, cut off his balls, and ram them down his throat!" Sam continued ranting, waving a butter knife, which could hardly do the job.

"That's enough, Sammy," Irma sobbed, loudly. "I can't take much more of this. Once again, my Harry has proven to be a public shame and disgrace. The last thing I need is my husband going nuts too."

"Mommy, I am so sorry, but this time it wasn't my fault. Please, you have to believe me," Harry cried, putting his arm around his wailing mother, wiping away her and his own tears.

"Then whose fault was it that you missed your own wedding? Tell me what happened, Harry. Did you get abducted by aliens?" Sam said sarcastically, attempting to contain his outrage for his poor wife's sake.

"Something like that, Daddy. I know I don't have a very good track record with these things, but this time what happened was completely beyond my control. You just have to take my word for it. I swear I'll explain the whole mess to you later, but right now I have to find Jessica," Harry answered, bravely looking his father straight in the eye.

"What makes you think Jessica would want anything to do with you after what you just put her through, Harry?" Sam stared at his son. "You're such an inconsiderate, self-serving, arrogant shmuck, it's unbelievable."

"I don't care what you call me, Dad. I love Jessica more than anything in this world. I owe her a major explanation and I still want to marry her," Harry said, jamming his sweaty hands in his pants pockets and clenching his fists.

"Harry, there is no way I'm letting you near that girl," Sam announced, no longer able to contain his temper. "You've done enough damage to all of us, the Ackerman family, and particularly Jessica. I'm taking you back to Los Angeles tonight and you'll never see Jessica again. That's final!"

"I'm not going anywhere until I speak to Jessica first," Harry countered, experiencing a rush of newfound courage. "If she wants me to disappear, then I will. But just so you know, I intend to put up a good fight and make her believe the truth. This was all a huge misunderstanding. Now, if none of you will tell me where she is, I will search this entire hotel myself and go out to Hamptons if I have to, but I won't give up until I find her," Harry stammered.

"She's in her suite. She said she wanted to be alone," Jerry Ackerman, Jessica's father, said quietly.

"What, have you gone meshuga, Jerry?" Sam blurted angrily. "I'm trying to protect *your* daughter from a moron like my insane son, and you're telling him where to find her? Have you lost your mind?" He hated the fact that his best friend since childhood and former business partner was undermining him. Sam didn't know who was embarrassing him more, his miserable son or Jerry Ackerman, who managed to remain cool, calm, and collected in the face of this unfolding drama.

"I know you're angry, Sammy. I'm angry too." Jerry didn't raise his voice.

"Yeah, well, you have a funny way of showing it," Sam said, once again attempting to steady himself and not to let Jerry outclass him.

"Look, Sammy, obviously something went very, very wrong here, but it's for the kids to work out, not us. Let Harry go see Jessica and at least let her hear him out, even if it's for the *last time*," Jerry emphasized, glaring at Harry. Secretly, Jerry wanted to believe Harry and see his little girl Jessica happily married, but he didn't dare let on his true feelings to anyone in the room.

"That sounds like a smart idea," Rabbi Harmon concluded, gently placing his hand on Sam's. "Let God's will be done." Not wanting to seem disrespectful to the rabbi, Sam purposely looked the other way, shook his head, bit his lip, and rolled his eyes in sheer disgust. At times like these, Sam Raider failed to understand why God had cursed him with a son like Harry. And once again Sam was powerless to stop his black-sheep boy's actions. Sam, the former raging lion, now shrugged his shoulders helplessly in retreat. "She's your daughter, Jerry. If that's the way you feel, then who am I to argue?" Sam drowned his words in a glass of water.

"Thank you, Jerry, thank you, Rabbi, and thank you, Dad. I know you really hate me right now, but I swear, you won't be sorry." Not wanting to appear too cocky, Harry bowed his head in gratitude, nodded slightly, and only half-smiled at the table before he ran out of the ballroom towards the hotel elevator.

★★★

Once on her floor, he ran down the hall until he arrived in front of Jessica's suite. A wave of sheer terror suddenly washed over Harry. *I could handle the adults, but I don't know if I can really face Jessica. I wouldn't blame her if she wanted to kill me or never see me again. Maybe my dad was right, she'd be better off without me. I probably should just disappear and get out of her life forever.* Harry looked down at his left hand and remembered his Piaget watch was gone. The sun had tanned all the way around the spot where it used to sit on his wrist, leaving him with the large white outline of the fifty-thousand-dollar timepiece that he had given away in a moment of desperation. The image of the old homeless couple filled his thoughts. Harry gently knocked on Jessica's door.

At first he just tapped lightly, but when he got no response, his pounding got more persistent and forceful. Finally the door swung open. Much to Harry's chagrin, it was not Jessica standing there. It was Chas.

"Oh my gosh, Harry! What are you doing here?" Chas whispered, not wanting Jessica to hear who was at her door.

"I thought Jerry said that Jessica wanted to be alone," Harry said, frustrated to find Chas inappropriately in the middle of yet another private moment in his life.

"Jerry Ackerman knows you're here and he let you come up?" Chas whispered again in disbelief, holding the door just slightly open behind him.

"As a matter of fact he did, Chas. I don't know what the hell you're doing here either," Harry shot back, trying to sneak a peek into Jessica's room.

"Well excuse *me*, Harry, but someone had to comfort *your bride*, since you obviously thought you had something better to do than make it to your own wedding," Chas said sarcastically, raising an eyebrow for effect.

"Look, Chas, I just went through hell with the family and I'm sure Jessica and I are not going to have the easiest of times right now, but the last thing I need is shit from you. So please, if you don't mind, get the hell out of my way and let me talk to her," Harry demanded, almost pushing Chas out of his way.

Jessica was stretched out on a lounger in the darkened room wearing her cream La Perla robe. The wedding dress had apparently been torn off and stuffed into a small wastebasket, tulle and satin in puffs on the floor. She stared out the window intently at the city lights, her little toy poodle curled up in her lap. Jessica looked particularly lovely with the luminous glow of Manhattan behind her. Slowly, Harry approached and knelt down beside her. She knew he was there, but didn't say a word.

After a few minutes of sitting in silence together, Harry quietly spoke. "Jes, I don't blame you if you hate my guts, want to murder me, or throw me out that window, but I swear to you on my life, what happened tonight had nothing to do with me. Even if you never speak to me again, you have to know how much I wanted tonight to be a success, how much I love you, and how much I want to marry you."

A sigh of relief came from doorway. Jessica looked up in surprise. Harry shot up, ran over, and flipped on the lights to find Chas standing against the door, trying to make himself invisible, but refusing to miss the drama of what he hoped would be Harry and Jessica's reconciliation. Harry wanted to slug Chas, but at this point he knew he couldn't afford to make any more enemies. "Chas, I thank you for taking care of Jessica while I was missing in action, but now I need to speak to Jessica privately, if you don't mind," Harry said solemnly.

"But of course, Harry. Jessica, if you need Chas, just holler. I'll be waiting out in the hall," Chas said smugly.

"Why don't you go home for the night, Chas? You did a great thing here, but Jessica and I need to be by ourselves right now," Harry shook Chas's hand and moved to escort him out.

Oh sure, use me like a maid to clean up after you, when Jessica was crying her eyes out and this room was an emotional ground zero. Now you come in like some kind of big hero, and it's time for old Chas to scram! Chas though to himself, as he collected his things. He hated nothing worse than to be left out of the action.

Harry was relieved to be alone with Jessica at last. "Jessica, I..."

"I don't want to hear it, Harry!" Jessica screeched in the most shrilling voice he had ever heard. She gave his face a good, hard slap.

How could such a big, ferocious sound come out of such a petite person? Harry wondered, as he felt the sting of her smack on his cheek. He expected his sweet Jessica to be crying, bawling, hyperventilating even, but he never thought she was capable of such anger.

"I don't know who the hell you think you're playing games with here, but if you think this disaster is going to ruin me forever, you've got another think coming, *motherfucker!*" Jessica raged. "I survived four years of misery with my last husband, and yes, there were times I wanted to end it all, but hey, I'm still standing," Jessica said, now up from the lounger and pacing back and forth. Her poodle Cindy had run under the bed. Never had she seen her mistress in such an angry and empowered state. "You are one sick fuck, Harry Raider, do you know that?" Jessica shrilled, waving her finger right in his face.

"Yes, actually I do," Harry admitted. He sat on the edge of the big bed, watching Jessica explode. Harry had never seen this rough and ready side of Jessica before; he was completely beguiled and even more turned on by her.

"But even though I've pulled crazy stunts in the past, I am absolutely not responsible for not being here tonight." Harry's body stiffened as he stomped his foot.

"Really? Why the hell do you think I would believe that, Harry?" Jessica tore into him mercilessly. She ran towards the bed with her fist in the air wanting to punch him, but grabbed a pillow and hit it instead.

"Because it's the truth, Jessica," Harry said in a straightforward tone. "Why would I lie to you then come here and beg for your forgiveness? If I wanted out, I would have stayed gone," said Harry, subconsciously fluffing up the rest of the pillows.

Jessica grew quiet. Deep in her heart she sensed he was being honest with her, but she just couldn't let him off the hook that easily. "Do you want to hear what happened?" Harry asked, hugging one of the pillows like it was a teddy bear.

"I don't know if I even care, Harry. What do you think of that?" Jessica crossed her arms triumphantly, believing she might be getting the better of him.

"I hope that isn't true, Jes. I hope, more than anything, you still care about me, and you'll let me explain."

Once again, Jessica was silent. She was doing everything she could to remain tough and not to start crying. She grabbed her shoulders in an effort to steady herself and then marched intently to the other side of the room. Jessica wanted to prove to Harry that shenanigans like this wouldn't be tolerated. *Why did he have to make it all so difficult?* She thought to herself as she positioned herself by the door. She knew she still loved him and was thrilled he had come back, but Jessica had her pride and didn't want to let Harry think he could walk all over her. She figured any story he told her, even if it was the truth, would only aggravate her more.

"Did your disappearance this evening had anything to do with your friends from LA? You know, those guys with the strange nicknames?" Jessica demanded of Harry sternly after a long moment of deadly silence.

"Yes it did, Jessica. How did you know?"

"Because all of their names were on the guest list, but Chas said he didn't see any of them at the pre-ceremony reception. I thought maybe they tried to sneak you out of here or something totally sinister like that. A group of non-stop partying bachelors can't be thrilled about losing their bank-rolling partner in crime." Jessica was beginning to let her guard down, as shook out her arms and slowly sank down to the floor. She was sitting with her back against the wall, staring out into space, wondering how the hell she was going to make this marriage work.

"You're a smart woman, Jessica," Harry smiled softly.

"Okay, Harry, they've shown me their true colors, so when we go back to LA, they are gone, out of our lives, forever! Do you hear me? Have I made myself one hundred percent clear?" Jessica said, clasping her hands like an old school marm and stamping her toes.

"Does that mean we're getting married, Jessica?" Harry asked, tears welling up in his puppy-dog eyes.

Jessica could no longer keep up anger. "I guess so," she replied. Slowly, she stood up and walked over to Harry. This was the last straw for her and she slowly began to break down. Tears flooded her green eyes. Soon they came on full force, and she found herself in her Harry's arms. The lovers held each other, cuddled, and kissed.

★ ★ ★

The passion of the moment was enthralling for both of them. Harry and Jessica were cuddling closely and were on the verge of making love. Just as they were about to consummate their reconciliation, there was a loud knock on the door. "Who the hell could that be?" Harry muttered, upset that an outsider was ruining his special moment.

"It's just me," said a voice familiar to Harry. "Is everything all right? We didn't hear anything from either of you downstairs and both families began to worry. May I come in?" It was Rabbi Harmon who'd come to check on what was going on. He thought that he might be able to pacify everyone with an official "Harry and Jessica" progress report.

"Come on in, Rabbi, it's good news." Harry and Jessica untangled themselves from each other's embrace and made sure they were properly covered before the rabbi entered their room.

"Baruch Hashem, Bless God. Meer hashem, God's will be done," said Rabbi Harmon, taking Harry's hand as he entered the room. He tried desperately to ignore the rumpled bed and Harry's disheveled "you caught me in bed" look. To him, these were all good signs that Harry and Jessica were back on track.

Harry didn't want to waste another minute. "Can you marry us right now, rabbi?"

"Now is as good a time as any," the happy rabbi exclaimed. *For once a Raider affair could end on a joyous note. Sam deserves a little nachus for all he's been through,* the rabbi thought. "Let me go downstairs and get your families and I can do the ceremony right here," the rabbi said enthusiastically.

"No, nobody else. Just me and Jessica, totally alone, right here, right now," Harry said, scooping Jessica up in his arms and kissing her on the cheek.

"Yes, it should be just me and Harry. No one else," Jessica said, smiling warmly and taking Harry's hand. After all the intrusion into her life she had endured, having a private wedding was a welcomed relief.

"Harry, both your families will be very upset if I marry you two while they are downstairs, wondering what has happened," the rabbi quivered, shaking his head, pleading with Harry to cooperate.

"Trust me, Rabbi, they'll be very happy, completely elated, when they hear that Jessica and I got married," Harry grinned mischievously.

Oy vey Harry, you're such a tummler. It always has to be a problem with you. You can't just make life nice and easy for everybody, the rabbi thought.

Harry begged, "Please, rabbi, I don't want to lose the

thrill of the moment."

"Do you have the ring, Harry?" the reluctant clergyman asked.

"Right here, Rabbi," Harry said proudly, pulling the gorgeous Cartier wedding bands out of his jacket's inner pocket.

"They're beautiful, Harry," the rabbi sighed, and shrugged his shoulders. "What can I say but all right already, I'll do it."

"Awesome! You are one righteous dude," Harry giggled, giving the rabbi a huge, uncomfortably strong bear hug.

"Jessica, would you like to get dressed?" the rabbi said, looking away to avoid staring at Jessica's half-naked body, covered by the small La Perla robe.

"No, rabbi, I want to marry her just the way she is. No dress, nothing fancy, just simple, beautiful Jessica," Harry, ever the romantic said.

Once again, the rabbi shook his head, plastered a pleasant look on his face, and stayed silent. *Well, at least he'll let her wear a robe. I should thank God he doesn't want me to marry them in the nude,* the rabbi thought as he pulled his prayer book from his pocket and opened it. Jessica took Harry's hand as he helped her off of the big bed. The couple took their places in front of the rabbi, by the big hotel window.

"Do you have anything we can use as a chuppah?" the rabbi asked as he glanced around the room.

"How about this?" Jessica giggled, as she took her wedding dress out of the wastebasket and held it over their heads. The rabbi raised an eyebrow and smiled weakly. He knew the best thing to do was just to go along with this extremely unorthodox marriage and make it as kosher as possible.

The rabbi did his best to stand straight and firmly in

front of Harry and Jessica. He closed his eyes and tried to imagine that the original wedding plans had gone off without a hitch and that they were now under the chuppah, surrounded by family and friends. When the rabbi opened his eyes, he saw Harry and Jessica's beaming faces shining beautifully before him. They were both filled with so much hope, love, and excitement that the old rabbi's heart began to melt. *So it's not a big fancy party, so what? Obviously these two meshuga kids love each other very much. If only their parents could see the look on their faces right now, there would be no more explaining to do,* the rabbi thought to himself as the hard look on his wise face began to soften. "Are you ready, my children?" the rabbi said in a sweet, fatherly voice.

"You betcha!" Harry exclaimed as he squeezed Jessica tightly. Once again the rabbi closed his eyes. He circled his arms in the space above Harry and Jessica's heads and sang quietly in Hebrew. Then after praying some more words in the ancient language, the rabbi asked God's blessing to join Harry and Jessica in holy matrimony. After a few magical, yet intensely private moments, Harry Raider married Jessica Ackerman minus the fanfare of an extravagantly decorated ballroom filled with glamorous guests, exquisite floral arrangements, a twelve-piece band, and Chas Greer taking advantage of every possible opportunity to get his picture taken with a celebrity. Simplicity and honesty were their greatest gifts to each other that evening as they quietly exchanged their "I do's."

"Does anyone have a glass?" The rabbi looked around the room hoping to complete the ceremony with the official culmination of a Jewish marriage.

"Here we go," Harry said, grabbing a typical hotel drinking glass. He deftly wrapped it in a pillowcase. "HI-YA!" Harry yelled and jumped on the glass with all of his might.

Harry picked up petite Jessica and kissed her lovingly. He carried her back to the bed and threw her down, totally oblivious to the fact to that the rabbi was still in the room.

"Okay, well, I see you two still have a lot of catching up to do, so I'll just excuse myself and go back downstairs to tell your families the wonderful news," the rabbi said. "Be fruitful and multiply. Baruch Hashem, bless God. Maybe tomorrow we'll have brunch," he said, letting himself out of the burgeoning pit of passion.

For the first time that night, Harry and Jessica made love as man and wife, with the bright lights of Manhattan glowing in the background and Cindy the poodle chewing up Jessica's five-hundred-dollar Jimmy Choo wedding shoes under the bed.

chapter six

*B*ILLIONAIRE BLACK MARKET BOTOX BRIDE
IN NEAR WEDDING BLOW-OFF!

*BOTCHED BOTOX BABE ALMOST ABANDONED
AT THE ALTAR!*

*HIGH SOCIETY SWEETHEART SO CLOSE TO
BEING SUDDENLY SINGLE!*

Luckily for Jessica, she was already en route to her European honeymoon when the rag sheets, gossip columns, and tabloids enjoyed a marvelous time at her expense. While her picture was splattered about every newsstand in the United States, Jessica slept comfortably, her head on Harry's lap, as she traveled across the deep blue sea. Someone in the hotel must have tipped off the swarm of reporters camped out on Fifth Avenue about what had happened. It wasn't too hard to figure out, since all the celebrities and other high-profile guests were caught leaving way too early to have enjoyed a full evening of dining, dancing, and wedding celebrations.

Whoever ratted Jessica out somehow knew that she and Harry finally did marry in the privacy of their hotel suite, so the articles the papers ran couldn't make her look like a total reject (even though they would have loved to). Even though all turned out well in the end and both sets of parents were relieved to have their kids married, there was still plenty of drama to be written about. The story of the Beverly Hills Billionaire Boy missing his star-studded wedding made big news from coast to coast. It was somewhat of a letdown in the end that it was all a terrible mistake, but even so, Harry and Jessica had provided enough excitement to get the ball rolling. Only a week ago there was little more than a slight degree of media fascination with the rich girl who almost OD'd on extra-strength Botox, but today Jessica Ackerman-Raider and her equally loaded husband Harry were the center of a firestorm. In this case, Chas Greer was right on the money. After all, what young, American couple could compete with their vast wealth, her elegant good looks, and his mischievous, reformed party-boy persona? In Europe, where Harry and Jessica were headed, there were young royal blue bloods emulating style, setting trends, and stirring up enough gossip to keep the paparazzi's tongue's wagging. Back at home, the high society yearned for someone to fill the emptiness left by the doomed JFK Junior and his gorgeous wife, Carolyn, who had been tragically lost at sea after an airplane crash several years before. Celebrity couples could come and go, but Harry and Jessica were now the closest thing the papers had seen to American royalty in a long time.

At this sweet point in the beginning of their life together, Harry and Jessica were still very much in the dark about their celebrity status, even as it was gaining momentum on American shores. Their plane landed in London, the first stop on their European tour, and they embarked on the honeymoon of a lifetime. Ah, what a trip it would be! Jessica's new stepmother had used all of her social and royal contacts to make sure the newlyweds had the red carpet rolled out for them in the grandest cities all over the continent. Jessica and Harry were treated like VIPs in Paris, Rome, Monte Carlo, Athens, Geneva, and Vienna. Whatever glitz these two bon vivants missed with their fabulous wedding plans turned topsy-turvy definitely came back to them in spades.

★★★

At the end of their lavish trip, the Raider's private plane glided across the ocean, effortlessly flying a sleeping Harry and Jessica back to hills of Hollywood. It was around six in the morning when the Queen Irma II was given clearance to land in the private jet area of the Los Angeles airport. Harry was snuggled up in Jessica's lap, with a new Frette sheet pulled up around his neck. He was snoring so loudly that he completely drowned out the sound of the descending airplane engines.

As the early morning sun poured into window, Jessica slowly awoke from a deep, Ambien-enhanced sleep. A jolt of bumpy turbulence startled her, but because she was resting so peacefully, she almost forgot where she was. "May I offer you some fresh orange juice, Mrs. Raider?" the private jet's uniformed attendant asked Jessica when the plane leveled out. She handed her a warm, wet towel while spritzing Evian air moisturizer in the area directly around Jessica's face.

"Sure, that would be great," Jessica yawned. "Do you know where we are now?" Jessica asked, taking a Waterford crystal glass filled with fresh pulpy orange juice off the attendant's sterling silver tray.

"We're just about to arrive in Los Angeles. It's a lovely day, Mrs. Raider, practically no smog. If you look out to your left, you can just about see the Hollywood sign," the woman said, smiling a Donny-Osmond-sized grin.

Gently, Jessica shifted Harry over to one side so that she could get a good look out the window. Below her lay her new town and a world of unexplored possibilities. Even while traveling extensively in her single days, Jessica had never spent much time in California. She traveled all over Europe, Israel, and the Far East, but with the exception of a few shopping trips to Beverly Hills' Rodeo Drive with her late mother, Jessica was a stranger to the City of Angels. Jessica gazed down at mountains that looked like they were dotted with dollhouse-sized buildings.

Somewhere down there was her new Sunset Boulevard, twenty-thousand-square-foot Beverly Hills palace with gardens and a pool, a wedding gift from Harry's parents. On one level, Jessica felt strange moving across the country into a house that was bought by Harry's father and decorated down to the last tea towel by his mother. But she knew this was just their generous way of making the transition as easy as possible for her.

Their giant home was decked out from top to bottom with every creature comfort the young couple could imagine. Irma even hired a full staff, including a variety of maids, a butler, pool cleaners, Japanese gardeners, Feng Shui artists, dog walkers, and weekly rotating chefs specializing in an array of California and international cuisine. Everyone employed by the senior Mrs. Raider was primed, ready to go, and eager to cater to Harry's and Jessica's every whim. When she arrived at her new Beverly Hills home, Jessica wouldn't have to lift a finger. She could just drop her purse at the door, walk up the massive pink marble staircase to her private dressing suite, and comfortably sink into a waiting, relaxing rosewater bath already drawn for her. If everything went as Irma planned, the young couple would enjoy a blissful introduction to married life in Beverly Hills and everyone would live happily every after.

As the Queen Irma II landed on the runway, a white limousine dutifully waited on the tarmac. "Wake up, baby, we're here," Jessica said softly, running her fingers through Harry's unruly frizz.

"Wow, really? Already? I can't believe it. It feels like we just left Rome," Harry said, enjoying a good, long stretch.

"That's because you slept the whole way, Harry. You even missed the landing. It was wonderful to fly in over the mountains and to see all of LA on a clear morning. It looks pretty fantastic," Jessica said with excitement. The bright sunshine and majestic mountains had given her a warm welcome, and she couldn't help but feel wonderful about beginning her new life with the man she loved.

"Great, I'm glad you're as psyched as I am about being here. I haven't been home in long time," Harry said as he helped Jessica schlep her Louis Vuitton carry-on down the exit stairs of the plane.

"I have to admit, I was a little a nervous about it at first," Jessica said, reaching into her Fendi purse for her Chanel sunglasses to block out the early morning glare. "I mean, I never really lived this far away from East Hampton before. But now that I'm here, I have a good feeling that I'm really going to love it," Jessica said confidently.

"And I love you, baby," Harry grinned, whipped out his latest digital camera from his Le Sport Sac and began snapping away at Jessica.

"I want to capture the essence of Jessica Raider taking her first steps in Hollywood. A brighter star this town has never seen!" Harry said, striking a series of silly poses, pretending to be a "stalkerazzi" celebrity photographer. "Maybe I can sell this picture to the *National Enquirer* and get enough money to buy another watch," Harry joked.

"No thanks, I've had enough press lately," Jessica said. "I think I'll shun the spotlight for a while." She took Harry's hand and walked toward the awaiting car.

"Great to meet you, Mrs. Raider. Welcome to Los

Angeles," said the chauffeur, an elderly, elegant African American gentleman, smiling mischievously as if he were hiding a big secret. He opened the back door and all of a sudden a white, fluffy ball sporting a big, red velvet bow came jumping out of the back seat, bounding towards Jessica. It was Cindy, Jessica's beloved toy poodle, smelling all nice and clean, fresh from the groomers.

"Oh my gosh! My baby!" Jessica squealed with delight, dropping her bags and scooping up her little pet into her arms. "I missed you so much, poochie poochie poo!" Jessica cooed, practically smothering the dog with kisses. Cindy, equally excited to see her mistress, licked Jessica's Italian-sun-kissed face enthusiastically.

"Lucky dog," Harry winked and playfully elbowed the chauffeur.

"I'm sure your lovely wife has plenty of affection left for you, Mr. Raider," the chauffeur said politely.

"Hey Frank, what is this Mr. Raider crap? You've been driving me around since I've been about four years old. Why are you so formal all of sudden, dude?" Harry slapped Frank on the back and looked at him, completely confused.

"Well, I just thought since you're all grown up and married now, you'd want a little more, respect, sir," Frank said, tipping his hat towards Jessica.

"Okay, like, don't become a total dork or anything on me, pal. Just because I got the old ball and chain here doesn't mean *anything's* changed. Isn't that right, Jessica?" Harry said, poking Jessica in the ribs.

"Well, I'm sure they'll be *some* changes," Jessica muttered nervously, subconsciously picking at Cindy's collar, doing her best not to sound too controlling.

"Oh, sure, honey, so I've calmed down a little, but it's still me, Frank! I'm still Scary Harry!" Harry said to the chauffeur, jumping into his unsuspecting arms and giving him a giant, inescapable bear hug.

"Well, I'm sure glad you're home and it's certainly nice to see you so happy," was all the aging man could say, blushing with embarrassment in front of the new Mrs. Raider.

"Me too, kiddo! Now let's roll!" Harry said, snapping a few shots of Frank helping Jessica into the limo while she clutched Cindy for comfort. Luckily for Beverly Hills' new golden couple, the traffic was exceptionally light this morning on the 405, the main freeway that brought the limo home from the airport. "Should I get off on Santa Monica Boulevard and make some time or take the scenic way on Sunset?" Frank asked Harry, who was so excited to be back in LA he could barely sit still.

"Take Sunset, definitely!" shouted Harry from the backseat. "I want to give my lady and her muffin here 'the official Harry Raider tour of terror'!" Harry chortled.

"What the hell is that?" Jessica blurted out anxiously.

"Relax, babycakes, it's cool. It's just that I used to be a real party animal, that's all. You knew that!" Harry gave her knee a reassuring pat.

"Yeah, I guess I did," Jessica admitted. Her eyes soon followed Harry's gaze out the window to the humongous, sprawling mansions arising along the twisty, turning, winding road that ran Bel Air into Beverly Hills.

"Wow, I've had so many rockin' experiences in these hellacious hills, man," Harry said, hanging his head out the window. "Driving through here brings back so many memories!"

"Well, the fact that you can actually remember what you did here is a good sign." Jessica smiled, forcing herself to stay positive. She wasn't about to let Harry's flashback ruin her first day in Los Angeles. *Okay, so he likes to reminisce about his bachelor days, so what? It doesn't mean he's going to go out and do it all over again. It's only natural, right? After all we've been through, I really do know he loves me. He won't fuck it up now,* Jessica told herself as Harry focused on his old neighborhood.

"See that driveway down there?" Harry said, pointing to a long but otherwise inconspicuous driveway behind a pair of large, imposing metal gates.

"Mmhm," Jessica said, nodding her head.

"That's Hef's place." Harry grinned like he was rolling a porno flick through his dirty little mind.

"Hef?" Jessica asked naively.

"Hugh Hefner, the granddaddy of the original good time. That's the Playboy Mansion. Hef, you're GOD!" Harry rolled down the window and screamed like a teenager on spring break, then sat back in a fit of laughter.

"Gee Harry, seems like you're really going to miss all of this. I'm so sorry to put such a damper on your lifestyle," Jessica said, beginning to pout. She didn't have a mean bone in her dainty little body, but she knew how to give a guilt trip like the best of them.

"Yeah, well, what can I do? I'm a married man now. Looks like the party's over for good. What a bummer."

Startled by his words, Jessica glared at Harry in disbelief. *Has being back in LA for such a short time, driving through his old neighborhood, made him think he made a horrible mistake? Does he really think that being married to me is really a bummer?* She felt a panic attack coming on. "Oh my God, Harry, I've got to get out of here!" Jessica panted, beginning to hyperventilate. She loosened her death grip on Cindy and frantically reached for the car door.

Before she could open it, Harry put his hand on hers and pulled her into his arms. "I'm sorry, sweetie, I was only messing around. Can't you take a joke, sweetheart? You can't take half the shit that comes out of my mouth seriously. You know that by now, don't ya?" Harry chided, caressing Jessica's soft hair.

"Yes, yes, I do Harry," Jessica sat back, cleared her throat, and pulled herself together. "I know you have a wicked sense of humor and I've got to learn to accept that and go with the flow." She picked Cindy up off the floor of the limo and firmly placed her back in her lap. Jessica was not about to blow it on her first day in Beverly Hills.

"I was hoping you'd do more than 'accept' me, I was hoping you'd love me. All of me, even the insane parts." Harry searched Jessica's green eyes and was only half joking now.

"I do love you, Harry, you know that. And I am really happy to be here in LA with you. It's just that when you talk about your past, even when you're only kidding, it makes me feel very insecure. I feel like you've given up a big part of yourself to be with me, and I really hope you'll think I'm worth it and will never have any regrets."

"You're more than worth it, Jes. You're my whole world now," Harry declared proudly. "Besides, I didn't just give up the partying lifestyle for you, Jes, or for my parents' money. I really did it for me," Harry admitted, softly.

"That sounds very healthy, Harry," Jessica replied confidently. She kissed him on the cheek and squeezed his hand supportively.

"I mean, I can't be a fuck-up my whole life, right? Thirty-nine years of total debauchery has got to be enough," Harry smiled sheepishly and let out a big yawn as they pulled into their new estate. *Okay, I guess this is home,* Jessica thought to herself. She tapped on the window of the limo like she was knocking on wood for good luck, a gesture that she hoped would keep Harry's old ghosts from haunting their new life together.

chapter seven

The limo slowly pulled up to a massive iron gate. Beyond it, Jessica could see a surrealistic white modern home on Sunset Boulevard just around the corner from the Beverly Hills Hotel. "I can eat breakfast at the Polo Lounge every day! They have the best eggs and hash there. I love it! I love it!" Harry shouted.

"I think your dad was hoping you'd join him in the mornings at Nate and Al's before you both go to the office," Frank noted, as Harry leaned out of the limo window to snap pictures of his new abode. Nate and Al's, a deli on Beverly Drive that served real New York Jewish haimish cooking, was a Beverly Hills institution. If a struggling actress needed an agent or a young screenwriter wanted to get his movie produced, the best chance they had to meet Hollywood's crème de la crème was over cream cheese and lox in this power breakfast pastrami palace.

"What do you mean, Frank? You never drove me to the office with Dad," Harry laughed, not wanting to accept what the chauffeur was hinting at.

"It's not my place to say anything, Harry," Frank said quietly, realizing he might have just made a huge blunder. It never occurred to him that Mr. Raider senior had not yet informed Harry of what was in store for him on the other side of those gates.

"Come on, Frank, my man. Clue me in on what's going on. Do you know something I don't?" Harry cajoled, snapping a close-up picture of the uncomfortable expression on Frank's face as he piloted the limo through the opening gates.

"As I said, Harry, I can't get involved in what goes on between you and your dad, but I'm sure y'all will have a good talk when you get settled in." Frank hoped he was being diplomatic, and that he hadn't just opened a can of worms with Harry.

"That's not good enough, Frankster. What's going down here, dude?" Harry persisted as Frank parked the car in front of the large, imposing front door.

"Oh, I don't know what to tell you, Harry," a flustered Frank continued. "Look, there's your mother. Maybe she can have a word with you before you see your pop." Frank exhaled, relieved to see Irma Raider come rushing out of the mansion, thrilled to welcome her son and his bride to their new home.

Irma, a cosmetically enhanced Joan Rivers clone, tried to look California casual but she was decked out in new, white Nike sneakers, a designer velour track suit, and about two hundred and fifty thousand dollars worth of diamonds from the waist up. Even as Irma jumped up and down excitedly and waved her hands over her head to give her kids a big, exuberant hello, her Jose Eber-coiffed, golden-streaked hairdo simply did not move.

As Jessica observed her new mother-in-law's energetic joy and enthusiasm, she saw a little bit of Harry in the aging beauty. It was obvious that Irma's son's magic marriage merger had put the bounce back into her step, even if her hair didn't follow suit.

"Welcome, welcome!" Irma gave Harry a huge hug and pinched his cheeks, attacking him as he got out of the limo. Harry couldn't remember the last time his mother had been so physically affectionate with him. It was like a new, loving spirit had inhabited her tiny body.

"Whoa, easy, Mommy, you're embarrassing me in front of my new bride." Harry wasn't sure how to handle his own mother's display of love.

"That's okay with me, Harry. You did your share of embarrassing us over the years. If a little squeeze from your mother is going to make you blush, then let's say we're even," Irma laughed, once again playfully pinching her son's nose. She was so thrilled that Harry was home with his wife that Irma was willing to forget the near forty years of trouble and heartache he had caused the family.

"And, Jessica, my shaineh maidel, so glad to have you as my daughter," Irma beamed as she leaned forward to throw her arms around a very surprised Jessica. "You know I always wanted a little girl, but after Harry the doctor said I couldn't have any more children. We were going to adopt, but Sammy got so busy with the business, I didn't want him to take on another responsibility, you know. So, my dahling, I've been eagerly awaiting the day when my Harry would find himself a lovely girl and start a family of his own."

Jessica managed to plaster a smile on her face and nodded dutifully at Irma without saying a word. Jessica knew better than to confront her mother-in-law about choosing to wait before being fruitful and multiplying.

"Can we see the house? It was such a generous gift, we can't thank you enough," Jessica tactfully asked, changing the subject.

"Why, of course. It was our greatest pleasure, dear. Sammy and I are just delighted to have you as part of our family."

Irma took Jessica's hand, as Frank unloaded the bags from the limo and Cindy relieved herself in a nearby bush.

Irma opened the door to a massive California paradise. The grand foyer featured beautiful foliage arranged elegantly in a large Ming vase atop a circular glass table centered in the room. To the left was a long passageway with floor-to-ceiling windows, leading to an oak-paneled den, the French-themed formal dining room that sat thirty, the stainless-steel professional chef's kitchen with top-of-the-line appliances, and then continued out to the canopied breakfast courtyard, the coquina-stone sun patio, swimming pool, and cabana. To the right was an expansive living room/art gallery filled with museum-quality works by world-famous artists including Miró, Chagall, Agam, Calder, Rauschenberg, Degas, de Kooning, Norman Rockwell, and Andy Warhol.

Jessica's eyes lit up. She saw that her in-laws had obviously gone to great length and expense to surround her with such fantastic artwork. She realized that not only did they spend a fortune to acquire such pieces, but they also must have put in a lot of time to locate them all. *Wow, they must really want me here if they went to all of this trouble. Some of these paintings couldn't even be found at the top galleries in New York. They must have had curators all over America and in Europe looking for this stuff. It's unbelievable!* Jessica thought as she studied the signatures on the paintings with an artist's eye. All of a sudden, standing there in *her* house surrounded by the masters, Jessica began to feel at home.

"Hey, Jes, I thought you'd like these paintings! I told my mom nothing but the very best for my favorite *arteest!*" Harry said, coming into the living room sipping a Coke and chewing on a salami sandwich he picked up from the kitchen.

"This is the most fabulous private collection I've ever seen," Jessica said, turning to see a beaming Irma.

"Let's just say Sammy and I called in a few favors from some of the top dealers at Sotheby's and Christie's. When we were on our trip to Europe last summer, we acquired some very important pieces, you know. Sam says you can't go wrong with art, it's a rock-solid investment," Irma continued.

"Shouldn't they be hanging in your own home?" Jessica felt a pang of guilt.

"Oh no, we've got a house full of things we've collected over the years. Besides, you and Harry can't be Beverly Hills' new 'it' couple without a top-notch art collection. I know you young people pretend not to care about these things, but one day you will!" Irma laughed, trying to sound hip.

Jessica stared at her mother-in-law with a look of total bewilderment. "What are you talking about, Mrs. Raider?" she asked.

"Mrs. Raider, that was *my* mother-in-law, may she rest in peace back in Brooklyn. Please call me Irma, or if you like, you can call me Mom. I'd like that very much," Irma's eyes began to well up with tears.

"Okay, Mom," Jessica said hesitantly. "What do you mean by 'it' couple?

"Oh, you know dear, the high-society young couple everyone wants at their parties, movie premieres, gallery openings, fashion shows, charity events, weddings, Bar Mitzvahs, that sort of thing. Sammy and I were that couple once, many years ago. I'm so glad to see that it's already happened for you and Harry. It brings back so many memories of wonderful times we shared together," Irma said wistfully.

"I don't want to disappoint you, Mom," Jessica said, struggling with the word Mom. Jessica's mother had died many years ago, and it was still hard for her to imagine that anybody else should be called that name. "But, since I just moved to Los Angeles and don't know anyone, it might take me a while to meet new friends. I wasn't really very social back home. I know Harry loves to get out and about, so I promise to make an effort to be more social," Jessica said shyly. "But I wouldn't call us an 'it' couple by any means."

Irma practically roared with laughter at Jessica's cluelessness. Didn't she know that the Beverly Hills gossip columnists had been chronicling her every move from the fiasco before the wedding to the European honeymoon? Could she really be that naive? Irma looked at Jessica with total disbelief. And then it hit her: Jessica was as sheltered as she appeared to be. She had no idea what she was in for. Not only were the Beverly Hills society papers about to watch the new Mrs. Raider like a hawk, but they could also have a lot of fun and sell a lot of papers at her expense if she stepped one foot out of line.

And there was another awful truth Irma didn't exactly want to confront Jessica with. Before he got married, Harry Raider was considered the hottest catch in town. An endless stream of barracuda-like mothers from the Pine Valley Country Club, Beverly Hills' B'nai Brith, and her Hadassah Women's group had approached Irma over the years, begging for an introduction to her wayward son for their surgically perfected daughters. Some of the less subtle mothers would even come right out and say to Irma that the reason Harry got into so much trouble was because he wasn't married to the "right" girl. "Right," every time, meant their daughters.

One particularly forward woman proposed that her little girl, a recovering heroin addict, would go with Harry to rehab and support him through his own recovery process. Even Irma, who wanted nothing more than for Harry to shape up and settle down with a nice Jewish girl, could see the absurdity in all of this. She knew that the only reason these heartless, merciless women shamelessly pushed their daughters on Harry was because of the vast Raider fortune. Irma was no stranger to this phenomenon, since it was these same shallow women who would steal her own husband away from her given the chance.

Irma didn't want to scare Jessica by telling her that there were women who would smile to her face then do anything behind her back to take Harry away. All the scheming mothers and daughters in Beverly Hills who had lost out on a marriage to Harry Raider would now be seeking revenge. At Pine Valley, Irma had already heard women gossiping on the tennis court that it wasn't fair that two young kids like Harry and Jessica should have so much money. The general consensus seemed to be that tremendous wealth like the Raiders' and the Ackermans' should be spread around a little. Nobody in Beverly Hills' society wanted to see this marriage work.

"I'm sure you'll find that Californians are very welcoming," Irma offered with a big, fake smile. "Why don't you go upstairs and take a look at that little office I set up for you near your dressing room? There's already a bunch of things waiting for you," Irma continued.

How can that be? Who even knows I'm here? Jessica wondered as she made her way up the pink marble staircase. When Jessica walked into the cheerfully decorated office Irma created, Jessica couldn't believe her eyes. There were piles and piles of elaborate party invitations filled with confetti, sparkles, and pop-out figurines, addressed to Mr. and Mrs. Raider, just waiting to be opened. If that wasn't overwhelming enough, lining the back of the room were goody bags filled with promotional products from local publicists. Each bag was filled with samples from companies who wanted Jessica, Beverly Hills' newest hottie, to be seen in public donning their wares or chatting up the goods to her influential friends. There was everything from aromatherapeutic and soul-cleansing bath salts, herbal-infused hair gels that glowed in the dark, top-designer makeup kits and long, twisted hairpieces to rhinestone-studded costume jewelry, personally monogrammed T-shirts, cashmere sweaters, Fila tennis socks, gold and silver funky shoes, and brightly colored, naturally perfumed spandex workout clothes that were guaranteed to never to smell of sweat. There were even gold-encrusted gift cards for free deep-pore-busting facials, artichoke-enhanced seaweed wraps, spiritual healing massages, electric aura readings, fat-free candy mix-in frozen yogurt sundaes, trips to an organic raw salad bar, expensive cocktails at posh hotels, and Japanese manicures that came with a free sushi sampler platter and a pot of antioxidant green tea. Jessica had never seen such an overflow of unnecessary California crappola in her life.

I can't believe this. Where did these all come from? Jessica wondered as she sifted through the first pile. Just then the phone rang. It was Chas Greer, calling from New York. Finally, there was a familiar voice amidst the insanity. Although he was over three thousand miles away, Chas had to be the first friend to secure his permanent position in Jessica's new life.

"Hello, glamour girl. How's Hollywood? Is it faaaaaaaaabulous?" Chas whined in his inimitable saccharine tone.

"I got a stack of invites here and I literally just walked in the door. I don't get it. Why have we been invited to all these events?" Jessica asked, tearing open envelope after envelope.

"Jessica, darling, you can't be serious. I told you, Harry and you totally outshine even the biggest star on Hollywood Boulevard. You guys are American royalty and don't you forget it, girlfriend!" Chas flattered her.

"I don't think I can even if I wanted to," Jessica muttered under her breath as she made her way through the piles that never seemed to end. "I still don't understand how all these people know we're here."

"First of all, Jes, the Raiders are very established people in the Beverly Hills community. Second of all...did you open the package from me yet? It's in a purple FedEx. Surely you can find it under the mountain of stuff on your desk." Jessica could sense Chas smirking smugly on the other side of the phone, insinuating that his correspondence was so much more important than anyone else's.

"Ah, yes, here it is. Let's see what's inside," Jessica said, purposely opening the package extra slowly to tease Chas and make him wait. The little devil in Jessica loved to taunt Chas anytime she could.

"Well hurry up, honey, I don't have all day. I have a major appointment with Melania Trump uptown and I don't want to be late," Chas said, taking Jessica's brief pause as a good opportunity to drop a big name.

"Oh my God, how did this happen?" *I'LL TAKE THAT ONE! SORRY DARLING, IT'S NOT FOR SALE! THE FRESH PRINCE OF BEVERLY HILLS AND HIS BOTOXED BRIDE BLOW THROUGH BUCKINGHAM PALACE,* said the *News of the World,* Britain's most notorious rag sheet. If these gaudy headlines weren't enough, underneath was a picture of Harry and Jessica admiring some extraordinary artwork during their private tour of Buckingham Palace.

THE HONEYMOONERS—BEVERLY HILLBILLY STYLE: BOTOX BRIDEZILLA AND BILLIONAIRE BAD BOY BUY THEIR WAY THROUGH EUROPE. This horrible headline found in a national celebrity gossip magazine was accompanied by a picture of Jessica and Harry walking down the Left Bank in Paris carrying hoards of shopping bags from designer stores.

BON VOYAGE BOTOX BRATS! HARRY AND JES-SICA RAIDER WHINE AND DINE IN MONTE CARLO.
This one, perhaps the nastiest of them all, was found in a local Beverly Hills society paper, written by a gossip columnist who was always extremely jealous of the Raiders' good fortune. How this curmudgeon reporter got a picture of a sour-faced Jessica briskly shooing away a wine waiter and Harry yawning at the table of a fancy five-star restaurant on the Riviera, Jessica would never know. What she knew was that she had been closely followed when she was abroad and never had any idea of what was going on. Needless to say, this kind of negative attention scared her immensely. No one cared what she did or where she went when she was living in the Hamptons. The media's sudden fascination with her life was an unwelcoming surprise and she didn't know how to make it go away.

"How the hell did they get these pictures?" Jessica was astonishment. "I never saw anyone flashing a camera at me while we were away, except Harry of course. I know he didn't send his pictures to the newspapers, we haven't even got the film developed yet," Jessica continued.

"Of course it wasn't Harry, silly girl. Don't you know that the paparazzi, especially the European ones, have cameras equipped with heavy-duty zoom lenses? You could be naked in your hotel room and they could take a shot of you while they were sitting in a café all the way across the street. Look what they did to Princess Diana. Those pictures sell for big money, honey. I'm sure many a paparazzo put his kid through school with just a shot of the princess getting out of the car!"

"But I'm not Princess Diana, I'm just me. I still don't understand what all the fuss is about," Jessica said, sliding all the invites into the top drawer of her desk in one fell swoop.

"You will soon, kiddo. And you may not be Diana but

you sure are a hell of a lot better looking than Camilla, and that's the best that they have over there now. It's no wonder they were so interested in a pretty, young American heiress," Chas giggled.

Jessica flopped down in her chair. "I wish you were here with me, Chas. I know it would be a lot easier to get through all this with your help," Jessica caught herself saying. If those invites had come to her back in East Hampton, she would have just thrown them out, like she did for years as a single woman and during her first failed marriage. But now that she was Mrs. Raider, she saw that her days of being a social hermit were over. She couldn't take Harry, the life of the party, away from every bash in town and expect him to be happy. He sure wasn't the type to sit at home in front of the television every night talking back to CNN, like her last husband. The only way to make this work was to let him enjoy himself somewhat safely and controlled. This was her only chance of keeping him from seeking out the pleasures of LA's underworld after hours.

"Oh, I wish I was there with you too, little Jes. It would be so exciting to tag along with you and Harry to every hot party in town. Remember, I grew up out there and I still know everyone who's anyone. I could be a real help, sweetie," Chas said.

"I know, Chas, I wish I could just move you out here with us. What would that take?" Jessica said, almost seriously.

Chas smiled into the phone. "Well, my business has really taken off in the past six months. You'd have to pay me more than I'm making catering to all of my clients, new and old. That would run a small fortune. But I know you can afford it."

Jessica threw her hands up in the air in frustration. She felt that she needed Chas so badly, but she just couldn't come to grips with the extra expense. "Yeah, but I really can't justify it right now, you know. I have to prove myself here first. Harry loves you, Chas, but if he thinks that I can't function in his world without you to hold my hand, he'd lose respect for me. I have to show Harry that our love is the only thing that matters and I am capable of being a strong, independent wife that he can be proud of," Jessica declared, straightening up in her chair. "I'll really miss you, Chas. I hope you'll have a reason to come to California soon," Jessica said softly.

"Oh, poopie, you know I'll come out there every chance I get. My mom isn't getting any younger, and I have to come to Beverly Hills to get her to the best plastic surgeons. Also, I do have quite a nice coterie of bicoastal clients now. So many trendy LA girls are into getting sophisticated Manhattan chic." Chas puffed on his clove cigarette.

"That's great, Chas. Of course, I can still fly you out here each season to put together my wardrobe. I wouldn't dream of getting a new personal shopper or stylist. You'll still buy all of my clothes for me and you can stay here anytime you want. We've got a huge house, there's plenty of room for you and Juan," Jessica replied enthusiastically. She was so happy to be talking to someone she knew, she didn't even care that it was conniving, catty Chas Greer.

"Terrific, sweetie, we may just take you up on that," Chas said, lifting his arm in the air victoriously and pouring himself another glass of Chardonnay. He so loved it when his clients needed him! The more desperate, the better.

"Great, I hope I get to see you," Jessica didn't even try to hide the neediness in her voice.

"You will, darling, you will," Chas breezed.

"Who you talking to?" Jessica heard Harry ask as he dashed up the stairs.

"I better go now, Chas, Harry's coming. We'll talk soon?"

"Of course we will. Ciao, baby." Chas let out a confident giggle as he hung up the phone. Oh, how he loved to hook them in. Any fears he had about losing Jessica Raider to a new Beverly-Hills-based stylist had just completely been assuaged. No one could ever take Chas's place in his ladies' charmed lives! Chas had perfected the art of hand-holding to a T and not even the professional ass-kissing celebrity "handlers" were as good at coddling their clients. Cocky and comfortable as the Cheshire cat who just watched his dinner get caught in the mousetrap, Chas Greer smiled triumphantly, stretched out on his big white leather couch, and sipped his Chardonnay.

★★★

Back in Beverly Hills, Harry entered his wife's new office to find her standing there totally bewildered. "Wow! Look at all this great stuff!" Harry proclaimed, attacking the goody bags like a kid at Christmas. "Check out these running shoes!" Harry put a terry-cloth headband around his frizzy hair and forced his feet into a pair of sneakers that accompanied a pass for a free one-month membership to a local gym.

"Harry, I think those are for women." Jessica couldn't help but be amused by her husband's enthusiasm. What seemed to her an overwhelming burden was all fun and games to him.

"No way, these are unisex. They fit great!" Harry exclaimed, jogging in place, lifting his knees practically all the way to his chin. "What else have we got here? Wow, look at this!" Harry had discovered some bubble bath that came with two plush, monogrammed robes, an herbal neck rest, and a multi-colored loofah. "Hey, Jes, how bout you and I slip these babies on and head for some fun in the tub?" Harry grinned devilishly.

"Sure, why not? A bath actually sounds like a great idea." Maybe a little escape with Harry was exactly what she needed at the moment.

"Right this way, madame!" Harry smiled as he held the door open and led her down the hall towards their bedroom. When they reached their boudoir Jessica was pleasantly shocked. Though her living room was filled with paintings created by the great masters, her very own works of art adorned their bedroom walls. Some of her favorite watercolors of Cindy playing in her East Hampton garden and of the two them frolicking carelessly by the sea had been prominently displayed above the big brass bed.

"This is incredible!" Jessica gazed at her own work like someone visiting a museum for the first time. "It was so thoughtful of your mother to ship some of my stuff all the way across the country. Having these paintings here makes me feel so much at home," Jessica sighed.

"Hey, wait a minute now. Where's your portrait of me?" Harry asked, looking around the room.

"You mean the nude one I painted of you posing in the sun, like an Adonis?" Jessica giggled.

"Yes! Frankly I must say that it was your finest work yet, my dear. Don't you agree?" Harry searched his wife's eyes for a hint of the truth about how she saw his naked body.

"Of course it was, Harry," Jessica squeezed his hand supportively. "I can't see Irma Raider unwrapping it and hanging it in our bedroom though. I'm sure she left it back in East Hampton."

"What a bummer!" Harry took off his shoes and socks and started to undress in preparation for his romantic bath with Jessica. "Come, baby, it's time to hit the tub of love," Harry said seductively as he sauntered over to Jessica and rubbed her neck and unhooked her bra. His hands made their way around her shoulders and then around her petite torso. Harry ran his fingers gently around Jessica's soft, pillowy female parts while massaging the rest of her form firmly. This was a move he knew would drive her wild.

Jessica let out a sigh of sheer pleasure, then rolled her head around in response to her husband's warm touch. She finally began to relax into the moment. That was until she caught sight of a doorway that led to a smaller room that appeared to be an annex to her super-large bedroom. "What's in there?" she asked Harry curiously, as she continued to enjoy Harry's magic hands.

"Do you really care right now?" Harry whispered into her ear, licking the edges of it.

"I guess not," Jessica murmured, as she felt herself getting moist with excitement.

Without ever facing her, Harry slid his hands down the back of Jessica's pants and lowered them to the floor. While still fondling her he kissed down her back until he reached her ample buttocks. His brazen tongue kept exploring until it eventually found the essence of her womanhood. Since Harry was bold enough to take an unorthodox route to the source of all of her desire, Jessica had become crazy with excitement. She screamed wildly as Harry bent her over and plunged himself inside her. Her fingers gripped the edge of the bed as she hung on for dear life, loving every minute of the intimacy she shared with Harry.

As he continued to make love to her, Jessica managed to grab a towel and place it underneath herself, so it hit the "love mound" just right. Pretty soon she was sharing Harry's ecstasy. Even though he had reached his climax, Harry made sure to keep pleasing his wife, so that she too could feel an uninhibited release of passion. In a matter of seconds, Jessica felt like it was the Fourth of July between her legs, although it was approaching early December. The erotic connection that Jessica shared with her new husband was definitely enough to take her mind off of the stress and pressure she associated with becoming a Beverly Hills matron. At least for now, they could be just "Jessica and Harry" all alone in their little love bubble, or so she thought.

chapter eight

Harry and Jessica lay on their massive king-size bed, entwined in each other arms. After a few moments of rest, Harry was ready to get on with the show. Unlocking himself from Jessica's loving embrace, he popped off the bed, put on the freebie plush robe, and walked into Jessica's office. Rummaging through one of the goodie bags for the best-smelling bubble bath, he called out, "What are you in the mood for today, honey? The scent of Georgia peach or wild honey maple oak?"

"I don't know, you decide," Jessica let out a big yawn and stretch.

"Okay, I'll surprise you!" Harry grabbed a bunch of different bath bottles and marched purposefully towards the bathroom. Jessica got off the bed and put on the other gift robe. Instead of following Harry directly towards the tub, she wanted to check out the little room she had spotted from the corner of her eye before her husband enraptured her. Jessica pushed open the large oak door all the way.

Tastefully decorated in yellow and white was a fully outfitted nursery, complete with bassinette, canopied crib, changing table, music box, children's toys, rocking horse, and collection of teddy bears. There was even a happy little smiley-faced bag filled with diapers, baby wipes, natural baby-friendly shampoos and hypoallergenic aloe-based lotions. Obviously a yellow décor had been chosen since Irma couldn't know the sex of Harry and Jessica's child, who wasn't even a thought in Jessica's heart yet.

Oh my goodness, this is totally nuts. I mean, it's even a little creepy. Jessica eyed a pair of Raggedy Ann and Andy dolls she swore were looking right back at her. *Okay, it's one thing to allow her to decorate my house down to the last doorknob—after all, she did pay for it. But it's certainly another to let her control my womb! Harry's still a big baby himself. How can she think he could nearly be ready for the responsibility of fatherhood? Can't she give us at least five minutes to make sure we can make it as a married couple?*

But as taken aback as she was at the surprise of finding a children's paradise on the other side of her newlywed boudoir, Jessica felt surreally comfortable in this ready-made infant FAO Schwartz. Jessica couldn't help but flip through some of the children's books and poke around the softness of the variety of dolls. *Maybe this isn't so terrible after all. I mean, all this stuff looks kind of harmless. It's really sweet, even.* Jessica folded a baby's receiving blanket that had fallen off a white wicker rocking chair. While Jessica stared at the smiling stuffed faces of Winnie the Pooh and Paddington Bear, simple but serious maternal thoughts ran through her mind.

As she wound up a merry-go-round music box, Jessica's heart began to melt. Strangely enough, she felt happier in the nursery for her imaginary children than she did in her so-called office filled with invitations and free stuff.

Stopping for a moment to take it all in, she realized that she wasn't the only one who was going to be a little more than freaked out to see what Irma had concocted. *How the hell is Harry going to react to this?* Jessica started subconsciously humming along to the tune coming from the merry-go-round. *Well, one of two things is going to happen here. This is going to totally blow his mind and he's going to jump out the window and head for the nearest party in the hills. Or he's going to think these toys are for him,* Jessica chuckled to herself.

Jessica tiptoed out of the nursery and quietly shut the door behind her, as if the spirit of her yet-to-be-conceived baby was already asleep in there.

Back in the safety of her bedroom, Jessica was about to slip off her fluffy robe when she heard a quiet knock. "Come in," Jessica said, quickly pulling the robe back around her tiny body. Irma Raider opened the big door just a crack.

"I hope I'm not disturbing anything," Irma whispered, still standing in the doorway.

"No, no, it's all right, come on in." Jessica opened the door fully for her mother-in-law to enter.

Despite Jessica's welcome into her and Harry's private oasis, Irma stood respectfully in the doorway, and wouldn't enter the sacred space. *My grandchildren will be created in this very bedroom,* Irma thought as she gave Jessica a warm, motherly smile. "I'm so sorry to disturb you, Jessica. I just wanted to say goodbye before I go home to Sammy. I sincerely hope everything in this house is to your liking."

"Oh, yes, it's beautiful. Again, thank you so much for this amazing gift and for preparing it so wonderfully for us." Jessica smiled and nodded her head in approval. Because her family background was so similar to Harry's, she knew she would probably be thanking her in-laws for the house every time she saw them, every day for the rest of their lives. The only thing the Raiders enjoyed more than spoiling their son and daughter-in-law was hearing how grateful the kids were to have such giving parents. Jessica knew her father would have done the same thing and behaved absolutely the same way, if Harry and Jessica had chosen to live in East Hampton instead of California.

"Have you had a chance to have a good look around the whole upstairs wing?" Irma asked subtly, looking around and unable to meet Jessica's direct glance.

"Um, no, not quite yet, but I will this evening," Jessica said sweetly, watching Irma's face drop in disappointment. Immediately Irma began picking at the Chanel buckle on her belt with her long, manicured nails and rubbing one Ferragamo pump on top of the other, as she crossed her legs in an attempt to hold her anticipation. She also began nibbling on her bottom lip, swallowing a large glob of pink shimmering lipstick.

She inhaled a big breath and held it until she looked like a blowfish about to explode. Jessica decided not to torture the old woman any more. "I did manage to see this entire side of the upstairs, though. I saw the whole bedroom suite and the gracious rooms adjoining it," Jessica said, raising an eyebrow and pointing directly in the direction of the nursery.

"Um, hm," Irma mumbled, still frozen in position. "Well," she forced herself to continue while running her twenty-carat-diamond-ringed fingers through her highlighted hair. "What do you think?" Irma concluded and finally was able to look Jessica straight in the eye.

"I think it's lovely. I absolutely adore the whole thing," Jessica replied. She shut her eyes and lowered her head, giving Irma a little bow of reverence. This silent gesture was an acknowledgement that she was ready to do her duty, whether that was her real truth or not. Jessica felt that the easiest thing to do at this moment to wave the white diaper in retreat and let it be known that she was a willing captive in her own home.

"That's wonderful!" A joyful Irma clapped her hands together and let out a huge sigh of relief. "I'm so glad to know you're comfortable with, uh...everything," Irma stuttered and cleared her throat. "You and Harry and... um... well, you know... will be so happy here!" Irma gazed longingly towards the nursery. She pulled a rumpled tissue from her pocket, blew her nose, and dabbed at the tears that welled up in her eyes, careful not to smear her mascara. "Okay, well I should be going. I don't want to overstay my welcome." Irma turned around and sprinted down the corridor, waving her hands in excitement.

Jessica went out in to the hall and watched Irma fly down the long winding staircase. "Please take it easy, there's no reason to rush," Jessica called down after her. Noticing the look of sheer horror on Irma's face, Jessica realized that she had been gravely misunderstood. "I mean, Irma, there's no reason to go home so soon. You ran down the stairs so quickly I was afraid you'd hurt yourself," Jessica said sheepishly, as she shrugged her shoulders and grinned apologetically.

"Oh!" Irma said, totally relieved. She felt a little embarrassed. "I'm sorry, dear, I don't know what I was thinking. I have to hurry up anyway. There's a brisket, some stuffed derma, and a beautiful chicken in a pot waiting for me at Canter's on Fairfax. I want to pick it up and get it home to Sammy while it's still hot. That way I don't have to go through the bother of reheating it." Irma hurried out the door into the circular driveway.

"This from a woman who has a staff of twelve at her estate just waiting to put fire under a matzo ball," Jessica muttered under her breath, as she watched Irma climb into the back of her Silver Cloud Rolls Royce.

★★★

With her mother-in-law safely out of the house, Jessica was eager to chill out with Harry in a relaxing tub. In the bathroom, she found him wearing a pair of funky dark sunglasses, blowing bubbles with the scented bubble bath, and sipping what looked like champagne from a plastic champagne glass. "Harry, what are you drinking? Where did that come from?" Jessica demanded, fearing that her newly clean and sober husband had just jumped off the wagon.

"Well, there you are, sweetie. What took you so long? I was getting so impatient to be honored by your adorable presence, I was almost forced to down this whole bottle by myself," Harry laughed and hiccupped erratically, pretending to be under the influence of whatever was in the near-empty bottle.

"I was seeing your mother out, that's all," Jessica proclaimed, stomping her foot and planting her hands on her hips. "Now, are you going to tell me where you got this?" She grabbed the bottle out of Harry's hands and inspected the label. "Green Goddess's Sparkling Apple Cider. A 100 Percent Nonalcoholic Divine Nectar," Jessica read out loud.

"Sorry, Harry," Jessica admitted, softly tapping the bottle against her head while she let her robe fall to the floor.

"It's okay, honey, I know what it looked like. I was just teasing you a little, that's all," Harry grinned mischievously, as he reached out his hand and helped Jessica submerge in the warm, sudsy water. Jessica let out a relaxing sigh and lay back into Harry's waiting arms. He poured some of the apple bubbly into another plastic cup and held up to Jessica's lips as she took a long, seductive sip.

"Mmm. This actually tastes great. Who sent it to us, anyway?" Jessica purred, closing her eyes and nuzzling her head under Harry's chin.

"Mom had it waiting for us. Isn't she fantastic? She thinks of everything," Harry said.

"She certainly does. You think this is something, you should see the nursery." Jessica laughed at the absolute absurdity of it all.

"The *what?*" Harry exclaimed, sitting up straight and practically drowning Jessica.

As Jessica spit out a mouthful of bubble bath she almost swallowed, it dawned on her that she had gotten a little too comfortable. *Oh shit, what did I just do? How the hell am I going to get out of this one?* She watched Harry's face as it turned from a healthy sun-kissed tan to an ash gray at the very mention of fatherhood.

Harry popped out of the tub and wiped himself off hastily while frantically searching around the bathroom for his baggy Calvin Klein boxer shorts. Harry ran into the bedroom, grabbed the first pair of jeans he could find in the closet, put them on, and then went back in the bathroom.

"You're on the pill, aren't you?" Harry demanded. This was the first time he had ever spoken even remotely rudely to her since they first met in the Hamptons the past summer. "Please tell me you're on the pill, Jes," Harry begged, softening up his tone when he saw tears streaming down her face.

"Yes, I'm on the pill, Harry," Jessica answered fighting back the tears that were flowing from her sea-green eyes.

"Phew! That's a relief. You know, it never occurred to me to ask you about birth control. I just figured a hip chick like you would know how to protect herself. It's not like you had to get knocked up to trap me or anything like that, so I just figured whatever you were doing to keep the little monsters at bay was your business, babycakes." Harry chuckled with relief as he sat down next to the bathtub where Jessica sulked.

"Monsters, huh? Is that what you think of our future children?" she sobbed uncontrollably, getting more soap in her eyes as she attempted to wipe the bubbles off her face.

"No, no, of course not. I didn't mean it like that," Harry handed her a fresh face cloth and helped her out of the tub. "It's just that I'm, like, in no way ready for fatherhood, Jessica," Harry said quite firmly as he gently dried her off with another big, white towel.

"Are you telling me you never want to be a dad?" Jessica asked him directly, planting her arms on his shoulders.

"Of course not, Jessica. I could be into having a bunch of little Harrys, or Harriets for that matter, one day, just not right this minute. I'm still a big kid myself, you see?" Harry flashed his irresistible little-boy grin and playfully wrapped his towel in a turban around Jessica's head.

"Aaaahhh, Mrs. Raider, my favorite genie has escaped her bottle. Come and let me take you on magic carpet ride into a mysterious land far, far, far away," Harry said in his best Arabian accent, twirling Jessica around in place.

"So when do you think you will be ready?" Jessica pursued him, not letting her husband off the hook.

"Jesus, Jessica, I don't know!" A befuddled Harry thudded down to reality. After pacing back and forth a little bit in silence, Harry walked into the bedroom and flopped on the bed. He put both his hands over his face and began to rub his eyes.

"You know what, Jes, I guess we should have talked about this before we got married." Harry hid his face behind his two palms.

"If I said that I wanted kids right away, would that have changed everything?" Jessica asked him quietly, standing squarely at the foot of the bed.

"No, not really." Harry sat up bravely and propped himself up on a giant pillow. "I would have definitely still married you, if that's what you wanted to know." Harry smiled at his worried wife, and opened his arms for her to jump in.

This time Jessica was not so quick to jump into Harry's arms. She needed more answers and she needed them now.

"What's wrong?" Harry asked, as he saw his wife was not moving.

"Did it ever occur to you to ask me if I would still have married you if I knew that you weren't ready to start a family right away?" Jessica folded her arms to regain her self-esteem. Harry laughed irreverently.

"Look, Harry, to be honest with you, I actually wasn't thinking about starting a family right away either. But when I saw the sweet nursery Irma created, it got me thinking, that's all. Let's remember that I'm the one who moved all the way out here and was willing to start a whole new chapter in my life, just to be with you. If anyone needs time to get adjusted to this whole thing, it's *me!*"

"Is it so terrible here?" Harry waved his arm around the room to show her what a spectacular home his family had provided for her.

"Of course not. It's fucking breathtaking, all right? But any way you slice it, I'm still on new ground here and it's totally Raider territory," Jessica continued.

"You're a Raider too, Jes." As cocky as Harry was at times, he knew that Jessica was one woman he couldn't manipulate.

"Yes, Harry, I'm your wife and I'm going to do everything I can to build a happy home here with you. But in my perfect world, life *does* include children, or at least one child. So I just want to know, what kind of time frame did you have in mind?" Jessica asked, pointedly.

Oh my God, she is not giving up. I never had any kind of "time frame" or anything even close to that. Harry stared at Jessica with a perplexed look on his face. "I don't know what to tell you, Jes, except I guess we should do it when the time feels right, for both of us." Harry desperately hoped that his vague answer was enough to satisfy Jessica, even just for now.

"I guess I'm going to have to accept that, even if it is a bullshit answer," Jessica cracked a smile. She knew she put Harry on the spot and there was only so far she could push him, at least in their first discussion. "Will you at least come take a look at the nursery?" Jessica said, flashing her own devilish smile.

"What, now?" Harry asked, putting two pillows over his head.

"Come on, silly." Jessica grabbed the pillow and smacked him playfully, like she wanted to start a pillow fight. *If I make it a game, the whole thing won't seem so scary to the big baby I married*, Jessica thought to herself as she tickled Harry's stomach.

"All right, all right, I'll take a quick peek." Harry rolled off the bed and put on his Stubbs and Wooten monogrammed slippers.

Hmmm, looks like I just might make a good mother after all. Jessica smiled triumphantly as she took Harry's hand and led him into the white and yellow nursery.

★ ★ ★

"See, this isn't so bad," Jessica said softly, gently stroking Harry's back. She could see that he was holding his breath as he looked around the room. "Just breathe, Harry, please," Jessica whispered in his ear. "Why don't you check out some of these toys, they're actually pretty cool," Jessica continued, taking a big stuffed musical teddy bear off of a rocking chair and handing it to Harry. "Go ahead and squeeze its tummy. It plays twenty different tunes you'll recognize." Jessica put her hand over Harry's and pressed the toy together between his fingers.

A small smile of amusement slowly broke over Harry's

face at the variety of kid's songs that came out of the bear's stomach. The kid inside of Harry wanted to keep pinching it to make the music play faster and faster. Before he could get bored with the bear, Jessica introduced him to a rocking horse, then a baby gym set that held his attention for a good ten minutes. She walked him over to a blue *Finding Nemo*-themed "fishy chair" that had an aquarium in it filled with plastic dolphins that made soothing ocean sounds. This toy particularly tickled Harry, as he carefully tried to sit in the child's chair without breaking it. Resting his arms on the deep-green, fluffy "seaweed" side pillows, Harry began to relax.

"Irma picked out pretty cool stuff, huh?" Jessica said, plopping herself down on an oversized yellow smiley-face beanbag next to Harry. "I hope you're not getting seasick," Jessica joked.

"Nope, I always liked marine-life toys, that's probably why I became such a happening surfer dude," Harry said, balancing himself on the chair like he would on a surfboard.

"I bet you'd have a killer time teaching little Harry junior how to catch the waves." Harry grew absolutely silent and kept pressing the buttons on the aquarium to make the dolphins dance and sing.

Maybe I spoke too soon, Jessica worried. She picked up a coloring book and began to doodle with crayons to appear distracted.

"Or Harrietta," Harry said, staring straight ahead at the twirling fish, avoiding Jessica's look.

"What?" Jessica asked, surprised by Harry's delayed reaction.

"Harrietta, Harriah, Harriet... you know little girls can be surfers, too. Not that I would want those scumbag beach bums chasing after our daughter, who will probably be hot if she looks anything like her mother." Harry grinned at Jessica with a new, yet soulful twinkle in his eye. Wary of pushing him for more information than he was ready to give about his feelings, Jessica searched Harry's expression for his true meaning.

"And a huge heart of gold, if he or she is anything like his or her father," Jessica said, happily, happily tearing up. She sensed that Harry was warming to the idea of father-hood, even if he had not yet come right out and said so.

"Okay, kiddo, you win. We'll fill the world with little Harrys," Harry said, pulling Jessica off the beanbag, lifting her into his arms, and seating her on his lap, looking absolutely ridiculous as they sardined themselves into the child's fun-tastic chair. "So how many do you want, ten, twelve, twenty-one?"

"I hope you're kidding, Papa Bear," Jessica giggled with delight. Her whole being glowed with a warm energy. To Jessica, there was nothing more perfect than sitting with her husband planning their family's future in the peaceful serenity of a baby's nursery. Never did Jessica experience such a level of closeness and intimacy with her ex-husband, Freddy, who coldly viewed procreation as a way to secure his financial future with the Ackerman family fortune. Even if Harry wasn't exactly ready for diaper duty on that day, she felt that when the time came, her future child would have the very best playmate and daddy anyone could ask for. Jessica knew this to be true, just as much as she knew that Harry was her soul mate.

"Well, I was thinking, if we are going to do this, we might as well do it right. Why not have a whole tribe of Harrys? I think we could achieve world domination through the Harry seed!" Harry said, mimicking the voice of Dr. Evil from the *Austin Powers* movies.

"Slow down there, Mr. Raider. I didn't say that I wanted

to be responsible for a whole new race. I was thinking more along the lines of one, maybe two especially cute ones, but I think I'd put a cap on it after that."

"Oh, all right, I guess it will have to be whatever you say. I mean, you are the official child bearer, the womb of wonderment, the mother ship as they say. I guess I can't tell you how many people you have to pump out of there," Harry said, lovingly sliding his fingers between her legs.

"Mmmm, that feels good," Jessica murmured, rocking herself back and forth. "Does that mean you want to get to started right now?" she asked.

"Uh, no. Not right this minute," Harry quickly removed his hand from Jessica's private spot and lifted her up off of him. Jessica dared not show her disappointment. A part of her wanted desperately to get wrapped up in the moment, make love, and conceive right there in the *Finding Nemo* baby chair. Yet the more sensible part of her knew it would be better for both of them to wait until they got more adjusted to their new life together before she could stop taking the pill, and they could embark on the parenthood journey.

At the very least, Jessica felt a wave of relief that she managed to get Harry in the right frame of mind. This should have been enough, but Jessica needed one more vow of reassurance before she could leave the nursery and continue exploring her house.

Before she could ask him anything else, Harry scooped Jessica up in his arms and carried her out of the nursery. "What are you doing, Harry?" Jessica giggled, caught off guard by her husband's romantic gesture. "I'm carrying you over the threshold. Isn't that what newlyweds are supposed to do in their new home?" Harry asked, exiting the nursery quickly.

"Why don't we go for a swim? There's a rockin' pool out back and I bet I could convince the chef to rustle up a few burgers and fries, maybe even run some Coke and ice through the blender to make a Slurpee. Doesn't that sound great? How 'bout it, Jes?"

"That sounds great, Harry, but I have to ask you one question," Jessica said, smiling innocently. "How long do you think we should wait before we start trying to have kids? The only reason I'm asking you this is because I'm almost thirty-five years old. Even though I know women are having babies when they are in their forties today, I just don't think we should put it off much longer."

Harry tried to hide the annoyed look on his face. "Okay, before you turn thirty-five we can start trying. Just please don't tell me you are turning thirty-five this week. You see, Jes, this topic makes me so nervous, I've forgotten your birthday," Harry admitted sheepishly.

"My birthday isn't until the end of May. You have at least six months of getting used to me, before anything has to happen. Is that fair?" Jessica asked directly.

"Absolutely fair, Jes! Now can we go out and play?" Harry was relieved that this conversation was finally coming to end and Jessica was pacified, at least for now. He could feel the sweat trickling down his back. All he wanted to do was jump out the bedroom window and land in the pool.

chapter nine

Harry grabbed his bathing suit and rushed down the stairs, hopping two at a time. He wanted to spend the rest of what started out as a very intense day chilling on his back on a floating raft in the pool. Harry sprinted through the downstairs corridor until he came to the sliding glass door that led to the stunning backyard. There lay a crystal-clear, aquamarine, Olympic-sized swimming pool, glistening in the California light.

Surrounding the elaborate gunite hole of water in the ground were comfy lounge chairs with monogrammed black-and-white striped cushions, picnic tables, and an open cabana with a shower, barbecue grill, a non-alcoholic mini-bar, and kick-ass stereo system. The sight even impressed spoiled Harry. "Aw, sweet!" he exclaimed as he gazed at his outdoor paradise. Harry flung himself headfirst into the pool. Within seconds he bobbed up and hopped onto one of the floating lounge chairs fit for a king and his queen. Just as he was about to lie back and get comfortable, Frank, Sam's chauffeur, walked out to the pool area.

"Frank, my man, how's it goin,' dude?" Harry didn't have a care in the world.

"Very good, sir. You must be enjoying the pool after your long trip home," Frank said politely with a bit of hesitation in his voice.

"Are you kidding? This is great! I can't believe Mom did all of this for us. She rocks!" Harry pretended to splash the family's loyal retainer standing at the water's edge.

"Yes, I know your mother put a lot of work into your new home, sir, but don't forget your father had a lot to do with it too." Frank forced an uncomfortable smile.

"Oh yeah?" Harry asked casually, spinning himself around in the chair, to see if he could make still water into waves. "What did old Sammy do with this place, besides sign the checks?" Harry laughed. He knew very well that his workaholic dad probably hadn't even set foot in his new home.

"I know your father wants you to be happy here, Harry."

"Good, well you tell him the next time you see him that Jes and I are absolutely thrilled with the place. You can even tell him that he's welcome to stop by anytime. There, how's that? Am I a grateful son or what?" Harry chuckled.

Harry loved Sam, because he knew that deep down Sam also really loved him, but over the years he never took the time to show it. Sam always seemed too preoccupied with some business deal, and when it wasn't work, he wanted to socialize with his friends at the club. And of course there were rumors of the many mistresses Sam kept all over town. So there wasn't much time for Harry. Although he could never verbalize it to anyone, not even his closest friends, Harry felt that Sam was embarrassed and ashamed of his wayward son. Harry learned at an early age that the way to get his father's attention was to pull crazy stunts and cause trouble. The more trouble he could get himself into, the more Sam would be forced to stop whatever he was doing and save Harry's ass. Yet as prevalent as this push-pull dynamic was in Harry's life, it was a delicate, hidden part of his psyche that he chose to block out. Even at the ripe old age of thirty-eight, Harry never really understood why he always felt so compelled to be such a fuck-up.

"Harry, I hate to ruin your day, but your dad sent me here to pick you up for lunch. He would like you to join him at Nate and Al's in fifteen minutes," Frank said awkwardly. He hated the fact that his boss had sent him to do his dirty work and not spoken to his son directly regarding his afternoon plans. Frank didn't know how Harry would react to his father's demands, and had no desire to get in the middle of a father and son standoff. Frank had worked for the Raiders since before Harry was born and he didn't want to lose his job at this late stage of the game.

"Oh, that is just bullshit right there, Frank. You tell my father, I'll see him tomorrow or even later on for dinner if he wants, but there is no way I'm getting out of this pool to go down to that crowded restaurant and drown myself in chicken fat. As a matter of fact, I'd rather drown myself right here than go into town now." Harry dove off the chair and held his breath underwater for as long as he could. Frank knew better than to be alarmed at Harry's antics. He had dialed 911 so many times over the years to save Harry from all sorts of life-threatening situations that all the operators knew him by name. Frank just stood there calmly until Harry had no choice but to come up for air.

Without another word, Frank went into the cabana and brought out a large blue pool towel and a pair of rainbow-colored flip-flops. He held the towel open and stared at Harry directly. "Don't make me come in there and get you, sir. You know when your dad says he wants to see you, he means business," Frank said firmly, taking his cell phone from his chauffeur's jacket and waving it at Harry.

"Oh, you're not actually going to call him, are you, Frank?" Harry pleaded, a tone of sheer dread in his voice.

"If you're not out of the pool in about three seconds flat, you'll leave me no choice, Harry. If you won't listen to me, then you can listen to him scream at you for making him lose his favorite booth because you were late," Frank said firmly. Even though Sam Raider spent every day of his life at Nate and Al's, on many a crowded Saturday morning, even Sam Raider, children's clothing king of the world, had to take a number and wait in line like the rest of the crowned kings of corned beef.

"Okay, okay, you win. Nothing's worse than Sam Raider when he's had to watch other people being seated at table number twenty-two, especially on an empty stomach. Let me get my shoes and a shirt and we'll leave. I'll tell Jessica to hurry up and get dressed. I'm sure it won't take her long." Harry darted out of the pool and dried off with the towel Frank handed him.

"Uh, I'm sorry, Harry, but your father did specify he wanted to see you alone this time."

"You're kidding, what the hell for?" Harry asked, a little confused.

"I think I better let Mr. Raider explain," Frank said, wanting to avoid the subject all together.

★★★

The Silver Cloud Rolls Royce made a left onto Beverly Boulevard and pulled up in front of Nate and Al's Delicatessen. Strangely enough, there was no line outside, a good sign that Harry wouldn't have to deal with his father's impatient need to be seated immediately upon entering. *The restaurant is unusually quiet today, probably because of the glorious weather,* Harry thought to himself as he entered and searched around the room for his father. *Only a total shmuck like me would have to be inside on this gorgeous day and be berated by my dad.* Harry hustled up to his father's booth like an obedient St. Bernard and planted a kiss on Sam's aging, wrinkled cheek. Harry opened his arms to give the old man a great big hug before sitting down across from him. As Harry was greeting his father, he noticed Jerry Seinfeld wearing a baseball cap and noshing on a bagel, sitting in the corner with two men who appeared to be his agents or business managers. In the booth behind Jerry were Lenny Kravitz and Usher surrounded by a few funky-looking music types. At a small table facing the two celebrity-laden booths was an eighty-something Jewish lady with bright orange hair and long fake nails, wearing a loud leopard print from head to toe. She obviously had no idea that she was sitting so close to such heavy-hitting modern-day celebrities. That was part of what made Nate and Al's so special. Famous or not, everybody was treated like a star.

Sam was not normally one who went for open displays of physical affection, but he reached up to hug his son back, a gesture that he had never before done in public.

Okay, the old man's in a good mood today, probably because he got his table quickly and has been munching on some sour pickles to hold him over. Maybe we can just get some quick chow and get out of here, so I can get back to my pool. Harry dove into the plate of pickles and ate three of them at the same time.

"You look as though life has been treating you well, son." Always the competitor, Sam ferociously attacked the pickle plate with his fork, not wanting to let Harry get the last one.

"Yeah, the honeymoon was great, but I've only been gone about a month," Harry smiled. Not to be outdone, he picked up his knife, knocked the last pickle off of his father's fork, and shoved it in his mouth. Sam let out a proud laugh.

"That's my boy. I didn't know you had such a fighting spirit. Married life seems to have a good effect on you." Sam smiled and signaled to waitress to bring more pickles. "Can't complain. Jes is a great girl. She scared the shit out of me this morning, you know, with pregnancy stuff. I don't think she'd even thought about it until she saw Mom's nursery. I can't believe Mom did that, by the way. Does she want to do me in? What was she thinking?" Harry gulped down some ice water to put out the pickles' garlicky flames in his mouth.

"What do *you* think your mother is thinking? She wants to be a grandmother, ASAP. Can't say I blame her. We're not on the earth forever you know, Harry." Sam looked his son directly in the eye. Harry didn't even want to think about his father's mortality. They had their differences and troubles, but Sam was a constant pillar of support for Harry. If not emotionally, certainly financially Sam was always there to protect his little boy. Harry figured as long as Sam was around, one way or another, everything would always be all right.

"Okay, Dad, I hear ya, but does that mean we have to start increasing the population on Sunset Boulevard tonight?" Harry asked.

"Of course not, Harry. First get used being married and living a clean and sober life. I know it's going to be hard for you not to revert to your old ways now that you're back home, but you've got to do it, Harry. This time there are no second chances." Sam switched to a deadly serious tone. Harry just stared at his father in stone-cold silence. Part of him wanted to jump in and assure his father that the wild party days were way behind him. But Harry was never a very good liar. He couldn't look his father in the eye and make a promise he wasn't 100 percent sure that he could keep.

"What will it be, Sammy?" a good-looking waitress asked. She was tall and blonde, in her late forties, and she embodied the essence of a hard-edged Hollywood beauty who never got her big break. "You know my son Harry, don't you, Jeanie?" Sam said to the waitress, who was doing her best not to look at Harry. Harry got the feeling right away that for whatever reason, this woman did not like him. *Maybe she's pissed that I ate all the pickles without ordering first,* Harry thought naively.

"Sure, good to see ya, sweetie," Jean rasped in her smoker's voice. She would not look up from her note pad. "So, what are you boys having today?" Jean scribbled away nervously.

"Make it two of the usual," Sam said.

"What are you, nuts?" Jean swatted Sam across his bald head with her order pad. "The doctor told you to stay away from those kinds of foods. A corned beef and chopped liver sandwich soaking in chicken fat could slam shut those arteries in one fell swoop!"

"Come on, honey, it's just one sandwich. It won't kill me. Besides, we're celebrating. Harry's come home to Hollywood. My son is home for good." Sam beamed. This comment seemed to upset Jean even more than Sam's request for a corned-beef-laden land mine. She coughed loudly and cleared her throat, while shooting Sam an accusatory look that made him squirm in his seat.

"Jeanie has a wonderful son too. He's in college, an economics major at Harvard, an honor student with straight A's. He's something to be very proud of," Sam added, avoiding all eye contact.

"That's great, Jeanie," Harry said, smiling generously, wanting to break Jean's icy exterior. "I bet he's so smart, he got a full scholarship," Harry continued, enthusiastically.

"Didn't have to. He's got a rich father," Jean smiled

wryly at Harry, then turned around and rushed towards the kitchen before the Raider men could say anything else.

"What was that about, Dad?" Harry asked.

"How should I know? Women are strange creatures. Haven't you figured that out by now?" Sam purposely changed the subject.

Sam, you dirty dog. Where have you been dipping your salami after hours? Do I have a half-brother with his head buried in the books back in Boston? Harry thought. With everything he had just been through with Jessica, he didn't need anything more to complicate his life right now, or ever, for that matter.

In a matter of moments, two mile-high corned beef, chopped liver, and chicken fat sandwiches were placed in front of Harry and Sam. "So tell me, how do you like the house?" Sam asked with chopped liver dribbling down the sides of his mouth.

"Oh, it's great, Daddy, really fantastic. Thanks so much. We can't get over it," Harry said gratefully. Like Jessica knew she could never stop thanking Irma, Harry knew he would be groveling to Sam for the house every time they got together for the next fifty years.

"I'm glad you like it. May you, Jessica, and my future grandchildren spend many years there in good health. L'Chaim!" Sam toasted, raising his cream soda to toast Harry.

"L'Chaim, Dad! To a long life!" Harry raised his big glass and downed half of his celery soda. Sam looked at his son wistfully. "Harry, I brought you here today for a reason."

"Well I sure hope so, Dad. I mean, I was just about to enjoy a killer day in my brand-new pool when Frank yanked my ass outta there and drug me down to this mecca of matzo balls," Harry wisecracked, stuffing more of his sandwich into his mouth.

Sam slammed his sandwich down on the plate. "Are you saying it's more important to float around like a total schmuck than to have lunch with your father? Do you know how much that pool cost me? I had fifteen schvartzes working around the clock getting that damn thing ready for you!"

"I know what that word means," a Gucci-clad African American woman sitting in the next booth said. "You should be ashamed of yourself," the women scolded, waving her long fingernail at Sam.

"You're right, I should. I'm sorry," Sam said, embarrassed. The woman paraded out the door.

"You are a really a great guy, Dad. I'd skip time in the pool to hang out with you any day." Harry winked at Sam. He was so happy that the woman gave him a cool reprieve from Sam's fury and some time to charm his way back into Sam's good graces.

"I'm glad you feel that way, Harry. Knowing that makes it easier for me to say what I have to say to you. Harry, I would like you and Jessica to take time and have a period of adjustment to your new life here in Los Angeles. The holidays are approaching and your mother and I really want you two to enjoy yourselves and get into the swing of things," Sam said.

"Sounds great to me, Pop." Harry managed to smile and take another bite of his corned beef at the same time.

"Then when the first of the year comes around, I'd like you to come work for me."

Harry's throat closed around a dangling piece of meat. He couldn't seem to swallow or bring it back up. He was completely paralyzed. His face began to turn blue.

"Harry, please, be careful. My god, you're going to choke. Here." Sam handed Harry his soda, which Harry sucked down. Fortunately the drink washed the rest of the sandwich down and once again, Harry could breathe freely.

But that moment would have offered an easy way out. The thought of going to work with his hard-nosed "legendary businessman" father was much scarier than walking through the pearly gates.

"Gee, Dad, I don't know. I know I said when I was in the Hamptons that I would try to work when I got home, but maybe that's not the best idea for me, you know. I'm more of a man of leisure." Harry made a funny face and giggled. Underneath his joking he desperately hoped his adorable little-boy act would carry him without having to face grown-up responsibilities.

Sam laughed ironically and took a sip of coffee. "Harry, I don't think you understand. You don't have a choice. You *are* going to work with me, beginning the first of the year. I'm not getting any younger and it's time you were trained to take over. That's it, no more questions asked." Sam raised his coffee cup like he was toasting the official commencement of Harry Raider's life as a responsible, productive human being.

"But Dad...you don't want me in the office. I'll screw things up. You have a totally rockin' business. I don't know a thing about making kids' clothing. You know the whole idea of fatherhood and anything to do with kids freaks me out. Just ask Jessica! Why would you want your fucked-up kid in there to blow it all to hell? I'm a loser, remember? A lost cause. A total schmuck!" Harry begged for mercy. He was so nervous that he slipped his feet out of his shoes and flexed his toes up and down to relieve some of his tension.

"So what are you suggesting, Harry? I hold the position open for Jeanie's brilliant son at Harvard? Should I leave him everything?" Sam said sarcastically, and winked in Jeanie's direction. He knew that Harry was anything but a schmuck and totally understood what was going on.

"What would Mom say about that?" Harry shot back as he pointed his butter knife at his father's throat, in his last ditch attempt to "play" his Dad. This time, Harry Raider was way out of his league.

"I think your mother would have a nervous breakdown if her son would have to move out of his house because he couldn't make the mortgage payments," Sam stated, matter-of-factly. He nonchalantly took the knife out of Harry's hand, dipped it in some mustard, and spread it on his sandwich.

"There's a mortgage on the place? Why?" Harry asked in disbelief. Rich folks like the Raiders didn't need to borrow money like mere mortals.

"The mortgage will be paid by your salary. No salary, no payments, no house. Get it, Harry?" Sam looked up from his plate and fiercely stared down his shaken son.

"Jessica's rich, she could always make the payments," Harry retorted, hiding his quivering lips behind a chopped-liver–stained napkin.

"Oh really? Do you think you'd remain so attractive to your wife if you had no money and she had to support you? Come on Harry, grow up! Any woman, especially a wealthy girl like Jessica, wouldn't put up with that. She already showed you that she had no problem getting rid of a man that didn't meet her standards. Look how quickly she was willing to leave her ex-husband when she fell in love with you. If you don't live up to her expectations, who knows what she'll do next?" Sam picked up a napkin and wiped his hands, rolled it up in a ball, spit on it, and then threw it on the floor. "Like that, Harry." Sam was pulling out the big guns. He had aimed and hit his son where he lived.

"That's different!" Harry yelled, shaking his head in disbelief. He took the straw out of his soda and began to chomp on it like his father did with his cigar. "Freddy was a complete asshole. He treated her like crap and she didn't want to put up with it anymore. I treat Jessica like gold and she knows that. She would never leave me." Harry was sweating and fighting back tears.

"And what about when you don't have any money to support the children she wants so badly? Being a good father means being a good provider, Harry," Sam continued coldly and he started eating again.

"Yeah, well, there's more to fatherhood than just paying the bills," Harry accused Sam. He put the straw down and began to chew the ice in his drink as he spoke. Harry wanted his dad to hear him but at the same he was terrified to confront him, so talking with a muffled mouth full of ice seemed like a pretty good solution.

"What, are you the expert all of a sudden, Harry? Two minutes ago you said you didn't know a thing about father-hood. Now you're giving *me* advice?" Sam shook his head and grabbed a pickle. Harry was at a loss for words. He didn't have it in his heart to blast his father for ignoring him most of his life. Deep in his heart, he knew that Sam was not trying to punish him. In fact, he realized that his father was trying to do the right thing.

I guess he doesn't think that I'm such a lost cause if he trusts me enough to come into his business. That says something right there. Maybe he doesn't think I'm a waste of his time after all. He could be right about Jessica too. She wants to be a mother so badly, how do I know that she wouldn't dump me on my ass if I couldn't pay the bills? Even though she doesn't need my money, she still has to respect me. How can she do that if I'm a total loafer? Harry thought, pushing his empty plate away.

"All right, Dad, you win. I'll go to work for you. But I'm not coming in until ten, and I can get out early to play ten-nis at the club if it's a really nice day," Harry demanded.

"As long as you get all your work done, I don't give a rat's ass when come or when you leave, Harry. It's quality, not quantity, I want from you, son." Sam smiled.

"Fine, and if I do a good job then Jessica and I get a month off in the summer to go back to the Hamptons," Harry continued his negotiations.

"Harry, if you are willing to finally pull your weight, the world will be your oyster," Sam said.

"Okay, Dad. I'll do my best not to ruin the billion-dollar business that you've built up over the past forty years," Harry chuckled.

"Thank you, Harry. I knew you'd see things straight. Now how about a little dessert?"

Back at the house, Jessica was again on the phone with Chas as she sat behind a huge pile of party invitations strewn across the desk in her private office. *Okay, the new Mrs. Harry Raider is going to come out of her shell and take this town by storm! I am not going to be afraid anymore and I'm determined to make Harry proud,* Jessica thought, deciding whether to attend a star-studded movie premiere, a celebrity chef's private tasting, or a multi-million-dollar gallery opening—all of which were scheduled on the same night.

"Why not go to all of them, Jes?" Chas suggested. "First you must pop over to the chef's for hors d'oeuvres and champagne. He'll understand that you couldn't possibly be expected to stay for the whole thing and believe me, honey, he'll be thrilled that you came at all. Afterwards, meander over to the theater on Hollywood Boulevard. Get your picture taken arriving and walking down the red carpet with Harry, then slip out the back entrance before the boring movie starts and head over to the gallery. It's all very simple, my pet, isn't it?"

Although Jessica had psyched herself up to be gung-ho about attending as many Hollywood events as possible, it was not in her nature to tackle such a feat alone. She needed help, guidance, and support from the master of the high society, a man whose life was one big social whirlwind from New York to LA. She needed none other than Chas Greer.

"Did you get my latest shipment yet?" Chas gushed. "I FedEx'd it so it would be there when you first arrived. I even enclosed instructions for the maid to follow on which clothing needed to be pressed and how everything should be arranged in your closet. I thought a closet full of gorgeous, perfectly put-together outfits, accessorized to the hilt with hats, shoes, and bags, would make you feel more at home. I wanted my little Jessica to feel totally secure and empowered enough to begin her takeover of Sunset Boulevard." His lover Juan was giving him a pedicure as he lounged on his white Shabby Chic sofa back in Manhattan. Chas stretched out like a pampered prince, puffing on a clove cigarette while eyeing the padded invoice he'd sent Jessica for the extravagant package.

"Yes, yes, everything got here just fine." Jessica nibbled on her nails and twisted the phone cord around her tiny fingers.

"Uhm, great, so then you'll have no trouble figuring out what to wear. The garment bag for each outfit is marked very clearly by event. Some say 'movie premiere,' some say 'cocktails only,' etc., etc.," Chas continued. His attention to detail and making life easy was part of what made him the real superstar.

"Oh, yes, but it's a little confusing, Chas."

"What?" Chas shouted into the phone. *I spent hours slaving over how to put together ensembles to make that short, little elf-like woman look like a supermodel. How dare she question my creativity?* Chas thought to himself. He practically kicked Juan in the face as his foot shot up from the pail of rosewater. "I mean what's to understand, sweetie? It's all very clear. All you have to do is unzip the bag, pull the stuff out, and put it on. Is that such a drama?" Chas said, gulping Chardonnay and promptly returning to his ass-kissing persona. He didn't dare let Jessica or any of his clients know that their stupidity bothered him. The hand-holding part of his job was what really paid the bills. It was almost more important than the clothing or anything else he supplied.

"I know that, Chas, but you just told me that I had to go all three events in one night. What I am supposed am I supposed to do, come home and change between each party? If I do that, my night won't end until breakfast," Jessica fretted. She was genuinely baffled by the demands of her new lifestyle. Secretly she worried about everything ranging from what she was going to wear to making aimless cocktail chatter to looking good in the inevitable photographs. Oh, how Jessica wished that she and Harry could have just continued to live in the sanctity of her East Hampton garden, with no one to bother them but her toy poodle. Those quiet, simple days of summer were behind her now, and it was time to step into Hollywood's unforgiving spotlight.

"Oh, darling, you can't be serious," Chas chuckled in a cocky manner, as he carefully submerged his foot into its aromatheraputic soak. He was relieved to find out that Jessica's bewilderment was due to her own limited lack of imagination. "Okay, sweetie-kins, let me teach you the first rule of achieving social stardom. Are you listening carefully?" he teased, enjoying himself.

"Go on, Chas." Jessica knew full well she had played right into his hands. She had worked herself into such a state of social anxiety that she had no choice but to swallow the medicine she had begged to be given.

"All right, here it is: fashion's golden rule. Overdress to impress! That means wear something appropriate for the most elaborate event you are attending that night. That way you look appropriately hot for the big one and the guests at the other parties will wonder where else you're going and what they're missing. The truth is, dear, that no one will ever reach the level of social glory that's meant only for a power couple like you and Harry."

Jessica giggled nervously and let out a huge sigh. Chas knew very well her problem with social phobia. *Why is he saying this shit to me now?* Jessica thought. *Is he just egging me on to just to wind me up or does he think all this bullshit flattery is somehow going to help me calm down? He's so smooth sometimes, I just can't figure him out.*

"Jes, are you there honey, or have you had a panic attack and passed out?" Chas piped, hoping to sound genuinely worried.

"No, I'm here, Chas. Continue with the fashion rules; I just grabbed a pen to write it down." Jessica did not want to share her fears with Chas right now.

"Well, since the movie premiere is the hottest ticket for the night, I suggest you don the Valentino gown with the Harry Winston jewels and the Chanel slippers. I know that a lot of people, even the stars themselves, go for the grunge look when going to these things, but that look just won't do for you, dear. My professional recommendation is that you always go for the old-Hollywood glamour-girl look. That way you'll never take a bad picture. And, let's remember, you're not some poor white trash starlet who just got off the bus from Kansas, slept with a director and his wife, then became a star. You are Hollywood's new royalty and therefore you must always look regal. People will expect that of you, dear."

"Seems like everyone out here expects something else of me," Jessica caught herself saying. Chas's mind started working. *Oh, this is interesting. She's not even there one night and she's already feeling the Hollywood heat. I sense a fabulous opportunity for Chas to come to the rescue.* Chas put out his cigarette and lit up another one.

"What's going on, dear girl? You can tell Chas." Chas knew the best way to disarm Jessica and get her to spill her insecurities was to speak to her like a little girl.

Jessica took a piece of her curly hair and twirled it around her fingers like a little girl. "It's just that there are so many forces pulling at me at once. All of these people who sent these invites and goodie bags must expect me to be an older, married version of Paris Hilton. You say that Hollywood society expects me to be the next Jackie O. Then there's Harry, who expects me to jump into the Beverly Hills lifestyle and totally forget about his past, even though some reminder of it is lurking around every corner. Irma, God bless her, expects me to get pregnant, this evening at the very latest!" Jessica laughed, realizing the irony of it all.

"Oh my goodness, Jessica. Are you going to have a baby? How fantastic!" Chas spewed. "I met a guy from England at Shari Lane's son's bris who can get you a great deal on a Silver Cross carriage, the Balmoral edition. Oh my, and Burberry has such an elegant kid's line now—Madonna's kids are photographed in it all of the time. This is going to be so exciting!" To him, any addition to the Raider family meant another paying client. If he was really lucky, he'd hit the jackpot and she'd have twins.

Jessica waved her hands in front of her face to clear the air. "I don't know that I'm ready to do it right away, but I don't want to put it off too far into the future. I'm very glad you're enthusiastic, because Harry is totally flipped out by the thought of the whole thing. You know, I can't believe that he didn't think that a woman of my age wouldn't be at least thinking about having kids sooner rather than later.

Could he be that clueless?" Jessica asked.

"Honey, with Harry Raider, anything is possible. Up until now, he's pretty much lived in his own little drug-induced universe. It's almost as if he's been on a continual acid trip for thirty-eight years. Only now has his spaceship landed here on earth with the rest of us. Give him time, sweetie; he'll come around. I bet Harry would make a marvelous father. Think of how much fun he would be!" Chas giggled mischievously.

"Well as soon as it happens, you'll be one of the first people to know," Jessica chuckled.

"Oh Jes, I'm very hurt. I thought I'd be on the phone with you when you took your first EPT test. I want to be there when you first read the results," Chas whined, shamelessly pulling out the big emotional guns. He quickly put his hand over Juan's giggling mouth. *She can't think we're laughing at her problems or are being anything but totally sincere. If she thinks we are making fun of her, that will blow everything. She's got to trust us!* Chas thought as he pushed Juan away and handed him the rest of his wine.

Of course, Chas knew that spoiled Harry would never be able to give Jessica the love and support she needed during a pregnancy, especially, heaven forbid, if there were any problems. So as usual, he was right there to volunteer his services. *The closer I get to Jessica and her future offspring, the more financially solid my future will be. Might as well catch them as they're coming down the birth canal. Better yet, nothing wrong with hooking them when they're growing in the womb. Can't grab a client young enough these days,* Chas thought, while Juan sat pouting on the edge of the couch.

"That's really sweet of you, Chas. I'll remember that when the time comes. Right now, however, I think I better forget about bottles and diapers and concentrate on being the life of the party. Let's face it, I have to be Harry's hot Hollywood wife before I can be a mother. I mean, that's the only way I'm going to get laid around here. Right?" Jessica joked.

She was beginning to lighten up about what her life was going to become. Somehow, knowing that she could at least spill some of her guts to Chas made her feel much more relaxed. Most of the time Jessica saw Chas for who he was, but this afternoon, his voice was a port in her personal storm. She wanted to believe that deep down, underneath all of his pretentious crap and conniving, Chas Greer was a truly decent man.

After giving Chas a three-thousand-mile air kiss goodbye, Jessica diligently returned to the pile of invitations, trying to pump herself up to paint the town "Harry." *What have I got to complain about? I know a million girls who would die trade places with me right now. Hey, it could be worse. He could be a boring tight-ass like Freddy. At least with Harry, I know I'll always have fun.*

But she was not the only one getting in the mood to party that night.

chapter eleven

About a half an hour west of Beverly Hills, in the tony seaside town of Malibu, all hell was breaking loose at a drugged-up, boozed-up orgy taking place in a large new beach house. The stark white and glass edifice located in the Colony, Malibu's most exclusive neighborhood, belonged to Harry's buddy Mike Roman. Harry's old gang were the hosts of the evening of debauchery, and relishing every minute of it.

They charged their guests fifteen hundred dollars per couple and a thousand dollars for singles to join the fun, and there was no shortage of people willing to fork over that kind of cash to indulge in a night of carnal pleasure. Members of Hollywood's elite underground party circuit were there: everyone from the high-profile celebrities who paid extra for their hosts' vow of privacy to big-wig producers and studio heads.

Like every good Hollywood party, there were the celebrity ass-kissers, the rich people outside the industry who'd do anything to get in and rub their naked shoulders with Hollywood's hotshots. This group, made up mostly of plastic surgeons, lawyers, publicists, and bored businessmen looking to finance independent "projects," and it was usually made up of the wildest and most demanding attendees. They were always the first to notice if the lines of coke were cut too thin or the liquor wasn't a top-shelf brand. The rest of the revelers were too far gone to care about such trivialities.

Mike Roman was naked underneath a pile of people. There were so many nude bodies around him that he couldn't even see who was doing what to him or what gender they were. A big, double D, silicone-chested woman, clad only in a police helmet and spiked heels, straddled his chest, grinding herself on his nipples and gently whipping his face with a tasseled cop's stick. He felt his toes plunging into some kind of wet crevice, but he didn't know who or what this moist cave belonged to.

With Mike so wasted and whacked out, someone had to run the show and make sure all of the guests were getting what they paid for. That someone was Todd Krane. Forever the entrepreneur and especially charming when he had taken a hit of ecstasy, Todd, dressed only in a leopard loincloth, went around to the voyeurs who were watching the love fest and offered them more lines of coke on a Tiffany crystal dish. Donny Mayberry, the most hard-core drug user of the four, had stuffed himself into a closet and was freebasing crack by himself. An underage Mexican hooker who was generously offering her services gratis tried to join him twice, but a good blow job or anything else was of no interest to him when good drugs were available. Sex was something he only settled for when he couldn't score a hit.

As usual, Bill Ladd had taken two girls—a thin, flat-chested Asian one and a voluptuous, corn-fed "girl next door" type—into a huge marble bathroom upstairs. He was painting their faces with exotic cat-like makeup. Once he had turned them into sparkling, glittering beasts, he coaxed them to crawl all over his body, lightly clawing his face, penis, and balls while making ferocious animal sounds. After his "night in the jungle," Bill and the girls jumped into a bubble bath, where they proceeded to "groom him" with an herbal loofa and an aromatherapeutic sponge.

The bad boys' weekend of forbidden festivities was going splendidly until about six o'clock the next afternoon when the doorbell rang four times. All guests had been clearly instructed to ring only twice, a pass code to be allowed entry. Todd, whose ecstasy high was slowly wearing off, got extremely nervous. Fearing the worst, he thought that maybe the police had been tipped off about what was going on. Even more dangerous than the local fuzz, who could most of the time be bought off with a signed celebrity photograph or a free pass to Universal studios for their kids, was the paparazzi. If a reporter from *Star, Globe,* or *National Enquirer Magazine,* got wind of how the "Who's Who" of Hollywood spent their free time, the shit could really hit the fan. This type of scandal could top anything from Michael Jackson to Heidi Fleiss, so Todd knew he had to be exceptionally careful before opening the door.

Stepping over naked people satisfying their lust and others who had passed out from too much partying, Todd made his way across the living room and bounded up the metallic staircase. He went out onto the back balcony and carefully climbed onto a slanted part of the roof, where whoever was out front could not see him. Todd was relieved to see a familiar black Mercedes stretch limo with darkened windows parked in the drive. This "black on black," as Todd called it, was his drug dealer's vehicle of choice. He quickly got down from the roof and went back in the house. Todd knew that if he didn't get down there fast to let the dealer and his men in, they would start shooting down the door.

"Welcome, gentlemen. Wish you would have come earlier. You missed a glorious time," Todd said with a big smile on his face, opening the front door. Standing dead still on the front porch was a short, balding, salon-tanned man in a black Armani suit and dark sunglasses, smoking a huge Cuban cigar. On either side of him were two overgrown Neanderthal-looking thugs with greasy shellacked black hair, also wearing black suits and dark shades. Long gold chains hung around their necks and dropped down to the middle of their barrel-like chests. One of the goons was chewing gum so loudly that the cracking noise was starting to give Todd a headache.

"We don't have time to waste, Kranks. We have a plane waiting to take us back to Vegas in thirty minutes, so we're just here to collect. Where's the dough?" the tough little man in the middle said. He spoke with a harsh New Jersey accent that effectively made up for his lack of physical stature.

"Right this way, gentlemen," Todd said coolly, confident that he had raked in enough admission money to pay off the drug dealer and have some to spare. Todd and his crew had been such good customers in the past that this particular dealer would front them the drugs and allow them to pay after they took in the money from their paying party guests. That way the boys didn't have to reach into their pockets and the dealer could charge a higher price for waiting time. This arrangement worked well for everyone, especially Mr. Kranks and company, who could no longer count on their old friend Harry Raider to pay for the whole shebang upfront.

Todd escorted the three men into the den. They remained unfazed as they walked through the orgy room with a matter-of-fact sense of purpose. Kranks brought the men into a den filled with white leather furniture. In the corner was a glass bar stocked with every kind of liquor imaginable. "Why don't you gentlemen make yourselves a drink and enjoy the view while I go get what you came here for?" Todd said, handing the small wiseguy a scotch on the rocks.

"As I said, we're in a hurry," the man said and downed the booze in one gulp, placing the glass on the table with a hard slap.

Todd left the three men in the den and sprinted back through the house. Actually, he wanted to get the dealers out of there as quickly as possible. He didn't want their ominous presence to frighten the guests or ruin the party mood. Todd went upstairs to the bedroom closet. When he opened the door, he found Donny Mayberry sliding in and out of a crack coma. "Ah shit, Mayberry, move your fat, buzzed-out ass away from the stash. The dudes are here from Vegas and they want their payday." Todd pushed his wasted friend out of the way—to find the door of the safe wide open.

"What the fuck is this?" Todd screamed at the top of his lungs.

"Whaaaaaaaaa?" slurred Donny, too dazed and con-fused to be jolted by his friend's rage.

"What the fuck is the safe doing open and where the hell is the money, man?" Donny just shrugged his shoulders and slumped over a pair of Bruno Magli shoes.

"Wake the fuck up, you fat fucking slob. Where the hell is the money, asshole? What the fuck did you do with it?" Todd grabbed Donny around the collar of his preppy blue-and-white-striped Brooks Brothers shirt and began to shake him like there was no tomorrow. "Tell me, man! Tell me! What did you do with it? How did you even know how to open this damn safe?"

Donny, still pretty delirious, could barely speak, but

somehow forced the words out of his mouth. "I didn't take it man. She did." Donny mumbled.

"She WHO? Who's SHE?" Todd yelled right in Donny's flushed face, as he grabbed his chubby cheeks and slapped him around.

"The girl, man."

"What girl?" Todd yelled even louder, as he became more and more freaked out.

"The little girl that was just here, man," Donny sputtered, pointing to the spot on the closet floor where the teenage hooker had been sitting.

"How the hell did you get in the safe, man? How the fucking hell did you get in?" Todd screamed, slapping Donny again.

"I didn't go in there... she did," Donny said, still feeling no pain.

Todd noticed out of the corner of his eye that the shoebox, where he had hidden the combination to the safe, was open and the paper on which the numbers were written was missing. "Holy fucking shit, man, do you know what this means? Do you have any fucking idea how dead we all are right now? Do you even care, you dopehead?" Todd exclaimed. He picked up the shoebox and threw it up in the air in a fit of frustration. "How could you let her go in there, man? How THE FUCK could you let her do that?" Todd said, pacing around the room like a man on death row.

"I dunno. She was young. She said she needed money, so I just said, take it, take it all, baby. You're a good little girl, go ahead," Donny rambled, not really having any idea of what he was actually saying.

"You fucking loser! You may have just got us all whacked, do you realize that? What the fuck am I supposed to tell those guys? What am I supposed to say, that doped up Donny gave fifty thousand dollars to a whore who sold him a pathetic sob story? Is that what I'm supposed to tell these guys?" Todd fell to the floor next to Donny, who had passed out. Todd's head was in his hands and he was crying. Never in his life had he been this scared, ever! He knew that the men in black sitting in his white den would not let him out of this alive. Not only did Todd not have the money that had been stolen, but he had no way of getting his hands on that amount of cash in time.

"Okay, I got to get my shit together and think of something. There has to be some way to get us out of this. Think, dude, think," Todd said, thinking out loud.

"Haaaaaaarrrrrrrrrrrrrrrry," Donny mumbled under his breath, as he rolled around in a drugged-out stupor.

"What the fuck are you saying now?" Todd said, pushing Donny's large body away from him.

"Haaaaaaaaaaaaarrrrrrrrry," Donny slurred again, unable to open his eyes.

"Harry? Harry? Is that what you are saying, you dumb fuck?" Todd said, glaring at Donny. For a minute Todd was silent. Would their old friend come to the rescue and save his life or would the "new and improved" Harry Raider want no part of this mess? Todd didn't know the answer but he didn't have time to ponder the question, either. He had to act and act fast.

Todd swaggered down the stairs and joined the men impatiently waiting in the den. "Where's the dough?" the small man said, obviously pissed off that Todd had come back empty-handed.

"Gentlemen, it seems my financial manager didn't think that it was in our best interest to keep all that cash here, with all these strange people partying, so he moved it to a much safer location," Todd said, flashing his smoothest smile.

"Where the hell is that?" the wise guy said, getting more

and more annoyed.

"Beverly Hills, sir," Todd replied confidently. "I have a private banker there who takes care of all my transactions. He's holding the money at his estate. I swear I can have it for you no later than tomorrow morning." Todd was hedging his bets that Harry would come through.

"Why so late, why not now?" the tough guy insisted.

"Because he left for Palm Springs, and he'll be back later this evening. I didn't know you guys were coming today; I thought you'd be here tomorrow. I wouldn't be stupid enough to jerk important men like you around, now would I? You'll have your money no later than midnight. I swear on my life," Todd said, doing his best not to let his panic show, even though large beads of sweat were dripping down his neck.

The wise guy didn't speak for what seemed to be the longest minute of Todd Krane's life. It was as if he were waiting to be sentenced to death or given a chance at life by a Mafia judge and hitman jury. Finally the little man spoke. "All right. Me and Sal are going back to Vegas. Vito, you stay here with this stugots until he comes up with the bread. Don't let him out of your sight. If he doesn't have all of it by twelve midnight or he tries anything funny, whack him. That's my orders," the wiseguy said flatly.

"That won't be necessary; I'll have the money, sir," Todd said, feeling the back of shirt dampen with hot, wet sweat.

"You better!" the wise guy shouted as he turned and walked out of the house with his goon in tow, without saying another word.

Vito, the other thug, sat down on the big, white, round leather couch and made himself comfortable. "You got anything good to eat?"

Todd nearly passed out from sheer relief. "Uh, I don't think so. I can run to the deli and get you something, if you want," Todd stuttered, nervously realizing he still had to a big job in front of him.

"No way. You're not leaving here unless it's to go get the money. And then, I'm going with ya. Got that?"

"Sure, of course. How about I nuke you a frozen pizza and then we can go into Beverly Hills and pick up the cash, all right?" Todd said, to pacify the beast.

"What-evah!" the goon said, disappointed that he'd have to settle for a microwave dinner while his boss and cohort would probably be dining in a fine Italian restaurant on the Vegas strip.

★★★

After Vito downed a half-heated meat-lover's special, he and Todd got into Todd's Porsche and flew down the Pacific Coast Highway towards Beverly Hills. Todd didn't say a word during the whole ride; he was too busy thinking about how to convince Harry to save his life. *Maybe I should make up some big elaborate lie about how I need this money to save my dying mother or get the son I didn't know I even had out of jail for a crime he didn't commit. The new squeaky-clean family-man Walt Disney version of Harry would take pity on a sorry-ass story like that,* Todd thought.

I can just tell him the truth and he'll help me out. Besides, if Harry is fooling everybody right now, he'll want to keep me around to start supplying him later when he gets back to his coked-up self. Todd smiled and prayed that Harry was still a low-down dirty dog, just pretending to be a prissy poodle until he was getting the whole bone.

Todd and Vito pulled up in front of Harry's new mansion and parked the car on the sidewalk in front of the large gates. "Why ain't we going in?" Vito asked suspiciously.

"I'm going in, Vito. If he sees you, he may get nervous. Trust me on this; I gotta go in there alone. Look, you see those big gates, man. It's not like I can escape or anything without getting past you," Todd begged.

"What do I look like, a fuckin' moron? I ain't leaving you alone for one minute. Ring the bell on those gates and get us in there, NOW!" Vito threatened pulling a gun out of his jacket and holding it to Todd's head.

Shit, this is getting more fucked up by the minute, Todd thought to himself, once again trying to keep his composure. "Okay, let's roll."

Todd announced himself into the intercom and the gates swung open. He drove the Porsche into the circular driveway and parked it behind Harry's blue Bentley. Jessica, wearing an elegant Ungaro evening gown and Jimmy Choo heels, was putting on an earring as she opened the front door. She didn't recognize Todd at first, which was probably a good thing, because she would have slammed the door in his face

"Horny Toad Kranks, what the hell are you doing here, man?" Harry yelled from the top of the staircase. He couldn't believe that Todd had the balls to show up uninvited after he ruined Harry's wedding. Harry was standing there, comfortably half-dressed in his tuxedo shirt, socks, Gucci loafers, and boxer shorts, fiddling with his bow tie.

Todd, however, was fighting for his life. He had to pretend like everything was just dandy between him and Harry, so that Vito wouldn't know that Harry actually had no clue of what was going on. "Harry, great to see you dude! Can I come up and speak to you for a minute? It's important business," Todd said, hoping and praying that Harry would see Vito, realize something was up, and show some mercy for his old friend.

"Uh, sure, who's your friend?" Harry said, trying to size up Vito. Harry was still very angry with Todd, but he got the sense that he was in real trouble, and it just wasn't his nature to turn his back on a childhood friend.

"This is Vito. He's a business associate from Vegas," Todd said, not skipping a beat.

"Um, wait a minute, now. I don't mean to interrupt, but Harry and I are on our way out for the evening," Jessica said, wary of Todd and the sleazy-looking swine he had brought into her home.

"This will only take a minute, Jessica, I promise. I really need to speak to Harry," Todd said, shooting Harry an intense look.

Harry recognized the distressed look. "Sure, come on up, Toadster. Honey, show Vito into the kitchen and have the chef make him a sandwich or something. He looks hungry," Harry said, before Jessica could have time to get another word in.

"Okay, Harry, but make it quick. We can't be late for the Feldstein Bar Mitzvah. It's a sit-down dinner and we've already missed the cocktail hour," Jessica said firmly.

"Don't worry, sweetie, it'll only take a minute of your hubby's precious time," Todd said as he bounded up the stairs. Vito smiled politely at a very miffed Jessica as she reluctantly led the creature into her beautiful new kitchen.

Upstairs, Todd jumped onto the bed while Harry finished dressing. "So how much do you need?" Harry said, after Todd poured his heart out and begged his friend for help.

"Fifty thousand g's by midnight or I'm a dead man. We'll all be dead, Harry. They'll whack us all—me, Mikey, Bill, and Donny. Even though that putz deserves it, I'd still hate to lose the sorry-ass bastard. You know what I mean. These fucks know no mercy and when they make a point, they have to make it big!" Todd said.

"Yeah, I understand. The problem is, I don't have access to that kind of cash anymore," Harry said, getting very upset. He honestly wanted to help his friend, but his funds were on hold until he started work.

"Harry, you're the richest guy in Beverly Hills. You gotta have something hid away somewhere. You know, for a rainy day, or some shit like that," Todd insisted. He couldn't believe that his friend, who used to blow fifty grand on a weekend, was totally tapped out.

"No, really, man. They won't give me anything until I start earning a salary at my dad's office after the first. Right now, Sammy's paying for everything. They're keeping me on a really tight leash. It's like I'm a guest in my own house," Harry said, pulling on his pants.

"Okay, well can't you ask your dad for a loan? Tell him you got in some kind of trouble that doesn't involve booze or drugs. Come on, Harry, Sammy can't think you became a saint overnight. There has to be some kind of room for a slip-up somewhere, as long as it doesn't fuck up Daddy's grand master plan for the rest of your life!" Todd said sarcastically, trying to shame his friend into coughing up the cash.

"I don't know, Toad. I can't risk it. I got everything on the line now, man. I have to be good," Harry sheepishly admitted.

"Oh, so you're telling me that you're gonna let me and the rest of the boys get blown away? You don't have the balls to put your ass on the line for us anymore, Harry?" Todd pushed on. "What the hell has happened to you, man? You used to be the hippest dude in town and now you've become a total wuss. Even worse, you got this new wife, new house, and new life ahead of you and you don't even care that all of your old buddies could wind up in the ocean wearing cement shoes. You are really a piece of shit now, aren't you, Raider?"

"Fuck you, Kranks," Harry screamed, raising his middle fingers on both hands, and stomping furiously across the room.

"No, fuck you, Raider. Oh big man, shooting me a birdie! That's probably the best you can do these days, you piss-ass mama's boy," Todd said, marching right up to Harry and getting right in his face. The two men's eyes locked, like they were trying to stare into each other's soul. Being that physically close to Todd, Harry could practically smell his fear. He knew that this was no game and Todd desperately depended needed him to survive.

Harry smiled gently, backed away from Todd, and opened up his arms.

"I'm still the same old Harry. I'm not going to let my buddies down, no way. I just have to think of a way to get the cash out of my dad. I'm seeing him tonight at the Bar Mitzvah. Let me see what I can do," Harry said, his voice softening. The intensity of the moment was almost too much for him so he had to do something clear his mind. Harry walked over to the mirror and put some gel in his hair to calm down the eternal frizz.

"Cool, but whatever you do, be sure you're back here with the money by midnight. Me and Vito have to hang out until you get back." Todd let out a big sigh of relief and relaxed onto a mound of Jessica's white lacy pillows.

"Okay, let me get out of here. The sooner I get to Sam, the better," Harry said, checking himself out in the full-length mirror. "How do I look?" Harry said, spinning around on his heels.

"Oh, you are just stunning, little Harry. You'll make Mommy and Daddy so proud," Todd laughed.

"Fuck you, man," Harry said, purposely messing up his once perfectly gelled hair in an attempt at rebellion.

"Hurry back, Bar Mitzvah boy," Todd cracked, as he went up to Harry and adjusted his bow tie. Then in a show of true friendship, Todd gave Harry a manly hug for at least trying to save him from the Mafia.

chapter twelve

Arriving fashionably late, Jessica and Harry made a grand entrance in the main ballroom at the elegant Beverly Hills Hotel. The whole place had been turned into Cirque du Soleil. Little Scotty Feldstein had seen the show on a school field trip and had been obsessed with it ever since. What else was there for loving Beverly Hills parents to do but to hire the entire Cirque du Soleil troupe to perform at their son's Bar Mitzvah, even if it set them back a cool million dollars?

Harry and Jessica posed with Scott's parents for pictures that were sure to appear in *LifeStyles* magazine, the glossy bible that chronicled wealthy Southern California Jewish events. They mingled with the best of Beverly Hills until Harry spotted his parents standing at the bar chatting aimlessly with the Bar Mitzvah boy's proud grandparents. "Oh great, there's my units, right this way!" Harry took Jessica's hand and dragged her through the glittering, bejeweled, surgically enhanced crowd of parents and their dolled-up brats.

Slow down, Harry. What's the rush? Gosh, I've never seen Harry so excited to see Sam and Irma before. Something weird must be going on here, Jessica thought, as she nearly tripped over some short pre-teenagers dancing a little too closely.

"Hiya, Daddy!" Harry said, enthusiastically slapping Sam on the back, almost knocking the miniature egg roll out of his hand. "Mom, you do look lovely, as always," Harry continued, taking his mother's hand and kissing it gallantly. Her thirty-four-carat diamond solitaire ring almost poked his eye out.

"Why thank you, Harry. You remember Sylvia and Henry Mendleberg, Scotty's maternal grandparents," Irma said, politely reintroducing her son to the aging but equally stylish couple.

"Nice to see you again. Sorry I didn't recognize you at first, but you look so much younger, I thought you were maybe some of Scotty's friends," Harry joked, laying on his best bit of Beverly Hills Bar Mitzvah schmooze.

"Irma, you have some son there. He's a real charmer!" Sylvia Mendleberg grinned.

"Yes, we're very proud of him. And this is his beautiful new bride, Jessica," Irma said, welcoming her daughter-in-law into their chatty circle.

"Pleased to meet you," Jessica said nervously. Jessica was never really at ease at big, lavish events. Tonight she was trying extra hard to play the lovely wife, but she secretly wished that she and Harry were back at home cuddling in front of the television or enjoying dinner al fresco by their new pool.

"Jessica and Harry will be having their own children very soon. Jessica's dying to be a mother, aren't you dear?" Irma said mercilessly, announcing to the Mendlebergs that she too would soon be eligible to enter in the unofficial Beverly Hills Grandparents' Social Olympics. In most other parts of America, this simple statement wouldn't have an underlying meaning. But in Beverly Hills, the Mendlebergs knew what Irma Raider was really saying was, "Pretty soon, I will have the chance to make a bris or baby naming that will make your shoddy Bar Mitzvah look like a day at McDonald's. And, if that weren't enough, in thirteen years, if I'm still alive, G-d willing, *meer hashem,* I will throw the Super Bowl of Bar Mitzvahs that will everyone will be talking about for centuries to come. And don't you forget it! Amen!"

As the unfazed Mendlebergs were taking their warning in stride, poor Jessica felt like she was about to faint. *How could Irma be so insensitive and put me on the spot? Doesn't she know that a comment like that could send Harry into a tailspin for the rest of the evening?* Jessica thought, her initial panic now turning to frustration and anger. *What the hell would she like us to do, go into the bathroom, fuck like rabbits, and not come out until it's confirmed that I'm with child?* Jessica thought while smiling her Beverly Hills party smile. "Ha, ha, ha, that's my mother! Always the one with subtle hints! Just one of the reasons why we love her!" Harry said, spreading his convivial mood and giving Irma a big kiss on the cheek.

Knowing how he really felt about the subject of fatherhood, Jessica was surprised to see Harry react so calmly to Irma's outspoken attack. *Something else really must be on his mind tonight, otherwise he would have been heading for the door by now,* Jessica thought as she breathed a huge sigh of relief.

"Daddy, can I talk to you a minute en prive?" Harry whispered in Sam's ear. Sam didn't like the sound of desperation in his voice. He raised an accusatory "what have you done now" eyebrow and gave Harry a look of absolute dread. "Please, Daddy, it will only take a minute. It's important," Harry said under his breath.

"Sure, Harry, let's go outside. Something tells me that it's time for a cigar," Sam said quietly to his son.

"Will you folks please excuse us? We're going out on the terrace for a little smoke. Jessica, why don't you tell everyone about your fantastic honeymoon? I'm sure the Mendlebergs would like to hear about all those royal events you attended in Europe. Jessica's stepmother is a very famous countess. Prince Charles is a close friend."

Harry and Sam stepped out onto the balcony. "Don't tell me you've had a problem with drugs again, Harry. I can't hear something like that now, you know," Sam said, lighting up his cigar.

"No, Dad, it's nothing like that," Harry assured the old man. "It's... it's... it's a girl!" Harry finally said. Harry had not stopped to think about why he was going to tell his dad that he needed the money.

"What happened? You get a broad knocked up?" Sam said coolly. He was somewhat relieved to hear that it wasn't something he considered to be serious.

"Exactly!" Harry said, going along with whatever his father believed to be true. *This is something he, of all people, has got to understand and be cool about,* Harry thought as he stood there with a guilty smile on his face.

"Jesus, Harry, you haven't gotten a broad knocked up since you banged the maid when you were sixteen. That's a pretty good track record. When did it happen this time?" Sam said, not looking up from his cigar.

"On my honeymoon!" Harry hoped he could create a story believable enough to fool his father.

"Are you telling me that you actually got away with shtuping another broad on your *honeymoon*, without your wife catching you? Harry, you're unbelievable!" Sam laughed as he puffed away on his stogy.

"I'm sorry, Dad, but I couldn't help myself. You know,

like father, like son!" Harry giggled, hoping his father would see the humor in the situation. Sam just winked back at Harry, never quite acknowledging his own bad behavior.

"We were in Italy and we went to a party at this outrageous villa that the countess got us invited to. Anyway, this young Italian princess wanted to give us, well, give me, the grand tour. Jessica was busy checking out all the Picassos and other fantastic art hanging on the walls, so I said 'Why not?' I mean, who could refuse a gorgeous, sexy, voluptuous eighteen-year-old Italian beauty? She was so gorgeous, she looked like a young Sophia Loren," Harry shrewdly said. At this point, Sam perked up. Sophia Loren was his favorite silver-screen siren of all time. He had tried on many occasions, unsuccessfully, to bed her.

"Anyway, her gorgeous bedroom was part of her house tour, and before I could stop myself, one thing led to another and bang! I was a total goner. She seduced me!" Harry hoped he had given his old man a shot at living out his ultimate fantasy vicariously through his bullshit story.

"That's incredible, Harry. I don't know if I actually believe it happened that way, but it's still quite an accomplishment." Sam and Harry snickered together. *Okay, now that he is on my side, it's time to go for the gold,* Harry thought, and he prepared to hit his dad up for fifty grand. "Anyway, she contacted me through a mutual friend and said I got her pregnant. She's young, and naturally she's terrified to tell her parents, so she needs some money to leave the country, have an abortion, and maybe take a little vacation with some girlfriends to recover from the whole drama."

"So, you're asking me for some cash to get you out of this mess?" Sam asked quietly.

"Exactly, and I need it right away, otherwise she'll have to go to her parents, who will in turn tell the countess, and then it's surely going to get back to Jessica. You see, Dad, if

I don't make this go away right now, it could ruin the rest of my life," Harry pleaded.

Sam Raider watched his son's body language. Harry was swaying back and forth nervously, chewing the inside of his left cheek. Sam could tell that there was obviously a sense of urgency to what Harry was saying, but something deep inside him didn't believe that Harry was telling the whole truth. Before agreeing to help him, he decided to put his son to the test. "How do you know it's yours?" Sam asked.

"What?" Harry said, caught totally off guard. He thought he had his dad eating out of the palm of his hand.

"How do you know that you are the one who got her knocked up? If she is in the habit of leading strange older men into her bedroom, maybe you are just one of her many conquests." Sam looked Harry straight in the eye. He was interested to see how his son could explain his way out of this question.

"She was a virgin!" Harry excitedly crowed, very proud that he could answer his father and cover his ass so quickly.

Sam laughed out loud. "You mean to tell me that instead of choosing an eligible, rich, young, royal European man, a sexy, eighteen-year-old Italian princess chose to give her virginity to you? Harry, that's the wildest story I've ever heard. You don't really expect me to believe that, do you son?"

"But it's true, Daddy, I swear! I think that's the reason she wanted to do it with me. I'm not part of her royal European circle. With me she could become a woman and explore her sexuality without getting a reputation as a total slut. She knew I couldn't tell anyone because I was married, so I was a safe bet. I guess she never figured that she could get knocked up on her first shot," Harry said, praying that Sam would follow his logic.

"How much does she want?" Sam asked, pretending to accept Harry's excuse.

"Fifty thousand dollars," Harry said calmly.

Sam was silent for what seemed like an eternity to Harry. Sam didn't believe one word of Harry's story, but obviously his son was in some kind of real trouble. "That's a lot of money, Harry. How do you know that if you give it to her, she won't ask for more?" Sam wanted to see just how hard Harry was willing to put up a fight.

"She's from a rich Italian family, Daddy. She doesn't need my money, except this one time so that she doesn't have to embarrass herself. Reputation is a very important thing over there, especially since they're Roman Catholics. I swear, this is just a one-time thing, to save her future, and mine for that matter. I mean, if we take care of this now, I won't have an illegitimate child walking around on this earth that I don't even speak to," Harry said, pulling out the big guns.

If my dad really does have a secret son he's been supporting all of these years, then this should hit him where he lives, Harry hoped.

Sam turned away from Harry, blew his cigar smoke over the veranda, and began to walk back into the party. Harry just stood there, paralyzed with fear and sadness.

Before Harry had a chance to run after him, Sam slowly turned around before he reached the door that led back into the ballroom. "In my cigar humidor, under the box of Cubans, is my secret stash. I got one hundred and fifty thousand bucks sitting there waiting for a rainy day. Take what you need and don't tell your mother," Sam confided before disappearing in a cloud of cigar smoke.

"Dad, you're the fucking best!" Harry yelled after him. Harry wanted so much to run up and give Sam a big hug, but he knew that would do more damage than good. Sam didn't want anyone else to know that he had just been worked over by his son.

★★★

When Harry returned, the party was in full swing. He was finally able to grab Jessica away from the boring Mendlebergs and pull her onto the dance floor. Harry and Jessica began dancing to the sounds of Britney Spears, who had been hired to be the entertainment for the night. Not only did she provide great music, but she also provided enough material for all of the fathers and sons in the room to fantasize the night away.

"Is everything okay, Harry?" Jessica asked, curious to learn what Harry and Sam's little tête-à-tête was about without appearing too pushy.

"Everything is just great, darling. You are the most gorgeous girl here tonight! Are you having a good time?" Harry asked.

"As good as can be expected. You know I'm not great at these kinds of things," Jessica said, moving to the beat of the music.

"Relax, kiddo, you're doing a super job. Besides, you're with Harry; that means you're automatically the life of the party." Harry laughed and kissed Jessica passionately. Jessica's stressed-out mood melted away now that she had her husband's full attention. All of a sudden, Harry felt a pinch on his ass, from a masculine hand he knew was not Jessica's.

"Hey, Raider, get a room!" Billy Schwartz, another one of Harry's old childhood buddies, said. Short, balding, "Dr. Beverly Hills Billy"—better known in these parts as "cosmetic dentist to the stars"—was boogying on the dance floor with his six-foot-three ex-Playmate-centerfold wife, Inga, right next to Harry and Jessica.

"Britney is so hot," Billy mouthed to Harry behind his wife's back. Harry just nodded in agreement. "This is so much better than those Bar Mitzvahs we used to have, huh, Raider? I'll never forget your father's face when he found out you were in Vegas with a couple of hookers that morning. What a fucking pisser you were!" Billy laughed. Jessica nodded politely and pretended to be amused by yet another crazy story from her husband's past. "At thirteen years old, you had the nerve to keep all of your family's friends and the Bee Gees waiting! You definitely showed them the real meaning of 'Saturday Night Fever,'" Billy shouted above the music.

"Yeah, well those days are long gone. I'm a happily married man now," Harry said, beaming at Jessica. "As a matter of fact, it's getting kind of late; I think we should be going home now. It's past my bedtime," Harry said to Jessica, pulling her off of the dance floor and heading towards the exit. He wanted to have enough time to stop by his parents' house, get the money, and bring it home to Todd before the clock struck midnight.

"But Harry, we haven't even had dinner yet," a baffled Jessica said, now standing outside of the hotel while Harry signaled for Frank to bring the car around.

"Oh, Jessica, don't tell me that you care about some lousy Bar Mitzvah dinner. The main course always sucks; after the hors d'oeuvres, it's a downhill slide. I thought you hated these things, anyway. Wouldn't you rather be home, having a late-night skinny dip in our brand new pool?" Harry asked, not so gently pushing his wife into the back seat of the Bentley.

"To tell you the truth, that does sound like a lot more fun. I just thought it was important to you to go to the party, that's all," Jessica said, adjusting her twisted dress.

"It's important that we pop in, say hello, and make an appearance, but we certainly don't have to torture ourselves and stay the whole night," Harry said coolly, relieved to be in control of the whole situation.

"Wow, that's good to know." Jessica was thrilled to hear she didn't have to play the dutiful-wife role all evening.

"Frank, do me a favor and swing by Dad's house before taking us home," Harry said, casually. "Sure thing, boss," Frank replied, delighted that father and son now seemed to be working as a team.

★ ★ ★

"I'll just be a minute, sweetheart," Harry said, tapping Jessica lovingly on her knee as he sprinted out the door, giving her no time to ask him any questions about the mysterious pit stop. "What's going on, Frank?" Jessica asked the driver, as she watched Harry dart into his parent's huge, faux-French-chateau estate with urgency.

"Heck if I know. I don't ask any questions. I just do what I'm told. Life around here is much easier that way, ma'am," Frank said sweetly.

"Not for everyone," Jessica said wistfully. She didn't mind going along with Harry's antics to a point if that's what it took to pacify him. But there was no way she was willing to live her entire life with her head in the sand, looking the other way, pretending to be unaware of Harry's shenanigans.

Within minutes, a very happy-looking Harry jumped back into the car and signaled Frank to get moving. "Home, James!" Harry said, in his best British accent. "Oh, yeah, I forgot your name isn't James! Home, Frankster, my man!" Harry chuckled.

He seems mighty pleased about something and I'm dying to know what it is. I'm going to hold my tongue and wait until we get home. Maybe after we begin to chill out a little bit, he'll confide in me, Jessica thought, looking curiously at Harry.

When they arrived home, Harry flew out of the car and

ran into the house. Jessica did her best to keep up with him. When she followed him into the downstairs den, she definitely didn't like what she saw.

Todd and Vito were stretched out on her new furniture. They hadn't even taken off their shoes, and both had their feet on the low, modern glass coffee table, imported from Germany. There were bowls of popcorn, chips, and M&Ms all over the place next to plates piled high with half-eaten sandwiches and empty beer cans. The whole place was a terrible mess. Harry seemed absolutely not bothered by the whole thing. He was shaking Vito's hand and giving him the envelope filled with cash when Jessica entered the room. She tried to keep a look of disgust off her face and made a valiant attempt at appearing somewhat pleasant, but really she wanted to scream. Jessica had tried to convince herself that Harry's hooligans were gone for good. When she was thinking rationally, she knew that wasn't realistic, but on the other hand, this asshole had ruined her wedding! *How dare he have the nerve to barge into her home in the middle of the night and invade her newly married life? Who the hell did Todd Krane think he was? Harry was a different man now, didn't he get that?* Jessica thought. She wanted to run up to Todd and slap his face, but a protective little voice deep inside warned her to get control of herself, immediately!

The bottom line was that Todd was part of Harry's old gang and even though he had sworn to stay away from them after the wedding, it was inevitable that one or two of them would pop into their lives every once in a while. If she wanted to make her marriage work, Jessica had no choice but to accept this fact and adopt an "if you can't beat them, join them" attitude, at least for the moment.

"Is there anything else I can get you boys?" Jessica asked, smiling lovingly at Harry. He was pretty amazed that she wasn't flipping out.

"No, Jessica, we won't be staying long. I just have some, well, uh, business to finish up with Harry, then we'll be out of your way," Todd said, somberly. He felt guilty about how nicely she was treating him after the stunt he pulled at her wedding.

"So sorry to hear you won't be staying longer. I hope to see you again. Now if you'll excuse me, I'll let you get on with it," a triumphant Jessica said, as she turned to leave the room.

"Ah, sorry about the wedding, Jessica. We were playing a practical joke on our old buddy. We never meant it to go so far and get out of hand." Todd felt compelled to apologize to Jessica and to Harry. Harry had come to his rescue and saved his life while Jessica welcomed him and Vito into her home.

"Oh, don't worry about it. It was actually very funny," Jessica, said controlling her sarcasm and letting out a fake laugh. *I better leave and quit while I'm ahead,* Jessica thought as she ran out of the room and headed up the stairs.

"She's some special woman," Todd said to Harry.

"I told you she was awesome, otherwise I wouldn't have married her," Harry replied, walking his old buddy to the door.

"Listen, I'm sorry I put you on the spot like this, dude, but I really had nowhere else to turn," Todd said.

"It's cool, man, I'm just glad I could come through for ya. You know, things aren't the way they used to be. I have to earn my cash like any other normal human being." Harry shrugged his shoulders, implying he had no idea what that really meant.

"No, really, man, I know you're doing the doting-husband, good-son thing right now, but if you ever get really bored with the whole scene, you know your boys are just waiting to take you back where you belong." Todd smiled slyly and poked Harry playfully in the ribs. The devil was doing his work this evening and came disguised as an old friend.

"What do you mean?" Harry asked. "Don't I belong here in my own home?"

"Of course you do, man. I'm sorry, I'm just not convinced that Harry Raider, party-animal extraordinaire, is going to be content to be living on a leash for the rest of his life. Something tells me that eventually, you may need some time out of the cage," Todd said, raising an eyebrow.

"No, no, no, those days are behind me now. I'm cool with the way things are," Harry said, halfheartedly, like he was trying to convince himself as much as he wanted to fool Todd.

"That sounds like Sam Raider talking, not Harry," Todd shot back. For a minute Harry was silent. *I'd like to be able to jump down your throat right now and tell you how off-base you are, but for some reason I just can't. Of course the old Harry would love to hop in that Porsche with you guys and go snort my brains out in Malibu, but I'd probably hate myself the next day. I need time to adjust, man, so you're going to have to give me a break,* Harry thought.

"I think you better get outta here, Toad. I promised Jessica a skinny dip and I sure as hell don't want to keep her waiting." Harry smiled. He hated telling his old friend to get lost, but he felt that he had no choice.

"Whatever you say, dude. Just remember we're here if you need us. Oh, and Vito and his boss in Vegas are like the most powerful dudes on the Strip. They can get the best of everything: grade-A coke, the hugest high-roller suites, the best tables, limos, and the horniest bitches on the Strip. If you want to spend a wild weekend in the desert, Vito is your man." Todd winked suggestively at Harry. He enjoyed his little game of tempting the beast, but he knew not to push it too far. Harry Raider had once again just proved to be a walking bank with an all-night ATM, so he didn't want to alienate the one person he knew he could count on to get him out of trouble when shit hit the fan.

Fuck! That sounds like a pisser! Sometimes I wish I could still do that shit and get away with it, but I'd lose my ass now, Harry thought, momentarily longing for the good old days. "As I said, it's getting late. I better go inside now," Harry said, hanging his head and purposely walking away from his friend.

"Whatever, man. We'll miss you," Todd yelled after Harry as he peeled the Porsche out of Harry's driveway and screeched down the street like a teenager in his daddy's car. Relieved to have temptation out of his way, Harry walked through his living room and headed out to the pool.

★★★

Floating in the pool, stretched out on a raft, was a completely naked Jessica, very definitely waiting for her husband to join her. A big, naughty smile spread across Harry's devilish face. *You see, there are rewards for being a good boy. Life doesn't have to be boring just because I'm not getting high anymore. There are other ways to enjoy myself,* Harry thought as he took off his clothes and jumped into the pool.

He swam over to Jessica's raft, tipped it over, and immediately pulled her on top of him. The newlyweds began making out and passionately fondling each other. "Do you want to tell me what that was all about?" Jessica whispered in Harry's ear, as she came up for air between kisses.

"Nope," Harry said, lifting her up on top of the pool's first step.

"What's the matter, Harry? Don't you trust me?" Jessica

said, as she nibbled on Harry's neck.

"Of course I do, but this was a private matter between old buddies. Just forget all about it, okay?"

"Okay, I just don't want you to think of me as your parole officer. I'd much rather be your partner in crime," Jessica purred. *There is no way I'm going to ruin this hot night with a million questions. One day I'll find out all there is to know about Harry and the boys, but tonight, my man remains a mystery,* Jessica thought. Seductively, she began slowly covering Harry's whole body with kisses, focusing on that one special place that drove him wild. Soon they were making love like a couple of hot teenagers by the side of the pool. Mr. And Mrs. Raider were screaming so loudly and enjoying each other so much that they didn't care if they woke up all of Beverly Hills.

All the hookers in Vegas got nothing on you, kiddo. I really think I'm going to be truly happy now, Harry thought later that evening as they cuddled together under a duvet on their king-sized bed. For the first time since her arrival, Jessica felt totally comfortable in her new surroundings and finally experienced a bit of peace.

Hollywood won't be such a scary place if I can fall asleep in Harry's arms every night, Jessica thought, as they both drifted into a lovely sleep. That evening Harry and Jessica's Beverly Hills multimillion-dollar mega-mansion on Sunset Boulevard had the intimacy and coziness of a hand-built log cabin hidden away deep in a wooded forest. Although Irma Raider had furnished the place from top to bottom and Sam had paid the bills, it was Harry and Jessica's love that made the huge house into a warm, nurturing home. At least for now, all was right in the new couple's world and nobody on either coast could put a price on their happiness.

chapter thirteen

Before they knew it, the holiday season was upon them. From the Halloween party on the Twentieth Century Fox Studio's lot to a pre-Thanksgiving bash on a music mogul's yacht in Marina Del Rey, Harry and Jessica were on a nonstop whirlwind of hitting the town. Invitations to all the top events never stopped pouring in, and neither did the gift bags filled with goodies like jewelry or free shampoo. With a lot of help from Chas's "care packages" and a fabulous team of hairdressers, makeup artists, and nail experts, Jessica looked absolutely ravishing every time she walked out the door. Much to her credit, she always smiled pleasantly for the paparazzi's cameras that flashed relentlessly in her face at everything from a lunch benefit for underprivileged children at Morton's restaurant to the celebrity-studded wrap party of a new animated movie.

During this festive time, Harry also could be commended for turning up not high and perfectly dry. He didn't even taste one drop of champagne for a toast, and passed up punch bowl after punch bowl of rum-laced eggnog. At every event, Harry was sipping nothing more than Coca-Cola. Even without drugs or booze he still managed to be the life of the party, entertaining Hollywood's bigwigs with his crazy camera antics and funny stories. When the Christmas rush rolled around, it seemed as though Harry and Jessica had been to a holiday breakfast, lunch, ball, or cocktail party of some sort almost every day since Thanksgiving. Cumulatively they had visited more homes in Los Angeles than Santa and the Hanukkah Fairy put together.

Jessica, who never used to leave her garden back in East Hampton, was absolutely exhausted. In her efforts to do Harry proud she had knocked herself out. The stress was really beginning to take a toll on mind, body, and spirit, and she didn't know how to make it go away. Harry, on the other hand, was enjoying every minute of their social merry-go-round. Thoughts of going to work for his father and being forced to become a responsible grown-up hung over his head like a black cloud of impending doom. The more he ran around all over town, the less he had to focus on the inevitable reality of what was right around the corner. He was so busy having as much fun as possible that he hardly noticed that Jessica was at her wit's end and desperately needed a break.

★ ★ ★

Returning by private jet from a New Year's Eve gala at the Caribou Club in Aspen, Harry and Jessica at last spent a weekend relaxing at home. On Sunday morning, the day before he was to begin working for his father, Harry woke up in an empty bed. He thought that maybe he'd surprise Jessica in the shower, but when he went into their bathroom, he saw that his wife was nowhere to be found. Since Jessica was not naturally an early riser, Harry began to get a little worried. He put on his favorite fluffy robe to look for her. Out of the corner of his eye, he noticed that the little white door to Irma's makeshift nursery was pushed open.

Jessica sat on the big sunflower beanbag chair, wearing nothing but her pink La Perla robe and Miss Piggy house slippers. Cindy, who had been very much ignored by her busy mistress over the last few crazy months, was curled up on Jessica's lap, happy to be the center of attention once more. Jessica caressed Cindy lovingly, twirling her curly poodle hair between dainty fingers, and didn't say a word when Harry knocked quietly on the door. "Should I come in, Jes?" Harry asked in a small voice just above a whisper. He wanted to believe that everything was fine, but instinctively he knew something was wrong.

"Sure," Jessica said, not looking up from Cindy's poofy poodle head.

"Are you okay?" Harry stood in the doorway. He had not once gone into the nursery since the couple moved into the house months ago. Subconsciously, he thought that if he went in that room, even to play with one of the toys, that he'd be giving Jessica the wrong message. "Aspen was a killer time, wasn't it?" Harry said, sitting down on a Kermit the Frog armchair next to Jessica, fidgeting a bit to make himself comfortable on the tiny piece of furniture.

"I guess so," Jessica answered listlessly.

"You spent most of night gabbing with Goldie Hawn and the rest of the time you hung out with Melanie and Antonio. You certainly looked like you were having a good time," Harry said, confused by his wife's sullen disposition.

"You know, Harry, there's more to life than being seen with movie stars and going to party after party. Don't you ever get sick of the whole thing?"

"Not really," Harry said honestly. "I didn't think I could have a good time being sober, but these few months have been a riot. I was hoping you were enjoying yourself as much as I was," Harry said, unwilling to face what he sensed that Jessica was about to lay on him.

"Harry, you know how proud I am of you that you haven't gone off the wagon and that you've kept your commitment to me. That's why I wanted so badly to be the ultimate party girl you could have a blast with. But you know what? That's not really who I am or what I want my whole life to be about," Jessica said softly.

Harry sniffled, shook his head, and cast his eyes down at his Gucci shoes. "Look, Jessica, on Monday morning I have to go to work for my dad. As you can imagine, I'm scared to death, because I've never worked a day in my life and Sam is the most famous children's clothing manufacturer in the world. I hope I don't totally fuck up the billion-dollar business he's spent his whole life building. I'm going to have to get serious at least during the day, Jessica. That's why I think that you and I should continue to have the best nightlife we can, so I have something to look forward to after Sam's done busting my balls." Harry smiled and played with a furry football he found on the floor.

"I understand that you are very worried about your new challenge, and I certainly don't mind going out once in a while, but I'd be lying to you if I told you I was really happy." Jessica was fighting back tears. She wanted so much to keep up her end of their unspoken deal, but deep down she knew she could no longer continue with the charade.

"Jessica, I love you so much. You know I can't stand to see you get upset. You know a million girls would kill to have your life. I don't know if they'd all want to be married to a freak like me, but I certainly do know that a lot of babes would love to be Beverly Hills' Most Beautiful Belle of Every Ball." Harry put his arm around Jessica and kissed her on the cheek, doing his best to be comforting. *I love Jessica, but for the life of me, I can't understand what the hell she has to complain about. We have everything: a gorgeous home, cars, parties galore—what the heck is wrong with that?* a frustrated Harry silently wondered.

"Don't think I don't know how lucky we are, but I'm sorry, Harry, it just seems so empty at times," Jessica said, now bawling. Harry took a big breath and turned away from her.

"I can't believe you could say something like that, Jessica. You make me feel that being married to me isn't gratifying," Harry said, unable to look her straight in the face.

Jessica covered her eyes with one hand and pounded the chair out of sheer frustration with the other. "Oh no, Harry, I didn't mean that at all. I am thrilled being married to you. I just want to add a deeper dimension to our lives. I love you so much that what I want is a family. Harry, I really want to have a baby," Jessica blubbered, handing Cindy over to Harry as she wiped the tears from her eyes with the belt from her robe.

Harry threw his arms up in the air. "Jessica, I don't know what to say. I'm just starting this new job, so let's see how that goes first before we make any big decisions. I need time, honey."

"No, Harry. It may not be that easy. We have to do something *now*," Jessica exhaled like she was letting loose a secret that she had kept bottled up inside of her for quite some time.

"What do you mean, Jes? We haven't even started trying!" Harry put down the poodle and walked over to the window. Jessica sat quietly with a very guilty look on her face. She nervously nibbled on her quivering lower lip and began again to whimper. "Jessica, please tell me that you've been on the pill this whole time. Please tell me you haven't been trying to get knocked up without telling me," Harry said, staring out into the garden.

The thought of Jessica becoming pregnant just as he was figuring out how to deal with Sam was overwhelming

Harry. He could feel the sweat building up around his neck and dripping down his back. He swayed back and forth but could not get comfortable. The hair on his chest, legs, and arms all began to itch, like he was breaking out in hives from head to toe. Even the tiny hairs in his nostrils and ears burned. He felt like he needed to escape. Being husband, businessman, and father was a burden way too heavy for him to handle all at once.

"I thought we agreed that we would decide *together* when the time was right to have a kid," Harry said, pacing around the room frantically.

"We did, but since I never got pregnant before, I was beginning to wonder if I even could. Chas said that sometimes it takes a while for your body to get back to normal when you stop taking the pill. I figured by the time you were ready, my body would be ready, but now it's been a long time and still, nothing, even though we make love a lot," Jessica sobbed.

"You're telling me that you discussed this with that asshole Chas Greer before you even let me in on what you were doing? This is completely nuts, Jessica!" Harry said, shaking his head in total disbelief.

"Don't look so damn upset," Jessica blasted at Harry, her tears now turning to pure anger. "I may not be able to have children, so you may get your wish, Harry!" Jessica ranted as she stood up from the beanbag and got right in Harry's face. "I may be totally infertile, so you may get to be the only big baby in this house for the rest of your pathetic life!" Jessica screamed and ran into their bathroom, locking the door behind her.

Because Jessica had been so patient with Harry, he had always tried to be the same way with her, especially when she discovered the nursery and brought up the baby-making topic on the first day they moved into the house. Now, unknowingly, she had pushed him over the edge. "I can't believe you'd do something as major as go off of the pill without talking to me about it. I thought I could trust you!" Harry screamed back as he slapped the bathroom door with both hands. "I thought we understood each other. You were the last person I thought would be sneaky and try to force me into something that I wasn't ready to take on," Harry exclaimed as his voice grew even louder.

"I'm sorry, Harry, but sometimes it gets really hard waiting for you to grow the fuck up!" Jessica cried, as she cracked open the door for a split second to yell at Harry, then once again slammed it in his face.

I feel totally betrayed by her, man. It's like there's a side to her that I don't even know and I certainly don't like, Harry thought as he threw his hands up in the air and backed away from the door. He began furiously pacing up and down the hall, stomping his feet and pounding his fists in the air. "I can't believe you'd do this to me after I've stayed sober for *you* all of these months. I could have easily gone and partied so many times behind your back and you might have never caught me. I could have kept a stash of coke somewhere in this fucking house and had a whore or two when you were getting your damn hair done, and you would have never even had a clue. I could have fooled you, Jessica dear, and my parents that I was on the straight and narrow, but no, I wanted to give it a real shot, because I didn't want to let *you* down. This so un-fucking-fair of *you.* Don't you have any idea of how hard it is for me to be back in LA and not go snort my brains out with my buddies? My boys are dying to get wasted with me like old times and I've walked away from them, all for *you!* What a fucking joke, man, what a fucking idiot I've been. What a waste of fucking time!" Harry yelled as he went into his bedroom, got dressed in a hurry, ran out of the house, and drove his blue Bentley like a madman down Sunset Boulevard, heading towards the Pacific Coast Highway.

★ ★ ★

After following the twisting, turning ocean road, Harry screeched up to Mike Roman's house in Malibu. Mike and Todd were lounging on the sun deck, nursing a post-New-Year's hangover. Todd took off his sunglasses and leaned up against the white railing. "Harry Raider, I don't believe it. Aren't you a sight for my red buzzed-out eyes? What the fuck are you doing here, man? Like I don't know…" Todd said laughing. An "I told you so" shit-eating grin spread across his suntanned face.

"What can I say, buddy? You were right. Harry needs to have a good time! I'm baaaaaaaaack!" Harry said.

Even though those treacherous words came out of his mouth, Harry felt a little sick to his stomach as he stood there helplessly looking up at Todd and Mike. On the drive out to the beach, he'd had time to think about what just happened. Harry realized that he probably overreacted to Jessica's hysterics. He almost turned around and went back home. But the old destructive side of Harry told him to keep driving. Now that he had arrived at his friend's house, he felt like there was no turning back.

"So what will it be, Raider?" asked Mike, as they walked into the large stainless-steel chef's kitchen. "How about a little mimosa to get things started?" Todd poured Harry a glass of champagne, adding just a little orange juice for color.

"Uh, no thanks, I'll just have a Pepsi," Harry said, pushing the glass away.

"Aw, come on, Raider. You didn't drive all the way out here for a soda, now did you?" Todd put the champagne glass back into Harry's hand. He picked up a long, twisted swizzle straw from the counter and placed it into the champagne bottle. "C'mon, I'll race ya! You know what they say, no better way to cure a hangover than to catch another buzz," Todd said before he started slurping the bottle dry.

One drink. I'm sure can have one drink without getting myself in deep shit. What harm could one little drink do? Harry thought and reluctantly took his first sip of alcohol since he nearly OD'd last August in the Hamptons. Three empty bottles later, Harry was wasted and ready for anything Todd, Mike, Bill, and Donny had in store. Harry's head spun so fast that he couldn't put up a fight when was shoved into a stretch limousine headed for the airport. Less than an hour later, a private plane dropped the gang off on a landing strip in Las Vegas, where another white limo was waiting to take them to a high-roller suite at Caesar's Palace.

★★★

The lavish gambler's paradise penthouse apartment on top of the Strip's most notorious hotel was decorated in wall-to-wall mirrors, plush circular couches, and two gigantic spinning waterbeds, which revolved beneath a strobe light. Stereos, flat screen televisions with DVD players, an extensive video library of pornography, and every other high-tech gadget known to man filled the room. The kitchen came with a fully stocked bar that had every type of liquor imaginable, lots of fruit-juice mixers, and free bottles of Dom Perignon champagne. In the refrigerator were large platters of imported cheese and fruit, piles of caviar, and shrimp cocktail. The grownup gang of boys had everything they could possibly want, except one thing...and that was soon to arrive.

Just as Harry was getting comfortable on a lounger equipped with a heat massager, the big golden front door swung open. Vito and his short, stocky Danny Devito-esque Mafia boss entered without even knocking. "I guess you gentleman found everything to your liking?" the short man said.

"Fucking fan-tab-u-lous," said Todd, looking around at his group of untamed party animals. Mike swilled more champagne and sat fixated in front of one of televisions, playing with the remote control. He had a variety of selections from the porn library and kept replaying the climax scenes over and over again. Donny was in the kitchen wolfing down plates of shrimp as he made piña coladas in a blender. Bill was experimenting with drag-queen makeup and wigs in the huge marbled bathroom while going through a pitcher of cosmopolitans.

"I'm glad to see everything is in order for your banker, Mr. Krane," the mob boss said, smiling at Harry, who was oblivious to what was going on. "Here's a little fun stuff, on the house. We hope to see you at the private high-roller tables within the hour," the Neapolitan Tony Soprano said as he threw a large Ziploc bag full of cocaine on the glass table directly in front of Harry.

"That's all blow?" Harry asked in disbelief. Even a veteran party guy like Harry Raider was shocked· by the large quantity of drugs before him. "There must be at least a half a million dollars' worth of coke there," Harry said, staring at the bag of drugs like a long-lost lover.

"Very good observation, Mr. Raider. No wonder these boys consider you the smart one. We're counting on you to play at least that or double at the tables. Let's just say this is our show of good faith." The mob boss looked directly at Harry. "I'll see you gentlemen later." He disappeared just as quickly as he came.

Harry couldn't speak. His champagne buzz was starting to wear off and he knew a huge choice lay in front of him.

I can either stand up, bust out of here right now, and go home before I do any real damage, or I can stay and play, Harry thought, his glassy eyes still transfixed on the cocaine bag.

"What are you waiting for, Raider? Dig in," Todd said, sitting down to Harry. "You better hurry up and get going before Mayberry puts down the shrimp and starts snorting up that bag like a vacuum," Todd said, pouring some of the coke out onto a silver tray. Like the pro he was, Todd chopped it up and divided it into thick white lines with his black American Express card.

"I can't gamble a million or even half a million bucks away like I used to. I certainly shouldn't be doing this," Harry said quietly.

"Who says you're going to lose, Raider? The house doesn't always win, you know, and as I remember it, there is no luckier high roller than Mr. Harry Raider. This is your chance to make some quick cash before you have to start working like a trained dog for Daddy. Did you ever think about what you would do if work didn't work out?" Todd asked, pushing a line in Harry's direction.

"What do you mean?" Harry asked, staring down at the glorious white temptation spread out in front of him.

"What if you ain't got what it takes to fill Sam Raider's illustrious shoes? What if you can't live up to what he expects of you and the whole thing explodes in your face?" Todd said, snorting line after line, without coming up for air. "What are you going to do then, Raider, live off of your rich wife? You could easily walk away with two, maybe three million here tonight, if the stars line up in your favor."

"And what if they don't? What if I lose a half a million bucks I don't have right now?" Harry asked, thinking out loud.

"So fucking what? Then you borrow it from Sam's business

and stay there and work it off as long as you have to. At least this way you have a good chance at having a serious Plan B, in case you can't stand answering to your daddy all day and your wife when you get home at night. Maybe two or three million bucks isn't a lot of bread in your world, Harry, but it's enough to guarantee that you'll always be a free man!"

"I never really thought of what might happen if Sam and I couldn't work together," Harry said, shrugging his shoulders and smiling sheepishly. "I guess you're right, it could be a huge disaster waiting to happen. I should have some of my own cash to cover my ass in case of emergency. I think if I'm going to play, I need a clear head," Harry said, turning away from the lines on the table. "What, are you kidding me, Raider? It's just the opposite. If you think too much about what you are doing when you sit down at the table, you'll get all nervous and fuck it up for sure. It's all a big game, man, remember? And when Harry's having fun, great things happen," Todd said, cutting another line of coke and moving it in Harry's direction.

Harry didn't say a word. *He's right, I can't sit there at the table and get all paranoid about what I'm doing or I'll lose my shirt. A couple of lines won't fuck me up for good, they'll just get me in the winning mood.* Harry took the rolled-up one-hundred-dollar bill from Todd's hand and snorted half the coke on the table. Within minutes, Harry Raider was feeling no pain.

★ ★ ☆

About three o'clock in the morning, Harry woke up completely dazed and confused. At first he had absolutely no idea where he was. He found himself half dressed, on the revolving waterbed, spinning slowly under the strobe light. Next to him was a sleeping Asian hooker in a lacy red bra.

"Holy fucking shit," Harry whispered as he got up from the bed and slowly walked around the suite. Even though all the lamps were turned off, the neon lights from the Strip outside the floor-to-ceiling windows illuminated the whole room.

After searching the living room, other bedrooms, bathroom, and kitchen, Harry realized he was alone, except for the hooker who was slowly waking up. As she untangled herself from the bedsheet, sat up, and began to put her clothes back on, Harry realized that "she" was a "he." Harry's head felt fuzzy and he thought he was going to toss his cookies right there. Amongst all of his wild and crazy sexual encounters, Harry Raider had only played for one team. The boy-boy love thing was something that had no appeal for him whatsoever, at least when his mind was his own.

"Relax, honey, nothing happened. Well, nothing happened with you, anyway," the hooker said, as she finished zipping her tight jeans and pulled a low-cut, revealing blouse over her head. "I was with your friend with the cool makeup, but wanted to crash for a while after he and the other guys took off. Hope you don't mind that I sacked out here for a while," she said, adjusting her wig and slipping into a pair rhinestone-studded stilettos.

"No, that's totally cool." A relieved Harry flopped down on to the bed.

"My name's Crystal, what's yours?" she said, going to the mirror to apply lipstick.

"Uh, Joe...Joe Blank," Harry replied, unwilling to reveal his true identity.

"Joe Blank? That's a classic!" Crystal laughed at Harry's obvious lie.

"Okay, it's not Joe Blank, it's Harry, Harry Raider." Harry was embarrassed that he had been so rude.

"That's okay, honey, my real name isn't Crystal either. It's Maralyn, used to be Marvin, but I like Crystal better. I call myself Miss Crystal Balls, because I give Tarot readings when I'm not working the casinos. That name gives me so much more dramatic flair, don't you think?" Crystal twirled around and struck a model-like pose.

"Definitely," Harry smiled.

"Well, I'll be going now to start working the lobby. This is prime time for me, you know. I get a lot of action. You enjoy the rest of your stay, sweetie," Crystal said, as she showed herself out.

"Wait a minute, do we owe you money?" Harry asked. He was so used to bankrolling everybody in the old days that offering to pay for his friend's hooker was just his natural reaction.

"No, sweetie, the other boys took care of me, but thank you anyway. They said that they could pay me because you'd be paying for everything else," Crystal said, shaking her head at Harry in pure pity. *Oh great, I have an honest hooker here, but my friends have no problem ripping me off,* Harry thought to himself and chuckled ironically as he opened the front door of the suite and escorted Crystal to the private elevator. "You behave yourself, sweetie," Crystal said, pointing at something behind Harry, as the elevator doors closed in front of her. Harry came face to face with Vito. Even at this wee hour in the morning, he looked ready to kill.

chapter fourteen

"Hope you're not thinking of going anywhere, Mr. Raider?" Vito said in a gruff voice.

"Of course not, where the hell would I be going? I'm not even dressed," Harry said, shrugging innocently.

"That's good, Mr. Raider, because you're not free to leave until you pay the house what you owe us," Vito said, smiling firmly. Vito played a very special role in Las Vegas. Up and down the Strip, he was known as "The Enforcer." While the hotels and casinos had to put up a legitimate front in order to operate legally, everyone knew that it was guys like Vito who kept the town profitable. If a high roller tried to split without paying his bill, a hit man like Vito was quietly called in to make sure the tab was covered.

At that minute it dawned on Harry that he had played and lost. He had been so high on coke for most of the night that he had absolutely no recollection of what went on, or how much money he lost. His boys left him holding the bag as usual, and Harry figured he had no choice but to pay the bill and get back to LA in time to show up at his father's office by 9 a.m.

If I put off facing Jessica until I get a good start with Dad, she'll be more likely to forgive me, so I won't have to deal with that until later on, Harry thought. He was actually more nervous about making amends with Jessica than paying off Vito and company. This was not the first time Harry Raider went on a big gambling binge and lost. The money was always there to bail him out, so in the past he never had anything to worry about. "Give me a couple of hours and I'll call my accountant to wire you the money." Harry walked away from Vito as he headed back to the suite.

Before he got very far, Harry felt a huge hand land firmly on his shoulder. "I don't think so, Mr. Raider. You left the tables around midnight and we've waited long enough. We are going to need that money within the hour. You can send money into the house account over the Internet and make sure we get online confirmation of the transfer. We've gotten very high tech here," Vito added.

"How much do I owe?" Harry asked, unprepared for the answer.

"Seven hundred and fifty g's," Vito said, looking Harry in the eye to see if he could detect any hidden fears. That number was big, even by Harry's high rolling gambling standards, but it was still under a million, so his father couldn't freak out too badly.

"Okay, fine, no problem. I'll call my guy and tell him to do it now. He's an older dude and he needs his sleep. I didn't want to get him out of bed," Harry said nonchalantly.

"He can relax later, because if we don't get that money soon, you'll be the one who'll be going to sleep for a long time," Vito said slowly. Harry knew he wasn't kidding, but still was not alarmed. Irving Freed, the Raider family accountant for over forty years, had come to Harry's rescue every time.

"I get what you're saying, but really, there'll be no problem," Harry said.

"I'm glad we understand each other, Mr. Raider. It's nothing personal, just business. We'll let you leave as soon as we know the money has hit the house account. Meanwhile, enjoy the view," Vito said, standing in the doorway, pointing to the sea of neon lights glowing over the Vegas Strip. He shut the door behind him and left Harry on his own. Harry didn't like what he had to do, but he knew he had no choice.

Harry dialed Irving's number in Beverly Hills. After about ten rings, Sylvia Freed, Irving's wife, answered the phone. "Hello? Who is this? Stanley, is that you? Is everything all right, bubeleh?" Sylvia's groggy, sleepy voice said.

"No Sylvia, it's not Stanley. It's Harry. I'm sorry to bother you at such a crazy hour, but I need to speak to Irving. It's urgent," Harry said to the old woman.

"Oh God, I thought it was my Stanley. His wife, Becky, is expecting twins any day now. I'm going to be a grandma, do you believe it?" Sylvia said, still managing to kvell on the phone to Harry in her sleep.

"I know, Sylvia, it's lovely. My mom and Jessica are having the shower, remember?" Harry was indulging his old family friend in polite chatter before hitting up her husband for help.

"That's right, Harry. You have a wonderful girl there. So tell me, when are you going to give Irma and Sam the same nachus that Stan and Becky are giving us? A baby makes everybody happy, Harry," Sylvia said, yawning.

"We're working on it, Sylvia, we're working on it. I promise you," Harry laughed, giving her the standard blow-off answer.

"You better be, Harry. Your parents aren't getting younger," Sylvia said, blowing her nose into the phone.

"I know, Syl, believe me, I know. Now may I please

speak to Irving? It's really important."

"One second, he's just coming back from the sitting on the pot. At his age, he goes all night." Sylvia handed the phone to her husband, who was too tired to be embarrassed by the "too much information" line she crossed every time she opened her mouth.

"Who is it, Syl?" Irving asked, as he coughed and cleared his throat before getting on the phone. "It's Irma's meshuga boy Harry, who else would call at this hour?" Sylvia said, handing Irving the phone without covering the receiver.

"Harry, what's wrong?" Irving cut right to the chase.

"How do you know something's wrong?" Harry asked, curious.

"Harry, even you're not nuts enough to call me at three o'clock in the morning just to say hello. What happened? How much do you need?"

"Seven hundred and fifty thousand dollars wired to the house account at Caesar's Palace," Harry said, opening the refrigerator door, hoping to find some milk and Captain Crunch.

"Oy vey es meer, Harry. Why the hell did you have to go and do that?" Irving said, practically falling off of his bed.

"What are you getting so upset for, Irving? It's under a million. I thought you'd be proud of me this time. I've lost more before." Harry was now searching the cabinets for any type of high-sugar cereal.

"Harry, you don't understand what's been going on. There's no more money." Harry heard the familiar "plop, plop, fizz, fizz" of the Alka Seltzer Irving was making.

"Don't be silly, Irving. I know I'm not supposed to get any cash until I start working, but I'll be back in LA in a few hours and I'll get to the office as soon as I can. Dad will see that I'm making an effort, so please just advance me the cash to cover my debts and you can deduct the whole thing from my salary. I'm going to be good from now on, Irving, you'll see," Harry said, chomping on a granola bar since he could not find his breakfast of choice.

"No, Harry, you don't understand. There's no more money at all! The business is totally bankrupt and your father is personally almost broke. I told Sammy he should have talked to you about this before you came into the office. Oy, oy, oy, what a fucking disaster," Irving said, downing the Alka Seltzer in one gulp.

"I never heard you say fuck before, Irving. You must be serious," Harry said in absolute disbelief. "How could Dad have lost all of his cash? He's supposed to be the smartest guy in the rag trade, a fucking genius." Harry felt his throat tighten and close up around the crunchy pieces of oatmeal. "I can't believe this is true. How could Dad allow this to go on?" Harry asked.

"It sure didn't happen overnight, Harry. It's been going on for a long time. I've tried for years to talk some sense into your dad, but he's a very stubborn man. Come home, Harry. You'll sit down with both of us and we'll tell you the whole story. It's not too late for Sam to save himself. There is one opportunity left, but so far he won't take it. Once you know the all the facts, maybe you can convince your father to do the right thing. Maybe he'll listen to you," Irving said, leaning back against a pile of pillows.

Harry spit out the granola. "I'd love to be on my way home right now, Irving, but I don't know how I'm going to get out of here alive unless I pay up," Harry said, trying to catch his breath. Never before had he been in a situation like this without a lump of cash to buy himself out. Just a few months ago, he took his father's last few bucks to save his best friend's life; now Harry wasn't sure how he could save his own.

"Harry, you have a rich wife, what are you worried about? Give her a call, make nicey-nice, and I'm sure she'll give you whatever you need," Irving said.

"I can't do that, Irving. She's really pissed off at me right now. If she found out was here, she'd divorce me for sure. The only reason she wouldn't want these guys to kill me is so she could have the enjoyment of doing it herself." Harry paced the room.

"You don't have a choice, Harry; she's the only one who has access to that kind of money. You know I'd give it to you myself, but I don't keep that kind of cash around. When I saw what was happening to Sammy's business, I gave my son Stanley all of my money to invest and I'm pleased to say he's done very well. We have a nice retirement account, but it's nothing I can touch. Sylvia signs all of the checks. I can't get into any trouble that way," Irving chuckled.

"You're damn right, Irving. Thank God, Baruch Hashem," Harry heard Sylvia mutter under her breath on another phone. Apparently she had been listening in on the whole conversation to make sure her husband wouldn't take pity on Harry and personally try to get him out of his mess.

"I guess I could try to put it on my credit card," Harry only half-joked.

"Don't even try to use them, Harry. I've been haggling with American Express for months now just to get them off of our backs. There must be someone else besides Jessica who can help you," Irving said, trying to assuage his guilt.

"No one I can think of, but don't worry, Irving. You and Sylvia go back to bed. I'll figure out something," Harry said, trying to think on his feet.

Harry hung up the phone and got dressed immediately. His first challenge was to find a way out of the hotel, then he could first start to think about how he was going to get back to LA. Slowly, Harry opened the door to the suite, just a crack and looked out into the hallway. He could see Vito's ominous figure guarding the elevators. On the other side of the hallway, Harry saw an exit sign that led to the fire escape staircase. Somehow he had to get down those stairs without Vito catching him. Lucky for Harry, a maid's cart wheeled out of the room next door and blocked Vito's view of the last part of the hallway. Harry snuck behind the cart, rushed down the hall, and quietly opened the fire escape door. Relieved to have made it past Vito, Harry wasted no time heading down the stairs as fast as his feet could carry him.

★★★

Forty-two flights of stairs later, Harry Raider reached the bottom. He was haggard and out of breath, but he knew he didn't have time to waste. If the maid saw him leave and said something to Vito, hotel security would be after him in seconds. That would be the beginning of the end. Harry carefully opened the door at the bottom of the stairs that led to the casino lobby. The floor was packed with conventioneers checking in, and it looked as though Harry could have a good chance blending in with the crowd. He furtively crept out and started making his way toward the hotel's front door. Soon he noticed the security guards roaming around the lobby floor, hanging out especially near the entrance. *It can't be safe for me to try and just walk out of here. There has to be another way. I need time to think of how I can get out of here alive,* Harry thought as he walked quickly towards the men's room.

I can hide in here until I come up with a plan, Harry thought as he splashed some cold water on his face. He was beet red from rushing down all those stairs and still not completely recovered from his wild night. As he was looking at his sorry self in the mirror, a door to one of the bathroom stalls swung open. Much to Harry's delight, it was Crystal Balls. She had come in to freshen up and change her outfit. Crystal was also carrying a makeup case and some clothes in a small, brightly colored suitcase. "Lordy, Mr. Harry. What are you down here with us pee-ons? I'd guess that suite of yours would have plenty of bathrooms. Don't tell me you had to come all the way to the lobby just to relieve yourself?" Crystal joked, as she opened her makeup kit and took out a razor and some shaving cream. She lathered up her face and began shaving. "Stubble, I hate it this early in the morning. What's a girl to do?" she joked between long strokes.

"So aren't you going to tell me what you're doing down here in this public area, Mr. Big High Roller?" Crystal asked, as she reached into her makeup bag and began to put on some new foundation and powder.

"I owe the house seven hundred and fifty big ones and I have no way of paying it right now. I've got to get back to LA and straighten this whole thing out, but I have no way of getting there or any money to by an airplane ticket. You could say I'm totally screwed," Harry said, looking at himself in the mirror and not liking what he saw.

"Hm, maybe I can help you out," Crystal said, putting on some glittery eye shadow.

"Don't tell me, you have seven hundred and fifty thousand dollars stuffed in your bra." Harry chuckled sarcastically at the thought of having to turn to a she-male hooker for help.

"Honey, if I was that good, I sure as shit wouldn't be living out of a suitcase in a hotel lobby." Crystal opened her suitcase and tried on a couple different pairs of leopard-printed high heels. "I've never been to LA before and I heard it's kind of cool. Do you think I have what it takes to be a star?" Crystal continued striking a pose in the mirror.

"Sure, why not? But then, what do I know? I'm just a spoiled brat who is a failure of a husband and not much good at anything else. Maybe I should let those goons do me in. Jessica would probably be better off," Harry said in a rare moment of self-pity.

"Now don't start overreacting on me. I'm the one and only drama queen around here." Crystal smiled and put her masculine arm around Harry. "Listen, if you can get me a place to stay while I'm out there, I'll drive you to LA in my van. I've always dreamed of strutting my stuff down Hollywood Boulevard. When a girl looks like me, who knows what can happen!" Crystal said, beaming at Harry.

"Really, you would do that? You could stay with my friends out in Malibu, you know, the guys you met earlier. They definitely owe me a big one. But I can't even help you pay for gas," Harry said.

"That's okay honey, I could use some time off. Malibu, huh? Très chic! Let's get going. I feel like a movie star already."

"Great!" Harry said as he started to walk out of the men's room. Crystal pulled him back in.

"Wait a minute, Harry, are you crazy? Those tough guys aren't going to just let you walk out of the hotel," Crystal said.

"Oh yeah, I almost forgot, I'm a walking dead man," Harry said, frustrated.

"You may be a dead *man,* but that doesn't mean you have to be a dead *woman,*" Crystal said, reaching into her suitcase and pulling out a floral sundress, a matching yellow sweater, and a pair of strappy sandals.

Harry figured this was his only hope of getting out of the casino alive, so he was willing to try anything. He grabbed the clothes out of Crystal's hands and put them on the best he could. Having never worn a woman's outfit before, Harry first tried to step into the dress, but soon figured out that wasn't going to work. He then awkwardly pulled it over his head and just about managed to adjust it around his manly torso. Luckily he was able to tie the straps and put the sweater over his shoulders to cover up his hairy arms.

Harry then picked up the shoes and looked at them inquisitively. Going for broke, he tripped, fell forward, and almost landed smack down on face as he stumbled into the sandals. However, with a little bit of forced determination, Harry was just about able to balance himself. Crystal took out a blonde wig, which she flopped onto Harry's pile of unruly frizz. Harry twirled around to get Crystal's approval. "Girrrl, you're looking better already. Amazing what a little fashion can do. I copied this outfit from *Vogue* magazine. Naomi Campbell was wearing the exact same thing. You'll look almost at hot as she did gliding down the catwalk."

"All you need now is a little makeup and we're good to go." Crystal grabbed her makeup bag and within minutes Harry Raider was completely unrecognizable as a member of the male gender. "You know something, Harry? You make a fine-looking woman," Crystal said, winking at Harry and pinching his butt.

"Uh, don't get any ideas," Harry said and tried to find his balance on his new footwear.

"Don't worry, honey, I don't give it away for free, remember? And right now, you're broke so you don't exactly fit the profile of a qualified customer." Crystal took Harry by the hand and led him out of the bathroom. *Great, I'm not even financially appealing to a hooker. I wonder how my wife is going to feel about me,* Harry thought. They made it safely out of the hotel, walked across the parking lot, and hopped into Crystal's beat-up old van.

"Can this thing make it all the way to LA? We're not going to get stuck somewhere in the middle of the desert, are we?" Harry asked, as Crystal put the key in the ignition.

"You better hope not, honey. When that makeup starts to melt it can be one ugly mess." Crystal laughed as she peeled out of the parking lot and headed straight for the highway. He wasn't traveling in first-class luxury like he was used to, but the trip home wasn't as bad as Harry would have guessed. Harry and Crystal listened and sang along with her collection of Broadway show tune CDs and the six-hour trip passed by faster than expected. For the moment, Harry felt lucky to be alive, yet he knew that the Vegas mob could easily track him down in LA.

Hopefully I will find some dough to pay them off before they knock me off, Harry thought as Crystal pulled up in front of his father's office building in Century City. Before getting out of the van, Harry handed Crystal a piece of paper with directions to Mike Roman's beach house. Underneath the address Harry wrote:

Here's a little souvenir from our Vegas trip. Be good to my friend, you bastards. She's a hell of a girl and more of a man than any of you losers will ever be. Love, Harry.

chapter fifteen

He gave Crystal a friendly hug and a goodbye quick kiss on the cheek and popped out of the van, carrying his men's clothes in a plastic bag he found under the back seat. Forgetting for a minute that he was still in dressed in drag, Harry marched purposefully through the lobby of his dad's office building. Before he reached the elevators, he was stopped by the guard at the security desk. "Can I help you, madam?" the guard said politely, not recognizing Harry.

"Hi Walter, it's me, Harry, Sam Raider's son!" Harry said jovially as the guard stared at him with a look of complete horror on his ashen face.

"Shall I buzz his office and tell him that you're on your way up, Madame... uh... sir?" stuttered the guard. Everyone knew that Sam Raider's son was a bit of a wild card, but no one would think that Harry was crazy enough to show up at his father's place of business wearing a dress.

"No, that's okay, I want to surprise him," Harry said, doing his best to keep a straight face. There was nothing Harry liked better than stirring up the establishment. He was thoroughly enjoying his moment of play before he had to go upstairs and face some very serious problems.

"Oh, I'm sure you will. Have a nice day, Harry. You know your way up," the guard said and pointed to the elevators. Working in LA, he had seen some pretty strange people come and go, but somehow Harry Raider always seemed to be the winner of the weirdo competition. Harry took the elevators up to the fifth floor where his dad's office had been for the past twenty-odd years. Before anyone could see him, he slid into the men's room, washed off all of his makeup, and changed back into his own men's clothing. The last thing Harry wanted to do was freak out his father by showing up in his office dressed like the daughter he never had.

As Harry was walked down the hall, he heard yelling coming from the vicinity of his father's office. As he drew closer, he could tell the voices belonged to his father and Irving. They were in the midst of a very loud, very heated argument. Instead of barging in, Harry chose to stand in the hall outside the door and listen in.

"Sammy, do you understand that you are absolutely broke? I am here as a favor to you, because there hasn't been enough money in the business to cover my salary for the last year," Irving said.

"Big deal, Irving. I've paid you enough over the past forty years to set you and your children and your children's children up for a long time!" Sam yelled.

"I know that. Why do you think I'm here, Sammy? I want to try to talk some sense into you to save your ass. The landlord here says that you're six months behind on your rent and if you don't pay it, he's throwing you out. The second mortgage you put on your house in Beverly Hills hasn't been paid either and the bank is definitely going to foreclose. What the hell are you going to tell Irma?" Irving bellowed.

"I don't know. She'll have to understand, that's all!" Sam shouted back at him. He was sitting behind his big oak desk. Sam opened his desk drawer, picked up a cigar, lit it, and inhaled, hoping the smoke would soothe his soul. "It won't be so bad. We'll move in with Harry and Jessica. There's so much room in that castle they won't even know we're there. I spent my last nickel buying that place," Sam said, leaning back and smiling.

Harry put his hand over his mouth to block the sound from the unsuspecting gasp he let out. Harry's stomach felt like it had come up to his throat and he almost fainted at what he was hearing. He was barely used to living under the same roof as his wife; throw his parents into the mix, and it had to be a recipe for disaster.

"Sammy, please, do you think a newlywed couple wants to live with their in-laws? I would never do that to my kids. How could you?" Irving asked Sam, who was turning red and shaking his fists like a madman. He hated it when people didn't see things his way.

"Don't you remember back in Brooklyn, when families used to live under one roof? It's just a temporary thing until the business turns around, until I can get back on my feet," Sam said, getting up from his desk, walking over to the window, and pounding the glass so hard that he nearly shattered his view of the Hollywood hills.

"That's just it, Sammy. You won't be able to start making money again unless you close down the factory in Pasito. The operating cost of that place has been draining billions out of you. I've been telling you for years that you can't afford to manufacture children's clothing in California—or anywhere in the United States anymore. You know that all of the competition has been making their goods in China. They offer the stores prices so low, we can't even begin to compete with them," Irving said, waving his hands over his head and pacing around the room.

"China, Shmina. If I had closed down the factory ten years ago, like you told me to, I would have put twenty thousand people out of work. I don't want to be in this business if I have to be a scumbag," Sam said wistfully, resting his head against the window. "Think of it, Irving. The livelihood of Pasito has been solely dependent on my company for almost forty years. If my factory shuts down, people will lose their homes, their savings, everything. I couldn't do that to them; they made me a rich man." Disgusted with himself, Sam shook his head and wiped a random tear that came streaming down his face

"Yes, maybe at one time, Sammy. But for the past ten years they've been draining every cent you have. The new generation has educated themselves in all kinds of technology and can get good-paying jobs elsewhere. They don't need us anymore," Irving said firmly, turning away from Sam. It killed him to see such a well-meaning, brilliant man get eaten alive by his pride.

"What about their mothers and fathers who have worked for me most of their lives? What's going to happen to them? They won't be able to find work anywhere else." Sam walked around his desk.

"You can't save the world, Sam; you have no choice but to save yourself and your family's future. You should accept the consulting position you've been offered with KIDCO. It's a no-brainer dream retirement job for you, Sammy. They'll pay you one million dollars a year, plus a performance bonus if sales go up, just to have a children's clothing legend like you on their board," Irving said, walking next to Sam and trying to reason with him.

"That's not what I want, Irving! Do you hear me?" Sam shrieked, practically pushing Irving away as he banged his fist against the desktop. "I have to borrow money from the bank to keep this business alive for Harry. He's a married man now, and I want to teach him the ropes. Maybe that's why my clothing lines haven't been selling. I could be too old for this business now. You know the department store buyers are kids in their thirties. They're Harry's age. That's why I think my Harry will be so great. He's a little nuts, but he has a fantastic, charismatic personality and the young buyers might really warm up to him. I'm going to go to the bank and take out a business loan to float me and keep the factory open until Harry can turn this business around," Sam said with a gleam of hope in his eye. When he spoke about his son, his whole demeanor suddenly changed. Harry was Sam's hope for the future. He clapped his hands together and raised them over his head like he was already declaring victory. "Harry has amazing potential, Irving. He's gonna surprise the shit out of you. Give him a chance to prove to everyone that he is truly Sam Raider's son," Sam said in a determined voice, nodding his head. He then picked up a picture on his desk of him and Harry on the beach in Acapulco and waved it in Irving's face.

Out in the hallway, Harry felt a lump in his throat. *I never knew that Dad had such faith in me. I always believed that he thought I was a lost cause. I can't tell him about the money I owe in Vegas. It would totally destroy him. Somehow I'm going to have to figure out how not to let him down.* Harry continued listening at the doorway.

Irving just shook his head. He felt so much pity for Sam that he could feel his stomach cramp into knots. "Sammy," Irving said quietly. "I don't how to tell you this without crushing your vision, but I have to tell you that Harry hasn't changed. Wife or no wife, he's still the same playboy he always was. He's not you, Sammy, so don't pin hopes on him he can't possibly fulfill," Irving said, looking at Sam solemnly.

Sam jumped up from behind his desk and pointed his finger at Irving. "How the hell do you know who or what my boy is? I'm telling you, Irving, he's a new man now. You would be amazed at his transformation," Sam said proudly as he crossed his arms and stomped his foot.

There were no words sad enough to describe Irving's overwhelming feelings of dread, doom, and gloom. It was one thing to tell Sam Raider he was making stupid, unrealistic, overly idealistic business decisions. It was something else to tell a man the awful truth about his only son. "Sammy," Irving said softly, with pure compassion in his voice. "Harry called me from Vegas." Irving forced the words out of his trembling mouth.

"Vegas? When the hell was he in Vegas?" Sam demanded.

"Last night. He called me around 3 a.m. and he sounded high as a kite," Irving said.

"Drugs? Are you *sure?*" Sam yelled, violently hitting the mahogany-paneled wall. As much as Sam didn't want to believe Irving, he knew that his old friend and accountant wouldn't make up a lie of this magnitude.

"I'm afraid it's true, Sammy. He said he needed money, a lot of money, to bail him out of a big gambling debt he owed the house. There was no money in any of the accounts to send him. This is very serious, Sam. Those people in Vegas don't mess around."

"How much did he hit you up for?" Sam asked, tears running from his eyes.

"Seven hundred and fifty thousand. I told you, Sam, he wasn't dealing with play money," Irving continued.

"Oh my God, my God, my God!" Sam uttered, trying to catch his breath.

Sam's face went from bright red to ash gray. He grabbed at the buttons on his sports shirt as a razor-sharp pain in his chest overtook him. Within seconds, Harry heard a huge thud. Harry rushed into the office to see his father listlessly slumped over his desk, like all the life had been thunder-bolted out of him. Irving stood frozen.

"Quick! Call a fucking ambulance!" Harry screamed at Irving, as he flipped his father's lifeless body over and started to perform CPR to the best of his knowledge. Irving finally snapped out of his daze and called for help, as Harry breathed into his father's mouth and pounded on his chest with all of his might.

★★☆

Harry rode with his father in the back of the ambulance on the way to Cedars-Sinai Medical Center, Los Angeles's finest medical institution. All the while, Harry held Sam's hand and whispered in his ear, "Daddy, I swear if you make it out of here alive, I'll go to work with you every day and do everything to help you turn your business around. I'll charm the shit out of the stupid kid's clothing buyers just like you said I could. We'll show them, Daddy. This time I won't let you down. I don't care if you lost all of our money, I just don't want to lose you."

Harry also prayed silently. *God, I know that I may be a total fuck-up and I've blown many chances, but this time, I swear on my life, if you let Daddy live, I promise, I'll make him proud of me,* Harry bargained. But this time it was too late. Sam Raider's time had run out.

Harry sat in the hospital corridor next to his mother, who was crying inconsolably. Harry's Aunt Shirley and Uncle Miles were there, attempting to comfort Irma to no avail. A somber-looking doctor came to speak to the family and break the bad news. Sam Raider was gone; there was nothing anyone could do. After absorbing the finality of the doctor's words, Irma passed out.

Shirley and Miles took Irma home in her big, black limo, but Harry stayed. Overwhelmed with guilt, feeling like his

Vegas trip has been the final straw on the camel's back that was his father's life, Harry sat on the bench outside the hospital with his head in his hands. He was completely broken.

Harry looked up to see a blue Bentley pull into the hospital driveway. Jessica was in the driver's seat. When she saw Harry, she parked the car at the curb. Without saying a word, Jessica sat down next to Harry and put her arms around him. Together they cried and shared their sorrowful intimacy.

"I'm so sorry about Sam, Harry. I came over here as soon as I found out. I'm sorry I didn't get here sooner," Jessica said with a lump in her throat.

Harry just shook his head and. "How can I blame you for showing up now, when I didn't show up at home last night? I can't even believe you are still speaking to me. If you want to divorce me, I totally understand, Jessica. I won't give you a problem," Harry said solemnly, clearing his throat and staring down at the pavement. *I can't imagine she'd want anything further to do with me after the way I've behaved, especially when she finds out Dad died broke,* Harry thought.

"Don't be silly, Harry," Jessica said calmly, stroking his back.

"No, really Jes, I've been a total asshole as usual. I've tried life clean and sober, but I fucked it all up now. I'm a total loser. I guess some things never change," Harry said, looking out at the car park, not having the guts to look Jessica in the eye.

"It's my fault too, Harry. I pushed you to it. If I didn't put so much pressure on you to start a family, you wouldn't have gone off the deep end. I've taken for granted just how much you've changed your life to be with me, and how hard it must be for you not to go back to your old ways, especially now that we're living in LA," Jessica said, sitting straight up.

"No, you have every right to want to have kids. You'd be such an awesome mom," Harry said, smiling softly.

"You really think so?" Jessica was not able to mask her sheer delight.

"Of course you would. You're sweet, caring, nurturing, warm, cuddly…"

"Oh God, no wonder you wanted to go and blow your brains out. You make me sound like your grandmother!" Jessica said.

"Are you kidding? No way, Jes! You're a lot of fun to be around," Harry said encouragingly.

"You mean, I'm not a boring, stuffy, prudish, naive little twit from the East Coast who's been nothing but a killjoy to party-boy Harry?" Jessica asked, as she nervously played with the lace of Harry's sneaker.

"Prudish? What, you?" Harry laughed. "Have *you* slept with *you* recently? You're a wild woman, Jes! As good as any pro, if not better!" Harry joked. Injecting inappropriate humor and levity into a tense situation was his unique specialty.

"Well thanks a lot, Harry," Jessica said, sarcastically. Jessica took in a deep breath and looked around the parking lot, avoiding asking Harry the one question that had been eating away at her. Although she knew it was totally inappropriate to probe Harry about his excursion to Vegas right now, she couldn't help but finally blurt out the inevitable. "I probably shouldn't ask you this…but…while you were in Vegas…" Jessica continued, with a quivering voice.

"No, nothing happened. Absolutely nothing. Well, nothing sexual at least. I did some coke, which I shouldn't have, but Harry Junior was kept in his cage. That I swear to you on my life," Harry said. "I would never do anything to hurt you, Jessica, even when I couldn't stop hurting myself. That's how much I love you."

"I believe you, Harry. If you say nothing happened, then nothing happened."

Harry looked up at his wife in absolute amazement. "But I did lose a lot of money. Seven hundred and fifty thousand dollars to be exact, and that's money I don't have to bail my ass out," Harry said shamefully.

Jessica waved her hand in front of her face, as to dismiss the importance of the money. "Don't worry about it, Harry, I took care of it," Jessica said quietly.

"What?" Harry said looking up at her, totally confused.

"Vito and another thug came to the house early this morning looking for you. I recognized Vito from when he was there with Todd, and I knew right away that you were in some of kind of very deep trouble. They told me that you owed them a lot of cash and left the hotel without paying. So I wired the money to the hotel from my own account and they went away." Jessica tried to hide the fear in her voice. She had never seen anything like this back in East Hampton.

How could a beautiful, wealthy, kindhearted woman like Jessica still want to be married to somebody like me? She could do so much better, Harry thought, putting his hand over hers. "I can't believe you did that for me, Jes. I would have thought that you'd be the first one wanting me dead. I don't know how I can pay you back," Harry said, shaking his head and staring at the sidewalk.

"Don't even think about that right now. Look, I'm sorry that I asked too much of you. Harry, you don't have to worry about having a baby yet if you don't think you can handle it. It's okay if it's just you and me. Really, I won't bring it up again. You know I want to be a mom, but I'll let you come to me and tell me when you're ready. Is that fair?" Jessica asked, resolute.

"To tell you the truth, I wouldn't mind if we went home right this minute and got started," Harry said sentimentally.

"They say a Jewish soul can't really rest until he has somebody named after him. I think it would be kind of nice to have a little Sam or Samantha running around. It would be a nice tribute to my dad. God knows I've made his life miserable, the least I could do would be bring him some peace now that he's gone."

Jessica hugged Harry so hard she practically squeezed the life out of him. "That's a wonderful tribute to Sam's memory, Harry. And you know a grandchild would probably put ten, maybe twenty years on Irma's lifespan. There's no way she'd let anything happen as long as there was a baby to dote on. She'll probably outlive all of us," Jessica gushed, unable to contain her excitement.

"There's only one big problem," Harry said wistfully. "I'm totally broke."

"I know, Harry," Jessica said, seriously.

"How the hell did you know? I just found out myself." Harry was totally befuddled.

"Irving Freed called my father last month and explained Sam's dire financial situation. Irving wanted my father to talk some sense into Sam and get him to accept that offer from KIDCO, for Irma's sake and for us. Dad wanted to talk to me about it before he said anything to Sam. He didn't want to do anything that would cause unnecessary friction in the family. I told Dad that I'd support his decision whatever it was, but in the end he decided not to interfere. As much as my dad loved to compete with Sam in the past, he didn't have the heart to kick him when he was down. Dad knew that Sam would consider it the ultimate embarrassment, even if he were just offering his friendly advice," Jessica said shaking her head like she was proud of her father's compassion. "Anyway, don't worry, we'll be fine. Dad is on his way out here and he'll make sure everything is okay," Jessica said confidently.

Harry stood up and threw his arms in the air. "Oh great. You see, that's the problem, Jessica. How can I be a dad if my wife's dad still has to take care of us? What would my kid say if he or she ever got in trouble? 'Aw gee, I have to call my granddaddy because my father is totally useless'?" Harry looked up at the smoggy LA sky.

"Harry, don't be so hard on yourself. What happened to Sam is not your fault, and really, it's not even your fault that you've never worked before. If Sam wanted to raise you to be a junior version of himself, then he would have. Sam wanted you to enjoy the life he never had," Jessica said, sweetly.

"No Jes, not any more. I heard him say right before he died that he was counting on me to help him rebuild his business," Harry said.

"That's silly, Harry. How could he expect that of you? He knew that you had no experience. I think he just wanted for you to come to the office to keep you out of trouble."

Harry looked at his wife with a hurt expression in his eyes. "Maybe I didn't have my dad's know-how, but Sam thought my charm and enthusiasm would win over the younger generation of kid's clothing buyers. I heard him say that they would listen to me, because they would think I'd know what was hip and trendy. Sam said that in my own way, I could add value to his company. Maybe you don't believe in me, Jessica, but Sam Raider, my father, the legend, actually thought that I might have what it takes to make it."

"Whoever said I didn't believe in you, Harry? I'm still here, aren't I?" Jessica demanded.

"Yeah, I guess that's true," Harry said, putting his arm around her.

Jessica took his fingers and began to caress them softly. "I just think you should let my father go into the office, work with Irving to shut down the business, and tie up loose ends. Then you and he can decide what to do from there," Jessica said.

"I don't know about that, Jessica. I feel like I should do what Sam would have wanted. May be I should try to rebuild my father's company from scratch." Harry stood up to pace back and forth.

"Harry, please, I know you're very emotional right now, but you've got to be realistic. Just let my dad do what needs to be done," Jessica said in the same way one would try to calm an upset child.

"No, Jessica, I want to make my own decisions for once. And let me tell you something else. I won't have a kid with you, I mean I can't have a kid with you, until I know that I can take care of all of us, on my own. Do you understand that?" Harry said, pleading.

"I understand perfectly, dear," Jessica said, looking up and smiling sweetly. *He's just caught up in the moment right now, but he'll come to his senses soon enough. Poor Harry's heart is in the right place, but he has no idea what he is saying,* Jessica thought, as she took Harry's hand. "Why don't we go home and get some rest before the funeral. Irving is making all the arrangements; your father left him in charge of everything."

"Do we even have enough money for a funeral? Who's paying for it?" Harry asked.

"Your dad had all of his burial expenses paid for a long time ago. He didn't want you or Irma to have to worry about a thing, even after he was gone," Jessica told him as they got into the car.

"What about this car? Can we still afford it? Who's paying for gas?" Harry asked nervously.

"Will you stop worrying about money, Harry?" Jessica smiled as she pulled out of the hospital driveway. As sorry as she felt for her husband, Jessica was equally amused by his sudden interest in their financial well-being. She had never worked a day in her life and never even dreamed of it. Harry was the same way. But what she didn't know was that life with Harry Raider would never be the same again.

chapter sixteen

Sam Raider's Beverly Hills funeral brought out the who's who in the garment business from both coasts. Calvin Klein, Tommy Hilfiger, Ralph Lauren, Donna Karan, and many more design moguls crowded the pews of the prestigious Wilshire Boulevard Temple. These people were just pups when Sam Raider was a legend on Seventh Avenue, and he helped a lot of them get their start in the cutthroat world of fashion. As rich and famous as they were today, most of the stars of fashion would happily tell you that they would have been nothing without the help of Sam Raider. Not only was the whole shmatah rag-trade at Sam's funeral, but it also brought out the Beverly Hills society crowd from Pine Valley Country Club and a smattering of old-time celebrities.

Sam's popularity and generosity spread far and wide in the entire elite Hollywood community. He had backed many a picture and put together financing for film and television projects that otherwise would never have found their way onto the big or small screens. Sam's reputation as a Hollywood angel was perhaps why Kirk Douglas came to the memorial services, along with Mickey Rooney. Carl and

Rob Reiner sat next to Dick Van Dyke and Bob Newhart. Ed McMahon cried along with Dick Clark. Many a studio head and television network suit attended the funeral with their wives, dressed appropriately in black Chanel accessorized with subdued single strands of pearls. Even the flashiest of Beverly Hills decided to play it down, to show respect.

No one was more distraught that day than Irma Raider. She sat zoned out on Valium in the front pew with Aunt Shirley and Uncle Miles. Because his mother was in such a fragile state, Harry was busy ushering everyone in. He frantically searched the room for the arrival of Sam's mistress, the waitress from Nate and Al's, and God forbid, her son from Harvard. That was a confrontation Harry was not ready for, and he certainly didn't want to have to deal with it on this sad day. "Don't worry, she's not coming," Irving whispered, putting his arm on Harry's shoulder.

"How did you know who I was looking for?" Harry whispered back, keeping a pleasant but grieving smile plastered on his face.

"Harry, you've been staring everyone who walks through that door up and down, searching them from head to toe. Mary McFadden and Joan Collins got so excited about you hitting on them. Don't you think you've been a little obvious?" Irving smiled. "Relax, Harry. Your father may have fucked up his business, but he protected your mother's feelings. He was a real gentleman to the end. When he gave that waitress the hush money over the years, he made her sign an agreement that she wouldn't embarrass the family and ask for more or show up at his funeral. In his personal life, I have to say, he was a very shrewd man. I only wish he could have played that much hardball during his last years in business," Irving said, shaking his head in dismay.

"How much did he give her?" Harry whispered back, solemnly waving to Jessica, her father Jerry, and his countess wife as they entered the chapel.

"Three and a half million dollars," Irving replied under his breath, at the same time nodding and shaking hands with the rabbi.

"*What?*" Harry screamed, unable to contain himself. For what seemed like forever, a long silence fell over the well-dressed mourners.

"He's just a little overwhelmed with emotion today." Irving smiled and waved at the haute couture doyens. Within seconds, everyone was back to peering around the room to make sure they were seen at the most important funeral of the decade.

"You mean to tell me that we are broke and that waitress has three and a half million dollars?" Harry groused, once he regained his composure and his voice returned to a low whisper. "That just doesn't seem right. How come she's still working? You would think with that kind of money, she'd be hanging out at a condo in Palm Springs or something."

Harry was pissed enough at Irving for telling Sam about his Vegas trip, which eventually led to his fatal heart attack. He thought Irving was nothing but a slimy little "Yes Man" who would have been nothing without his father. The last thing he wanted to hear from Irving today was this kind of crap. "I think she believed that if she stayed in front of Sam every day, she'd get even more. What better place to capture your father's attention than in his favorite deli? Of course, she had no idea about what was really going on," Irving said, shrugging his shoulders. "Besides, she was lucky. She gave all of the money to her brilliant son to manage. I have to say he's done a pretty good job, too. From what I hear, they still have every penny and then some. He won't let her touch a dime until she turns sixty and is ready to retire. Apparently the boy's a real whiz kid.'"

"Sounds like your son, Irving. You and my Dad had that in common, you each had *one* son you could be proud of," Harry said, lowering his eyes and staring at the "In memory of Sam Raider" sticker, freshly placed in the front of all of the prayer books.

"Hey now, Harry, don't beat yourself up, kiddo. Your Dad was crazy about his little meshuga boy and he had big plans for you," Irving said, giving Harry a fatherly pat on the back.

"I know. May be in a weird way, it's a blessing that he died before I started working for him. That way he doesn't have to suffer through any more disappointment," Harry said, letting out a sigh.

"God Almighty works in mysterious ways, Harelah. Baruch Hashem," Irving said, chuckling and pinching Harry's cheek.

Harry smiled at Irving helplessly and shrugged his shoulders in a sign of total defeat. Standing there in the temple at his father's funeral, surrounded by the biggest names in the clothing business, the entertainment industry, and Beverly Hills high society, Harry felt extremely small. *Jessica was right. There is no way I could ever do business on the same level with all of these big-time successful people. They'd laugh me right out of the boardroom,* Harry thought, as he walked to the front of the temple to take his seat next to his mother and Jessica's family.

Before Rabbi Herman began speaking, the door of the temple swung open. The whole congregation turned around practically at once to see who had the nerve to arrive so late. One by one, simple looking, plain-clothed people who clearly didn't fit in with the rest of the star-studded crowd started to pile into synagogue. They were the grateful people of Pasito, the town sixty miles east of

Beverly Hills that Sam's factory had supported for over forty years. Fathers and sons, mother and daughters, two generations of families who had worked in Sam's factory came to pay their final respects to the man who went broke trying to save their future.

A wave of relief fell upon the crowd when Irving made it his business to whisper around to everyone about who these people were. The socialites reacted to the Pasito factory workers not with love and compassion, but at least with polite tolerance, the way they treated their own maids, butlers, and other paid servants. The upper crust seemed relieved to know that they weren't being ambushed by a gaggle of lower-class fans or groupies wanting to rub shoulders with their famous, grieving faces. The only one who wasn't at ease with the appearance of the Pasito factory workers was Harry.

Harry had been to Sam's factory twice in his whole life. Once when Harry was a baby, Sam brought him to Pasito to show him off to all the workers. "My pride and joy," Sam would say as he passed Harry around to the women behind the sewing machines as they took turns cuddling their boss's new boy.

The next time Harry was in Pasito was when he was fourteen and the cops busted him for driving drunk with a bunch of kids from Beverly Hills High School on their way out to Palm Desert for spring break. The kind cops had received generous donations to their local officer's fund from Sam over the years. They also had many relatives working at the factory. So they brought Harry and company to his father's office instead of throwing the underaged gang in jail.

After that incident, Harry was never invited back to his dad's factory. However, now that Sam had new plans for his so-called reformed son, Harry thought that Pasito would be the first stop on his agenda. Sam would have wanted Harry to see the faces behind the kid's clothing brand, so that he could speak more passionately when talking to the buyers about the "Raider high standards of quality manufacturing."

All this raced through Harry's mind when he saw all of the people willing to endure being treated like second-class citizens in order to pay homage to Sam. Harry felt a large pit in his stomach and a growing lump in his throat. He knew these people didn't expect anything of him. They realized that Sam Raider's reign of good times and prosperity had come to a definite end. Yet somewhere in his heart Harry felt he owed them more than just a friendly face in a sea of snobs or a "Hello, thanks for coming." He reached down and squeezed Jessica's hand for support. She gave him a comforting hug, having no idea what was going through his head.

As a respectful quiet finally fell upon the crowd, Rabbi Herman began his sermon. Everyone sat in silence listening to stories and recollections of Sam Raider's greatness, but Harry's mind was a million miles away. In the front row of his father's funeral, Harry thought about how he was going to raise the money to keep the factory going until he could get in front of the buyers from the biggest children's clothing chains around the world. He wanted to make millions, even billions of dollars worth of sales. *I'm a natural-born schemer. I've charmed the shit out of everyone my whole life, so how could those buyers resist me? I'll get someone, maybe one of these rich fuckers here today pretending to miss my dad, to give me a huge business loan and then I'll get out there and sell, sell, sell! I'll have us back on top in no time! Look out, Hollywood, look out world, here comes Harry.*

"What the hell are you smiling about? This is your dad's memorial service!" Jessica whispered in Harry's ear.

"Oh nothing, just remembering some of the good times," Harry said nonchalantly, not wanting to scare Jessica with his newfound resolution.

Two weeks after Sam's funeral and extended shiva, Harry and Jessica's life had already begin to change drastically. The bank foreclosed on Sam's Bel Air mansion. All their artwork and heirlooms were sold off at an auction to cover Sam's debts, and the staff had been let go. Irma moved into a guest room in Harry and Jessica's house. A mother-in-law down the hall would have been a major stress for any newlywed couple, but Irma was so comatose from all of the tranquilizers she had been given that she hardly left her room. Jessica's father, Jerry, insisted on paying for an around-the-clock nurse to be with her, and this was one gift Harry graciously accepted. He wouldn't let his pride jeopardize his mother's health.

Harry and Jessica were living on a modest income—at least by Beverly Hills' standards—from her trust fund. Their dramatic decrease in income meant that the golden couple spent more nights at home snuggling in front of the television with take-out food than they did showing up at every event on the Beverly Hills social circuit. This mellow, more intimate lifestyle suited Jessica just fine, so much so that secretly she didn't mind if she kept paying the bills for the rest of their lives. Harry had hesitantly agreed to this awkward financial arrangement, but was secretly keeping track of all of their expenses. He had every intention of paying Jessica back once he could find a way to restart Sam's business.

Once the endless stream of friends and relatives stopped dropping by to pay their respects, Harry felt it was time to set his wheels in motion. He woke up at 6 a.m. one sunny morning and playfully jostled Jessica. "What's going on, Harry?" Jessica yawned and pulled the covers back over her head.

"What are you doing this morning, my love?" Harry said, tickling her gently, making sure she couldn't fall back to sleep.

"I'm sleeping in, Harry," Jessica said, trying to fend him off.

"No. It's too beautiful a day for that, Jes. I have a terrific idea," Harry said, sitting up and pulling Jessica into his lap.

"Nothing sounds better than sleep right now, Harry," Jessica groaned, unsuccessfully trying to escape his grasp.

"Why don't you and I throw on some clothes, run over to Nate and Al's and grab some breakfast, then take a drive out to my dad's old factory in Pasito?" Harry asked, with the excitement of a little kid who was trying to convince his parents to take him to Disneyland. Jessica slowly opened her eyes. Suddenly, she was wide awake and unhappy with what she was hearing.

"What's the point, Harry? They've been shutting it down for a few weeks now. It'll just be depressing, like an old ghost town," Jessica said, yawning and stretching. "If you want to eat at Nate and Al's because it will make you feel closer to your father, that's fine, but afterwards, why don't we take a drive out to Malibu and go for a walk on the beach or even pop up to Santa Barbara? There's a new resort up there that's supposed to give great massages," Jessica coaxed.

"No, Jes. You don't get it, do you? I told you, I haven't made up my mind what I'm going to do about Sam's business yet, and I need to have a look at the factory," Harry said, now out of bed and getting dressed.

Oh shit, I thought he had gotten over this crazy idea already. You know what, it's probably a good idea that he sees first-hand what a massive undertaking it would be to restart Sam's business. This little road trip just may be the reality check Harry needs. Jessica got out of bed and headed towards the shower.

"Okay, Harry," Jessica said as she took off her night-gown and got under the warm water.

"Does this mean we can go to Pasito?" Harry asked, pulling the shower curtain around his head.

"Of course, why not?" Jessica said, pouring a Clarins body wash over her head, mistaking it for shampoo. The sight of his naked wife standing under a hot shower was too much for Harry to take.

"Jessica, I love you," Harry proclaimed, as he ripped off his pants and jumped into the shower.

★★★

Jessica and Harry borrowed Irma's nurse's Pontiac to make the trip out to the factory, because Harry thought that the blue Bentley would be too ostentatious. "How can I show up in a half-a-million-dollar car when the factory workers are losing their livelihoods?" Harry said to Jessica as they drove east on the Santa Monica freeway.

"That's very considerate of you, dear," Jessica said, rolling down the window to enjoy the sunshine. Harry was so consumed with the idea of becoming "Sam Junior" that he didn't even realize that his wife was simply placating him.

"You know, my father always said, never flaunt your wealth in front of the staff or the buyers, because these are the people who are making you rich, without ever getting rich themselves. Flaunting your money in their faces will do you more harm than good," Harry said, proud of himself that he could remember at least one piece of Sam's wisdom.

"I didn't know that you and your father ever discussed business much, Harry," Jessica answered, surprised to hear that Harry had taken notice of what his father had to say regarding work.

"Well, we didn't have a discussion about it, per se, but I did overhear him talking many times. My room was over the patio, so the mornings he ate out there, I could hear his business conversations on the phone. Sometimes he'd be talking to buyers or the factory manager or to Irving. It seemed like he could run the whole world from there," Harry said wistfully.

"Did you ever go down and ask him about what he was doing?" Jessica probed to see if Harry ever really had a serious interest in business before Sam's death.

"Nah, I was either too hungover, too buzzed out, or too tired from partying to find out what was going on. Besides, I didn't want to interrupt him. I figured the last thing he needed was his burned-out kid on his neck when he was trying to do a deal." Harry laughed. "You really look beautiful today, Jessica," he said, glancing at his wife while keeping an eye on the congested LA traffic.

"Why, thank you, Harry," Jessica said, smiling without opening her eyes.

"One day, you're going to be a mogul's wife again, just like you were when you were married to Freddy. Only I won't be as stupid as he was. I'll make you feel like a queen every day, and I'll never forget the support you're giving me right now. You make me feel like I can do anything, Jessica," Harry said, taking one hand off of the wheel and placing it on her knee.

Oh boy, he can't be serious. Well, at least he believes that I'm with him. But really I'm scared shitless about this whole thing. I pray he changes his mind before he gets us in deeper trouble, Jessica thought, as she took Harry's hand in hers and smiled without saying another word.

An hour and a half later, Jessica and Harry pulled into the little town of Pasito, California. Besides a cheap Mexican restaurant, a bank, and an old drug store, Pasito didn't have much to offer. When Harry and Jessica arrived at the factory, it was stark and desolate, just like Jessica had warned. The building was pretty much abandoned. The grounds were also in desperate need of a landscaping makeover. "I guess exterior cosmetics were the last thing on Sam's mind when he was trying to keep this thing up and running," Harry observed as he escorted Jessica through the front door and down the vacant, eerily silent hallway towards the manufacturing rooms. They were pretty empty except for some female workers in the process of lifting a few sewing machines and a couple of teenage looters on the lookout for whatever they could steal.

One of the women recognized Harry from the funeral and realized that she was being caught red-handed. "Mr. Raider, I'm so sorry, please forgive me. I didn't mean to steal anything; I just thought since nobody would be using this sewing machine, I could take it home and borrow it, until I heard what was happening to the factory," the terrified woman said with a trembling voice.

When the teenagers realized who Harry was they took off through a back exit, carrying whatever they could. Nobody had been at the factory since a few months before Sam died. The few souls who were still lingering around all came into the manufacturing room to see who the visitors were. An aging janitor who had worked in the factory his whole life, a few men from the loading dock who were clearing out boxes of material, and the straggling seamstresses now stood there in front of Harry and Jessica. In this completely awkward moment nobody really knew what to say to each other.

"This place has really seen much better days," Harry muttered to Jessica under his breath. "It would be a tremendous job to get it up and running again. The store orders for kids' clothing that we would need to support this place would be huge! It's a much bigger challenge then I could ever have imagined."

Thank God he's finally coming to his senses. This trip out here was a good idea after all. At least this way he will grasp the magnitude of this disaster firsthand. Now we can drive home and maybe hit the Polo Lounge to grab a bite to eat. Hopefully he will feel as overwhelmed as I do and need some comfort food, Jessica thought, as she looked sympathetically at Harry. She knew that she would have to keep playing the role of the supportive wife until he finally realized that he was in way over his head.

"Everybody, can I have your attention for a minute?" Harry requested in a booming voice, as if he was speaking in front of an auditorium full of thousands of people instead of in a mostly empty factory. "Ahem!" Harry said, clearing his throat in an effort to call attention to himself. He stomped his feet back and forth like he was a soldier calling his troops to order. "For those of you who don't know me, I'm Harry Raider, Sam Raider's son. As you might know, my dad spent his last dime trying to save this factory, because he loved you all so much and was so grateful for the good work you did for him over the years. I can tell you that before Dad died, he wanted me to come work for him to breathe new life into the business and turn it back into the hot, money-making cash cow it once was. Yeah, man!" Harry bellowed in a cheerleader style, screamed while he spun around, jumped up and down, and clapped his hands wildly. It was as if Harry wanted to psych everyone into a factory-wide pep rally. Unfortunately, his enthusiasm was greeted with a deafening silence.

"Okay, okay, settle down, everybody," Harry said, once again standing still. He held his arms up over his head and signaled for an already quiet group to be even quieter.

"Unfortunately, Sam passed away before he could realize his dream, but I came out here today to tell you that all is not lost. I have every intention of fulfilling my father's last wishes to get this place on its feet again. I can't tell you exactly how I'm going to do that, but I will promise you one thing. I won't stop trying until I get this place cooking with gas! So please tell all of your friends and family and anybody else you knew who used to work here, that pretty soon jobs will be available again, with bigger and better salaries and tons of extra benefits for everyone!" Harry said, like a politician energized from spouting his own bull-shit. Once again Harry jumped around and hooted and hollered like he was at a football game and his team had just scored a major touchdown. It was evident that Harry Raider actually believed every single word he was saying.

Jessica was practically falling off of her feet and cringing with embarrassment at her husband's crazy speech. Just as she thought that he was ready to throw in the towel and come down to earth, Harry had morphed into a scary combination of Tony Robbins and George Bush, making empty promises he had no way of keeping and vocalizing them at the top of his lungs. Jessica could barely contain her shock at Harry's absurd ranting. Some of the older men, who had worked at the factory since Harry was a boy, actually began to laugh out loud—they had heard the stories of Harry's wild-child drug-induced antics.

Everybody who labored in the factory knew that Sam's son had never worked a day in his life and was nothing but a useless bon vivant. Instead of being jealous of Sam, most of the men who worked for him pitied him because of Harry. They knew that no amount of money in the world could restore a father's pride in a son he had let go wild. The thought of this spoiled but well-meaning young man restoring his father's business to its former glory seemed as outrageous as Sam coming back from the dead and doing it himself. "What's so funny?" Harry asked, his face turning red with embarrassment at the men's reactions.

"I'm sorry, Mr. Raider, we don't mean to seem ungrateful for your good intentions, but we just want you to know that we don't expect anything from you. We all had some great years here and now it's time to move on," one of the men said. He obviously knew that it was quite something for Harry to leave his privileged Beverly Hills life to try to help these people out. The last thing anybody in that room wanted to do was hurt Harry's feelings or appear ungrateful for his interest in their future.

"Listen, we are all doing what we have to do to pay our bills right now. I even have to let my wife support me and I sure don't like doing that," Harry admitted, glancing over at Jessica, who was squirming uncomfortably and wondering when this madness would come to an end. "But I'm going to pay her back every cent, just like I am going to give you all of your jobs back, when I fix this whole mess."

The old man saw that poor Harry was not ready to give up, so he treated him with the patience and tolerance that he would show any young man with lofty dreams. "Okay, son, you keep in touch and let us know how you're doing," he said, going up to Harry, and patting him on the back before leaving the room.

The few folks still there began to follow the old man, wishing Harry the best of luck and making their own exits. Soon Harry and Jessica were alone in the beat-up old factory, surrounded by shut-down machinery and the cobwebs of days gone past.

"Let's go, Harry," Jessica said, dying to get out of the dingy surroundings and back into beautiful California sun.

"I'm going to do this, Jes," Harry said, taking one last look around.

"Okay, Harry," was all Jessica could manage to say. She knew that she still had a battle ahead.

★★★

When they got back to Beverly Hills, Harry and Jessica went to Sam's office to meet Irving Freed and Jerry Ackerman, who had stayed in town to make his kids an offer he hoped they wouldn't refuse. Like the factory, Sam's office was also almost empty. Pictures of Irma and Harry had been taken off the walls, Sam's famous cigar humidor had been wrapped up and sent home, and other artifacts had been boxed up and put away. All that was left were the four walls and Sam's big oak desk, which the movers had not yet taken away.

"Come back to the Hamptons with me, Harry. You and Jessica can have a wonderful life there. Think of all of the terrific friends you made last summer. I'm sure everyone would welcome you back with open arms," Jerry said. He held his arms open to Harry as to fully embrace the young man, but a stoic Harry wasn't budging. "My wife and I are happy to bring Irma back east too. We can set her up in a lovely apartment and you can see her every day. That way we'll all be together, Harry. I'm a very rich man. What good does my money do me if I can't share it with the ones I love?" a kindly Jerry said, putting his arms on Harry's shoulders and searching his eyes for an answer. Jerry was deeply hoping he could take care of his daughter and her wild-card husband under his own roof.

"Thanks, but no thanks, Jerry," Harry said firmly, as Jessica almost fainted in despair.

Jessica looked first at her father and then at her husband with absolute fear and dread in her eyes. *Oh my God, what the hell is wrong with him? How could he turn my father's offer down? Is he really that nuts? Please, God, don't tell me he still believes this insanity about rebuilding Sam's business. Sam was a genius. If he couldn't save that damn factory, what makes Harry think that he can? I don't understand him. It's like I don't even know who I married.*

Harry turned to hold Jessica. "I don't blame you for being afraid," he said, unable to avoid his wife's obvious trepidation. "If you want to go back to the Hamptons with your dad until I get this whole thing straightened out, I won't stop you. I can't tell you how long it will take to do it, but I'll fly back to see you—every weekend if you'll send your plane. I know this is not what you signed on for, so if you want to wait it out back home, I totally understand," Harry said, with quiet strength in his voice.

"Harry, you really should reconsider Jerry's very generous offer," Irving Freed said. "Your dad tried for years to save the factory, but with the competition from cheap manufacturing overseas, it's just not possible. Please do yourself and your family a favor—go back to the Hamptons. I hear it's lovely this time of year." He was secretly hoping that he'd get some kind of financial bonus from Jerry if he helped convince Harry to do as he was told.

"I'm not going, Irving. I'm sorry, Jerry, I have something to do here, not just for my dad's memory, but for me and Jessica. I appreciate the fact that you want to take care of your family, so please understand that I'm finally ready to take care of mine."

One part of Jerry Ackerman wanted to run over and shake some sense into Harry. But another part of him wanted to give him a hug. For the first time, Jerry saw that spark in Harry that he hadn't seen in anyone since he and Sam were fighting their way to success back in Brooklyn. It was refreshing to be around that fighting spirit. He knew that he had to let Harry do whatever he had to do, no matter what the consequences were.

"Follow your heart, son," Jerry said, as he shook Harry's hand and quietly left the room, tailed by an overly apologetic Irving Freed.

"What about you, Jes? I won't be upset if you want to go back east for a bit while I try to figure this out," Harry offered, trying to steady his shaking voice. He knew that he had to tell her that she could go, but he desperately wanted her to stay. He had grown rather accustomed to Jessica's comforting softness. Her gentle calmness and reassuring touch would help soothe him in the turbulent days ahead.

"Harry, I think that you are absolutely insane and that you are living in a dream world," Jessica said, crossing her arms and gazing out the window at the hills of Hollywood. "It's not that I don't believe in you, I just don't believe that Sam's business can be saved, based on what Irving and my father have said."

"I'm sorry you feel that way, Jes," Harry said, hanging his head and slowly joining her by the window.

"But then again, what do I know about business?" Jessica took a deep breath and turned towards Harry. "I'm an artist and I've never even had a real job. Who am I to say no?"

I'm sure this is going to be one big mess, but I can't go back east and leave him alone out here, Jessica thought as Harry took her in his arms. *This is a side of Harry I never thought I'd see. Maybe he's more of his own man than I ever knew.*

"You know what, Jes? I think I'm ready," Harry said, caressing her cheek and running his fingers through her curls.

"Ready to start to the business?" Jessica asked, as he kissed her face.

"Ready to start a business and ready to start a family," Harry said, scooping up Jessica and placing her on top of the desk.

"Harry, do you mean it?" Jessica asked, breathless and caught off guard.

"Sure, why not? We are two adults who can take care of ourselves. At least we have a roof over our heads and some cash to live on until I make my billions. That's a hell of a lot more than my parents had when they first were starting out," Harry said. He then proceeded to unbutton her Michael Kors shirt with one hand and unhook her Gucci belt. Before long, Harry and Jessica were once again making passionate love. As they breathlessly achieved a simultaneous climax, Harry felt in control of his life and their future together.

chapter seventeen

D own in Acapulco, Mexico, Luisa Mendez sat behind a majestic pink marble desk. The thirty-five-year-old heiress to the billion-dollar Las Castillas hotel chain, the most successful of its kind in the Latin world, she was the only child of Señor Oscar Jose Ricardo Rivas de Quevas Conquistador de la Cruz de Mendez—the richest man in all of Mexico and South and Central America. He was so powerful that people would just refer to him as "Señor Oscar."

Originally of Austrian Jewish decent, Señor Oscar was born Isaac Mandlebaum. His family escaped the Nazis during World War II and like so many Jewish refugees who were denied access to American shores, they settled elsewhere, specifically in Acapulco, Mexico. Señor Oscar's father, Jacob Abraham Mandlebaum, changed his name to "Jose Mendez" to make himself more employable. Eventually he worked his way up from houseboy to hotel manager in a small resort in the hills. He eventually saved up enough money to open a hotel of his own, and called it Las Castillas. Now the Las Castillas hotel chain offered the most posh accommodations in the Latin world. Not only did Señor Oscar own the hotel, he also owned all of the prime real estate in the top locations where his hotels presided. He owned the best of everything south of the border.

Señor Oscar's late wife, Cecelia Lilliana Santos, was a former Miss Mexico and one of the most gorgeous women of her time. Luisa was a drop-dead gorgeous mixture of both her parents' most appealing traits. With jet-black hair cascading down her back, crystal blue eyes, a goddess-like body, and sharp Mexican features, Luisa could give any supermodel a run for her money. Yet despite her breathtaking beauty, Luisa was no spoiled heiress. She had a sharp head for business and the steely resolve of Leona Helmsley.

Unlike most Latin women of privileged position, Luisa had been working for her father in some capacity since she was thirteen. Right after her parents threw the Bat Mitzvah of the century in their famous mansion on the Acapulco cliffs, Luisa was found taking lunch orders by the pool at Las Castillas Acapulco and working behind the reception desk alongside the concierge. When Señor Oscar retired seven years later, it was Luisa who was named chairman of the board at the young age of twenty. She then single-handedly took the business to new heights.

Because of her involvement in high-profile charity organizations, Luisa was respected as another Princess Diana. Not since Eva Peron was a Latin woman so revered.

This morning, Luisa had just finished checking the numbers from her new Las Castillas del Grande Capital in Mexico City, when her assistant, Estabania de la Paz, came in with the agenda for the day. "Buenos dias, Señorita Mendez, you have a very busy schedule today so we better get started," Estabania said, sitting down in front of Luisa and handing her a long computer-generated list. Luisa reluctantly picked up the sheets of paper and scanned over them with a blank look. Using the papers as a makeshift fan, she twirled around in her chair and stared out the window at the deep blue Acapulco Bay.

"Forgive me Señorita, but there are many meetings we must attend today. May I suggest we get going right away?" Estabania asked, trying to capture Luisa's attention.

"I am not interested in any more meetings," Luisa said resolutely in her deep, smoldering voice.

"But Señorita, you have the diplomatic delegation flying in from Mexico City, and a lunch with officials from the planning and zoning board, then at four thirty..."

"Stop, I've heard enough," Luisa said, slowly turning around to face her faithful assistant. "Every day it's the same thing, meeting after meeting, breakfast, lunch, and dinner, with all of these boring people. I am thirty-five years old and I have to ask myself, what am I really accomplishing?" Luisa considered, aloud.

"You are the most important woman in Mexico. Every day you are building your empire," Estabania said encouragingly.

"No, not in the way I should be. I could be doing so much more. Mexico, South America, they are like tiny villages compared to the rest of the world. What I am doing here is actually very small. I need a much bigger challenge," Luisa said defiantly.

"Will you be running for president, Señorita? You know the papers are calling here *todos los días*. Pretty soon we must give them your official answer. They won't wait much longer. Have you made your decision?" Estabania asked excitedly. The older woman had worked for the Mendez family for many years, and had become somewhat of a mother figure to the ten-year-old Luisa when her mother passed away. Estabania was the one person Luisa trusted and confided in. Luisa knew that Estabania would rather be thrown off of Acapulco's highest cliff than spill Luisa's secrets.

"Why would I want to be president of Mexico? That

would mean I would be stuck here," Luisa said, playing with a pen on her desk.

"Is that so terrible, Señorita? You have everything," Estabania said, bowing her head and lowering her eyes so as not to appear jealous of her mistress's high life, while she lived with her twelve children in a one-room shack in Acapulco's worst neighborhood.

"To some, yes, I am fortunate, but to others I am nothing. Las Castillas is just a little hotel chain, a drop in the bucket on the international scene." Luisa took a sip of her coffee, wrinkling up her nose in disgust when she realized it was going cold.

"I know it is not my place to ask you, Señorita Mendez," Estabania said, careful not to offend her boss, "but what is it that you want?" Estabania could no longer contain her curiosity.

"What I want, no, what I *need* is to take this business to the next level. I have a global vision for this company. I want to see a Las Castillas in places like Paris, Milan, New York, and Monte Carlo. I want to own the most exclusive hotel chain in the world," Luisa said, lowering her voice to just above a whisper, with an intense look on her face.

"You have big dreams," Estabania said, sighing and realizing that she was way out of her league.

"Papa Jacky had big dreams when he came here from Austria, as did my own father. That is why we have what we own today. But I want to take what they did and make it bigger than they ever imagined!" Luisa declared, getting up from her desk, gesturing toward the tranquil turquoise ocean outside her window.

"Excuse me for saying this, Señorita, but I don't think your father would ever let you leave Mexico and go out into the world all alone. Especially since you're not..." Estabania stopped, afraid to finish the sentence.

"Married?" Luisa filled in, fiercely staring down Estabania.

That Luisa Mendez was still single at thirty-five years of age was the only thorn in her gold crown. A social faux pas of this magnitude was enough to bring down Luisa's halo a few notches, not only in the eyes of the Latin people but also in the eyes of her father.

Luisa's old-maid status had people guessing what could be wrong with her. In the sophisticated sidewalk cafés of Acapulco and in the exclusive enclaves in Mexico City, hot gossip flew out of the mouths of those who were supposedly in the know about the personal lives of the rich and famous. Some said that Luisa was secretly a lesbian. Others insisted that she was having torrid affairs with a string of gorgeous lovers, who were in neither her class nor financial position, and therefore were unsuitable to marry. Among the uneducated, even more outrageous rumors were circulating. There was a cult-like group of people who actually believed that Luisa was a saint or the Virgin Mary incarnate. They wholeheartedly believed that when Luisa would finally have a child, it would be the equivalent of the second coming. Of course the truth about Luisa's single statue was more obvious and less dramatic than anyone could imagine. She simply had never met anyone who was good enough.

"Who am I supposed to marry?" Luisa said sarcastically to Estabania, when she was really asking herself the question. "All the wealthy Latin men are incredibly demanding and completely controlling. They don't want a dynamic, powerful woman, they want a wife who is an obedient servant, one who will keep her mouth shut and look the other way while they are out all night screwing every slut in town. Why should someone like me answer to a tyrant and be a prisoner in my own home? Ridiculous! Besides, most of the desirable Latin men are Catholic. Papa would never allow that. Where do you think I'm going to find a wealthy, permissive, wonderful Jewish man, who will appreciate somebody like me? Not in Acapulco or anywhere in Mexico or all of Latin America, that's for sure," Luisa said defiantly.

"Do you want to get married, Señorita?" Estabania boldly asked. Sometimes Estabania thought that Luisa enjoyed being the queen bee so much that she had no use for a man in her life.

Luisa raised an eyebrow, laughed ironically to herself, and nibbled on her bottom lip. "That is a good question. The answer is that I really don't know. Perhaps if I met a man who could entertain me and keep me amused, it might not be such a bad idea. After dating so many arrogant, self-important morons, it would be very nice to meet a man who doesn't bore me to death. I can't imagine such a person exists," Luisa laughed.

"What about children? You'd be a wonderful mother," Estabania said, biting her tongue. Estabania had serious doubts about Luisa's maternal urges or abilities, but she knew that Luisa would need an heir to keep Las Castillas going when she eventually retired. This alone was motivation enough to make a marriage.

"*Ay caramba.* And ruin my perfect body to pop out a gang of little annoying brats? Well I guess it's a sacrifice every woman must make sometime in her life," Luisa yawned, disinterested.

"You could always adopt. There are many children living in poverty here who could use a loving home," Estabania said enthusiastically, as though she was providing her mistress a solution to keeping her legacy alive while still keeping her figure.

"Don't be insane, Estabania. Do you think that I am going to pass all of this on to some whore's bastard child from the streets? My family has worked for two generations to build Las Castillas and I plan on expanding it even further. There is no way I'm going to hand it over to a stranger. No, I must have my own child, at least one, even if I have a plastic surgeon standing by to give me a tummy tuck right after I deliver," Luisa said, sitting back down at her desk and lighting a cigarette.

"So what are you going to do, Señorita?" Estabania asked, struggling to keep her composure and fight back the tears. Estabania had adopted three of her own children, and Luisa's words stung.

"I am going to go to Papa and ask his permission to go to the United States to open the first Las Castillas hotel outside the Latin world," Luisa announced, pouring herself a shot of brandy from a stash she kept in her desk.

"What does that have to do with finding a husband?" Estabania asked, confused.

"Everything, my dear Estabania, everything." Luisa smiled ruthlessly and downed her brandy in one smooth, swift swallow.

★★★

The sun was setting behind the mountains that surrounded Acapulco Bay as Luisa's chauffeur-driven Mercedes pulled up in front Señor Oscar's huge stone mansion. A butler answered the door and escorted Luisa to the back veranda overlooking the city. Señor Oscar, now in his eighties, was still debonair, seated at a dinner table for two, sipping cold sangria out of a tall glass. He was dressed all in white and wrapped in a finely woven Mexican *serape* to protect him from the evening chill. His old eyes lit up with joy when his only daughter bent down to kiss him on both cheeks. He signaled for her to sit down opposite him. All of Luisa's tough talk was left in the office. Tonight, for Señor Oscar, she was all sweetness and light.

"I'm dying to get married and give you beautiful grandchildren, Papa," Luisa said softly, as she picked listlessly at her sliced guava salad.

"This is good news, Luisa. I am an old man and nothing would make me happier than knowing you had a family to take care of you when I am gone." Señor Oscar reached across the table and took Luisa's hand.

"Oh, don't say that, Papa. I love you too much to ever think of losing you," Luisa said in her best manipulative little-girl voice, taking his hand and kissing it gently.

"Thank you, my darling niña," Senor Oscar said, glowing with paternal pride.

"Papa, you know there are no good eligible men in Mexico. All of the boys from the top Jewish families live in America. There is no one here for me. I guess I will always have to be sad and lonely," Luisa said, feigning despair.

"Ay, don't say that Luisa, darling. There is someone for everyone. God has good things in store for my *preciosa*. You will find your beshert."

"Where am I going to meet him, Papa? I am thirty-five years old and still he hasn't found me. I think Hashem will only help me get a husband if I go out and search for him." Luisa looked down at the plate of tilapia that the butler placed before her.

"My poor *preciosa* Luisa, I didn't know that you were so unhappy. Is there anything Papa can do to help you?" Señor Oscar asked, with a very concerned look on his weather-beaten face.

"You can let me go to America, Papa, to find the Jewish man of my dreams," Luisa said, looking at her father directly.

Oscar leaned toward his daughter and lowered his voice. "And if I say yes, where will you go?"

"Miami is no good," Luisa replied. "I need a fresh start. However, I think New York is too far, Papa. I want to be able to come home if you need me."

"Thank you, my sweet," Señor Oscar acknowledged, digging into his dinner, relieved to hear that Luisa didn't want to travel to the ends of the earth.

"I was thinking about Beverly Hills. There are many rich Jewish families there and it's not too far away," Luisa said, relaxing and beginning to enjoy her fish.

"And what will you do while you are in California? Who will run Las Castillas while you are away?" Señor Oscar wanted to know, starting to suspect there was another, deeper reason behind Luisa's move. He knew his daughter almost better than she knew herself. Judging by the way she had carelessly thrown over some of Latin America's top bachelors in the past, Señor Oscar believed that Luisa wouldn't want to go all the way to America just to find a man. Something else was cooking and he was beginning to see right through her little charade.

"I will take care of Las Castillas, of course, Papa. I would never let anyone else do that. I was thinking of opening a little office somewhere on Rodeo Drive, and who knows, maybe even a small hotel," Luisa said, nonchalantly.

The shrewd old man pulled a fish bone from between his lips and laughed out loud. He hadn't become a billionaire by being a fool. Señor Oscar knew exactly what was behind his daughter's desires to move to LA. She wanted to go global and he damn well knew it. Remembering the fight he had with his own father, Papa Jacky, when he was a young man and wanted to open a hotel outside Acapulco, Señor Oscar couldn't help but have warm feelings for his daughter. There was a true Mandlebaum macher, hidden somewhere beneath her Mexican-princess exterior. How could he hold her back, when he had to push so hard to fulfill his own dreams? It was because of the struggle he'd fought and won that Señor Oscar was able to sympathize with his daughter and let her spread her wings. He saw right through her scheming but didn't let on for a second.

"Okay, if you think you can manage keeping track of Las Castillas in Mexico and South America, while looking for a husband in Beverly Hills, then who am I to try and stop you? You may go, as long as you agree to search for a mate while you are there. I am not sending you so far away from home for a joy ride," Señor Oscar said sternly.

"Of course not, Papa. I intend to be very serious... about finding my husband, that is," Luisa caught herself. "Oh, and Papa, I was just wondering. What do you think about me opening a Las Castillas hotel in Beverly Hills? Do you think it is a good idea?" Luisa inquired innocently.

"Well, if you start out small and don't go over the top, it might be all right. I guess it would be a good experiment for you to see if a Las Castillas could compete in America," Señor Oscar said, pushing his plate away and sipping his coffee.

"Really, Papa?" Luisa exclaimed, bursting out of her seat. "Does that mean you'll give me the money and the backing to do it?"

"Only if you promise me that you won't spend your whole time working and that you will make finding a husband your first priority. Luisa, if you don't get married, I'm afraid I will have to send someone else to run your Beverly Hills hotel and bring you home. You know I can't bear to have my *preciosa* sent away for no good reason. The only way I can allow this is if I am sure that you will have a wedding and soon give me grandchildren," Señor Oscar said firmly.

"Ah *sí, muchas gracias,* Papa! I promise, I promise! *Con mucho gusto!*" Luisa squealed, leaning over the table and affectionately hugging and kissing her father. She had won his support and soon the crème de la crème of Beverly Hills would be at her feet. Hollywood was about to greet a rising new star.

chapter eighteen

The next morning Luisa got to the office bright and early to start planning her move to Beverly Hills. By lunchtime, Luisa was already in bidding wars on three exclusive properties in both Beverly Hills and Bel Air. One that particularly interested her was a sprawling old estate in dire dilapidated condition, near the top of Mulholland Drive. Despite its near tear-down status, the massive Spanish-style main house and guest houses on the property could be renovated easily into elegant suites with the latest state-of-the-art amenities. The estate also offered spectacular views ranging, on a clear day, from the Pacific Ocean in Malibu to the majestic skyscrapers of downtown LA. There was a serpentine-shaped pool that would require a massive updating and an untended Japanese garden that yearned to be restored to its once lush botanical beauty.

Because the property was in a choice location, but very much out of the way of mainstream traffic, Luisa imagined turning it into the perfect, elegant hideaway for Hollywood's big-name celebrities and the international royalty who sought the ultimate in pampering and privacy. She envisioned a twelve-suite boutique hotel, with the feel of a private club that would cater only to the very, very rich and famous. Luisa wanted to make this Las Castillas *the* most exclusive place in Hollywood, a place where a patron could get anything they wanted delivered to their door at the drop of a hat. When Luisa's offer of twenty-three million dollars was finally accepted, she was so excited she jumped out of her chair and tripped on her six-inch Jimmy Choo heels.

Luisa knew that lining up the best of everything for Las Castillas would be a major undertaking, and because she was a pro herself, she knew it wasn't smart to undertake it alone. Although Luisa's fame was legendary everywhere in Latin America, in the United States Las Castillas was unknown, and more to the point, so was she. Luisa quickly figured out that in order to tap into America's best resources, she needed an experienced point man, someone who knew his way around the lifestyles of the very rich and famous.

She recalled that the last time she had gone on a shopping trip to New York, someone had mentioned a personal shopper "everything guy" who was so powerful that no one in New York society made a move without him. Luisa also remembered that this magic man had loads of top flight connections in Los Angeles too.

As soon as she finished signing the documents necessary to purchase of the estate, Luisa picked up the phone and dialed her New York friend Penny Marks Levitt, whom she had met at childhood summer camp.

"Penita, *es tu Lulu aquí! Cómo está,* sweetheart?" Luisa said in her smoky voice. Her tone was lighter and more playful than usual.

"Oh my shit, Luisa, is that you?" an excited Penny practically screamed into the receiver. "I haven't heard from you in ages! What's up, *chica?* How the hell are you?" a very pregnant Penny cooed, while rubbing cocoa butter on her ever-expanding stomach's stretch marks.

"*Ay caramba, mi amiga,* I have so much to tell you. You won't believe what is going on. But first you must tell me, how are the little *niñas?*" Luisa said, taking another long drag on her cigarette.

"About to pop any second now and I feel like I'm going to explode. I'm nearly two weeks late and the doctor says if the twins don't come by the end of this week, he's going in and taking them out. What do I care about a C-section? It's not like I ever wear a bikini anyway. Can you imagine my fat ass in a bikini, after giving birth to twins, no less? Now that's a scary thought, enough to close down East Hampton's Main Beach for whale watching," Penny quipped, sipping her vanilla soy milkshake.

"Penita, you are so funny. When am I going to see you, my friend?" Louisa checked her watch. Even her oldest and dearest summer buddy was worthy of only so much of her golden time. "I wish you'd come to New York for the babies' naming celebrations. I'm having the lunch at Twenty One right after the temple service, and there is also a dinner at Daniel on Saturday night and a brunch at the Carlyle on Sunday for the out-of-town guests. Did you get the invitations?" Penny asked, wondering why she had not heard from Luisa sooner, since the weekend of parties had been planned months in advance.

"Of course I did. That is why I am calling you, to say I am coming," Luisa smoothly lied.

"Oh my goodness, I am absolutely thrilled to hear it. I'll call Freddy and see if there are any single available men in his new Wall Street firm who we can introduce to you while you're here," Penny said, enthusiastically.

"Oh, that won't be necessary," Luisa laughed and twirled around in her seat. "One day I should be as lucky as you are today, my beautiful friend. But I can't meet a man who lives in New York, because I am moving to Los Angeles. I am opening a new hotel there," Luisa said nonchalantly.

"OH MY GOD! You have to talk to Chas Greer, he knows absolutely everybody who is anybody. He'll totally hook you up with everything for your hotel. Give him like ten minutes and the whole world will be calling your place nonstop trying to get reservations. He'll have you sold out in seconds flat!" Penny graciously gushed.

"Who is Señor Chas?" Luisa asked, feigning ignorance, all the while gloating at the perfect unfolding of her plan.

"Chas Greer, the svengali of style! Don't you remember? I'm sure he could be an enormous help to you," Penny said, feeling good that she actually did something for somebody else today.

"Do you really think so, Penita? I could sure use his guidance," Luisa said softly, as Penny played right into her hands.

"Honey, when Chas Greer takes over, nothing can stop you. Your hotel will be the talk of both coasts!" Penny said, picking at a half-eaten organic oatmeal cookie that somehow got lost in her white leather couch.

"Well I am very grateful to you, Penita, for making the introduction," Luisa smiled triumphantly.

"Oh, please, don't be silly. It's the least I could do. After all, you're flying all the way to New York for my babies' naming weekend. I'll tell Chas you want to meet him, I'm sure you two will have a lot to talk about," Penny said.

"*Adios, muy linda Penita. Con mucho gusto,*" Luisa purred into the phone, and quickly put down the receiver, sure to quit while she was ahead. Always get the last word, Luisa reminded herself as she walked out of her office and instructed Estabania to make hotel reservations at the private towers at the Waldorf Astoria, one of New York City's best hotels.

Restaurant Twenty One was buzzing not only with its usual celebrity lunch clientele, but with the one hundred guests Penny had at her pink and white baby-themed tables. A week prior to this elegant soiree, she had given birth to fraternal twins Blaine Bettina and Bernard Bertram at Lenox Hill Hospital, Manhattan's most elite mecca of maternity. The B theme in her children's names was in honor of her late father, discount clothing king Bernard Marks and her younger sister, Bunny, who had died from a cocaine-and-bulimia-induced heart attack the summer before. That bulimia also started with a B was an irony Penny chose to overlook in order to preserve the cuteness of the matching names.

Penny's guests were mostly New York's top Jewish society. Making a grand late entrance was Luisa Mendez. Predictably, she had shown up at Temple Emanuel about two minutes before the service was over and had gone to her hotel to make business phone calls before sauntering into the luncheon just as the first course of pesto gnocchi was being served.

"There you are! I was wondering what happened to you. I was getting worried," Penny lied, as she stood up to greet Luisa. *Like it wasn't bad enough she paraded into the temple late, wearing that low-cut trashy black and red number, showing enough cleavage to give the rabbi a heart attack. Now she has the nerve to show up after everyone is seated,* Penny thought as she smiled widely and gave Luisa a big, warm hug.

"Come sit down. Chas can't wait to meet you." As promised, Penny escorted Luisa over to her chair right next to Chas Greer. Newly highlighted, perennially tan, and dripping in Armani from head to toe, Chas was as always the best-dressed man at the table. On the other side of Chas sat his lover, Juan.

"Chas Greer, it's certainly a pleasure to meet you. Your impeccable reputation precedes you. You are truly a legend in American high society," Luisa shamelessly flattered Chas, as he stood up to shake her hand and pull out her chair. Instead of sitting, Luisa pulled him closer and air kissed both his cheeks, a chic continental affectation. For once in his life, Chas was practically at a loss for words. No one had ever complimented him so generously before. Usually his new clients were barely polite in the beginning. After he got to know them more intimately, at the same time taking more and more of their money, they eventually let their true, spoiled, demanding dispositions hang out.

As Chas was getting bowled over by Luisa's flattery, Juan was beside himself. Having grown up in South America, he was familiar with Luisa's notoriety, and he felt like he was getting an audience with the pope. "Luisa Mendez, the queen of Latin America, it's an honor and pleasure to be in your company this afternoon," Chas said, as he pushed in Luisa's chair behind her. Chas knew that the Latin culture was a lot more formal than anything in New York or LA, so he did his best to come across as someone who could emulate the height of manners and grace.

"Oh, no, Señor Chas, the pleasure is all mine," Luisa smiled and looked Chas directly in the eye now that they were both sitting down.

"Luisa, I'd like to introduce you to my dear friend, Juan Carlos Gomez. He comes to Manhattan via Caracas. His grandfather, the diplomat Jorge Gomez, was almost elected president of Venezuela and his father, Luis Gomez, is one of the top plastic surgeons in his country," Chas said proudly, knowing how important upbringing and connections are to Latin and Jewish people.

"Ah *sí,* I've heard of your family," Luisa lied while nodding approvingly to Juan, bestowing upon him the ultimate compliment. Poor Juan bowed his head with gratitude and reverence towards his new regal lunch mate.

"*Muchas gracias,* Señorita Mendez, *muchas gracias.*" Juan couldn't even bring himself to call Luisa by her first name.

"What brings you to New York, Luisa?" Chas asked as he sipped his freshly poured bellini.

"The baby namings, of course," Luisa smiled and winked at Chas, taking a tiny bite of the gnocchi and pushing the plate away.

"You mean you traveled all that way just for this? My, what a wonderful friend you are," Chas stage whispered, grinning as he signaled a passing waiter to refill his glass.

"Well, not exactly," Luisa admitted, toying with the butter knife on her bread plate.

"I didn't think so," Chas gloated, now gulping his champagne-fruit juice mix. *One schemer can always catch another. You can't fool me honey,* Chas thought as he batted his long, perfectly curled eyelashes at his new Spanish soul mate.

"Chas, it's been a very long morning and I desperately need to unwind a little bit. Would you like to join me outside for a cigarette?" Luisa invited, slowly pushing herself away from the table.

"But of course," Chas quickly replied, getting up to finish pulling out Luisa's chair.

Chas guided Luisa through the crowded restaurant towards the front door. All of a sudden he felt a heavy hand slap down on his delicate shoulder. "Where the hell do you think you're going?" a pissed-off Penny yelled with a mouthful of gnocchi. There was no way she would let Chas leave her party, especially with Luisa in tow.

"Oh, for heaven's sakes! Would you relax, Pen? Luisa and I are just going outside to have a little smoke," Chas said snidely, as he took a napkin off an empty table and wiped some pesto sauce from the corners of Penny's mouth.

All at once, Penny felt very embarrassed and insecure. She didn't want Luisa to think that she gave a damn whether she stayed or left, but deep down she did. Today was not a mere luncheon to welcome her babies, it was Part Two of an extended victory party that began with her five-hundred-thousand-dollar, week-long wedding and month-long honeymoon on the ocean liner *Queen Mary II*. To Penny, who suffered through being "the fat ugly sister" until Bunny died, there wasn't enough she could do to make up for the time she had lost.

"I'm sorry, I guess I overreacted," Penny said, laughing nervously. "It's part of the hormone letdown after the pregnancy, you know. Some people get postpartum depression and turn crazy suicidal. I guess I just turned into more of a raving lunatic bitch than I already am!"

"It's okay, Penita, *mi linda,* don't be so hard on yourself. You just gave birth to two beautiful babies, of course you feel a little anxious," Luisa said sweetly, taking Penny's hand and air kissing her on both cheeks.

"Have fun," Penny waved, and Chas and Luisa skirted out the door.

Chas politely lit Luisa's cigarette before firing up his own clove, and the two slowly walked up Fifth Avenue.

"I want to make you a rich man, Chas Greer," Luisa said, stopping Chas in his well-shod tracks. "I am going to open the most exclusive hotel anyone has ever seen and you will work for me every step of the way. In a few weeks, I will move you to Los Angeles. You will bring me the best, most talented craftsmen and service people to make Las Castillas Beverly Hills the ultimate, unrivaled pleasure palace. When the hotel is ready to open, you will bring all of the glamorous Hollywood celebrities and New York power brokers through my front door, and then you will bring me the world!"

Chas puffed nervously on his cigarette, trying to remain calm. Never before had he been made such an amazing offer. He knew he was good, the very best even, at catering to the crazy whims of the rich and famous. But this one seemed like a hugely tall order to fill, even for a master like Chas Greer. For a moment he let himself fantasize about being the queen bee of Beverly Hills. Presiding over a prestigious hotel would do just fine. Chas imagined himself turning down celebrity publicists and A-lister's managerial "people" who'd call to make reservations. In order to secure a reservation, Chas would insist that he hear personally from each and every celebrity who would have to beg for a chance at prime occupancy.

Yes, all of the those horrible, spoiled brats who teased the hell out of him during his teenage years would now grovel at his feet. He remembered all of their names and if those born-and-bred Beverly Hills brats, now all grown up, wanted to rub shoulders with his celebrity guests, they could just forget it.

"Luisa, nothing would make me happier than to move to La-la Land and help you splash out your new venture, but I can't afford to just pick up and leave. I do have a few West Coast clients, referrals mostly, but my main business is based here in New York. I just can't drop everything and give up years of contracts. I can't lose that kind of income," Chas said apologetically.

"Weren't you listening to me, Chas?" Luisa asked, taking the half-smoked cigarette out of her mouth, stamping it under her feet, and quickly mouthing a fresh one. "I said I am going to make you a rich man. You will make more money working for me in one year than you've made in the last five here in New York. You will have everything you cannot afford here: a courtesy apartment, expensive company cars, a driver at your disposal, a spending allowance, and a fabulous six-figure salary to begin with. If we are successful and making money, then the sky's the limit and we can talk about big bucks for you. You will have no expenses, so almost everything you make will go right into your pocket. I don't know what else you could ask me for," Luisa said.

"How about a stake in the hotel? You know, a small piece of the action?" Chas said, brazenly, pushing his luck. Luisa abruptly spit the cigarette out of her mouth and didn't bother to sweep it away when it landed on Chas's Bruno Magli shoes. Chas jumped about five feet, irrationally fearing that he might go up in flames.

"How dare you ask me for such a thing? No one will ever own part of Las Castillas except my family. NEVER!" Luisa fired back in anger. She turned quickly on her heel and charged down Fifth Ave, leaving Chas to eat her dust.

"Luisa, wait a minute," Chas gushed as he ran after her. "I didn't mean to seem ungrateful for your generous offer, I just wanted to save you some money, that's all," Chas begged, desperately attempting to justify his previous over-the-top suggestion. "I thought it might be easier to give me a stake in the hotel than a high salary. I was just trying to lower your start-up costs, honey, that's all. I didn't want to seem greedy. Of course I want to work for you! It would be the thrill of a lifetime. I'd gladly put my business here on hold for a while to go with you. I'd do anything you ask!"

Luisa kept walking at her fast pace and didn't even turn around to acknowledge Chas's pleas. When he finally caught up with her at the door of Twenty One, Chas was out of breath and noticeably sweating.

Thinking he just blown a golden chance, Chas opened the door for Luisa and hung his golden head in defeat.

Without a word, he followed her back into the party and once again pulled out her chair. Luisa continued to ignore Chas when the waiter brought the second course of veal Milanese and vegetable risotto. Luisa began to eat with great appetite, paying no attention to the gentleman sitting on her left. Noticing the look of despair on his lover's face, Juan pulled on Chas's sleeve and raised his eyebrows as if to ask what had transpired with Luisa. Chas abruptly shooed away Juan's gestures, quietly signaling for him to control himself.

Glad to see that her two prized guest had promptly returned, Penny got up and walked over to Chas and Luisa and put her arms around them both. "So, did you guys have a good talk? Hope you didn't totally smoke each other out. You know what they say, second-hand smoke is worse than the first," Penny said, making casual conversation to show Chas and Luisa that she had settled down. Chas just grinned uncomfortably at Penny while Luisa remained silent, chewing away on the delicacies on her plate.

"Well, I'll just let you guys enjoy your food and I'll go back to mine," Penny said diplomatically, sensing the tension between her two friends.

Just as she was about to leave them and go back to her seat, Luisa stopped Penny and took her hand. "Penny, I want to thank you for inviting me to this beautiful party and sitting me next to Chas Greer. He has agreed to come to Los Angeles and help me open my hotel. I know he will do a great job and we will have a huge success. I owe it all to you my dear. *Muchas gracias, mi amiga preciosa!*" Chas couldn't believe what he was hearing. He was back on track and had another shot at the big time! He reached down and grabbed Juan's supple hand with all of his might.

"Oh, thank you, Luisa, you won't be sorry," Chas gushed uncontrollably. "I'll make your hotel the hottest, most desirable place to say in Hollywood, and everywhere else for that matter. It will be more fantastic than you could ever imagine. I'll bet my life on it!" Penny smiled politely, even though she believed that working for Luisa would be the kiss of death for Chas. *The poor bastard has no idea what he has just signed on for. He finally has met his match. Those two certainly deserve each other,* Penny thought as she gave Chas a congratulatory air kiss. This was a huge amount of ass-kissing, even for him, but Chas had learned a valuable lesson. Working for Luisa Mendez meant learning how to orbit in a whole new stratosphere. He would do as he was told and meet her every need even before she could figure out what she wanted. Chas had been given the ultimate challenge and he was ready to take the plunge. Luisa Mendez, Hollywood's newest star, had just snagged the man who would make sure that she would outshine everyone else.

chapter nineteen

D o you believe it? I'm really coming!" Less than one month later, Chas was on his cell phone chatting away with Jessica Raider as Juan was sadly helping him pack for his move to Los Angeles.

"I can't wait to see you, Chas; it's been way too long." Across the three-thousand-mile divide, Chas could sense Jessica's ear-to-ear smile through the receiver. "It will be wonderful to have a good friend here. The last couple of months since Sam died have not been easy," Jessica said, as she sat at the desk in her near-empty office. Where there were once piles of invitations and stacks of goodie bags from every publicist in town, there was now only a stack of bills for Jessica to pay from her own account.

"I know, sweetheart, there's been some big changes for you. It's not exactly what you signed on for when you married rich Harry Raider, was it, pookie?" Chas pretended to sympathize as he put the last of his crisp white polo shirts into one of his ten overstuffed Louis Vuitton suitcases. Chas was not yet a wealthy man, but because of the perks and kickbacks he got from every designer in New York, Chas was able to travel in style.

"It's okay, Chas. Actually. I'm enjoying the rest. I was really getting sick of having to go out every night," Jessica said while balancing her checkbook. Harry's family's bankruptcy had knocked the golden couple right off their luminous social pedestal. It wasn't enough that Jessica alone was still worth billions—their star-wattage appeal was based on the merger of two mega-wealthy dynasties. Even though Harry couldn't understand why they never were invited anywhere anymore, Jessica was absolutely relieved to get off the social merry-go-round.

"What's it like having Irma living right down the hall from you guys?" Chas probed. "Having your mother-in-law around all time must be a total drag, even though she is a really sweet lady, of course." The nasty part of him enjoyed the Raider's financial demise. Even though Harry was the only boy in Beverly Hills who befriended him growing up, Chas thought that nobody should have as much money as Harry and Jessica supposedly did together. If she would only complain, even just a little bit, he would start to feel better

"You know, it's not as bad as I thought it would be. Irma has totally changed. I'm more worried about her than anything. She doesn't come out of her suite of rooms unless I go in there and ask her to. It's a little creepy. I try to make time to do simple things with her like play cards or take her out to PCH for a drive to get some healthy ocean air."

"Well isn't that sweet of you. You're just a living angel," Chas said, sticking his finger down his throat and making the vomiting motion to an amused Juan. "Harry Raider was sure lucky to find you," Chas told her, stopping his packing to light a clove cigarette and share a glass of Chardonnay on the couch with Juan. "So tell me, what have you and Harry been up to?" he asked as he took a big gulp of his wine and stretched out his bare foot for Juan to massage.

"We've been doing easy, low-key kinds of things like cooking dinner or ordering pizza and watching TV. Sometimes we go for walks on the beach or get massages by the pool, than barbecue some hot dogs," Jessica said.

"Jessica, that really should suit you just fine. I know how much you hate all that high-profile stuff. It sounds like the life you've always dreamed of, so who cares if you have to pay for it," Chas said, sipping his wine, trying to hold in his mean-spirited giggles.

"Yeah, everything should be just great, and it would be, but there are some big problems too," Jessica said, sighing.

"Oh really, do tell me everything," Chas said eagerly, as Juan pretended to air slap his face. Juan was a sweet, genuine guy who was entertained by his lover, but didn't approve of his unshakable cattiness. Juan thought Chas should be a lot more sincere to his clients, who were also supposed to be his friends.

"Are you sure you really want to hear this? Don't you have packing to finish?" Jessica asked before unloading her burdens to Chas.

"What are friends for? Besides, I'm taking a break. What's wrong, darling? You can tell Chassy."

Jessica nervously ran her hands through her curls. Part of her couldn't believe that she was once again reduced to confiding in Chas Greer. "Well, Harry is basically miserable. He wakes up every day bursting full of energy, ready to take on the world. Then he spends all morning making phone calls to his father's wealthy friends and former business connections to ask for money to restart Sam's company. Although most of the people take his calls out of respect to Sam, nobody really takes Harry seriously. I can't say that I blame them, but it hurts me to see Harry shot down by lunchtime," Jessica said, catching a glimpse of her sad face in the mirror.

"Well, isn't that what you want? Maybe if Harry hears it enough times from important people he respects and knows that Sam respected, it will begin to sink dawn on him that he is not a business man," Chas said, leaning into Juan, signaling for him to do his shoulders.

"I know that, Chas, and yes, I'd like nothing better than to have Harry give up his crazy dreams. But you know what? I've actually got to hand it to him. Not a day goes by that he isn't trying to do something to restart the business or calling someone to borrow money. It's really pretty amazing, especially for a guy who's never worked a day in his life. Harry Raider is a very determined man when he finds something that he is passionate about," Jessica marveled at her own revelations about her husband.

"And what about you, my dear Jessica? I hope Harry has plenty of the passion left for his wife at the end of the day." Chas looked at Juan suggestively and leaned in to his firm, muscular chest.

"Yeah, Harry and I are doing fine in that department," Jessica said nervously, like she was hiding something. "We make love a lot and actually this weird time period has brought us closer, in that way."

"Gee, for someone who's getting laid night and day, you sure sound tense. If I was getting it that much I'd hardly be able to breathe, let alone talk in your pinched tone of voice," Chas joked, as Juan picked up an overstuffed pillow and smacked his lover of the head. Juan was very bashful and hated when Chas even hinted about their love life to another soul.

"Do I really sound that bad?" Jessica purposely lowered her voice an octave.

"Well, you don't sound like a woman who's making mad, passionate love to her husband every night, that's for sure, honey," Chas said, grabbing the pillow from Juan's hand and tucking it neatly back into place.

"The problem is I'm not getting pregnant," Jessica managed to spit out. "We've been trying for a while now. Actually, I went off of the pill long before Harry even realized, and nothing has happened. I don't know what to think," Jessica admitted, trying to hold back her tears.

Chas quickly got serious. "Honey, now don't turn on the waterworks, Chas's on his way out to you and everything will be okay, I promise you." Even he wasn't so heartless as to not feel sorry for a thirty-something woman who couldn't get pregnant. Besides, the more kids Jessica had, the more he could shop for them, so he had something vested in her getting what she wanted, in this case. "Have you been to any fertility doctors? I'm sure they have the best out there. Everything is so advanced in California," Chas said, sweetly.

"No, not yet. I don't want to put that extra pressure on Harry right now. He's so consumed with this business thing that I'm afraid if I drag him around to fertility experts and what not, and for some reason it doesn't work, Harry will go right off the deep end. I just thought that since we've been so intimate lately, something would happen naturally, but it hasn't and I don't know what to do," Jessica sobbed, searching the desk for a tissue.

"Oh Jes, just give it some more time. Let this thing with Harry's business obsession run its course and when he's finally over it, than tackle the baby deal. Meanwhile you can have a lot of fun trying, night after night," Chas encouraged.

"I guess you're right. There's no need to panic yet. I think I read somewhere that stress can affect a man's sperm count. Maybe Harry's got too much going through his head that his penis is not packing its usual punch," Jessica said, laughing a little bit at her own joke and relieved to have been able to share her frustrations with somebody other than her poodle.

"See, there you go, Jes. You made a funny. I'm telling you, babycakes, just play along with Harry until this whole stupid little trip of his passes and you'll be asking me to pick out baby booties in no time!" Chas said, smiling confidently.

"Do you really think so?" Jessica whimpered, finally finding a tissue stuck under the seat cushions and blowing her nose.

"Absolutely, pumpkin. Now why don't you give Harry a big hug from me and tell him that I'll be sitting by the pool with you guys, sipping virgin margaritas by this time next week." Chas grinned, got up from the couch, and looked around his studio apartment to make sure that he hadn't forgotten anything.

"You're the best, Chas," Jessica said, as she was about to hang up the phone.

"Oh, no, dear, it's all about you," Chas replied, blew her a kiss, and put down the receiver.

★★★

As Chas carefully waited for his designer luggage on the carousel in the baggage claim at LAX airport, he had a strange feeling that he was being watched. All of a sudden, walking towards him across the crowded room was a gorgeous, tan, muscle-bound, blond twenty-something stud in white linen. He looked like a golden California surfer boy who had been pulled off of the beach and stuffed into a suit to have dinner with his mom. His pearly white glistening smile and perfectly chiseled features were totally intoxicating to Chas, who couldn't believe that this breathtaking gentleman was strutting his stuff in his direction.

My gosh, he is beautiful. He reminds me of a young version of me. Am I imagining it or is he really about to hit on me? Maybe he likes older guys. He obviously has good taste, Chas thought, winking at the young man who now was practically right on top of him. Just as Chas was about to embarrass himself with an obvious pick-up line, the young man beat him to the punch. "Chas Greer," the young man said, putting out his hand.

"That's me," Chas said, shaking the boy's hand, when he so wanted to kiss it.

"I'm Rocky, your driver. Luisa Mendez sent me. Here, let me help you with that," Rocky reached down and pulled all of Chas's bursting-at-the-seams suitcases off of the carousel in one swoop.

The next thing Chas knew, he was in the back of a brand-new white Rolls Royce being chauffeured by sexy Rocky to his posh new digs on the tony Wilshire Corridor, LA's ritziest street of million-dollar apartments. Rocky carried his bags onto the elevator and up to the penthouse of the smartest building the Corridor had to offer. For once in his gabby life, Chas was absolutely speechless. This palace in the sky was like nothing Chas had ever seen before, even during all his years on Park Avenue. The floors were a sparkling white-and-gray marble and the floor-to-ceiling windows offered unprecedented views of the Hollywood Hills and the Pacific Ocean.

The furniture was low, sleek Italian import, accented with crystal Lalique vases. The bedroom had a clubby, gentleman's feel, with oak-paneled walls and appropriate Ralph Lauren blue-and-green tartan. There was even an array of plush robes to choose from in the black-marbled, mirror-walled bathroom, equipped with golden faucets and a Jacuzzi tub large enough to hold a small army. "Is this where Luisa is staying while she is in LA?" Chas asked Rocky, who followed Chas to the large, walk-in closet that was bigger than Chas's miniscule studio apartment back in New York.

"No, Luisa rented a mansion on Sunset Boulevard near the Beverly Hills Hotel. This is where you live." Rocky smiled, bringing in a couple of Chas's suitcases.

Chas almost passed out. Never in his life had he lived in such a lavish, luxurious dwelling. *I can't believe this is finally happening to me. Luisa Mendez is a godsend. She will not be sorry she brought me here. I will make sure she gets everything she wants and more. Just wait till she gets a taste of Chas's magic,* Chas thought as he gazed out at the panoramic view from his bedroom window.

"Is there anything else I can do for you before I take off?" Rocky said, looking at Chas seductively.

"You can come here, boy, if you'd like a big tip," Chas said, signaling the young man to come closer. *Okay, so I just left a crying Juan in New York, but he'll never know about this. Besides, I doubt that he'll be a saint either,* Chas thought. Just then, the phone rang.

"Hello?" Chas said breathlessly into the receiver, a little confused about what was going on.

"Be here in ten minutes," was all Luisa's husky voice had to say.

Chas couldn't believe that Luisa would need him for anything on Sunday, just minutes after he arrived.

"Luisa, I'm so glad to be here and thank you, thank you for this gorgeous apartment. I've never seen anything like it; I can't even believe that I'll be living here! And the car, oh honey, what a beautiful machine. It's almost as wonderful as the hot rod who's driving it, if you know what I mean," Chas giggled like he was dishing comfortably with one of his New York girlfriend clients. However, his new boss had neither the time nor the desire to hear detail. As far as Luisa was concerned, Chas was there to serve her.

"Ten minutes," was all Luisa said, flipping her cell phone closed and lighting a cigarette.

✫✫✫

Rocky drove Chas down Sunset Boulevard past the spectacular mansions. He pulled up to the old Raider estate. "Oh my God, this is the house that Harry Raider grew up in. Don't tell me that Luisa lives here now?" Chas asked in disbelief as they were buzzed in through the massive gates.

"Yeah, apparently the Bank of Beverly Hills foreclosed on this estate a couple of months ago. Luisa got a really good deal. I think she's renting it with an option to buy. I heard her tell one of her friends that she could pick it up dirt cheap," Rocky said, proud that he made himself privy to his boss's conversations.

For a fleeting minute, Chas experienced an unfamiliar feeling of sympathy and sadness. This was Harry's family home; it shouldn't have been taken away. Chas had been invited there many times during his youth and enjoyed himself immensely. To Chas, the house was a refuge that sheltered him from the mean, heartless, privileged children of Beverly Hills who teased the tennis pro's son to no end and always made him feel lower than the hired help. Somehow the whole situation didn't feel right. Unbeknownst to Chas, it was about to get even stranger.

With the exception of some new, rented furniture and the absence of the art that had been sold at auction to cover some of Sam's mounting debts, the house looked pretty much the same as Chas remembered it. A Spanish-speaking maid led him through the house and up to Luisa's bedroom. There, lying spread-eagle, getting the inside of her toned thighs massaged by a hefty-looking masseuse, on what used to be Sam and Irma Raider's bed, was a nude Luisa. When Chas entered the room, she didn't even bother to cover herself with a towel or close her gaping legs. Chas politely covered his eyes and turned around, wrongly hoping that she would put on a robe or something.

"What's the matter, Chas, haven't you ever seen a naked woman before?" Luisa asked, laughing at Chas's modest reaction to seeing her in the flesh.

"Oh yes, of course, I just didn't expect," Chas stuttered nervously.

"What's wrong with you, Chas? Why are you so embarrassed? Aren't you gay?" Luisa chided him.

"I am gay...but..." Chas said, still not turning around.

"But what?" Luisa said cutting him off mid-sentence. "If you're a fag, than my body shouldn't affect you one way or the other," Luisa teased him mercilessly.

"Well, it doesn't. I just thought you'd be more comfortable if you put something on, that's all," Chas said, twitching nervously.

"I'm perfectly comfortable the way I am. Turn around, Chas, NOW!" Luisa demanded.

Hesitantly, Chas turned around, cleared his throat, and sat down on a chaise lounge by the window. Doing his best not to appear put-off by Luisa au naturel, he crossed his legs and smiled the best he could.

"That is so much better," Luisa smiled and offered Chas a cigarette.

"Are you sure it's all right to smoke while you're getting a massage? Can't that be dangerous?" Chas was trying to make casual conversation. The masseuse just shook her head but wouldn't dare say a word.

"If it is, who cares? I'm too old to die young. I'm thirty-five, you know," Luisa shrugged her shoulders.

"You look much younger," Chas said, trying to focus his eyes on Luisa's face and not the rest of her supple body.

"Thank you, my dear. Now let's get down to business," Luisa insisted, rolling onto her stomach and wasting no more time.

"Great, what do you want me to do first? Get a land-scaper? A designer? Contractor?" Chas gushed, getting a little more comfortable in the previously awkward situation. "I can set up meeting with wonderful decorators. I just think once you take me to see the property, I can put together a team to begin the transformation. It's so exciting, Luisa. Las Castillas will be truly legendary!"

"I'm glad to hear you are so enthusiastic, Chas. It will make your job that much more interesting. However, we will not begin to work on the hotel for a few more weeks. First you have a more important job to do." Luisa smiled devilishly. *Hmm, what could that be?* Chas asked himself, as he waited for Luisa to give him his first assignment.

"You have three weeks to find me a rich, Jewish husband," Luisa said nonchalantly, as if she had asked Chas to pick up a pizza.

Chas was blown away. He had no idea where *that* had come from. He thought he was dealing with the Latin version of Leona Helmsley. *She's got to be kidding, right? I can't get this bitch married. Who in their right mind would want to put up with her?*

He had to quickly regroup. "Why would someone as fabulous as you want to tie yourself down to one very lucky man? I would think a powerful businesswoman like you would want many men. How could one meager soul possibly satisfy you?" Chas inquired, hoping to talk her out of it.

"You are very observant, Chas. I've never met one man who would be good enough for me, but Papa insists I get married or he won't give me money for my hotel and will make sure I return to Acapulco. So, if you'd like to keep your job, your new apartment, your Rolls Royce, and your lovely little driver, I suggest you find me somebody to marry so we all keep Papa happy. Do you understand?" Luisa shot Chas a deadly look.

Chas knew Luisa wouldn't joke about something as serious as this. It was "I do" or die. "Gosh, Luisa, I would have assumed that a brilliant woman like you would be able to appease your father in some other way without sacrificing your personal life," Chas said, desperately trying to wriggle out of having to perform this horrible task.

"There is no such thing as 'appeasing' Señor Oscar. Papa's word is gold," Luisa said firmly and shot a pathetic look at the clueless gringo who stood before her.

"Yeah well, may be it's that way for most people, but you're his only daughter, for heaven's sakes. He's still your daddy and believe me, honey, I've dealt with plenty of them in Manhattan and Beverly Hills. A lot of whining, even a few tears may be for effect and I'm sure you'll have him wrapped around your little finger and get exactly what you want. It's that way with all Jewish Princesses, isn't it?" Chas chuckled. For some reason, the usually shrewd Chas Greer was way off of his mark. Not only did he not seem to understand the Latin paternal culture of respect, he also way underestimated who he was dealing with.

"Get out of here, you lowly piece of shit. How dare you insult Papa! If you are not gone from my sight in one second, that will be the end of you!" Luisa threw her cigarette at him, stood up, and turned her back.

"Luisa, wait a minute, calm down. I was only making a suggestion." Chas dodged the cigarette coming directly towards his face and stamped it out as soon as it hit the floor. He realized he had just made his first big mistake.

"I said you're fired, now go!" Luisa yelled, pointing to the door without turning around.

Frozen with panic, fearing that he just blew an opportunity of a lifetime, Chas stood dead in his tracks. "Luisa, I'm terribly sorry. I just thought you really didn't want to be married, but now I see that is not true and what a fool I've been. Of course I can find you a rich husband. I know everybody who's anyone from New York to LA. I'll have the cream of the crop lining up at your door. Just please give me one more chance. I'm begging you," Chas pleaded. He never had to stoop so low in his life, but with all the money he stood to make, just this once, he felt it was worth it.

"How fast can you find me a husband?" Luisa asked. She finally turned around, lit another cigarette, and slowly sat back down. She still did not look directly at Chas.

"I'll call my friend Marvin Green; he's a publicist at the Beverly Hills office of the Jewish Federation. The wealthiest families give money to that charity and they are bound to have a singles membership division. Marvin owes me a favor: I got his mother a Birkin bag last year at half the price. He'll give me a list of the most desirable single Jewish people in town and I will invite them here for cocktails and hors d'oeurves. I also know a lot of makeup people, celebrity handlers at the studios, some producers, and a ton of managers and agents. They could definitely tip me off to who's hot and available in Hollywood. Consider this your official coming out party, Luisa. I bet I could fill your backyard with enough single, rich Jewish men for you to have your pick. Will that do, dear?" Chas's confidence returned and he was very proud of himself for coming up with great ideas on the spot.

"It better," Luisa replied sharply. "That will be all," Luisa told, him putting out her cigarette, getting up from the table, heading into the bathroom, and slamming the door behind her.

Chas looked at the masseuse for some sign of support or perhaps a bit of understanding about how belittling and abrupt Luisa could be. He got nothing from the woman, not even acknowledgement of his presence. Overwhelmed and completely bulldozed, Chas showed himself out.

Silently he got into the car and told Rocky to head back to the penthouse. As the car rolled out of the driveway, Chas felt a gnawing pain in his stomach that was hard to ignore. The house that was once his haven had now become his living hell.

chapter twenty

Chas spent the next three weeks leaving no stone unturned in his pursuit to find the most eligible bachelor in Los Angeles. As a result, he was also developing quite a reputation as "the man to know" on the Hollywood scene. Word spread around town that Chas Greer had been hand-selected by the Mexican heiress to commandeer the opening of her first American hotel, and he would soon be in a plum position to offer all kinds of perks to those worthy of his attention. Chas quickly become the darling of the Velvet Mafia, a powerful group of gay and lesbian movers and shakers who made the entertainment industry run behind the scenes. This underground group of producers, agents, managers, designers, and publicists were impressed by Chas's ability to pull together a coterie of affluent people who were the crème de la crème. Nobody who was less than perfect was allowed to enter Chas's rarified world and gain access to his much sought-after boss, Luisa.

Luisa was keeping a low profile until her party, which meant she spent her days working on plans for the hotel and got massages or relaxed alone by the pool in the evenings. She didn't want to risk gallivanting around the

Hollywood party scene without a potential husband on her arm and have that information somehow leak back to her father. One wrong move, especially out in public, and she knew that she would have to pack her bags for Acapulco.

While Luisa was sequestered away in solitude in her home on Sunset, Chas, on the other hand, had become the toast of the town. His apartment earned the name "the pretty-boy party penthouse," because when the sun sank below the hills Chas hosted a group of the sexiest homo hotties in Hollywood. And these young men sure knew how to have a good time. Every night there were wild orgies, guys loving other guys galore. Groping groups of two or more men took up every space in the apartment, romping on the living room floor, on the couch, in the kitchen, in Chas's bedroom, and of course in the Jacuzzi built for four.

Even while being surrounded by such unbridled eroticism every evening, Chas did not participate in the debauchery. He was mostly preoccupied by whether or not his most important guests were getting what they came for.

Also, the more secrets Chas had in his dirty little pockets about the extracurricular activities of his high-profile par-tygoers, the more favors he could curry in Hollywood. Now no one would ever be able to say no to Chas Greer, the man who supplied all the action after dark and kept his lips sealed—for a price, of course. Chas's payoff was access to anything and anybody he wanted. If Chas needed a rich husband for Luisa, then the married studio boss who was getting his cock sucked by the seventeen-year-old male model in the bathroom would make sure that all of the sin-gle up-and-coming heterosexual "young suits" who worked for him would show up at her party.

Though Chas chose to abstain from the devil's delights during his soirees, it didn't mean that he was headed for sainthood, either. Chas and his driver Rocky were enjoying quite an intense sex life that usually began around midnight and sometimes lasted into the wee hours of the morning. Since Hollywood was a notoriously early-to-bed town, Chas's wild parties usually started around five or six in the afternoon and were well over by twelve. There was always lots of champagne to go around. A sexy Asian sushi chef, wearing an open Oriental robe to show off his massive hairless chest, created scrumptious delights in the kitchen. The youngest, hottest, tannest, most well-oiled group of male models moonlighted as waiters. Dressed appropriately in only red leather G-strings, the dutiful servants passed around plates stacked high with fancy hors d'oeuvres and cocaine galore. The party was never slow to get going and the action started as soon as the first group of men arrived. Some of the married guys would get there early and stay only for the happy hour, before going home to dinner with their wives and kids. The sexy single boys also had to be home early, since their high-pressure jobs sometimes meant being in the office early in the morning. When the last guest was gone, Chas and Rocky would have a private party of their own.

Rocky was no idiot, either. Like most drivers, waiters, and other service people in Los Angeles, he was an aspiring model/actor. He knew that if he were a regular at Chas's sexy evenings, he would become used, old hat, and yesterday's news to the powerful people at the parties who could easily make him a big star. Rocky liked to appear fresh and clean, a new find when he went on an audition for a movie, television show, or commercial. That didn't mean that he wouldn't gladly oblige if a casting director or producer asked him to drop his pants. Like most actors, Rocky would do whatever he had to do to get the part. Still, being a bimbo on the casting couch seemed a lot better and more effective than simply being passed around like a party favor.

Rocky also believed that he would go a lot farther if he became Chas's official boyfriend, at least in Los Angeles. Rocky was well aware of the late-night phone calls and hysterical weeping messages Chas received on his voicemail from a distraught Juan.

"Why don't you just tell him to get a life?" Rocky said to Chas one night, lifting his head from the pillow.

"Juan is a very sensitive little thing. I can't just drop him; he'd break and smash all over the floor like a carton of raw eggs. I have to let him down easily, you know, pull away slowly. In time, he'll move on. It's only been a couple of weeks. In a few months, he'll forget all about me," Chas said, thinking aloud. Deep down he did really care for Juan, as much as he could care about anyone besides himself.

"Yeah, sure. Whatever, dude," Rocky replied sarcastically. He then got on his knees, arched his muscular back, and spread his legs seductively, signaling that he was ready for Chas to mount him and take him for a ride. As Chas enjoyed the naughty pleasures of Rocky's meaty flesh, the thought of Juan and his wailing was a million miles away.

★ ★ ★

Three weeks to the day after Luisa gave Chas her orders, her backyard was jam-packed with the wealthiest, most desirable single men in LA and a host of other sought-after people to ensure that her cocktail party was a huge success. Among the crowd of Hollywood swells were none other than Harry and Jessica Raider, making their return to the party scene.

Chas had been too busy taking care of Luisa to spend any time with them since he moved to LA, so he thought the party would present an opportunity for them all to catch up. Chas also knew that even though Harry was broke, he would lend a certain flair to the party, especially since he grew up in the house that Luisa was now renting.

Chas turned out to be exactly right, but just how accurate he was would come to shock even him. Harry was thrilled to be invited to a hot party again. Once the news got around that he had lost his fortune and was living off of his wife, Harry hadn't been invited into the heat of the scene for what seemed like ages. Therefore, he wasted no time making the most of the evening's festivities.

Almost as soon as he and Jessica arrived, Harry went around to all the different groups of mingling guests. He said hello to old friends and introduced himself to the people he didn't know. Once he had their attention, Harry laughed loudly and told jokes to anyone who would listen. In a very short time, Harry had made himself the center of attention and become the life of the party.

Unafraid to make fun of his unfortunate financial situation, Harry stole one of the waiter's trays and ran around taking drink orders. He then put on one of their aprons and began serving people hors d'oeuvres. He had the whole stuffy crowd roaring with laughter and his antics actually won him a thunderous applause. Harry thrived on this kind of frenetic energy and wanted to keep the ball rolling. Without even asking Luisa's permission, he'd grab a group of party guests who looked bored and lead them on tours of the house while regaling them with funny stories about some of the crazy things he had gotten away with in happier times. Little did Harry know, Luisa had been watching him the whole evening. Like everyone else, she couldn't help but be totally captivated by Harry's charismatic persona. Because she was so amused and entertained by his audacity, she didn't stop him when he went marching through her new home without a second thought. Harry was out of control and brazen and Luisa loved that. He obviously didn't feel like he had to impress anyone or apologize for who he was and what had happened to him. This was a huge turn-on to the heiress.

Harry stuck out like a sore thumb amongst the crowd of Hollywood heavy hitters who stayed cool, calm, and collected under all circumstances. The more of an attraction he made himself, the more Luisa's curiosity intensified. The other single men at the party reminded her of the stiff, stuck-up, arrogant men of Mexico, who behaved like they were God's gift to women. Harry was quite a contrast. He was a free spirit who didn't appear bound by social rules and obviously didn't give a damn about keeping up appearances.

Harry wasn't the only one Luisa was watching like a hawk. Jessica Raider was not exempt from Luisa's scrutiny either. Luisa couldn't help but notice that Jessica seemed to feel awkward and strained in the crowd of strangers and didn't make any effort to keep up with her husband. *Could she be so confident about the loving state of their marriage that she just sits there like useless deadwood and lets him go off with a group of strangers? I don't understand why she doesn't follow him, laugh at his jokes, or at least try to be somewhat amusing herself. What could a man with so much gusto possibly see in that silly little girl sitting in the corner whispering away with one of my servants?* Luisa thought as she stood on the balcony outside her bedroom.

When Luisa saw Harry carry a plate of food and some drinks to Chas and Jessica, Luisa felt it was right to make her move. For all the time she had spent spying on Harry and Jessica, she had not introduced herself and had no idea who they were. All Luisa knew was that Harry seemed like the most exciting man she had ever seen and Jessica looked like a little mouse she could dispose of in one stomp.

"Aren't you going to introduce me to your friends, Chas?" Luisa said in her sweetest voice as she sidled up to Chas and the Raiders. She appeared so warm and gracious as she held out her hand to Harry that her extreme switch of personalities threw Chas for a loop. Luisa took the art of schmoozing to a whole new level.

"These are my dear friends Harry and Jessica Raider. I know Jessica from New York, but funny enough, Harry happened to grow up in this very house. It used to belong to his parents before it came up for lease," Chas said, subliminally hinting to Luisa that Harry's family had to let the bank take the house. Chas also wanted to signal Luisa not to spend too much time on the Raiders when there were plenty of rich, single, marriageable candidates there for her taking.

"Harry, I was upstairs finishing getting dressed when I caught part of your house tour. It was hilarious! I was laughing so hard I could hardly get my dress on," Luisa said smiling seductively, grasping Harry's hand. "Can you imagine? I was standing there in my bedroom, naked, when I heard these people coming down the hall and this funny voice talking about the time he lost his virginity in the hall closet. I thought maybe you were going to walk in on me. Now *that* would have been something!" Luisa said, raising an eyebrow and heaving her bountiful cleavage in Harry's direction.

Harry's eyes practically popped out of his head. "Wow, I didn't know that anyone was actually in the house. I guess you're pretty pissed off at me. It's just so weird, because I grew up here and I had so many fantastic adventures that I wanted to tell everyone. I thought it would add to the fun of the evening, if your guests knew about this house's rockin' Raider party history," Harry said enthusiastically.

A nervous Chas wanted to head off what he thought was a potential socially explosive situation. "Luisa, that is Harry's unique way of apologizing for breaking and entering. I hope you aren't too angry," Chas explained in his usual saccharine, condescending tone.

"Not at all. I rather enjoyed what I could hear of Harry's stories." Luisa eyes never left Harry's. "As a matter of fact, if you would be good enough, I'd love it if you'd take me on a private tour of this house and tell me all about the trouble you got into growing up here. It sounds like you know how to have a good time."

"We were just about to leave," Jessica finally spoke up. Because she knew that Chas depended on this woman for employment, Jessica had remained quiet and polite. Now, however, enough was enough, and it was time to take Harry home, before any real damage was done.

"Oh, please, Jessica, give Harry another five minutes," Luisa implored. "I'm sure it is very sad for him not to be able to come back to his family home anymore. Let him enjoy himself one last time before you take him away from here."

"Whatever Harry wants to do," Jessica heard herself say as she forced a smile onto her face.

"It'll only be a few more seconds, Jes, I promise. Just let me have another whirl around my old stomping grounds before we pack up for the night." Harry put his arm around his wife and kissed her on the cheek.

"Sure," Jessica acquiesced, sitting down next to a confused Chas.

"Wonderful, please come with me. I want you to show me everything," Luisa said, winking at Harry, putting her arm in his, and heading him back into the house.

"I wonder what the hell that is all about," Chas said, as he took a glass of wine from a passing waiter's tray. "There are over two hundred rich, Jewish, single guys here for Luisa to meet. What could she possibly want with Harry?"

"Oh, I don't know, maybe she doesn't want a partner of

her own. She's probably just one of those typical Beverly Hills bitches that gets off on stealing other women's husbands," Jessica snipped, nervously chomping on the ice in her soda.

"Oh, no. Luisa doesn't have time for those kinds of games. She has to get married, otherwise her father will pull the plug on the money. She's not going to jeopardize her whole future by wasting time with a married man," Chas assured Jessica and himself. "Maybe she met someone here tonight who she really likes and she's just using Harry to make him jealous. From what I know about Luisa, that seems like something she'd do to get a man's attention. Trust me Jes, that's a much more plausible situation. You have absolutely nothing to worry about."

"Frankly, Chas, I wasn't really that worried about it. Harry's not exactly in a position to support a high-maintenance, expensive Beverly Hills wife right now. Besides, our marriage is really good and has gotten much stronger over the past couple of months," Jessica said, smiling confidently and patting Chas on the back. Chas smiled back, but inside he wasn't so sure.

★ ★ ★

Nearly an hour went by before Harry and Luisa finally emerged from the grand old house, laughing and joking. Jessica refused to give Luisa the satisfaction of seeing how pissed off she really was about being left there for such a long time. She smiled lovingly at Harry as he and Luisa approached her and Chas.

"Hi, honey, sorry that took so long. I got carried away with my stories as usual." Harry grinned and gave Jessica a hug.

"No problem, Harry, I didn't even realize how long you were gone. Chas and I had a great time catching up on all of the New York gossip," Jessica said, making sure her voice kept its levity.

Luisa gave Chas an unexpected continental kiss on both cheeks. "Thank you, Chas, for keeping Jessica entertained while I had such a fascinating time getting to know Harry and hearing all about this glorious house I have rented. Harry, I only wish you were still here to keep the fun going." Luisa looked at Harry and gave him the once over. An uncomfortable silence fell upon the foursome. Jessica wanted to slap Luisa's face, and Harry had no idea what to say.

Chas knew he had to say something to keep this situation from going down like a lead balloon. "Well, maybe you can invite Harry and Jessica for dinner sometime and you guys can double date with your new man," Chas enthused.

"Ah, yes, if I could only find someone as charming as you, Harry. I'd marry him in a minute," Luisa said, laughing.

"Well, I'm sure you can easily do that tonight. You have here over two hundred of the most sought-after single guys in all of Hollywood. There must be somebody that interests you," Chas said gesturing toward the crowd of good-looking, rich, successful people.

"What can I say? Why is it that all of the good ones are taken? Good night, Harry. Good night, Jessica. It was lovely to meet you." Luisa kissed Harry and Jessica on both cheeks, before going off to introduce herself to a tall, handsome man getting a drink at the bar.

"You see, she isn't into wasting her time," Chas laughed, breathing a sigh of relief. "Perhaps this whole night was too much of a meat market for her and she just needed a break. Harry, thanks for giving my boss some comic relief. Husband hunting can be very overwhelming, even if you're Luisa Mendez."

"Hey, no problem. She's a great lady. If she has any more parties, make sure we get invited," Harry said as Jessica took his hand and led him to the valet parking.

"Sure, guys. Thanks for coming. Have a great night." Chas waved as he watched Harry and Jessica get into the blue Bentley and drive away.

Later, Chas was standing at the bar getting himself another cocktail when Luisa grabbed his shoulders. "I want you in my living room at eight sharp tomorrow morning for an emergency meeting," Luisa demanded with her usual intensity. She was standing so close to Chas that she was almost spitting in his face.

"Okay, my pleasure. Is everything all right? Are you having fun at the party?" Chas said, praying that she would be satisfied with the first big event he put together for her.

"As far as I am concerned, the party is over. But don't worry, darling. It was a great success." Luisa smiled triumphantly at Chas, walked into the house, and locked the door behind her. Chas had no idea why she seemed so pleased, but he didn't want to question it. Instead he raised his glass in Luisa's direction and decided to enjoy the rest of the evening.

chapter twenty-one

I'm going to marry Harry Raider," Luisa said matter-of-factly as she sat in the living room that Harry grew up in, going over some paperwork.

"You can't be serious, Luisa. That's just plain silly!" Chas laughed, walking over to the French doors, opening them a crack, and lighting up a clove cigarette.

"I am dead serious. He is the first man that I've ever met who made me laugh so much. He is just the sort of person I need to compliment my life. I can't picture him being demanding of my time and energy," Luisa answered, occupied with some construction estimates she was reviewing.

Chas spun around on his heels and puffed on his cigarette. "Sure, you might find him amusing in the beginning, but I'm sure his crazy antics would get old after a while. He's like a big kid, Luisa. He's definitely not man enough for a powerful woman like you," Chas said, assured Harry was just a passing fancy for his boss.

"Who are you to judge Harry? So what if he doesn't flaunt his strength in front of everybody like a macho pig? He has quiet power, the kind you don't need to advertise," Luisa said firmly. "Most important, he behaves like he is totally free and doesn't need to prove anything to anybody. Which is perfect, because it is not his nature to want to control a woman. He will let me lead my life and not get in the way."

"Luisa, you know Harry is totally broke. Why do you think his family doesn't own this house anymore? The bank took it. Why would waste your time with a penniless man who's already married?" Chas thought whole thing was just too absurd. He had invited over two hundred of the richest, most successful single men to Luisa's party and most of them showed up. Why, with a room full of hotties to chose from, would Luisa focus in on a nut job like Harry Raider? Harry would only be a liability and Luisa didn't seem like the kind of woman who would be happy to carry someone along for the ride.

"You call that a marriage? That nothing little girl he calls his wife should be put out of *his* misery immediately. It is obvious that he only married her for the money." Luisa put her paperwork away and picked up a wedding magazine from the coffee table.

Chas waved his finger in the air and shook his head no. "Afraid not, dear. Harry married Jessica while he still thought that he was rich. He could have had any woman in Los Angeles, Manhattan, or the Hamptons he wanted, but he sincerely fell in love with Jessica. And, Jessica has really stood by Harry's side through his whole ordeal. With her money, she could get anybody now, but she still wants her marriage to work. This is a heart-to-heart soul mate thing. It can't be undone. You'll just have to find someone else," Chas told her, like he just told her to choose another dress for a party.

Carrying the wedding magazine in her hand, Luisa walked over to Chas and slapped him over the head with it as hard as she could. "Ouch!" he screamed, after the shock wore off. "What did you do that for?" Chas asked, dropping his cigarette out the window and cowering by the drapes.

"Don't you ever tell me what to do, Mr. Chas. I brought you to Los Angeles to serve me. You do as I say and don't ask any questions. Are we clear?" Luisa screamed. "You are going to put an end to that sham of a marriage and bring Harry to me."

Chas was getting fed up with Luisa's ridiculous demands. He had seen his spoiled clients through many a temper tantrum in his day as a personal shopper for the rich ladies of Manhattan and the Hamptons, but this was the first time in his illustrious career that he had been physically attacked. "I don't know if that's a fair thing for you to ask me to do, Luisa. I can't control other people's lives. What if I can't do that, Luisa? What if Harry just won't leave Jessica?" Chas readjusted his shirt in an effort to compose himself.

Just as Chas felt like he had it all together, Luisa went back over to Chas, grabbed him around the collar, and spit in his face. She then sent his lithe body reeling on to the floor. "If you don't break up Harry's marriage, you will never feel safe another day in your pathetic life. There are men in Mexico who will consider it an honor to get rid of somebody who doesn't please me. If you don't bring me the husband I need to satisfy Papa, then you will have destroyed me. And there is no way in holy hell that I can let that happen. Do you understand me?" Luisa said, slowly backing away from him.

"Are you threatening me?" Chas asked Luisa in total disbelief, while he brushed himself off and slowly stood back up.

"Why do you look so surprised, *gringo?* When you work for the Mendez family, you will have more money than you could possibly enjoy in one lifetime, but you MUST be dedicated for life. Got it?"

Fuckin' shit, what have I gotten myself into? I've witnessed many tantrums and have been called every horrible name under the sun, but no one ever wanted to have me killed. This is completely insane. How the hell am I going to get away from this bitch in one piece? Chas, now practically paralyzed with fear, thought as he grabbed his Hermès briefcase from the glass coffee table. He walked back over to Luisa, took the wedding magazine out of her hand, and threw it in the garbage.

Luisa recoiled in shock. She was stunned to see Chas approach her like that. Most of her servants ran out of the room crying after being subjected to one of her tirades and also being physically abused. She had no idea what he'd do next.

"My clients have their wedding dresses personally made, no off-the-rack crap. I'll call Vera Wang and tell her to clear her schedule. I'm sure you'll keep her busy with your specifications. If it's Harry Raider you want, than it's Harry Raider you'll get." Chas quickly left Luisa's home before she could suspect he'd been so scared he nearly wet his white Polo pants.

Well I'm still breathing, at least for today...Out of all the single men in Beverly Hills, why does she have to want psycho-boy Harry Raider? But if I am going to live to enjoy Luisa's hefty paycheck, I need to make as much money as I can and then get the hell out. I'm sure as shit not going to spend my life as this woman's punching bag. Sorry, Harry. It's now your turn to become Luisa's piñata.

When he returned to his apartment, his phone was ringing off the hook. Chas rushed into the kitchen to pick it up, only to find it was Rocky checking in to see when he could come over. "Not tonight," Chas said solemnly, pouring himself a big glass of Chardonnay and searching the cabinets for a Valium or any kind of sedative that perhaps someone had left behind. "Oh baby, you gotta be kidding me. I have a ton of boys from my new modeling agency I've invited over later. Besides, I also said my new print agent could come, too. Come on Chas, I really need to show this guy a good time," Rocky begged over the phone.

"Well, I'm sorry, sweetheart, but I'm not in a very festive mood tonight. I have some very serious work to do for Luisa and I need some quiet time to think," Chas said sternly, running his fingers through his golden, streaked hair, then rubbing his temples. Chas's life was on the line and he had no interest in having fun. He was completely frazzled. Besides being terrified of what Luisa would do to him if he didn't deliver, Chas also had an ache in his stomach when he thought about trying to break up Harry and Jessica. Chas wasn't one who was big on guilt, but being responsible for ruining two people's lives was too much for even a schemer like him to justify.

Luisa really doesn't love Harry, she just needs someone "easy" to marry to pacify her bank-rolling father. Harry and Jessica on the other hand, really do love each other. But there are serious dents in their marital armor. If Harry doesn't give up his nutty idea of restarting his father's business soon and start spending more time at home, Jessica could get really frustrated and sick of paying the bills for a husband she hardly ever sees. If Jessica starts to pressure Harry about giving up his dreams, Harry might rebel and run away from her. Then there is the baby issue. Jessica really wants one and Harry isn't really ready yet, even though he reluctantly agreed to try, somewhat against his will. Since the two brats can't both have their way at the same time, somebody has to give in and let's face it, neither party knows how to compromise. Therefore I have a good chance of causing enough mischief, Chas reasoned with himself.

"Chas, will you stop acting like my grandmother and get ready for a wild night? God, you sound like you're going through menopause or something, dude. Why don't you lighten up?" Rocky teased on the other end of the phone, as Chas nervously paced around the kitchen.

"No, I can't. Listen, I'll call you tomorrow. All right?" Chas said tersely. His head was swimming and he had to get this punk off of the phone.

"Okay. Whatever, dude. Later," Rocky huffed as Chas quickly hung up.

All the late nights were beginning to catch up with Chas. *I've forgotten how shallow everyone can be out here. It's all about business, all of the time. And they say New York is the city that never sleeps. Hm,* Chas thought. He hated the position he was in. He was usually the one manipulating everyone for some material gain. Now Luisa had outdone even him. As he sank into a black leather recliner, Chas tried to figure out why this bothered him so.

For the first time, Chas was beginning to experience what it was like to be wanted for his possessions. This was a very foreign feeling to the man who spent his entire career using everybody in New York City for what they could do for him. Now he found himself on the other side of the equation and he didn't like it one bit. Because he was usually doing the manipulating, he could see right through the users and losers and would be extra careful not to give anybody one damn inch. After all that, he had to sell his soul to gain his new wealth and this was something he couldn't get past.

Chas needed to be tough as nails and twice as ruthless to accomplish this task, but all that could begin tomorrow.

Tonight, he needed a soft shoulder to cry on and someone who could provide comforting reassurance. Chas found himself picking up his cell phone and dialing Juan's number. He hadn't spoken with Juan at length since he had moved to LA. Chas had basically ignored Juan's whining, desperate messages and only spent a few minutes pacifying him when he absolutely had to. Now it was Chas who needed Juan, the man who loved him, just for himself, not his cool new apartment.

"Juanita, pick up, it's me," Chas whispered into the phone.

"*Dios mío.* Oh *mi Jesus, Maria, y Jose,* it's Chassy! *Caramba!* I am so happy to hear your voice, baby. I miss you so much!" Juan squealed with delight into the receiver. He was screaming and crying at once.

"Would you calm down, honey? I just called to say hello. Sorry I've been so busy, but Luisa totally busts my balls day and night. She is one tough bitch," Chas said, crossing his legs and propping them up on some Versace pillows.

"Oh, Chassy *mi amor*, don't let that bitch boss you around. Why don't you come home to me? I make it all better and you will forget about Señorita," Juan pleaded with his lover.

"I'm afraid I can't do that, honey. Well, at least not yet. Luisa is paying me a lot of money and I have to do what she asks. I have a lot riding on this. Look, as soon as I deliver what she wants, I will have secured my position with her financially. Then I'll bring you out here!" Chas told him.

Juan screamed and jumped for joy. "Calm down, sister, it's not time to pack yet. I have to do something terrible, and then we can celebrate," Chas said, stoically.

"What could be so terrible for all of that money?" Juan sputtered out.

"Luisa wants to marry Harry Raider and I have to break up Harry and Jessica's marriage. I can't believe I have to do this. If not, she will basically have me knocked off. So either I'll be a rich man or a dead man." Chas stared out at the Hollywood Hills.

For a long moment, Juan was silent. He was absolutely mortified at what he had just heard. Juan's gut instinct made him want to tell Chas to forget the whole thing and that the money wasn't worth it. He also didn't quite understand the severity of the situation. To Juan, Luisa Mendez was almost a saint. She could never hurt anyone, especially not Chas. Juan thought it had to be all about the money Chas was making working for Santa Luisa. He knew how much Chas hated being poor and how much he desired the high life. For once in his life, Juan thought, he had to think with his head and not his heart. It would be the only way to secure his relationship with the lover he was just about convinced that he had lost to the hills of Hollywood.

"You must do it *muy rapido* and not even think about the Raiders. Neither Harry nor Jessica care about you, Chas. Everything you have done for them and they have never repaid you," Juan said.

"That is quite true, but still I hate the fact that Luisa is *ordering* me to do this. Nobody *orders* Chas Greer around," Chas said, attempting to regain at least one shred of his male pride.

"Listen, honey, Luisa Mendez is a powerful woman, but at least she is generous. She wants what she wants and she is willing to pay for it. What is wrong with that? It's about time somebody paid you what you are worth, no?" Juan said, slyly.

"No. I mean, yes, of course. You are absolutely right. I am sick and tired of working for these ungrateful people for peanuts. Luisa may be demanding, but you're right, she is willing to put her money where her mouth is. A lot of money! I'm glad I called you, darling, Juanita. You are the only one who understands me," Chas said sweetly, so relieved that Juan had helped him temporarily assuage his overwhelming sense of guilt.

"So...can I come to Beverly Hills to help you get Harry to marry Luisa?" Juan asked cheerfully, pushing his luck.

"Not just yet, sweetie. Let jazzy Chassy work his magic and then once I have the moolah, I'll fly you out first class," Chas assured him

"No, no, no! I want to come now. I am sick of waiting. I want to be with you!" Juan cried, starting to get overly emotional.

"Juan, please, cut me some slack," an exhausted Chas begged. "Just let me focus and we'll have the rest of our lives to travel the world and live like kings. Just a little while longer and you won't even recognize your life anymore."

"You promise you won't forget me when you make all of that money?" Juan said, with fear in his voice.

"Yes, Juan, I promise." Chas hung up with Juan, went into his bathroom, and turned on his Jacuzzi. A long soak and a good night's sleep would hopefully help ease his troubled mind and hardened heart. *Juan is really quite insightful for a young lad. Rich people only care about themselves. They've never done anything for me out of the goodness of their greedy little hearts. Now let's see, what does jazzy Chassy have to do to make this whole mess work to his advantage? Well, Harry Raider likes drama and excitement and oh boy, will Luisa give him plenty of that. Hm....*

chapter twenty-two

Le Femme Bouche Art Gallery on hip La Brea Street, the heart of lesbian Hollywood, was swinging the night that Chas brought Jessica there to meet his influential friend in the art business. Androgynous waiters with long hair and long white coats served haute cuisine raw vegan appetizers. Wine and sparkling water were passed around along with a selection of freshly squeezed exotic juices like guava/kiwi/mango and blueberry/pomegranate/blackberry. The "power dykes," and the people in the art world who needed their patronage, milled around the huge, industrial-looking warehouse that had been given an extreme makeover by an all-girl team of contractors, who morphed it into LA's sexiest gallery. Tonight, the paintings featured were created by a group of Afghani women who had used art to express their new freedom after the fall of the Taliban. Their images were profound and moving, while still managing to be bright and colorful pieces that one might even consider hanging in the living room.

"Jessica, meet my dear friend Billie Blaine, the most prominent woman on the Los Angeles modern art scene. If you want to get your paintings shown in this town, this is *the* woman to know," Chas said, as he introduced Jessica. Like Jessica, Billie was petite in stature, but that's where the comparisons stopped. Where Jessica's body was round and soft, Billie was a pumped-up, muscle-bound, rock-solid little soldier of a woman who looked like she lived at the gym.

But in spite of Billie's short, spiked blonde hair and tailored men's Armani suit and Hermès tie, there was something comforting about her hard-core presence. Jessica normally would have been put off by Billie's extreme appearance. Yet once she looked directly in Billie's crystal-blue eyes, Jessica felt safe in her presence. "Chas told me about the wonderful exhibitions you put on here," Jessica said to her.

"Oh yes, I normally don't do a show in this gallery unless part of the proceeds go to some international women's cause or it has a deeper women's theme. Art for altruism, as they say. Chas tells me you are a wonderful artist and that you had a very successful show in the Hamptons last summer." Billie smiled sincerely at Jessica.

"Well, I don't know how successful it was, compared to what you are doing here, but it sure was a great evening," Jessica replied, wistfully remembering the fun she had before all the trouble in her new life began.

For the first time since she had been in LA, somebody had mentioned her painting. Jessica had been so overwhelmed that she didn't have a minute to indulge in her own passion. Harry was staying in to watch some sports game on television this evening, so Jessica had come to the gallery alone with Chas. But while Jessica thought that she was giving herself a little reprieve from the intensity of living under her own roof, what she was really doing was playing right into Chas's master plan to break up her marriage.

"I'd really love to see some of your work, Jessica," Billie said, smiling confidently. "If it's as wonderful as Chas tells me it is, maybe we can do a new-artist show here and I can get you some celebrity clients to help get you started."

"Started with what?" Jessica asked curiously, biting into an hors d'oeuvre that had just been offered by a waitress.

"Your art business, of course. You'd be surprised how many movie and TV stars love to buy work by local artists. You'd think they'd spend their big bucks on acquiring the masters, but most of them are really still trailer-park hicks who got lucky and they're afraid to splurge on something they know nothing about. At the same time, they've been told by their agents and managers that art is a smart investment, so they like to start small with something they can afford and like. That way if you make it big, they can say they bought your work when you were an unknown. They love stories like that." Billie signaled a waiter to bring Jessica another glass of wine.

"Gee, I never thought about doing anything like that out here. I'd love to start painting again. I think I'll get some supplies and start tomorrow," Jessica said with a renewed sense of vigor.

Chas smiled deviously and patted Jessica on the shoulder. "You see, Jes? I told you Billie is terrific! This is just what you need to recapture your spark. You can't spend your whole life worrying about Harry, especially after all he's put you through recently. It's time you did something for yourself for a change."

Twitching in place, Jessica felt extremely awkward with Chas mentioning Harry in a negative light in front of a perfect stranger. But it didn't seem to bother Billie. Smiling sympathetically, seemingly without judgment, Billie took Jessica's hand and gave it a loving squeeze. "Honey, life is too short not to live your passion. Why don't you take a look around at some of the fantastic work here, while my old buddy Chas and I do some catching up?" Billie pointed

Jessica towards the half of the gallery she yet had not seen.

"Good idea, I'll see you guys in a bit. And thanks, Billie," Jessica said to her new friend.

"You got it, baby. Don't you worry about a thing." Billie winked at Jessica as she walked away. Billie pulled Chas into the corner. "Is she really that rich?" Billie whispered to Chas with an air of excitement in her voice.

"She's the heiress to about four billion dollars. Gee, I don't know, Bill, is that considered rich these days?" Chas chuckled.

"Mm Mm, all that money and great looking too. Are you sure she's gay? Why did she get married?" Billie whispered.

"I told you she had to marry Harry to satisfy her old man, to make sure she'd get all of the money. Now that she's done her duty, she's ready to start satisfying herself," Chas told her.

"Yeah, but how do you know she's gay? She doesn't seem to be," Billie demanded.

"Let's just say I know these things. She has tendencies. I've seen them. I can't tell you the number of time I've caught her checking out the naked models' bodies when I brought her backstage shows during Fashion Week. She's always commenting how hot she thought they were, especially the younger ones. It was like she was hinting to me to fix her up, but was afraid to really go through with it, because everyone knows who she is in New York and she was scared they'd blackmail her for cash," Chas lied to Billie through his teeth. He knew there was nothing more Billie would love to do than introduce a billionaire's daughter to new joys of womanhood. "I know it's been a long time for you, but do you think you can you handle a virgin, Bill?" Chas teased her mercilessly.

"Well, I don't know, can I cream in my La Perla panties right now? Do you think Jessica would notice if I took them off and slipped them in her bag?" Billie joked.

"Okay, down girl! Don't be so damn aggressive. I told you if you want to win her over, you have to start slowly. Jessica is still a tender little girl at heart and the one thing she needs most in life is some heavy-duty nurturing. This is also what she's definitely not getting at home from her spoiled-brat, self-absorbed husband, Harry. It's starting to take a toll on her and she is definitely beginning to crack. I see it in her eyes. She's tired, Billie, and if someone doesn't save her from that horrible, draining sham of a marriage, she's certainly headed for a nervous breakdown," Chas confided, solemnly looking into his wine glass and sadly twirling a swizzle stick around in it.

Maybe I should go into the industry. I think that one was worth an Oscar, Chas thought, as he observed Billie unable to take her eyes off of Jessica.

"What a waste of a good woman to be stuck in some freak show of a marriage. I ought to castrate him, bronze his balls, and hang them from my rearview mirror. Just wait until Jessica becomes *my* wife. I'll treat her so well that she'll wish she never wasted one precious moment with that useless beast," Billie said intently.

"Now, now, Billie, watch your temper. Remember, the way to Jessica Raider's heart is all sweetness and light. Take the bull out of dyke and think loving, gentle fairy god-mother. Once she realizes you can take care of her in so many ways that Harry can't, she'll be all yours. I'd bet my life on it."

Chas nervously searched his men's purse for a cigarette. *I better be right about Jessica's ability to jump the fence and her desire to be "mothered" both sexually and emotionally. I have too much invested in his plan for it not to work out,* Chas thought. Chas had known Billie for many years and he had watched her work her way up from a secretary to a true mover and shaker. He was counting on the fact that when Billie was determined to get what she wanted, she'd let nothing, especially not a man, get in her way.

★★☆

With Chas's help, Billie and Jessica became fast friends. While Harry was busy investigating more business opportunities or sneaking out to see his friends in Malibu, Billie would come over to the house and encourage Jessica with her painting. The ladies sat in the garden for hours while Jessica filled canvas after canvas with beautiful floral scenery. Billie would tell her how talented she was and bring her gourmet picnics to share by the pool. Jessica was extremely happy during these quiet, creative days, because they so much reminded her of the peace and tranquility she enjoyed back in her garden in East Hampton. Billie's nurturing presence was indeed helping her take her mind off of her troubles.

Many evenings when Jessica was looking forward to being alone with her husband, Billie had other ideas. There were gallery openings, private showings in celebrity homes, dinners with potential clients, and many other exclusive art-centered events that Billie would escort Jessica to. What Jessica didn't realize was that because Billie and she were always seen together, people were beginning to think they were a couple. The paparazzi who placed photos of Billie and Jessica in the various society columns would encourage the editors to write suggestive captions under their pictures.

JUST GOOD FRIENDS: MRS. JESSICA RAIDER AND AGENT BILLIE BLAINE AT THE LACMA ANNUAL GALA; WHERE'S HARRY? MRS. JESSICA RAIDER ARM-IN-ARM AT THE OPENING OF A NEW LA BREA ART GALLERY WITH AGENT BILLIE BLAINE; GIRLS NIGHT O.U.T. JESSICA RAIDER AND BILLIE BLAINE SHARE A 'FRIENDLY' KISS HELLO AT THE YOUNG

ARTIST'S PREVIEW AT THE HOME OF SARAH JONES AND JANE FEINBERG

None of this seemed to bother Jessica, who remained clueless about Billie's real intentions. When someone who knew Harry asked Billie if Jessica was still "Mrs. Raider," Billie went ballistic and banned that poor soul from further being in Jessica's company. Even with all the hoopla being made around her paintings, Jessica craved some quality time at home. She loved her new friend Billie and all that came with her, but sadly, she felt remorseful about missing Harry. Jessica was deeply afraid that she and Harry were growing apart.

"Jessica, if you are going to become a prominent Los Angeles artist, then you have to show your face around town. As much as I want to help you, I can't do it all for you. You need to help me by honoring the right people with your exquisite presence. Aren't you enjoying yourself? You seem to be glowing every time we go out and people talk about your seeing your work. Aren't you much happier now?" Billie asked lovingly, as she brought Jessica some new silky dresses as a surprise gift.

"Of course I am, Billie, and I can't thank you enough for giving me this fabulous life, but I miss Harry. I haven't spent any time with him lately. Either he's busy trying to figure out the business or I'm doing something with you. I think that Harry and I need to reconnect," Jessica said, trying on the beautiful clothes that Billie selected. Hearing that Jessica still had an interest in her husband didn't make Billie very happy, but she was not going to blow it by losing her cool. Billie wasn't afraid to take a gamble, and tonight she was going be a high roller with her romantic future.

"All right, Jes, honey, I understand. But tonight's young collectors' dinner at the LACMA is a must for anyone in the Los Angeles art world. The tickets were a fortune and I can't let you miss it. Why don't you bring Harry along? He loves a good party. There will be food and music there; I'm sure he'll have a good time with us." Billie forced a smile.

"That's a wonderful idea, Billie. Let me ask him right now."

Jessica darted down the stairs towards Harry's den, while Billie sat in Jessica's room, holding her breath. The last thing she wanted to do was spend an evening with boorish, vulgar Harry Raider. She had even been contemplating making her first move with Jessica tonight. But now she guessed that the good stuff would have to wait until Harry ignored and disappointed his wife just a little more. Lucky for Billie, that time was coming faster than she had anticipated.

Cheerfully, Jessica popped into Harry's den to find him chomping on some nuts, totally engulfed in a game of football. "Honey, Billie's got some tickets to a great party tonight at the museum. Why don't you go upstairs, throw on a tux, and we'll go. You don't even have to take a shower." Jessica smiled, hoping Harry would move from his couch-potato position and show some enthusiasm.

"Nah, I think I'll pass. I just ordered a few pizzas and the guys from Malibu might drop by. You go ahead though, and have a great time," Harry said, not even looking up at Jessica, his eyes still transfixed on the television.

Disappointed, Jessica left the den without saying a word and went back to Billie. "He said he doesn't want to go. I guess it's just you and me," Jessica said with a look of rejection in her big green eyes.

"It's okay, honey. You look like you need a hug." Billie took Jessica softly into her arms and gently stroked her thick, auburn curls. Doing her best to control her sexual urges, Billie cradled Jessica like a baby who needed to be soothed and comforted. As angry as she was with Harry for not making an effort to be with her, Jessica found solace in Billie's tender embrace. Right there in her marital bedroom, the seduction of Jessica Raider had begun.

★ ★ ★

When Jessica came home from the party, she snuck upstairs to find Harry fast asleep. She was still upset that he blew her off to be with his friends, so she wasn't particularly quiet while changing into her lingerie. A sleepy Harry slowly awoke to see his beautiful wife lying next to him in a pink silk camisole and matching G-string undies.

"Wow, you look beautiful," Harry told her, coming alive and kissing Jessica's bare shoulders.

"I really missed you tonight, Harry," Jessica admitted, finding herself enjoying her husband's affections.

"I missed you too," Harry said, kissing his way down to her neck and beginning to fondle her breasts.

"Then why didn't you come with me?" Jessica asked, moving his hand away.

"Hey, relax, Jes, I didn't think it was any big deal. You were with your friend Billie. I didn't think you really wanted me to come," Harry said.

"Of course I wanted you to come. Why else would I have asked you?" Jessica wanted to know but stopped fighting him off.

"I don't know, you guys have been having so much fun lately with this whole art thing, I didn't want to get in your way or make you feel you had to baby-sit me. This was a good event for you to show off at. I thought you were just being nice by inviting me, but I really thought you wanted to let Billie introduce you around." Harry held Jessica closer to him.

"Harry, I want you to enjoy this time with me. Billie's done so much for me, but you're the one I want to share my success with," Jessica said, searching her husband's eyes.

"That's really sweet, Jes. And I'm sorry if I've been distant lately or appear uninterested. It's just that I feel like

I've been running in circles. I can't seem to find a light at the end of the tunnel. But anyway, that's my problem. I want you to know how proud I am of you, Jessica, and how much I love you," Harry murmured sweetly in her ear.

"Oh, Harry, that means everything to me," Jessica said, smiling warmly. As they made love, their eyes locked and they reconnected.

"Nothing's happened yet, you know," Jessica said, grabbing Harry's hand, enjoying the afterglow of passionate, intimate lovemaking.

"I know, Jes. Maybe I have a low sperm count because I've been under so much stress." Harry felt a little less than manly.

"I'm not sure about that, Harry. I think it may be me. I've never been pregnant; maybe I just can't do it," Jessica said sadly.

"Listen, I doubt that's true. Let's not stress ourselves out about it, and just keep trying. It's not like we can't enjoy the process." Harry gave his wife a goodnight kiss.

"I guess so. Goodnight, my love," Jessica said, glad to have her husband's full attention again.

"Goodnight Jessica, sweet dreams of me," Harry joked, and the lovers drifted off into a deep sleep.

★★☆

The next day as Jessica painted in her garden, she seemed rather distracted. Billie noticed right away that Jessica was not herself that day. "Jessica, I don't mean to pry, but I can tell something is bothering you. What is it, honey? You can tell me." Billie put her arm around Jessica, lightly massaging her shoulders.

"It's Harry," Jessica said flatly.

Oh boy, this is it. The moment I've been waiting for. She's fed up and she's going to leave. Hallelujah, good-bye

Harry, Billie thought.

"What happened, honey? What did he do now to let you down?" Billie asked, whispering in Jessica's ear. She wanted so bad to blow in it and kiss her neck, but she thought it was best to wait until Jessica got whatever was bothering her off her chest.

"He can't seem to get me pregnant. We had a really good heart-to-heart talk last night, before we made love, and we are both going to make an effort to spend more time with each other. But still it's been months now, and nothing's happened. I think there might be something wrong with my eggs." Jessica would not look up from her painting. "I think I'm going to make an appointment to go see a fertility doctor next week. I'm dying to have a family with Harry as soon as possible."

Billie almost fell backwards. It never dawned on her that Jessica was still sleeping with Harry this whole time. Billie wanted to believe that Jessica was responding to her caresses and would soon be ready for a full-on encounter. But now she had just been blown out of the water.

Billie wanted to smash Chas Greer's head in. She was so upset that wanted to grab Jessica's canvas and rip it to shreds. Instead, Billie picked a bunch of flowers from an unsuspecting bush and began to pick the petals off, one by one. Swearing to herself that she wouldn't let Jessica see her lose her cool, Billie had no choice but to excuse herself. "Will you excuse me, doll face? I forgot, I have to make an important phone call," Billie said. She threw down her bouquet, got out her cell phone, and walked towards the front of the house.

"Why didn't you tell me she is still sleeping with her husband? I've opened up the entire LA art world for this girl and she may not ever be available. Have I been wasting my time and energy for nothing? What the hell is going on here?" Billie screamed at Chas, who was helping Luisa pick out tiles for the entranceway to the new hotel.

Oh God, Luisa and I are having a relatively uneventful day, the last thing I need is a furious lesbian on the rage, Chas thought to himself. When he heard it was Billie on the phone, he sneaked off to the bathroom so they could speak without being overheard. He had promised his boss that he would deliver Harry to her very soon, but he just needed a little more time. *Shit, I thought it would be best to reintroduce Harry to Luisa once Billie had begun to work Jessica over, but now it is pretty clear that Plan A isn't going too smoothly. Time is running out; I need to take some serious action,* Chas thought to himself.

"No, Billie, relax, everything will be fine. This is just a small snag, that's all. It's time to pull out the big guns. Don't fret, my dear Bill. As soon as my boss gets her hands on Harry, he won't know what hit him. Jessica will come running into your arms for sure."

"You better be right, Chassy. My last girlfriend left me for some rich bitch producer on the *Ellen DeGeneres Show.* I can't take any more rejection right now," Billie stammered.

"Don't go burning your bra just yet. Pretty soon, little Jessica Raider will be in deep need of some true sapphic support," Chas said reassuringly.

"How can you be so sure? Just when I thought that I was about to score a home run, I realize that I am still miles away from the finish line." Billie voice quivered as she brushed away a stream of tears.

"Oh Billie, don't be such a drama queen. You're not going to let a little setback like this get your way, are you? What happened to that tough chick with the brass ovaries that I've grown to love?" Chas cajoled, hoping to pacify her for the moment.

"I guess I'm still here," Billie said, blowing her nose and managing to crack a smile.

"Well that's good to know, baby. Now don't you worry, Chas has the solution that will take care of this matter once and for all," Chas said, running the water purposely so that Luisa couldn't hear any of his conversation.

"You promise?" Billie asked.

"I swear. I'll call you soon. Ciao for now," Chas said, shutting his phone off for the rest of the day, and returning to an afternoon of redecorating the lives of those around him.

chapter twenty-three

I think it's a brilliant idea to restart your father's business," Luisa said in a voice no louder than a kitten's purr as she showed Harry around the Bel Air property that would soon be the new home of Las Castillas. "I am so glad that Chas insisted you come here today to talk to me. It is nice to meet a man who is a visionary like me." Harry gazed around the once glamorous but now falling-down estate. Even though the cosmetics of the building itself were decrepit, the structural bones were still a work of majestic beauty. The grounds were a bit overgrown and neglected, but with a little landscaping and replanting, they could easily be restored to the former state of unparalleled elegance. Harry could understand why Luisa chose this property, and even though she had her work cut out for her, he knew the end result would be nothing short of spectacular.

"You do? I can't believe it. For months, everyone in the fashion business has turned me down flat. Even people who my dad started off wouldn't work with me," Harry said, gazing up at Luisa like he had just met his personal savior.

"They are small-minded people, Harry, who are scared to take a risk. They don't have the vision to see the bigger picture. And who knows, they may actually be afraid of you too," Luisa said, as the hilltop views of the majestic Pacific Ocean painted the perfect background scenery.

"Why the hell would anybody be afraid of me? If I swat a bee I feel guilty," Harry giggled with delight.

"Ah yes, Harry the joker. This is part of the deceptive image that you love to portray to make people believe that you are harmless." Luisa smiled knowingly.

"Really?" Harry replied, shrugging his shoulders, a little confused.

Luisa turned and looked at him straight in the eye. She then placed her hands firmly on both of his shoulders. "You are first and foremost a Raider; Sam Raider's son, no less. Don't you think people know that? In a sad way, some people may be secretly relieved that your dad is gone. With a giant like Sam out of the way, the lesser ones can breathe easier. However, the thought of Sam Raider's son stepping into his shoes must be absolutely terrifying to anyone who wants to stay in the children's clothing business," Luisa said.

"I never really thought of it like that. I just thought that nobody wanted to back me because I had no business experience," Harry said with excitement.

"Experience means nothing. All that can be gained over time. What matters most is where you come from and who your family is. You can change a lot of things, but you cannot change genetics. You are a Raider, just like I am the daughter of the brilliant Mandlebaum family. In that respect, we cannot change who we are, Harry. You and I are one in the same." Luisa looked Harry right in the eye and slowly reached for his hand.

Harry pulled his hand away and put it in his pocket. He was so nervous and excited by Luisa at the same time that he didn't even realize he was doing it. "You know my wife, Jessica, she's really the best and I love her madly, but she doesn't understand this whole thing at all. She is a very generous woman and would be happy to support me for the rest of our lives." Harry stared at the ground.

"Is that what you want, Harry? To be kept under lock and key? Do you want to be a male servant and have to answer to your wife's every whim and desire?" Luisa looked at him with pity as she pulled away and lit up a cigarette, instinctively knowing it was time to back off a little bit.

"Oh, she's not so bad. I'm sure there are a lot of women with her wealth who would be a lot more demanding," Harry said uncomfortably.

"Okay, well if that's what you want, to spend your life as your rich wife's butler, then I won't try to get in your way," Luisa said, turning away from Harry and beginning to walk back to her car. "I had what I thought was a wonderful business plan to present to you, but if you are not interested, then I understand."

Harry ran after her. "Wait a minute. Of course I'm interested. I was just saying how supportive Jessica has been through this whole thing financially, that's all. There is no way I want to live off of her money for the rest of our lives. Maybe she doesn't understand that now, but I bet she'd sure appreciate it if I was a big hit in my own right," Harry said.

Luisa turned back to Harry. "Maybe she doesn't think you can do it. Maybe she married you because she thought that you'd be a good playmate for her and that you'd never amount to anything on your own." Luisa searched her fifteen-thousand dollar Kelly bag for the keys to her Aston Martin.

"I don't know why she married me, frankly. I haven't exactly been husband of the year. But all I know is that I need to make my dad's old factory a success again, whether she understands that or not," Harry said firmly.

"Good. Now maybe we are ready to talk business," Luisa said seductively as she got into the driver's seat.

"What did you have in mind?" An anxious Harry placed his hands solidly on the door, so that Luisa couldn't blow him off and pull away.

"Do you really want to know?" Luisa asked, putting on her sunglasses.

"Of course I do," said Harry.

"Then get in and let me take you for a ride," Luisa answered, unlocking the door with her long, red, lion-like nails.

★★★

Harry and Luisa zoomed through the winding roads of the Hollywood Hills at a pace that would make a professional race-car driver fear for his life. "I love this car!" Luisa screamed above the wind in their faces and the sounds of a crooning Enrique Iglesias on her CD player.

"I see that," Harry replied. *Wow, this chick is nuts. I love it. Being with her is like being on a roller coaster. You never know what's going to happen next,* Harry thought, as they almost drove off the side of Coldwater Canyon.

Finally Luisa brought the car back to her property and parked in front of the imposing wrought-iron gate. The sun was slowly setting and there was not a cloud in the usually smoggy Los Angeles sky. "This place is going to be mind-blowing, I can feel it in my bones," Luisa said, proudly.

"I'm sure it will be, if you're behind it," Harry said with total admiration.

"That's very nice of you, Harry. I'm glad you believe in me, because I believe in you. Would you like to hear what I am thinking for *our* new business?"

"I'm dying to hear what you have in mind," Harry replied, finding himself falling under her hypnotic spell.

Luisa smiled devilishly and winked at Harry. She knew that she had him right where she wanted him. "I own a few working factories just outside of Acapulco. They make all kinds of embroidered fabrics and blankets there. It would be easy for me to start making children's clothing. Because I am so well-known in Latin America, I can use my name as the label and sell it into every department store. I could call the brand something like Luisa's Niñas. I am sure every mother who wants her child to look chic would buy my clothes. Anyway, once the line was making a lot of money in Latin America, I could bring it to the U.S. With a going product line, we'd have plenty of money to open your father's factory and make the clothes for the stores in the United States, right here," Luisa said, smoothly.

"Luisa, that would be incredible! But I don't understand what you need me for. If your factory in Mexico is making the clothes, why start making them here?" Harry said, curiously.

"Because American department-store buyers love to see that 'Made in the U.S.A.' label. It makes them feel less guilty. Besides, Harry, let's face it, I am only one woman and I cannot run my hotel business and be responsible for overseeing a children's clothing line as well. I know you have what it takes to get us to the top and I'm going to make sure you get there," Luisa said, touching Harry's hand lightly.

This time he did not pull away. "Thank you so much, Luisa. You won't be sorry. Everybody thinks that Harry Raider is a total fuck-up, but you'll see how wrong they are." Harry shook Luisa's hand in a businesslike manner. *Damn, I feel like I can do anything with this chick. I've never felt that way with anybody in my entire life before. Being around her is like being on an endless adventure,* Harry thought, as he started to get out of her car.

"Oh, Harry, now that we are going to be partners, I'd love to get your opinion about what Chas is doing for my hotel, too. Can you join me for a quick drink before you go home?" Luisa asked nonchalantly.

"I'm really supposed to be home early. I think Jessica has some kind of special dinner planned," Harry confessed.

"It will only take a minute. Please, Harry, I desperately need your advice," Luisa piped her best little-girl voice, the same one that she reserved for her father.

"Well, OK, as long as it doesn't take too long." Harry got into the driver's seat of his wife's Bentley and followed Luisa down the steep canyon.

★ ★ ★

The Beverly Hills Hotel was Hollywood's favorite watering hole for the rich and famous. Chas was waiting in Harry's favorite booth in the Polo Lounge, and so happy to see the new business partners arrive with smiles on their faces. "I'm guessing that Harry liked your idea," Chas said, sipping a Perrier and lime. He was slightly hungover from the night before, when he consumed the three bottles of wine after Jessica said she wanted to go to a fertility doctor.

"Yep, and I owe it all to you for bringing Luisa and me together. We are going to make a great team," Harry told Chas, pawing into a bowl of peanuts on the table.

"So glad to hear it," Chas said, winking at Luisa wryly.

Luisa took the bowl of peanuts away from Chas. Making no excuses, she ferociously grabbed a handful and downed it, like she hadn't eaten in a week. "And now that Harry and I will be working closely together, I want him to know everything that's going on with the hotel-opening party. Chas, I know that you have been speaking to every publicist in town and we have all the top celebrity names coming to the opening, along with the best caterer, the hottest band, and press lining up to get coverage," Luisa said, speaking shamelessly with her mouth full. "However, Harry was born and bred here in Beverly Hills, therefore I think he will be able to let us know if there is something more we should be doing." Luisa took out a cigarette and lit it. She inhaled twice and flicked her ashes into the peanut bowl, ruining any chances Chas thought he had of getting another snack. "I want this to be the party of the century, the biggest blow-out that Beverly Hills has ever seen and I think Harry could be quite influential to making that happen. Don't you agree, Chas?" Luisa gave Chas a swift kick under the table.

"Oh, yes, definitely. Harry is the LA party king. If anyone knows how to have a good time, it's certainly him," said Chas.

"No, no, I've retired from all of that. I don't party anymore at all, I'm just an old, boring, married man," Harry joked, checking his watch and realizing that he was soon expected home.

"I'm sorry to hear that," Luisa said, signaling the waiter and ordering a round of margaritas with extra tequila shots on the side. "I was hoping that you would show a single girl how to have a good time in Los Angeles, Harry."

"Well that depends. How wild you want to get?" Harry laughed, as the waiter delivered the drinks. *I was only going to have a Diet Coke, but these margaritas look so awesome. Besides, I'm right around the corner from my house. I can leave the car here and walk home if I get a little buzzed,* Harry thought, swallowing the drink and the extra kick on the side.

"The wilder the better. In my country, people talk too much, so I always have to be on good behavior. Here in America I feel free to have a good time and enjoy all of the naughty things I've been missing," Luisa said, seductively sucking on her straw. As hard as he tried not to be obvious, Harry couldn't take his eyes off of Luisa. Somehow the top buttons of her silk blouse seemed to have come undone, giving him an unblocked view of her fabulous, tanned cleavage. He could even see one large, brown, pointy nipple, somewhat poking through her flimsy black lace bra.

Luisa sensed Harry checking her out and felt like she had him right where she wanted him. "Chas, I think you have your own plans for the evening. I won't keep you any longer. Thank you for joining us here. You are dismissed," Luisa said.

"Sure, you bet, I'm outta here. You guys have fun," Chas squealed, relieved that he didn't have to bear witness to the unraveling of Harry's marriage.

As soon as Chas was gone, Luisa furtively slipped off her panties and passed them under the table to Harry. "Does this tell you how wild I want to be? I feel like a caged animal that has finally been set free. I want you to show me everything, Harry. Don't hold anything back," Luisa said, licking her lips.

Harry's hands were beginning to sweat as he held onto her red lace thong with a death grip. *Shit, what am I going to do now? If I do anything, I'm a dead man and my marriage will basically be over. But if I refuse her, I run the risk of insulting her and then she won't want to back my business. How the hell did I get myself into this situation?* Harry wondered and ordered more drinks.

"Luisa, I know a group of guys in Malibu who will do anything for a good time. They have insane parties every night. I can hook you up with them and I promise you'll have the time of your life." Harry hoped this would offer some kind of a solution.

"I don't feel comfortable partying alone with a group of strangers. That's no fun, Harry. I want you to come with me. Something tells me you want to come too," Luisa said, taking her panties out of Harry's hand and rubbing them on the crotch of his pants.

"If you want to party, sweetheart, then you better follow me," Harry told her, pushing himself away from the table and getting up in one swift move. *I better get us the hell out of here,* Harry thought as he threw some money on the table to pay for the drinks, grabbed Luisa buy the hand, and lead her towards the valet.

Harry tipped the valet a hundred dollars to bring his and Luisa's cars around ASAP. He normally wasn't that free with Jessica's money. "I'll see you in the 'Bu, stay right behind me," Harry said to Luisa, quickly jumping into the Bentley. The BU was the ultra-hip nickname that native Los Angelinos gave to Malibu.

"Don't worry, baby, I'm all over your ass," Luisa purred.

Harry just nodded politely and pulled the car onto Sunset Boulevard. *Okay, I'm still a little buzzed and shouldn't be driving, but I have to get Luisa set up with my boys out in the BU. They'll totally show her a good time, and then she won't need to be all over me. Damn, she's so fucking hot. I'm a married man, I'm a married man, I'm a married man,* Harry repeated to himself.

After forty-five minutes of fighting Friday night traffic on the Pacific Coast Highway, Harry, followed by Luisa, finally pulled into the gravel driveway in front of Mikey Roman's beach house. When he escorted her to the front door, he noticed that it was unusually quiet, especially for the beginning of the weekend.

Harry took the hidden key buried under a cactus plant near the front door and let himself in. Soon Luisa and Harry were all alone, standing in the middle of the huge, white living room overlooking the sparkling waves. "I guess they're not here," Harry said, fidgeting uncomfortably. "Maybe they went to Vegas, or took a road trip to Palm Springs. They do that sometimes. I'm sorry I dragged you all the way out here, but at least you know where the house is, so you can find it anytime you are in the mood to party. My friends usually have something going on here day and night. Just tell them you are a friend of mine and believe me, they'd be happy to have a hot chick like you join right in." By this time the liquor had worn off and he wasn't sure how he was going to get himself out of the situation.

"I'm glad you think I'm hot, Harry, but I wish that we could be more than friends, don't you?" Luisa was, moving closer to him, soon taking his hand and moving him onto the white leather couch.

"You know Luisa, I would love to be with you, but I'm married. I can't. I'm sorry," Harry said, summoning up all of what was left of his inner strength.

"Oh, that is too bad. You know, it's been so long since I've been with a man, Harry. It's not every day that I find someone as interesting and, well, exciting as Harry Raider, king of Hollywood. Can you blame me for wanting to have you ravish every inch of my body?" Luisa uncrossed her legs and twisted gently on the white leather.

How the fuck am I going to walk away from this? I'd have to be a flipping monk not to jump her right now, Harry thought as he felt his manhood rise to the occasion.

Just then the front door swung open and a buzzed-out Todd Krane entered with two unopened bottles of Merlot under his arm. "Well, Harry Raider, great to see you, dude. It's been too long, Brah! Who's the babe?" Todd asked, smiling mischievously.

"Uh, this is Luisa Mendez, my new business partner. She just moved here from Mexico and she's looking to meet some cool party people. Did I mention that she and I are business associates?" Harry mumbled nervously, repeating himself.

"YEAH RIIIIIIIIGHT!" Todd laughed out loud. "Look, me and the boys are down the street at this rockin' party. You won't believe this, but La Crema Models, they're like the hottest lingerie modeling agency in LA, rented a house out here to put up some of their new girls from Europe. Is this a fucking dream come true or what? Anyway, if you guys want to join us, it's number 24, okay? See ya," Todd said, as he grabbed a bottle opener and raced out the door.

"Let me take you down there to meet everyone, okay, Luisa?" Harry said, jumping up, excited that he had been given a real way.

"Only if you promise we can continue where we left off later," Luisa said, smoothing out her tight skirt and pulling herself together as she stood up and followed Harry out the door.

"Let's see what happens. You may be having so much fun, you may never want to turn back." Harry and Luisa walked a few doors down to another modernistic wood-and-glass beachside mansion. The castle by the sea was filled with young girls with foreign accents and the rich, male modelizers who followed their every move, hoping to bed as many beauties as their testosterone levels would permit.

Techno music was blaring as Harry brought Luisa over to the bar where an obviously underage Russian girl with green eyes and flaming red hair was pouring vodka and ice into a blender. "Just stay here one minute and I'll find my friends," Harry said, searching the room for a familiar face.

"Yo, Harry, in here," Bill Ladd called out from the oversized Jacuzzi in the black marble bathroom. Bill was having his usual threesome, this time with a long-legged Portuguese stunner and a blonde, blue-eyed, six-foot-two creature from Iceland. The sight of his friend having raucous sex with such wild abandon wasn't making it any easier for Harry to want to control himself. *God, these guys have it made. They party night and day, get their rocks off with whomever they want to, and don't have to answer to anybody the next morning. What a life! What am I missing?* Harry wondered, as he was transfixed by the sight of the Icelandic giant bobbing her head up and down underwater as she sucked Bill's cock, only coming up for air when absolutely necessary.

While he stood there contemplating the wild life he had willingly traded for a shot at wedded bliss, Harry felt someone rubbing up behind him and could smell Luisa's earthy, musky, alluring womanly scent fill the space around him. "Looks like fun," Luisa whispered in his ear. Harry turned around to see Luisa standing there totally nude. Her mocha-cappuccino-colored breasts, dark-cocoa hardened nipples, and goddess-like proportions were more magnificent than he had fantasized. Without saying a word, Luisa unbuttoned Harry's shirt and then unzipped his fly with her teeth. Before he could protest, she was sucking his manhood with her red painted lips and scratching his balls playfully with her long, cat-like nails.

It happened so fast, he couldn't stop her or have time to think about what he was doing. An out-of-control Harry exploded down her throat. She quickly got up, took Harry's hand, and led him over to the Jacuzzi.

After experiencing what felt like total ecstasy, an exhausted Harry stopped himself from doing any more damage. "I'm sorry Luisa, I just can't. Not tonight, anyway," Harry caught himself saying as he pulled up his pants.

"Suit yourself, darling," Luisa said, licking her lips and slowly walking into the Jacuzzi.

"I'm really sorry to have to rush off like this, it's just…" a nervous Harry stammered, when Luisa cut him off midsentence.

"Thank you for a wonderful evening, Harry. I'm sorry if I made you late for dinner. I won't keep you any longer. I know you have to get home to your wife." Luisa smiled wryly and seductively bobbed under the bubbling water.

As Harry fumbled his way out of the orgy, a part of him felt like there was no going back to being Jessica's good boy. Somewhere in his soul, Harry Raider had reached the point of no return. He had played with drugs when he shouldn't have, but he had never cheated on Jessica since he had committed himself to her the summer before in the Hamptons. Last summer, when he first found true love, seemed like a lifetime ago. So much had changed, yet the old Harry Raider, a man who lived only to satisfy his naughty urges, seemed to have stayed the same.

As Harry drove himself home, through his mind ran a litany of self-destructive thoughts. *I can never be the man Jessica wants or needs. I have to tell her what happened and ask her to divorce me. She'd be so much better off. Luisa is a hot piece of ass who's obviously been around. There's nothing I could do to shock a sophisticated chick like that or ruin her life. She's seen it all. Maybe that's what I should have—a sexy, ruthless bitch, who's a tough business partner and a wild lover. That way we both can have a good time and no one gets hurt. I knew it was too good to be true with Jessica; eventually I had to go and fuck it up.* Harry reached his and Jessica's estate and buzzed himself in through the big, imposing gates that falsely appeared to protect his family from the rest of the world. He quietly tiptoed into the house.

★★★

Harry found his wife sitting on a stool at the long, granite island in the middle of the kitchen. Harry could barely look Jessica in the eye. Instead, he picked up Cindy the poodle, who faithfully sat under Jessica's stool, munching on the crumbs of a stale prune Danish. "I'm sorry I missed dinner. I can explain," Harry said, nervously petting the pooch, who didn't look happy to be taken away from her late-night snack. "Chas introduced to me to his boss, Luisa Mendez, and she wants to back my business," Harry said, staring down into the perfectly groomed tuft of hair on Cindy's head.

"That's great, Harry. I know that's what you really want," Jessica said stoically, not looking up from her coffee. Harry was completely unnerved by his wife's overly calm reaction, so he decided to push the truth a little further. "You know she's new here, so she wanted me to take her to some parties and introduce her around, so I took her out to Malibu and…"

"That's okay, Harry, I'm not mad. Actually, I needed this time to be alone and think." Jessica took a slow, steady sip of her coffee while still not looking at her husband. *Okay, here it is. She's totally fed up with me and she's finally going to dump me and go back to East Hampton. I just ruined the best thing that's ever happened to me and now I'm about to get what I deserve,* Harry thought as he put the whining pooch back down under Jessica's stool and let her happily return to her sticky crumbs.

Jessica went over the microwave and started to make herself a cup of hot cocoa. "I think we should go see a fertility doctor. We've been trying for months now and nothing's happened. I made an appointment for lunchtime tomorrow. I hope you don't mind that I didn't talk to you about this first, Harry, but because of both our ages, I really feel like it's time to take stronger action," Jessica said resolutely, looking up at Harry.

Harry just stood their trying his not to look too shocked by what he had just heard. He was faced with the choice of a lifetime. *Okay, obviously somebody likes me up there and wants me to have a second chance. I can either go along with Jessica, act like nothing happened with Luisa, and try to figure out a way to save my marriage, or I can tell Jessica what really happened and cut my losses before I cause her any more disappointment,* Harry thought, as he walked over to the sink and threw some cold water on his face.

"Harry, are you okay? You look like you are going to pass out."

"I'm fine, Jessica," Harry said, running some cold water through his wavy hair, wanting to wash away any part of Luisa that might still be lingering.

"Listen, I know this is a lot to spring on you, but, Harry, I really think the time is right to do this now. Please don't let me down." Jessica got up from her stool and handed Harry a clean dishtowel to wipe himself with.

How can I, Jes? How can I? Harry thought as he hopelessly gazed into Jessica's sea-green eyes. He realized how much he still loved her. Luisa intrigued him and supplied the excitement he desperately craved, but Jessica was the only one who could really touch his tattered soul. She reached for Harry's hand, looked at him lovingly, and searched his face for what she hoped was the right answer.

"Let's go for it," Harry said, shrugging his shoulders and putting the towel in the sink.

"Harry Raider, you're the most wonderful husband in the world!" An exuberant Jessica jumped into Harry's arms and covered him with kisses. "As much as I want to make love to you right now, we really shouldn't in case the doctor wants a sperm sample or something. You know, you should give him a fresh batch," Jessica laughed. Her eyes now danced with sheer delight and she was overcome with joy at the thought of becoming a mother. "Let's go up and get right to sleep, so we'll be nice and rested for tomorrow.

It's going to be a beautiful day," Jessica chirped, as she practically skipped out of the kitchen and ran up the winding staircase. Harry followed behind her like a dutiful husband. *I must have done something right in another lifetime,* Harry thought, as he climbed into bed and put his arms around Jessica. As he fell asleep, Harry envisioned a cleansing tidal wave sweeping through Malibu, washing his sins of the evening safely out to sea.

chapter twenty-four

Y ou want me to give them blanks?" a shocked Dr. Scott Pierce, Hollywood's top fertility man, asked when Chas Greer stopped by his office. Dr. Pierce was responsible for producing more celebrity offspring than God himself. His reputation was worldwide. Yet like everyone who catered to the rich and famous, the last thing he wanted to do was piss off an "insider" who could get vicious, like catty Chas Greer.

"That's right. Shoot her up with dead sperm or sugar water for all I care. Just make sure there is no way that Jessica Raider gets pregnant, do you understand me?" Chas spoke in a loud whisper, making sure the doctor's nosy receptionist wouldn't hear him through the paper-thin walls.

"How do you know that Jessica Raider is even coming here? My patients usually like to keep their visits strictly confidential," Dr. Pierce told Chas.

"Confidential to the rest of the world maybe, but not to Chas Greer. Some very powerful people in this town don't make a move without consulting me first. How do you think I knew that Jessica Raider was coming here today?

Hmmm? Think about that one, Doc," Chas said, raising an eyebrow while pretending to look down at the medical degrees from Harvard hanging on the wall.

"But if I do that, and the treatment doesn't work, she'll just go to another specialist," replied a confused Dr. Pierce, shaking his head and rummaging nervously through his desk drawer.

"Not necessarily, my good doctor. My hope is that Jessica will just give up and realize it's just not meant for her and Harry to have children," Chas said, matter of factly.

"Chas, I know how influential you are in those high-flying circles, but do you think it's fair for you to be playing God?" Dr. Pierce asked, trying to reason with someone who was being quite unreasonable.

"Why not? You do it every day, don't you? What's the matter, you don't like it when somebody else can also work a few miracles?" Chas waved his fingers at the doctor like he was waving a magic wand. "Let me tell you something, Dr. Pierce, I know what's best for my clients. I've known Jessica Raider for many years and I am telling you, there is absolutely *no way* she is mentally stable enough to handle having children. Especially with a professional playboy like that juvenile delinquent, Harry Raider. He *is* her *baby*, do you understand that? While Harry Senior is out screwing every whore in town and snorting lines of cocaine, his offspring will be left in the care of a cold nanny, who won't give a rat's ass about what happens to the poor little thing." Chas paced around the room.

"Chas, I still can't give a patient 'blank' sperm, even if you assure me that it's in everyone's best interest. If word got out, I'd be ruined," Dr. Pierce said, slowly closing his drawer.

"Dr. Pierce, if you don't do this, by the time I get through with you, you'll never make another baby in LA, New

York, or anywhere else where there are rich, desperate, barren women," Chas said, confidently sitting down in the armchair in front of the doctor.

"Are you threatening me?" Dr. Pierce countered, refusing to be intimidated by Chas's grandstanding.

"Now, Dr. Pierce, there is no need to get testy. Have I forgotten to mention that I've come with a peace offering?" Chas said, changing from a demanding diva to a voice as sweet as honey. Chas slowly reached into his Luis Vuitton men's purse and pulled out a large, unmarked manila envelope. "Two hundred and fifty thousand dollars cash, our gift for your trouble, sir. That should help ease your conscience a little or at least make the pain go away, don't you think?"

"I don't think I should open this," Dr. Pierce said with a lump in his throat, nervously running his hands through his hair.

"Go on, Doc. Nobody would expect you work for free. You're really doing these people a big service. They just don't know it yet," Chas said, sliding the envelope across the doctor's desk.

"Chas, I really can't," Dr. Pierce said, staring down at the temptation that lay before him.

"*You must, Doctor!* You'll be very sorry if you don't. That I promise you," Chas insisted, lowering his voice to just above a whisper and pushing the envelope right into the doctor's lap.

The doctor reluctantly took picked it up and held it tight. "It's only because I have four kids of my own in college at the same time that I'm doing this," he said, looking down at the money and shamefully putting it into a safe he kept hidden under his desk.

"Whatever you say, doc. So I'm assuming we have a deal?" Chas asked, heading for the door.

"Reluctantly so," Dr. Pierce conceded, shaking his head

in embarrassment, far from comfortable about what he had done. "Just one question, Chas. You said 'our gift.' Who is 'our'?" Dr. Pierce asked.

"That is none of your business, doctor. Have a good day," Chas replied and showed himself out of the office.

Once in the parking lot, Chas quickly got in the passenger seat of a black Porsche that was idling in the driveway. "Take off! Let's get out of here before he sees you!" Chas exclaimed as the hot rod peeled onto Beverly Boulevard.

"Did he take my money?" asked the driver, anxiously.

"Of course he took your money. It's Hollywood, honey. Everyone is for sale. Nobody should know that better than you; you're an agent for heaven's sakes," Chas told Billie Blaine as she raced through the streets of West Hollywood. "Looks like your best friend Jessica is really going to need you for support," Chas said sarcastically, donning his coolest shades and blasting Cher's *Farewell Tour* CD on the car's raging stereo system. Chas and Billie treated themselves to breakfast at the Polo Lounge before they both had to begin their day jobs. For now at least, the power broker and the power player were making the world go round, turning obediently in the right direction.

★★★

During the next three months, Harry Raider led a double life, and he secretly loved every minute of it. His days were spent tagging along with Luisa, watching her put the finishing touches on her hotel and getting everything ready for the grand-opening party. At first there was just some harmless flirting going on between them, but that escalated into a suggestive squeeze here and there. As time went on the hugs got longer and closer, and the kisses on the cheeks became pecks on the lips, and then a little tongue was slipped in. Harry was slowly but surely getting drawn into

Luisa and falling deeply under her magnetic spell. Harry found himself wanting more and more of her. He would masturbate in his car thinking about her and it was Luisa's face he saw when he had "married-trying-to-procreate" sex with his wife.

Finally it all got to be too much for Harry, and like any good drug addict, he gave in to the overwhelming temptation that provocative Luisa flashed in face every time they were together. Harry and Luisa began having a full-on affair. They would sneak away whenever they could for a little afternoon delight. They had passionate, Earth-shattering sex everywhere from the back seat of her Aston Martin to the construction site of the hotel to what was perhaps the naughtiest place of all, his parents' former bedroom, which was now Luisa's personal pleasure pit.

In the evenings, Harry would have to go home to Jessica. Jessica was happy to keep to herself all day, painting or checking out galleries with Billie, so she didn't really miss Harry's presence during the daylight hours. She also had become so obsessed with having a child that her interest in lovemaking just for the fun of it had lost its appeal. Poor Jessica just wanted to get pregnant already. She regularly took Dr. Pierce's bogus fertility drugs and waited for a miracle. Sex became only a means to an end. That was fine with Harry, because he was getting the excitement he needed from his nasty afternoons with Luisa. And Luisa knew just how to work Harry over and play him like her own personal toy. If he ever dared to show up tired or worn out from all of the sexual activity that was required from him both at home and on the work front, Luisa would get him aroused anyway.

She would suggestively drop hints about how she had started her children's clothing line in Mexico, and how orders were beginning to ship to department stores all over

Latin America. Soon there would be enough profits to bring her business to Los Angeles and reopen Sam's factory, she would remind Harry if he didn't perform as she desired. This thought alone was enough to turn Harry into the Energizer Bunny so he could hump Luisa until she was satisfied. Strangely enough, even though Harry had never really worked a day in his life, he got a raging hard-on from the thought of being financially successful.

Another interesting thing was happening to Harry Raider. Since he began his affair with Luisa, he had no more desire for drugs or even the occasional drink. Harry had discovered something actually more addictive than a line of coke or a salty, cold margarita: the allure of forbidden sex. Harry thought he was one lucky man and was hoping that life as he knew it would continue on down this smooth and sultry road. He believed he had the best of both worlds and never thought about the day that his charmed existence would ever be threatened. Once again, Harry Raider was due for a serious wake-up call. And it came sooner than he expected.

★ ★ ★

Harry woke up and tiptoed into the bathroom, so as not to wake Jessica. He thought he could quietly get dressed, sneak some breakfast, and then be off. Much to his dismay, when he came out of the shower, he found Jessica sitting on the toilet, sobbing hysterically, holding yet another negative pregnancy test in her tiny hand. "You shouldn't be so upset, Jes. It's only been a few months. I read somewhere that some people have to try for years before anything happens. Don't you think you're overreacting a little?" Harry caught himself saying, trying his best not to sound insensitive.

"Sometimes I think you just don't care if we ever have a baby, Harry. I'm beginning to feel like I'm the only one who wants this," Jessica cried as she threw the sad-news pregnancy test into the garbage.

"That's ridiculous, Jes. I told you that I am ready to be a father now that I know that the factory will eventually open again. But there are other things I have to focus on right now, like starting my own business. You wouldn't be so impatient if you had more of a life, Jes," Harry said, losing patience a little too soon, as he hurried back into the bedroom and put on his clothes.

"What the hell is that supposed to mean, Harry?" Jessica screamed after him, her sadness turning to rage at her husband's flippant attitude.

"I mean, maybe you should be a little more serious about advancing your art business. All you do is paint and hang out at galleries. You haven't let Billie set up any shows for you and you don't even try to sell your work."

"Why should I, Harry? Those things aren't important to me. Having our baby is. I decided to put on everything in the art world on hold until the baby comes and maybe indefinitely. What's wrong with being a stay-at-home mom? I think that's the greatest job on earth. It's not like *I* need the money," Jessica needled him as she searched for a tissue to wipe her eyes. This was the first time since Harry lost his fortune that she had reminded him that hers was still very much intact. It was the farthest thing from Jessica's true nature to throw her vast wealth in anybody's face, especially her own husband's, but right now her unshakable billions seemed like the only thing she could count on.

"Yeah, well, Jes, there are lots of rich women who want to be successful. Just because you still have all of your money, doesn't mean you shouldn't try to be..."

"Be WHAT? More like Luisa?" Jessica screamed at the top of her lungs and gave Harry an accusatory look. Up until this horrible morning, Jessica had chosen to keep her head in the sand about the time her husband spent with the Mexican temptress so that she could focus on getting pregnant. Now it was painfully obvious to her that Harry was slipping away. He darted around the room, frantically searching for his shoes, his eyes glued to the floor so he wouldn't have to look her in the eye. "I'll never be like her, Harry," Jessica said, sorrowfully noticing the look of relief on Harry's face, as he removed his Bruno Maglis from Cindy's mouth.

"Yeah, yeah, I know, Jes," was all Harry could say as he put on his dog-bitten loafers and rushed out the door. *Holy shit, I feel so damn guilty, but I just can't face this whole thing now. How can she understand that Luisa is the only person who will give me a chance to prove myself in business, eventually? How can Jessica expect me to just walk away from an opportunity like that, when she doesn't want to do anything but stay home and have babies?* Harry thought as he moved down the stairs as quickly as possible and ran out the door.

Jessica sat alone on the big feathered bed that used to be her and Harry's private sanctuary. *I am such an idiot! It's unbelievable not to have realized what's been going on. How could I think that Harry wouldn't be swept up by Luisa?* Jessica thought as she cried uncontrollably.

"Go after him," Jessica heard a shaken, feeble voice say. "Go after him, Jessica. He's a man, and men are weak. His father was exactly the same way."

Irma Raider stood in her Armani bathrobe, resting on her cane in Jessica's doorway. Since Irma had moved in with Harry and Jessica, she had stayed out of their way and never once interfered in their marriage. She had rested in her suite, watching television, reading classic novels, and looking at scrapbooks filled with pictures of happier days. Today was different. Irma was determined to step in and help. "Now get your sorry ass out of bed and go bring Harry home," Irma advised Jessica sternly, as she turned and wobbled back down the hallway. Jessica couldn't help but laugh at her mother-in-law's attempt to recapture her old self, for the sake of saving her son's marriage. *Once a Jewish mother, always a Jewish mother,* Jessica thought to herself, taking Irma's advice. She was determined to kick some serious butt. A re-energized Jessica did the "high five" sign in Irma's direction. The younger Mrs. Raider was psyched and ready for action.

In a matter of minutes Jessica was dressed and about to get into her Bentley. Before she could take off, though, Billie Blaine pulled into the driveway. "Where you going, Jes? I thought we were going to go for a walk on the Santa Monica Pier and then to look at the new galleries on Venice Beach. I took off work for the whole day, just to be with you," Billie called, sticking her head out of the window of her black Porsche.

"I can't hang out, Billie. I have to go see Harry at Luisa's. It's urgent. I'll call you later on," Jessica yelled to her friend, as she got into her car and raced down the street.

When Jessica was safely out of sight, Billie rang Chas on her cell phone. He was working downstairs in Luisa's office as Luisa and Harry were upstairs enjoying breakfast in bed. "You mean she's on her way here right now? Oh my God, this is perfect. She'll catch them in the sack fucking their brains out and their marriage will be over. Of course, I'm sure I can count on you to be there for sweet little Jessica, to comfort her in her time of need." Chas let out an evil little laugh.

"My arms are wide open, Chas baby, just make sure all goes as planned," Billie smiled, and took a sip of her freshly squeezed guava-kiwi juice from the to-go cup that sat in the cup holder near the front seat.

"I'm on it," Chas said, inhaling a huge puff of his clove cigarette as he heard Jessica's Bentley pull into the driveway.

Chas stood still and gazed out the window for a moment, watching Jessica walk purposefully up towards the massive front door. Everything had played right into his hands, just the way he needed it to. Harry was upstairs with Luisa and soon, Jessica would walk right in and catch them. Jessica would most likely throw Harry out and he would have no other choice but to marry Luisa, especially since she had promised him so much—at least professionally. Jessica would go running back to East Hampton, heartbroken. Chas, having delivered Luisa a husband to keep her father happy, could go on living the California high life, even if he had sold his soul to the devil to do it.

Chas should have been thrilled that everything worked out in his favor, but for reasons he could not explain, he was anything but. There was a deep pit in his stomach, his head was beginning to throb, and his hands were uncharacteristically shaky and sweaty. He knew he could run upstairs and warn Harry that Jessica was coming, or try to get her to go away. He had the power to salvage what was left of this sad situation, or at least stall for time and let Harry and Jessica work it out.

I hate feeling like this. Guilt is so unattractive; it's an emotion that should remain strictly for peasants. Chas nervously lit another cigarette. *I mean, why should I care about them? Do they care about me? Well, they pretend they do, but they don't actually. All those spoiled rich brats care about is themselves. Why should I give a rat's ass about who marries who, as long as I get what I want, and that's Luisa's fine salary? It's a hell of a lot more cash than cheap-ass Jessica ever paid me. Oh, bloody hell, why do I feel so bad about doing this? I shouldn't feel this way.* Chas took one big last drag and defiantly stubbed the smoke out on the marble floor instead of neatly in the ashtray.

Chas was there to open the door before Jessica had a chance to ring the bell. "Hi there, honey, I saw you coming. Harry's upstairs with Luisa, uh, working on something for the clothing line... I guess. Why don't you go on up and see what they're doing. I've gotta run. Ciao." Chas air-kissed Jessica as he flew past her before she could even say hello. "Rocky, I've gotta meet a designer on Melrose. I'm late, let's go, *toute suite!*" Chas yelled to his hot driver, as he snapped his fingers and got in the back seat of his white Rolls Royce. Sensing the urgency of Chas's command, Rocky put on his chauffeur's cap, and got in the car to drive without even putting his shirt on. This didn't seem to bother Chas in the least. All he wanted to do was to get out of there before Jessica caught Harry in bed with Luisa and the shit hit the fan.

chapter twenty-five

Jessica knew something was very wrong, right away. It wasn't like Chas to run off without schmoozing a while, even if he was going to be late for his next appointment. Jessica felt she had no choice but to stay and confront whatever was happening upstairs.

Slowly, Jessica climbed the stairs. As she approached the top, she heard sounds of unbridled passion coming from the master suite. Her heart fell as she recognized those sounds as the same ones that once filled her own bedroom. Even worse, brazen Harry and Luisa had left the door open, as if to tell the world that they didn't care who knew that they were lovers.

As Harry collapsed and rolled to Luisa's side, he saw Jessica standing in the hallway out of the corner of his eye. Lying there and trying to catch his breath, Harry thought that he was just seeing things. Soon he realized that indeed, it was no mirage: Jessica was there in the flesh, standing in the hallway, and she silently turned and walked down the stairs to go home.

"Oh my God! Jessica, wait!" Harry screamed, as he wrapped a sheet around his lower half and started to go after her.

"Stop it, Harry. Just let her go," Luisa said, roughly pulling on Harry's arm and knocking him back onto the bed. Before he knew it, she had pounced on him and pressed her naked breasts against his chest so hard that he could barely move. "You don't need her anymore, Harry. You have me. We belong together. It's time for us now," Luisa said, pinning Harry to the bed like a professional wrestler.

"I gotta to talk to her," Harry gasped, using what was left of his strength to release himself.

"Harry, you are testing my patience. Get back in this bed RIGHT NOW!" Luisa demand in a fit of frustration as she pounded on the headboard like a spoiled child.

"I'm sorry, but she's my wife," Harry said, getting dressed as fast as she could.

The next thing Harry knew, Luisa was running around the room like a crazy woman, smashing Cartier vases against the wall and trying to break a Tiffany china bowl over his head. "Do you think you can just fuck me like some dirty, useless slut and then go running back to your stupid little boring wife? How dare you insult me like this! In Mexico I could have you killed for disrespecting me and damaging my honor. You have done a horrible thing! A man like you should be dying to marry me!"

Harry froze in complete shock. He hadn't seen Luisa lose her cool before and he certainly never thought she could behave like this. "I thought you were all about your business and didn't want to get married! I thought we were just having fun. You don't want to marry me Luisa, really you don't. You deserve better than me." Harry tried to reason as Luisa threw a twenty-four-thousand-dollar antique chair over the balcony and into the hedges. Luisa climbed up onto the railing and acted like she was going to throw herself over the balcony as well. She made sure she faced the area that overlooked the hard cement driveway, with nothing to block her fall.

"Luisa, please, come down from there. Let's talk about this. Please!" Harry cried as he tugged on her leg.

"You have disgraced me, Harry. How can I possibly live with myself?" Luisa moved her feet a little bit, like she was getting ready to jump.

"Luisa, if you just come down from there, I promise we can work something out," Harry pleaded, afraid that she really might go over the edge. A part of him felt that she was crazy enough to really do it.

"Are you saying you will marry me if I come down, Harry?" Luisa asked, as she swayed back and forth.

Okay, Raider, try to think straight. Just say something, any-thing, to calm this crazy bitch down. Tell her what she wants to hear, Harry thought. "Right now I'm still married, but who knows what will happen? Jessica probably doesn't want me anymore after what she's just seen. Please, Luisa, give me a chance to figure this whole mess out," Harry begged.

Now that she was finally making headway, Luisa decided it was time to stop faking. "Take my hand, Harry," she demanded, and Harry helped her off of the railing and led her off of the balcony into the safety of the bedroom. "Harry, please don't leave. I have waited so long for us to be together. If you go back to Jessica, I'm afraid I'll never see you again. We could have such a wonderful future together. I wanted to help you build such a tremendous empire, something that your father would have been so proud of. Jessica wouldn't do that for you, Harry, only I would. Jessica doesn't love you and understand you the way I do, Harry. Haven't I shown you that?" Luisa forced herself to cry in Harry's arms.

"You have shown me how much faith you have in me, Luisa, and I so much appreciate that, but..." Harry mumbled, not knowing what to say, as he held what he thought was a fragile Luisa close to his chest.

"Isn't that what marriage is supposed to be about? A man and a woman who would do anything to help each other fulfill their dreams?" Luisa asked, in the manipulative voice she saved for moments like these.

"Yes, Luisa," Harry replied, stroking her thick, wavy hair.

"I love you, Harry. I'd do anything for you, *mi amor*," Luisa gently purred, as Harry rocked her back and forth.

Harry sat with Luisa in silence. He knew he was in way over his head and didn't really know what to say. *On one hand, Luisa is totally right on. She has gone the extra mile and started a kids' clothing line down in Mexico, with the hopes of helping me open my factory here. She didn't have to do that. Jessica never really believed that I could make it on my own. Yet, I know she really loves me and wants to start a family. Both of these women are terrific in their own way and I don't know what to do. I just don't know,* Harry thought to himself.

Luisa made sure that Harry stayed with her the rest of the day. Every time he tried to leave she'd pretend to get really upset. To prevent another balcony scare, Harry remained by her side. Only when Harry promised that he'd be back to spend the night with her did she let him go home.

★★★

It was around six thirty in the evening when Harry got back to the house he shared with Jessica. Things were eerily silent. Harry walked around the downstairs, feeling like an intruder in his own home. Finding no trace of Jessica, he went upstairs and headed towards their bedroom. The housekeeper had made up the room and the bed looked like no one had ever slept in it. Harry wanted so badly to flop down and collapse on top of it, but he didn't dare.

Somehow he felt going near Jessica's bed at this point would be adding insult to injury, so instead he just stared out the window, wondering how he let his life become such a mess. Harry couldn't help but notice how the sun was slowly setting behind him, illuminating the entrance to the untouched nursery. Harry felt himself pulled towards the little room that Jessica wanted so much to fill with the joyous sounds of a new life blossoming. After everything that just happened, there was something strangely comforting about being in the nursery, even if the chances of having a family with Jessica were pretty much lost. It was at that point that Harry saw the note attached to the beanbag chair.

"I had a feeling you'd come in here, but it's too late, Harry. God didn't let me get pregnant because He knew that we didn't belong together. Pack your bags and be gone by morning. Don't worry about Irma; she'll be fine with me. I never want to see you again. Jessica." Harry's hands trembled as he read Jessica's harsh words one more time to let it sink in.

What else could I expect? I finally pushed her too far. It's really over. I knew it was too good to last forever. Of course I had to fuck it up. That's what I do. I guess that will always be who I am. A loser, Harry thought to himself, as he walked into the hallway, carrying the note in one hand and a full suitcase in the other. The door to his mother's suite cracked open and a pale, sickly looking Irma poked her head out.

"Oh, Ma. I've lost her for good. I can't believe what I've done," Harry said, with tears welling up in his eyes. He wanted for Irma to come out of her room and offer him a hug and some motherly advice, but the tough old bird wasn't giving him an inch.

"Goodbye, Harry. Good luck, son," Irma said, shutting her door.

"Wait a minute, Ma! You can't stay here with Jessica. You're my mother. You should come with me," Harry pleaded, knocking feverishly on Irma's locked door, feeling like he was losing everyone who mattered to him all at once.

"Goodbye, Harry, and good riddance. I'm staying here. You've ruined your life and I'm not going to let you ruin mine," Irma said icily from the other side of the big oak door.

She has a point, Harry thought. *Why should she leave? Jessica will take good care of her and I can barely take care of myself. Besides, who knows what Luisa would do if I showed up at her front door with my mother?* And so, without anymore more fuss, Harry let himself out of what used to be his happy marital home. He went back to the house he grew up in, where the mischievous Mexican goddess now ruled the roost. And even though his surroundings were old and familiar, Harry Raider felt like a stranger in his own life.

★ ★ ★

"Did I really do the right thing? Are you absolutely positive?" Jessica managed to say through her uncontrolled waterworks. Next to her, handing her tissue after tissue and tenderly stroking her hand, was Billie Blaine. She had been long awaiting the time when Jessica's marriage would finally unravel. Now she was there to pick up the pieces of Jessica's broken life.

"Of course you did the right thing. As a matter of fact, you did the *only* thing you could do under the circumstances. I mean, you caught your husband in bed with another woman. How much more evidence do you need that Harry Raider is no good? You did the only thing that any self-respecting person would do and that is throw him out of your house and out of your life," Billie said, stamping her foot for emphasis.

"Maybe I should have tried to talk to him about what was going on and try to find out why he was cheating on me, instead of just getting rid of him?" Jessica sputtered, helplessly.

"Are kidding? You're his wife, not his damn psychiatrist! Who the hell cares why he can't keep his dick in his pants?" Billie retorted, getting angry with Jessica for wanting to give Harry the benefit of the doubt.

"Well, there must be some reason he went to her. We were having good sex, or at least I thought so. There has to be some other..."

"All right, Jessica, do you really want to know why Harry cheated on you with the whore?" a frustrated Billie interrupted Jessica's babbling.

"Yes, I do," Jessica said, blowing her nose hard and hoping Billie would say something, anything, to explain and make sense out of the horror of this dreadful situation.

"Harry cheated because he is a no-good, lying, out-of-control, horny bastard. That's just the pathetic creature he was born to be. He can't help himself. The notion that all men are strong characters is just a myth. Harry is weak and basically useless. Harry is no more advanced than snakes or any other primordial beast." Billie paused to see if Jessica was listening. She went on.

"He smells a pussy he wants to fuck and he does it, without ever stopping to think about the consequences. The bottom line here, Jessica, is that men are pigs and they can never be trusted. The only person you will ever be able to trust is another woman." Billie softened her voice and looked into Jessica's bloodshot eyes.

"Why is that, Billie? Why are we women so different?" Jessica asked, pulling herself upright and trying very hard to stop crying and come to her senses.

"Women are superior beings, Jes. We have evolved farther along the food chain, psychologically and spiritually. Think about it, Jessica, men are the hunters. It doesn't take many brains to go out and kill something to eat. Women, on the other hand, are the natural caregivers. We nurture things and people, physically and emotionally. Why do you think we are the ones who carry children? It's because only a woman could handle all the changes the mind and body go through during those nine months. Do you think men could endure all that? No way! And what about labor? HA! Forget it!" Billie laughed at the thought of a man giving birth.

"Well, I wouldn't know. Harry and I had been trying to have a baby, but nothing was working. Maybe that's why he went to Luisa. Maybe he thought that because I couldn't give him a child, there was something wrong with me," Jessica wailed hysterically.

"Don't be silly, Jessica. I'm sure that has nothing to do with Harry's bad behavior. In fact, I bet the opposite is true. I bet that secretly Harry didn't even want kids; he really never seemed like the fatherly type. He probably wanted to fuck Luisa because he could do so without worrying about her getting pregnant. I doubt a ruthless, female version of Donald Trump like that woman never even thinks about having babies, let alone having babies with a joker like Harry Raider. She probably sees him as a play toy, someone she can fuck without any strings attached, and he probably feels the same way. Either that or he's doing it for this business she's promised to back him in, but so far has done nothing. Whichever, Jessica, you should be glad to be rid of him. Those two schemers deserve each other. You should have someone who can give you much more," Billie said, wiping the tears away and seductively touching her cheek.

"How can I, Billie? All men are crap," a confused Jessica muttered while trying to catch her breath.

"That's right, they are, Jessica. That's why you'd be much happier if you could fall in love with a woman. Think of how you feel when you and I are hanging out. You're happy and feel free to be who you really are, without worrying about pacifying stupid Harry. I see the look in your eyes when we spend time together. You are so much more relaxed and comfortable," Billie said, slowly moving both her hands onto Jessica's shoulders. Taking her time and making sure she didn't scare Jessica, Billie massaged Jessica's arms and worked her way down to the small of her aching back.

"I don't know if I could ever do that, Billie. I'm just not that way," Jessica said, enjoying Billie's physical affection, but not experiencing the desire to go any further than a friendly massage.

"Sure you could, Jes. Look how much you're loving the way I touch you. I bet if the right woman, a loving, tender woman, came along and showed you how to enjoy yourself sexually, while still feeling safe and protected, you would be surprised to find out just how incredible and satisfying lesbian love can be," Billie boldly stated while her hands flowed up Jessica's sides and around to her breasts.

"I don't know, Billie. I don't know if we should be doing this," Jessica said hesitantly, but doing nothing to stop Billie's now sexual advances.

"This is exactly what we should have been doing all along, my dear. Just let yourself go with it. You know you really want me. I've felt your energy for some time now. It's time you stop denying it, baby," Billie whispered into Jessica's ear, while licking the outsides of it, and unhooking her bra. Soon Billie's fingers were circling and pulling on Jessica's nipples, while cupping her breasts in both hands.

Jessica let out a wanton sexy sigh and let herself fall backwards into Billie's passionate embrace.

Billie turned Jessica around to face her and lifted up her shirt. Without waiting for Jessica's reaction, Billie began licking and sucking on Jessica's nipples until Jessica was writhing and moaning with sexual pleasure. She pulled down Jessica's jeans and panties, and Billie's demanding tongue left Jessica's heaving cleavage to quickly move down Jessica's stomach to her mound and wet clitoris.

Jessica's tiny hands gripped Billie's head, desperately pulling at her short hair, while shoving Billie's face as deep inside her as it could go. As soon as Jessica let out a screaming climax, Billie ripped off her own pants, climbed on top of her new lover, pressed her clitoris hard against Jessica's, and humped her until she too experienced a long-awaited, powerful orgasm.

Jessica and Billie collapsed into each other's arms and fell asleep on the couch like an old couple who had been together for years. As Jessica drifted off into a post-coital snooze, it occurred to her how right it felt, that moment, to be with Billie.

Maybe she's right. Maybe the only person you can trust is another woman. Maybe I should be with Billie. Besides, we have all the same interests; we both enjoy the art world and she probably would be willing to carry a baby if I couldn't. Maybe this is what I really want, not Harry Raider, Jessica thought as she fell into a deep, restful sleep.

★★★

NO LONGER WILD ABOUT HARRY: JESSICA RAIDER IN LESBIAN LOVE MATCH, screamed the *Beverly Hills Gazette.* **YOU GO GRRRRLS! JESSICA RAIDER LEAVES HUSBAND HARRY FOR LESBIAN LOVER,** said the social column of the *LA Times.*

SOCIALITE'S SAPPHIC SWANSONG: JESSICA RAIDER'S A WOMAN ON THE MOVE read Page Six of the *New York Post.* Within the next week, victorious Billie moved right into Jessica's house and Jessica's life. She made sure that everyone in Hollywood knew about their new love connection and that she and Jessica were seen at the chicest gay and straight parties on the LA art scene almost every night.

Jessica may have hated going out before when she had to force herself to play the part of Harry Raider's perfect socialite wife, but this time she seemed to bask in the lime-light. Jessica loved being part of the hottest girl-girl couple in town. It made her feel hip, cool, and desirable. Jessica didn't know if she could spend the rest of her life without making love to another man. But for the time, being in this radical world of people who weren't afraid to lead uncon-ventional public lives empowered her.

I'll show you, Harry Raider. You think that your Luisa is so together and exciting. I'll show you what real excitement is. I'll show you that I'm not some stupid little naive girl from East Hampton. I'll prove to you that I'm not afraid to live on the edge, Jessica thought when she saw the photos of her and Billie in the celebrity gossip papers. *If only he could see me, if only,* Jessica thought to herself, as a reporter from *Entertainment Tonight* filmed her chatting with Portia de Rossi at the GLAAD awards.

chapter twenty-six

As Luisa got out of bed, quickly got dressed, and headed downstairs to her office, Harry lay alone, feigning sleep. It had been about a month since he had moved in with Miss Mendez, and life was not as sexy and adventurous as he had imagined. It seemed that once she got him where she wanted him, she treated Harry just like one of her servants. She would often speak to him in the same demeaning tone as she used with Chas. While Chas enjoyed seeing the previously rich Harry Raider being demoted to a live-in love-slave houseboy, he also felt genuinely sorry for Harry and the hell Luisa was putting him through.

Before Harry moved in, he and Luisa couldn't wait to have sex in outrageous places. But now he was lucky if he got it in the bedroom they shared. The opening of the hotel was only a couple of weeks away, and Luisa was generally too exhausted in the evenings, or any other time of day, to fuck wildly. And then there was the question of the children's clothing business. Harry didn't want to put too much pressure on Luisa right before Las Castillas opened its doors, but still he was beginning to wonder when she would give him the money to open his factory. Every time he asked her how Luisa's Niñas was doing in Latin America, she would brush him off and change the subject.

Harry made a promise to himself that after the big opening party for Las Castillas, he would get tough with Luisa and press her for an answer. But this morning in particular, he felt especially lonely and sad, regretting that his once perfect life with Jessica had ended in disaster. As he lay in bed with the red satin covers pulled over his head, it was as if he could hear Sam speaking to him. "Harry Raider, you schmuck! How could you fuck up your marriage with a lovely girl like Jessica just for the sake of that damn business? Don't be a putz like your old man. I sacrificed my life, Harry, don't sacrifice yours." Harry grabbed the remote and turned on the television to drown out his late dad's scolding.

What flashed across the small screen brought a smile to Harry's troubled face. He couldn't believe what his tired eyes were seeing broadcast on the local news. There, in living color, was Jessica! She was holding hands with Billie Blaine and waving a big banner while riding on top of a huge float in the Gay Pride Parade right down the middle of Santa Monica Boulevard. Harry let out a big huge laugh. In his heart of hearts Harry knew that Jessica was not really a lesbian.

Not only do I respect her for being so brave, I absolutely can't stop missing her. I don't know what to do first, but before I can even make an attempt to speak to Jessica, I better be in control of my own life, Harry thought. Harry got out of bed and jumped in the shower, hoping the rain of warm water would energize him into action. Not even bothering to get dressed, Harry tucked a towel around his waist and marched purposefully into Luisa's office.

"Luisa, we have to talk NOW," Harry said, dripping water on the papers that Luisa and Chas were inspecting.

"Harry, can't you see we are busy? Go shopping or play golf or something. I can't see you until later," Luisa snarled around the cigarette in her mouth, not aware that Harry wasn't even dressed.

"It can't wait, Luisa," Harry insisted. He began twisting and shaking himself, so that the water on his body rained down on Luisa's documents and dampened her cigarette.

"Harry Raider, you fucking little shit. What the hell is wrong with you today? Have you gone crazy? This is a very important contract that I have to read, sign, and fax back within an hour. Now what the fuck am I supposed to do? Maria, take this into the bathroom and see if you can dry it off with a blow-dryer," a pissed-off Luisa complained as she practically threw the paperwork at a maid who was dusting nearby.

"I need to know EXACTLY when you plan to give me the money to open the factory in Pasito and bring your kids clothing line to the United States," Harry said.

Luisa just laughed at him, refusing to take him seriously. "Oh Harry, is that all you wanted to know? Poor baby, you're not worried, are you?" Luisa smiled seductively and mischievously at the same time.

"Uh, no, of course not. I just need to get some idea when this is actually going to happen. You've been promising we'd do it for a long time now, and yet, you haven't done anything about it," Harry said accusingly.

Luisa sat back in her big chair and yawned. "You know, Harry, you are so cute. You really are. You are such an adorable little boy. I could just kiss you all day, if I didn't have so much to do," Luisa smiled, signaling for Chas to pull out a chair for Harry.

Luisa knew she could only boss Harry around to a point. He was raised as a prince, and even though he didn't have any money behind him anymore, old habits were hard to break. As much as Luisa wanted to slap him as punishment for disturbing her, she knew she couldn't push him too far. She still had to marry him to keep her father happy, so that meant babying him and indulging his requests for her attention every once in a while.

"Harry, sweetie, nothing would make me happier than to open your factory in Pasito, start making my line there, and give all of those deserving people their jobs back," Luisa said, as Harry sat down in his designated chair opposite her. "But as you know, we have just gotten started with the department stores in Mexico and they take a very long time to pay. Six months, maybe a year. But, Harry, I promise as soon as I receive some profit, I will get started here with you. Okay, *mi amor?* I love you," Luisa said sweetly, reaching across her desk for Harry's hand. Harry found himself totally unnerved by Luisa's display of tenderness.

"I'm sorry I barged in here like this and got your contract wet. I know you have a lot to finish before the opening party for Las Castillas, and I really should have waited until after," Harry mumbled, feeling a little guilty that he jumped all over her when she was in crunch time.

"That's okay, my darling. I understand, business can be very frustrating. Can't it, Chas?" Luisa put out her cigarette and got up from her desk.

"Oh, it can indeed," Chas dutifully replied. Luisa walked around her desk and gave Harry a long, sexy hug, shamelessly grinding her pelvis into his. "Now, why don't you go upstairs and finish your shower. How I wish I could join you. Maybe tonight, we'll be able to get wet together," Luisa said, grabbing Harry's butt.

"Yeah, maybe," Harry said, pulling himself away from her. *I should be getting a raging hard-on right now, but I'm not,* Harry thought as he looked deep into Luisa's dark eyes. *I don't trust this chick. I really don't have any reason not to believe her; maybe I'm just feeling guilty and para-noid. I better finish getting dressed then go for a drive to the beach. I'm so confused I really need to clear my head,* Harry thought to himself, as he went through the motions of kissing Luisa goodbye then walked out of her office.

Just before he was about to head upstairs he saw Maria the maid blow-drying Luisa's wet contract in the down-stairs bathroom. She seemed to be signaling for him to come in there with her. Harry walked into the marbled and mirrored powder room to see what Luisa's maid could pos-sibly want with him.

"Señor, she is telling you a lie," Maria whispered in Harry's ear, just loud enough so that he could hear her above the noise of the blow-dryer.

"What are you talking about, Maria?" Harry practically yelled. Maria quickly put her hand over his mouth in an effort to shut him up.

Maria had been furtively listening to their conversation, pretending to clean just outside the doorway. "Please, Señor, I can't afford to get caught. But you need to know, she is lying about her children's clothing. She is making money, a lot of money. A huge amount of money, so much you wouldn't believe it. I know, because I hear her speak-ing in Spanish to her banker in Mexico every day," Maria whispered, and shut the bathroom door to make sure no one could see them.

"What? Are you sure?" Harry mumbled through the maid's hand. "I am positive, Señor. I also know this is true, because my brother lives near her factory and told me that she has people working there day and night. Young people, very young. It is very sad," Maria said, getting very upset.

"You know if Luisa found out you were talking to me about this, you could get fired or sent back to Mexico. So why the hell are you telling me?" Harry asked seriously, removing the maid's hand from his mouth. He couldn't get angry at Maria, because he was really mad at himself. In his gut, he knew Luisa was stringing him along, but he couldn't bring himself to question her even when he knew she was lying to his face. *Am I that gullible or do I just totally become an idiot when faced with a pair of great boobs and a rockin' body?* Harry wondered.

"I know I could lose my job or worse if you turned me in to Señorita Mendez, but I had to take a chance. It is horrible what she is doing in that factory and somebody must stop her. That somebody is you, Señor," Maria said, tears welling up in her eyes.

"I'm not sure what you mean by that, Maria. What could be so terrible with the factory?" Harry asked, handing Maria a tissue.

"I'm sorry, I can say no more. Why don't you go down there and see for yourself. The factory is in a town called Bolita, about ten miles outside of Tijuana. She keeps her dirty secret far away from her palace in Acapulco."

Maria and Harry were interrupted by Luisa screaming for her newly dried contract to be brought to her at once. "I'm sorry, I have to go now. Please, Señor, go to Bolita. Please do something to stop her." Maria shut off the blow-dyer, took the paperwork, and headed back to Luisa's office, leaving Harry alone with his thoughts.

I have no idea what she is talking about regarding Luisa's Mexican factory. I should go down there and see what is going on. If she has some secret to making a fortune, I want to know what it is, Harry thought as he went upstairs and put on his clothes.

★★★

A few minutes later he took the keys to Luisa's Aston Martin, drove onto the 405 Freeway, and was in San Diego two hours later. He kept on driving and soon crossed over into Mexico. Harry drove past Tijuana and looked for the signs that would lead him to Bolita. Finding nothing to show him the way, he pulled over to a taco stand by the side of the road. Taking a gamble with the health of his stomach, Harry scarfed down two enchiladas while the aging man who ran the stand told him approximately how to get to Luisa's factory in Bolita, only a couple miles away.

Bolita was worse than he expected. It was a shantytown of broken-down huts with no electricity or running water. Besides the skinny, underfed chickens running around in the hot sun, looking desperately for something to eat or drink, there wasn't much sign of life.

Finally Harry saw what could be a factory, although it was nothing like his father's facility in its heyday. Like everything else in broken-down Bolita, the unmarked building was in very poor condition, and certainly didn't look like the sort of place that was making beautiful children's clothing.

Harry got out of the car and walked towards the factory. As he got closer he heard the sounds of machines. As he got to the door, he heard something even more confusing and disturbing. It was the sound of children crying, fussing, and making the usual noises that kids do when they are hot, tired, and cranky. For a moment, Harry thought he had made a mistake. Perhaps this old, grungy building was some kind of Mexican day-care center the local mothers put their kids in while they were off working in Luisa's factory. When Harry opened the door, he couldn't believe his eyes. There in a hot, dusty, crowded, dimly lit room were hundreds of children, some as young as five and others in their late teens. They were dressed in ragged hand-me-downs, looking tired and hungry as they sat and worked in front of sewing machines. The children of the factory were just as surprised to see Harry, yet none of them dared to stop working, even to stare at the American stranger in their midst.

"Can I help you, Señor?" a perky voice asked in nearly perfect English. Harry turned around to see a young man, about twenty years old, standing behind him. He wore a multi-colored poncho and had lovely brown skin, but his blue eyes, prominent pudgy nose, and frizzy brown hair were an obvious indication that his blood was not entirely Mexican.

"Can you tell me what's going on here?" Harry asked him, coming out of his state of shock.

"We are working, Señor. That is all."

"But some of these kids are so young. They shouldn't be doing this. It's a crime. You should go to the police," Harry said, staring straight ahead, not being able to take his eyes off of the kids behind the machines.

"It's a crime if we don't work. The police will put us in jail if we stop," the young boy said, matter-of-factly.

"That's crazy! Who owns this factory? What are you making here?" Harry raised the two questions he already knew the answers to. But he had to hear the awful truth for himself.

"Why should I tell you? Who are you?" the young man asked, a curious look in his eye.

"I'm Harry. I'm a reporter from the *Los Angeles Times*. I am here to do a story on children working in factories. If you tell me who you are working for, I can get them in a lot of trouble and shut this hellhole down," Harry lied, sincerely.

"If I tell you too much, the police will take us away from our families and put us in detention. If you think this factory is bad, you should see where they would put us. It's ten times worse," the young man said firmly.

"Why would they do that?" Harry asked.

"Because they really work for the rich family who owns this factory. They control everything in Mexico, especially us. The police are paid by them to make sure we work in the factory night and day. Anyone who doesn't do what they say gets taken away," the young man answered, a sad look in his eyes. Normally he would have been terrified to speak so candidly to someone he didn't know, but there was something comforting about Harry's persona that put him strangely at ease.

"So what do you do here?" Harry probed, trying to make sense of the situation.

"I'm the factory manager. I've been working here since I was ten years old. I make sure everything goes okay. I try to make it as fun as possible for the little ones; you know, like we are playing a game or something. It works for a while, then they eventually catch on, but by that time they are used to their work load," the young man said.

Harry let out a big sigh. He knew that somehow he had to win this young man's trust if he was going to get anything accomplished here. "You speak pretty good English," Harry told him, looking into the young man's dancing eyes, trying to figure out what to say to win him over.

"My mother was a maid in Beverly Hills, but there was some kind of problem with the people she worked for. They gave her money to go away so we moved back here right before I was born. She taught me," the young man said proudly.

"Well she did a very good job. I hope she told you that all Americans aren't so bad. Some of us are pretty cool." Harry smiled brightly.

"My dad was American, but I never met him. I don't think his family wanted us around," the young man said coldly.

Harry was at a loss for words. Not only had this poor kid been abandoned by his father, but he had also been sentenced to a life of doom and gloom working in a crumbling sweatshop. *What kind of asshole would walk away from his own kid?* Harry thought.

"Hey, you want go for a ride in my really cool car and grab some lunch?" Harry said to the young man.

"Well, I really shouldn't leave," he said, smiling mischievously as he saw the Aston Martin parked in front of the factory.

"Come on. I know a great taco stand close by. They serve tequila with the worm still in it. Isn't that cool?" Harry said.

"Okay, but only if you promise to bring me right back," the young man said, running around Harry and going towards the car. "WOW, this is so awesome," the young man said, staring at the Aston Martin like it was a space ship from another planet that had just landed.

"Hop in!" Harry said enthusiastically.

"Can I drive?" the young man asked.

"I don't see why not," Harry said, handing him the keys. Soon Harry and the young man were eating bad tacos, drinking Cokes out of glass bottles, and becoming fast friends. "Hey kid, you ate like ten tacos and you didn't even tell me your name. That's not fair. At least I deserve to know who I just bought lunch for," Harry joked, taking a bite of a Mexican treat.

"It's Javier," the young man, taking the last taco out of Harry's hand and quickly shoving it into his mouth.

"Want to see something cool?" Harry said, walking over to the car and pulling out his latest high-tech camera. "This takes pictures and makes movies, with the sound, all at once. It's a digital miracle. Want to see how it works?" Harry asked.

"Sure," Javier answered curiously. Harry loaded up the camera's buttons and gave it to the man behind the taco stand. He put his arm around Javier and told him to say cheese.

The flash went off, and within seconds Harry was able to show the picture on the camera's screen to a very impressed Javier. "That's really awesome, Harry. I never have seen anything like that before," Javier said, as Harry put the camera in his hands.

"You know, if you'd let me take some pictures of the factory, I could bring them back to the United States and show them to some pretty powerful people. Once they get out, the factory would have to be shut down and I could almost guarantee the kids would be safe and wouldn't have to work anymore, ever!" Harry said, smiling big. *Don't you worry, kid, I'll stop at nothing to give Luisa exactly what she deserves. I hate her more than you could possibly imagine,* Harry thought, not letting his angry thoughts disturb the happy look on his face. Javier just kept staring at the ground. There was something wonderful about this American stranger that he wanted so badly to trust. But letting Harry take pictures of the children at work could jeopardize all of their lives.

"Have you heard of the Mendez family? Luisa Mendez owns the factory and controls everything in Mexico. If she finds out I let you do this, I'm a dead man," Javier said in a scared voice.

"Don't worry, I know all about Luisa Mendez," Harry said, putting his arm around his new friends' shoulders. *Nobody wants to take that bitch down more than I do. She's ruined both of our lives,* Harry thought to himself. "Believe me, she may run the show down here for now, but once I expose her as the heartless tyrant she really is, she'll be the one who'll be afraid for her life, not you, and certainly not the children," said Harry.

"Why should I believe you?" Javier asked Harry.

"Because..." Harry stuttered. He wished he could tell the young man the whole truth, but he knew he couldn't do that. Somehow he had to win the boy's confidence. "Because, it's my job to put people like Luisa Mendez out of business. Believe me kiddo, this story means more to me than you will ever know," Harry said, with a sincere look in his eye.

"Well, I probably shouldn't believe you, but somehow I do. I know you're telling the truth," Javier responded hopefully, looking up at Harry.

"You bet I am. So what do you say? Can I photograph your factory?" Harry grabbed the boy's hand for reassurance.

"Let's go for it," Javier answered with a new sense of steely determination to his voice.

"Awesome, my friend! You totally rock!" Harry gave Javier a big bear hug and tried to swing him around in his arms. Javier drove Harry back to the factory where he clicked away until he got enough footage of the young children. When he was done, he reached into his wallet and gave Javier the five hundred dollars that he stole from Luisa's purse before he left Beverly Hills.

Javier just stared at the crisp hundred dollar bills with astonishment. He had never seen so much money in his life. "I shouldn't take this from you, Señor Harry, since you are doing so much to help us." Javier counted the money over and over again.

"Oh, please, it's the least I could do. Besides, it's not really my money," Harry laughed.

"Oh really, then whose is it?" Javier asked.

"Let's just say that it belongs to a lady who owes you a lifetime of overtime," Harry smiled. He gave Javier a hug goodbye, got back into the car, and drove back to the San Diego airport. Instead of going back to Beverly Hills, Harry booked a flight to New York.

chapter twenty-seven

Harry was going back to the Hamptons. His dear friends there would be the ones to come through for him, at least one more time.

He called Luisa on his cell phone. "Honey, I'm in Vegas with the boys for a guys' weekend. I'll be back in a couple of days. Sorry I didn't tell you I was going, it was a last-minute thing. I hope you're not mad, baby doll." Harry forced the words out of his mouth while he was waiting for his rental car at JFK Airport on Long Island, New York.

"No, it's all right, Harry, I have so many last-minute details to handle before the opening of Las Castillas next week that I could use some time to myself," Luisa replied. Honestly, she was relieved to have Harry off her hands so she could tend to business without worrying about how to keep him happy and occupied.

"Great, I'll miss you, darling, and I promise to keep myself out of trouble."

"Okay, Harry, got to go, Chas is here with the caterer," a distracted Luisa said. In reality she couldn't have cared less what Harry did in Vegas as long as he kept himself alive long enough to marry her and please her father.

With Luisa taken care of, Harry made the trek down the Long Island Expressway until he came to Exit 70, then onto Montauk Highway, which would take him straight out to the Hamptons. Harry had flown the redeye from California, and when he arrived in New York it was a glorious, sunny spring morning. After being stuck in an insane amount of traffic, Harry was glad to reach the beach, and he rolled down his window to catch a whiff of the fresh ocean air. As he drove through Southampton, on his way to Bridgehampton, Harry began to remember all the wonderful times he had shared with his new friends the summer before. He couldn't yet bring himself to drive all the way to East Hampton, because that's where he had fallen in love with Jessica. Those memories were just too painful to deal with just yet.

Harry's first stop was Sag Pond Farm, one of the most gorgeous equestrian facilities on the East Coast. He knew that was where he could find Milly Harrington Cohen, the Wall Street Wonder Woman who had become one of his closest friends the summer before. When Harry got to the stable, he was shocked and thrilled to see Milly not riding, but five months pregnant and picking out ponies.

"Harry Raider! What a marvelous surprise! My God, I haven't seen you in ages," Milly cried and she gave her old friend a big hug as a groom paraded a fat, dapple gray Welsh pony by them.

"Oooh, he's a cutie," Harry said, patting the pony on his forehead.

"Yeah, he sure is. I just can't wait until my little girl comes. I'd bring her straight from the hospital to the stable and throw her right on a pony if David would let me," Milly laughed.

"I'm sure David would love to have a little girl who is a great equestrian just like you," Harry said, putting his arm around Milly.

"Yeah, maybe, but his mother would kill me if we went too quickly from the cradle to the saddle," Milly laughed. "So what brings you here, Harry?" Milly asked somewhat seriously. Being married to David Cohen, whose family was exceedingly prominent in New York's Jewish social circles, Milly heard all the latest gossip. She knew Sam Raider died broke and that Harry had left Jessica for Luisa Mendez. Personally, she thought he was crazy, but Milly said nothing about all this, until, of course, Harry brought it up.

"Well, to be frank with you Milly, I need money," Harry confessed, looking down in shame at the sawdust, and making circles in the hay with his shoes. "I've been trying to restart my father's business and reopen his factory for months now, but I've had no luck. At first I tried to going to all his old business contacts, but no one would take me seriously." Harry chuckled and shrugged his shoulders. "I even went to some of the people he helped get started out in the business, thinking that I could cash in on some favors, but some of them didn't even return my phone calls, and the others just wanted to hear about the parties I've been to." Harry shook his head in disgust. "So Chas introduced me to Luisa, who promised to get me started, but all she did was steal my ideas and start her own kids' clothing line, using child labor no less! She has turned out to be such a nightmare I can't even begin to tell you." At the mention of Luisa's name, Harry's whole body shook and quivered uncomfortably, like he wanted to shake off her evil energy.

"Harry, why didn't you come to me sooner?" Milly asked.

"I guess I was too embarrassed. I wanted to show my friends, and Jessica, that I could do this on my own." Harry watched another plump Shetland pony walked by.

"That's so silly, Harry, what are friends for? I'm a venture capitalist, for pete's sakes. I could have raised you the money and put someone in there, a financial expert in the clothing business, to oversee everything. All you would have been responsible for was sales, and believe me, Harry, with your personality, I bet you could sell kids' clothes to a nun!"

"Milly Harrington Cohen, you don't change. Thank goodness! I owe you everything for this, Mills. I'll never forget that you were the one to put me on my feet." Harry gave Milly another hug.

"Harry, I know a salesman when I see one. I'm like a bloodhound, I can smell someone who can make a lot of money." The two friends laughed as they walked back out to Harry's car. "Hey, I have a great idea. You know who you should really talk to..." Milly stopped to think.

"Who's that?" Harry asked excitedly.

"Penny! As you know, she's had twins and she's become an absolute maven about children's clothing. Not only does she buy enough stuff to outfit a small country, but everybody consults her on where to get the chicest kids' stuff. All the kids' clothing stores, and even some of the biggest department stores, know about Penny. Trust me on this, Harry, if she calls a kids' clothing buyer and tells them that they should start buying merchandise from you, you'll have it made in no time," Milly said with wild enthusiasm.

"I don't know if I can go to Penny. I doubt she'll want to help me," Harry admitted sadly.

"Why wouldn't she, Harry? You guys were inseparable last summer, like brother and sister."

"Yeah, that was last summer. So much has changed since then. Penny went to school with Luisa, she is married to Jessica's ex-husband, and is very good friends with both of them." Harry shook his head while opening his car door.

Milly smiled and raised her finger to her lips, like she was about to give Harry top secret social information. "I know for a fact that Penny can't stand Luisa. She was absolutely appalled that Luisa came to her baby naming just to poach Chas, and she was even more pissed that she spent the whole time outside smoking, then left early. Penny told me at a luncheon last week that she hopes she never sees Luisa again, and she wishes you'd get rid of her," Milly told Harry bluntly.

Harry wiped his hands together and then made a fist like he was ringing Luisa's neck. "Don't worry, I'm going to get her out of my life, but not without teaching her a lesson first," Harry said, smiling devilishly.

★ ★ ★

"Harry Raider... OH MY GAWD!" Penny screamed as she handed her little baby boy to a nanny standing by, and gave Harry a bear hug. Penny's mother, Reba, sat on a white sofa on the deck overlooking the ocean, cuddling the baby's twin in her arms. Nobody thought Reba Marks would ever recover from the shock of her daughter Bunny's death, but the arrival of the newborns brought the old lady back to life.

"Penny, you look gorgeous," a thrilled Harry said, after receiving such a warm welcome. "You already lost all of the baby weight and I must say that you've kept some on in all the right places," Harry teased, squeezing her milk-engorged breasts.

"Hey, cut that out unless you want to get squirted in the eye. I'm breastfeeding, Harry, and I feel like a moving cow," Penny laughed, escorting Harry into the nursery. "Milly called me from her cell phone and said you were on your way over. She said that she was backing you in business and that you'd want to see my kids' wardrobe," Penny said, opening a walk-in closet that was as big as a suite at the Waldorf.

God, she's good, Harry thought to himself about Milly.

"This is the girl's side and this is the boy's side," Penny said, glowing with maternal pride.

Harry was stunned. In his whole spoiled life, he had never seen such a collection of designer kids' clothes. On the boy's side were racks and racks of the latest apparel by Ralph Lauren, Tommy Hilfiger, Petite Bateau, and Absorba, just to name a few. The girl's side of the closet overflowed with Lilly Pulitzer, more Ralph Lauren and Absorba, Dolce and Gabbana, Burberry, Zannia, and Saks Fifth Avenue's own high-priced line of baby goodies. "Wow, Penny, you don't mess around," Harry said, inspecting a pair of baby Guccis.

"No, I don't, and everyone knows that about me too. When you get your line ready, I'd be happy to make a few phone calls to help you out, Harry. I'll even give a party to introduce your products and really kick it off," Penny said beaming.

She genuinely loved crazy Harry and considered him at least partially responsible for the wonderful way her life had turned out. After all, if Harry had never come to the Hamptons, he never would have met Jessica, and Freddy would never have been free to marry her. If that weren't enough, when Harry and Penny were supposedly "dating" that fateful summer, Harry made Penny feel gorgeous, sexy, and desirable, even though he never laid a hand on her. For restoring her self-confidence and treating her like a supermodel, Penny would always consider Harry a very special friend.

"So aren't you going to totally ream me out for being such a schmuck to Jessica?" Harry asked, as he and Penny sat in the kitchen indulging in one of their delicious pig-outs.

"I wasn't going to say anything unless you started," Penny said, dipping a slice of pita bread into a mound of fresh hummus and spreading some olive tapenade on it.

"Do you think she'll ever take me back?" Harry swallowed hard.

"I'm not sure, Harry. You really fucked up big time," Penny said, chewing a piece of fried chicken.

"Yeah, I know. I guess it's over, huh?" Harry said, putting down a lobster tail and losing his appetite.

"It doesn't have to be," Penny told him.

"Really?" Harry said hopefully.

"I'd go see the old man. I think he's the only chance you got left," Penny said, pouring Harry a Diet Coke.

"Jessica's father? Oh, no, I can't face Jerry. Not after everything I've put him through. Besides, he'd probably have me shot if I walked onto his property."

"Sounds tempting, Harry," an old man's voice said behind Harry.

Harry turned around to see an angry Jerry Ackerman standing in the kitchen doorway. Harry immediately jumped off of the kitchen stool and practically stood at attention. "Jerry! I mean Mr. Ackerman, sir. How did you know I was here?" a confused Harry asked. As scared as he was, Harry was almost relieved to see Jerry in the safety of Penny's kitchen. If this confrontation got nasty, at least Harry wouldn't have to endure the torture of driving up to the Ackerman estate and wondering if he would be allowed entrance.

"Freddy called me," Jerry said sternly.

"Sorry, Harry, but you know how much I love to punish you," a nebbishy, balding Freddy Levitt said, only half joking. "Besides I couldn't leave you alone in here with my wife, all the good food would be gone." Dressed in an Izod shirt and baggy Polo shorts that Penny had picked out for him, Freddy walked into the kitchen, put his *Financial Times* down on the countertop, and began to make himself a sandwich.

"What the hell have you done to my daughter's life?" Jerry demanded. In the past, Jerry had always been Harry's understanding ally in difficult situations, but this time Harry had alienated him for good.

"I know you're probably furious at me for what's happened, but..." Harry stammered,

"I'd like to kill you, you son of bitch. Who the hell do you think you are, leaving my Jessica for some whore? And after all that she's done for you?" Jerry yelled at the top of lungs. His face got so red, everyone feared the old man might have a heart attack while exploding with anger.

"I'm sorry, sir, I'm not sure I understand what you're saying. What exactly has Jessica done for me?" Harry said, looking Jerry Ackerman straight in the eye.

"WHAT? Are you a total moron or just a complete idiot? I mean you were living pretty good on our money, Harry. A big house in Beverly Hills, servants, I think Jessica is still taking care of YOUR MOTHER! We do all of this for you, and what do you do? Leave Jessica? You ungrateful little bastard, I hope you die and rot in hell."

Even though his actions with Jessica had been terrible, something inside of Harry wouldn't allow Jerry Ackerman to intimidate him. "For your information, Mr. Ackerman, sir, I didn't really leave Jessica. She threw me out," Harry said.

"Can you blame her?" Jerry screamed again.

"If you think that I should have stayed with Jessica because she was paying my bills, then I'm glad she threw me out. I'm glad that's over. I never wanted your charity, Jerry. What I wanted was your support," Harry said with a newfound strength. Silence fell over the room. Penny put down her piece of olive bread and finally stopped chewing. Not even Freddy, who was not-so-secretly enjoying Harry being annihilated by Jerry Ackerman, could say anything now. "I wanted you and Jessica to support me in restarting my father's business and trying to reopen his factory. But neither one of you would do that. All you did was try to convince me to shut everything down and spend the rest of my life being a playmate on your daughter's payroll," Harry said. "You didn't think I could do it, or do anything for that matter, and frankly neither did Jessica. Not once did she stand up to you and stand behind me in business. Both of you think of me of a useless playboy with big dreams. I never wanted to take anything from you or Jessica. I wanted to be a good, successful husband who could provide for her. I didn't want to be a hanger-on. I didn't want to be a loser!" Harry was shouting now, and Jerry Ackerman stared at the young man with total amazement. As Harry stood there speaking, Jerry saw shades of his old best friend, former partner, and fiercest competitor. Jerry saw in Harry a young Sam Raider.

Jerry shook his head and stared at the veins of gray in the white marble floor. He didn't quite know what to say to Harry. He felt guilty about not giving Harry the support he needed. But despite Jerry's regrets, there still was the question of his daughter and the mess that had become their lives. "So what do you plan to do now, Harry?" a somber Jerry asked.

"Now I plan to take Milly Cohen's venture capital money and with Penny's help with the buyers, start my own kids' clothing business and reopen Sam's factory," Harry said, wiping the sweat from his forehead with the wet washcloth Penny handed him.

"I don't mean about the business, I mean about my daughter. Do you still love her, Harry?" Jerry continued, not looking up.

"Of course I do. I wish I'd never let this whole damn thing get so out of control." Harry was now more apologetic than angry. He honestly loved Jerry and sorely missed Jessica.

"Unfortunately for me, Jessica seems pretty happy in the relationship she's got now, so I don't know what kind of chance I would have to get her back," Harry shrugged his shoulders helplessly.

Jerry pulled out a kitchen stool and starting to make himself comfortable. "I think you have a damn good chance, Harry. Don't get me wrong, I like Billie very much. She's a lovely girl and she's been very good and loving towards Jessica through this whole mess. But Jessica isn't a lesbian. Not really. I flew out there to meet Billie, and frankly, they seem more like sisters to me than lovers. An old man knows these things. If I thought Billie could make Jessica happy for the rest of her life, then I'd give her my blessing, but I think this is just a reactionary phase Jessica is going through to get even with you, Harry."

"So what do you think I should do, Jerry?" Harry implored softly.

"I think you should finish up anything you have left to finish up with this Luisa girl, then give Jessica a call. Take her to lunch and see if you two can at least start talking again. Take things slowly and see where you go from there," Jerry suggested, pouring himself a cup of coffee.

"That sounds like a good idea, Jerry. I'll do that," Harry said, a grateful tear welling up in his eye.

"I'm sorry I doubted you, Harry, and I'm sorry I never took your business ambitions seriously," Jerry said wistfully.

"That's all right, Jerry, it's hard to bet on a dark horse." Harry smiled devilishly.

"Are you kidding? The only place for Sam Raider's son is in the winner's circle. Your dad would have been very proud of you," Jerry said.

"Thanks, Jerry. That means more to me than you'll ever

realize." Harry got up and reached over to give Jerry a hug.

"I know, son, I know." And at that moment, the two estranged men became family again, over a smorgasbord of gastronomic delights.

chapter twenty-eight

Back in Los Angeles, things in Chas Greer's world were going from bad to worse. It was now one week before Las Castillas's grand opening, and Luisa was making Chas's life absolute hell. Chas was accustomed to her usual tirades, but now she had crossed the line and subjected him to intolerable humiliation.

It all began when Luisa barged in on one of Chas's gentlemen's parties. While Harry was away, Luisa arrived unannounced at Chas's apartment and let herself in. Stepping over and walking right past the most powerful players in the Velvet Mafia, Luisa grabbed Chas by the back of his collar. "You're coming with me," she screeched so loud some of the men stopped what they were doing to take notice. She proceeded to march Chas out of his own home, throw him in her car, and force him to spend the night at her home, cleaning up her kitchen and bathroom and doing her laundry because the maid left early with a cold. She even made him clean out her filthy hairbrushes and hand-wash some of her personal undergarments.

After totally degrading Chas and making him substitute for the maid, Luisa turned as sweet as sugar and begged him to stay to watch movies with her and eat popcorn. She was lonely with Harry gone and needed the company. Chas had no choice but to go from slave to girlfriend, all the while pretending to enjoy this evening of physical and psychological torture.

Word spread like wildfire throughout the gay community that Chas Greer had become no more than Luisa Mendez's lady-in-waiting. Overnight Chas's reputation as the man to know disappeared. He was immediately reduced to servant status in the eyes of the powerful, successful Los Angeles gay men who had risen to the top of their professions by outsmarting their straight counterparts. It completely turned them off to see one of their own so publicly disrespected. What made them even more furious was that Chas didn't put up a fight.

Chas, who was always socially smart as a whip, was painfully aware that he had fallen out of favor with his elite gay connections. No one would return his phone calls and dinner dates were refused immediately. When he tried to organize another party at his house, he received call-backs from the assistants of the people who used to ring him personally. Feeling like a broken man, Chas wasn't sure how he could ever fix this horrible situation. *Perhaps if the hotel is a big success, people will think I'm on top again. That is, if they don't think I'm the janitor,* Chas thought in the elevator on the way up to his apartment after a long day with Luisa. Rocky had taken the afternoon off, supposedly to go to an audition, so Luisa's driver dropped Chas off at his building.

When Chas walked through his front door, he thought he heard laughter coming from his bedroom. *I must be hallucinating. Who the hell would be here? Nobody wants anything to do with me anymore.* Chas went into the kitchen and searched the fridge for an open bottle of Chardonnay.

As the giggling continued, Chas realized that he wasn't hearing things. Someone else was in his house. Quietly he crept down the hall and stood outside his master bathroom, making sure he was hidden.

"Yeah, isn't this a great place? I love this huge Jacuzzi tub; it's practically as big as my whole apartment," a male voice said. "I think Luisa pays like ten thousand dollars a month for this place for Chas, isn't that unbelievable?" the voice continued. "Just you wait, honey, until I'm a famous actor. Then I'll get us a place twice this big. That's the only reason I'm still fucking Chas. You should see some of the power players that show up at his orgies. If they think I'm Chas's boyfriend they might give me an audition. That's really the only way for a straight guy like me to get anywhere in this town. I have to keep pretending I'm gay until I make it."

"What the hell do you think you're doing?" Chas screamed as he flew into his bathroom to see Rocky enjoying himself under a pile of suds with another lover—a young woman!

"Chas, dude, settle down. I didn't think you'd be back this early. This is Angie, my partner from acting class. We were, uh, only rehearsing a scene, doing some improvisation. I didn't mean a word I said. You know I love you," Rocky pleaded.

"GET THE FUCK OUT OF MY HOUSE AND MY LIFE, before I beat the shit out of you, you worthless piece of trash!" Chas's words echoed off the tiled walls as he turned purple in anger.

"Okay, okay, don't worry, man. We're out of here." Rocky and Angie got out of the tub as quickly as they could and put their clothes on over their still soapy bodies. Chas swigged from the bottle of Chardonnay out on the terrace until the two scoundrels were gone. He looked at the Hollywood Hills and wondered how his neat little life became such a horror show. Chas would have done anything to trade those mansion-dotted mountains he saw in front of him for his old friend, the New York City skyline.

He had left Gotham City at the top of his game. While he once controlled the best of Manhattan society, in Hollywood he had become nothing more than a glorified houseboy. And then there was Juan, who may have well been the love of his life. Juan too had been left in the dust so Chas could pursue his dream. And now it had all blown up in his face. Chas felt hopeless. What could he do now to turn his life around?

★★★

Harry flew back to San Diego and drove as fast as could up to the 405 freeway to Beverly Hills. It was around midday when he reached Luisa's house. Much to his delight, Harry found it totally empty. *She must be at Las Castillas,* Harry thought, a broad smile stretching across his face. Luisa and Chas had built the once-crumbling property into a magnificent masterpiece, and the elite Los Angelinos were already calling it the Taj Mahal of Mulholland Drive. *They're probably up there getting ready for the opening party, this is excellent!* Harry thought as he scurried into Luisa's immaculate office and turned on her computer.

Within seconds he had transferred all of the pictures he had taken of the children slaving away in Luisa's factory onto the big screen and turned his collage of shots into a jpeg file. Harry was no writer, but his passion provided just the words for a helluva press release:

FOR IMMEDIATE RELEASE: HOTEL HEIRESS HEADS UP CHILD LABOR CONCENTRATION CAMP. WOULD YOU LET YOUR KID WEAR CLOTHES MADE BY THESE CHILDREN?

Luisa Mendez, heiress to the Las Castillas hotel chain, forces children to work in her clothing factory under sub-human conditions.

The Mexican police, who are financially controlled by the powerful Mendez family, have threatened parents in the poor town of Bolita that if they don't send their children to work in the Mendez-owned factory, they will be jailed, starved, beaten, and sexually abused.

The factory operates twenty-four hours a day and the children are paid minimal wages; Ms. Mendez has very low manufacturing costs and sells her clothing line to stores at rock-bottom wholesale prices that undercut her competition. This is the dirty little secret behind Luisa's Niñas, the incredibly successful, affordable children's clothing line that is sweeping Latin American department stores and is scheduled to hit the U.S. soon.

It's time that the Mexican government, the United States, and human rights organizations around the world crack down on this horrible tragedy and slap the Mendez organization with heavy fines and possible jail time for Ms. Mendez herself, who knowingly opened a juvenile sweatshop.

Journalists who are interested in exposing Luisa Mendez as the heartless, cruel, ruthless power-monger she really is are invited to the opening of the Las Castillas Five-Star Hotel in Beverly Hills. The children of Bolita thank you in advance for your participation, and so do I.

Sincerely,

A Friend of the Kids

Harry read his words proudly out loud and hit the save button. He started looking through Luisa's computer files to find email addresses of her list of heavy-hitting international press contacts.

Just then, his search ended as he heard a door slam behind him. "What the hell do you think you're doing,

Harry?" Chas's whiny voice asked.

Oh shit, I'm totally busted. Fuck, how am I going to get out of this? Harry thought as he sat there in silence, a guilty look on his face.

"I was just going to send an email to some of my friends about the opening party, that's all," Harry said, nonchalantly.

"Oh, yeah? Well, isn't that nice of you," Chas answered sarcastically. "Now do you want to tell me what you were doing in New York when you were supposed to be in Las Vegas?" Chas accused him, as he crossed his legs and leaned against the door, trapping Harry in the room.

"How do you know that?" Harry blurted out, sensing he was in a lot more trouble than he initially realized.

"Let's just say a little birdie told me," Chas said.

"Cut the crap, Chas. How did you know where I was? Does Luisa have her people following me?" Harry asked, nervously putting his hands in pockets and feeling beads of sweat drip down his back. *Holy shit, what if I was being watched the whole time and Luisa already knows exactly what I've been up to? God knows what she'd do to those poor kids and even worse, what she'd do to me. I'm probably a walking dead man,* Harry thought, chewing on his bottom lip.

"Harry, are you back on cocaine?" Chas probed.

"No? Why?" Harry stammered.

"Because you're biting your lips like they are completely numb and you've become totally paranoid," Chas spat.

"What do you mean?" Harry jumped a little in place.

"Do you think that Luisa would actually spend the money to have someone following you like a bloodhound? Believe me, with everything she's got on her mind for the hotel opening, she's certainly not worried about you. She knows that you'll come when she calls," Chas said viciously.

"You still didn't tell me how you know I went back east," Harry persisted.

"I have a friend who works as a riding instructor at Sag Pond Stables. He said he overheard you talking to Milly Cohen about borrowing money to start a children's clothing business. He also heard you say that you made a big mistake with Luisa and you were implying that you wanted to get back with Jessica. Hend was so excited to be the first one with this kind of dirt, naturally he had to call me to dish right way," Chas leered at Harry.

"So, did you tell Luisa that I went to the Hamptons?" Harry asked, dreading the answer.

"No, I didn't. I didn't tell her anything about what I heard," Chas said, shifting his stance. He slowly uncrossed his legs and now folded his arms, firmly.

"Chas, you are one fine dude," Harry said affectionately, running over to give him a hug.

"Wait!" Chas said, holding out his hand and blocking him. "Harry Raider, you're going to tell me exactly what you are up to, and you're not going to spare one detail. If I find out that you are lying to me or even worse, that you left a valuable piece of information out, then I swear, I'm going to go straight to Luisa," Chas laid it on the line.

Harry didn't say a word, but his head was on fire. *Should I take a gamble and confide in Chas? I know that he is making a fortune but he hates Luisa as much as I do. Even so, he's not going to walk away from her money. Hmmmm, I think I have an idea,* Harry thought as the blood returned to his pale face.

"Chas, I am going to tell you what's going on and I'm not going to spare you any of the horrors. I didn't just go to the Hamptons, I went to Mexico first," Harry said confidently.

"You're kidding, why?" Chas asked, intrigued and perplexed.

"Because I needed to find out the truth about Luisa, and about her kids' clothing business," Harry said, taking a step back and opening his arms wide. "What I saw down there was shocking," he said, shaking his head, biting his lips, and angrily rubbing his fist in his hand. "So, I want you read something. But before you do, you should know that if you help me out now, when I open my factory and start my own children's clothing line, there will be a good job for you. You could be the creative director and help me with sales. You'd schmooze over all the buyers, I just know it, and you'd be able to design the hippest stuff! You could be the next kids' version of Calvin Klein. Milly is giving me a lot of money, so I could pay you a decent salary to begin with and later a percentage of all of your sales. Eventually, you'd make a lot more working for me than you would with Luisa, and you'd get your dignity back. That has to be priceless." Harry stared Chas right in his beady little eyes.

Chas Greer couldn't believe what he was hearing. Could somebody be offering him a way out of the hell his life had become? He wanted to rush over and hug the shit out of Harry Raider, but he didn't dare. He knew that his power, and his position to negotiate, was dependent on keeping his cool. "Sounds very interesting, Harry, but I can't make any quick decisions off the cuff. Why don't you show me whatever it is you want me to read, and then give me some time to think it over?" Chas said slowly, as he walked over to the computer.

"With great pleasure," Harry replied, as he pointed at the screen. Thinking he was in control of the situation, Chas gave Harry a cocky "just you try to impress me" smile.

But even Chas was not ready for what the press release said and the gut-wrenching pictures that accompanied it. At first, he was naturally sad and disgusted at how low Luisa was willing to stoop to achieve success. For a man who spent his life manipulating others and kissing ass, even this was way over his limit of distastefulness.

And slowly, Chas remembered what it was like to go to work as his tennis-pro father's ball boy when he was only five years old—not that the lovely green courts of Pine Valley Country Club could compare with a run-down harsh Mexican sweatshop. Still, Chas vividly recalled thinking that it wasn't fair how he had to work while the spoiled rich kids, who teased him mercilessly, got to play all day. Finally, Chas couldn't help thinking about Juan. The beautiful cocoa-skinned children with their dark soulful eyes reminded him of the pictures Juan showed him. Chas knew that if Juan got a load what was going on, he'd insist Chas take action.

Chas suddenly realized that he missed Juan and their old life together, so much. They hadn't spoken in months, and Chas suspected that Juan had most likely moved on with his life and found another boyfriend. It was probably someone who was younger and richer, Chas figured. Juan was such an authentic sweetheart. There was no way he'd stay single for long. But deep in his heart, Chas harbored some hope of reconciliation. *If I help Harry show Luisa's sins to the world, and I go to work for him, may be I can bring Juan out here to live with me, if it's not too late,* Chas thought, as his eyes fixed on Harry's horrid pictures.

"So what do you say, Chas? Do we have a deal?" Harry asked, putting his hand on his old friend's shoulder.

"We certainly do, Harry. Watch this." Chas hit a few more buttons on the computer. In a matter of seconds, Harry's press release was magically sent to hundreds of influential reporters at newspapers, magazines, and television shows all across the world.

"You've done the right thing, man," Harry told him, shaking Chas's hand.

"So have you, Harry. I'm sorry I've been such a little shit to you. It's just that I've been under so much pressure and..."

"Say no more, Chas. If anyone knows what it's like to live under Luisa's rule and be at her beck and call, believe me, it's ME," Harry laughed.

"Well, not that I deserve it, but anyway, thanks for giving me a chance to start over," Chas acknowledged humbly.

"We all need that right now, Chas. Let's hope Jessica will give me the same."

"That's going to be a tough one, Harry," Chas sympathized.

"Yeah, I know, but I'm going to give it one hell of a try," Harry smiled as they walked out of the office to go about their business as usual, and silently wait for the shit to hit the fan.

chapter twenty-nine

One week later, Las Castillas was shining brightly and ready to show off to the world that it was indeed the jewel in Luisa Mendez's crown. An hour before the opening party, Chas worked extra hard and made sure the whole place looked spectacular so that Luisa wouldn't notice him fielding confirmation calls from reporters around the globe. Chas even convinced Luisa that it would be in her best interest to put up huge movie screens outside on the red carpet so that the pictures of the celebrities entering the soiree could be seem from every angle of the hotel. Naturally Luisa loved the idea.

Harry, too, did his best to be unusually attentive and loving to Luisa. Lucky for Harry, she was too tired and stressed out to have sex most of the week before the party, so he only had to satisfy her needs twice. Both times he closed his eyes and pretended it was Jessica. The night he had been waiting for had finally arrived and he felt an enormous wave of relief that he would never have to touch Luisa again.

The sommelier had just cracked open the first bottle of Dom Perignon when Luisa and Harry arrived at Las Castillas.

True to form, Chas had arrived early to make sure everything was perfect and the stage was set to bring Luisa to her knees. Luisa was overjoyed when she spotted all the reporters from CNN, *The Today Show, Good Morning America, The Early Show, 60 Minutes,* and some producers from *The Ellen DeGeneres Show.* Representatives from every major paper in the United States, Europe, Asia, and Latin America were camped outside the hotel gates.

The first to arrive, in a black limousine, was Luisa's father, Señor Oscar, who had flown up from Acapulco for his daughter's major event. Señor Oscar walked proudly past the media, who flashed pictures of him and rolled cameras in his startled face. Far from thrilled at the media attention for tonight's event, the clever old man knew right away that something was very wrong. "All this for my daughter's hotel?" Señor Oscar whispered to the aide who escorted him into hotel's elegant courtyard reception area.

"I am sure everything is fine, Señor. There will be many celebrities here tonight, that is why there is so much press. There is nothing to worry about," his aide said, reassuringly.

Luisa's eyes lit up at the sight of her father. She grabbed Harry, who was sipping a Coke by the bar, and began to push him through the gold French doors into the courtyard. "Harry, Papa has arrived. We must greet him at once! I can't wait to introduce to him to you. This is the most important night of my life," Luisa said excitedly, talking to herself and almost ignoring Harry. "Papa!" Luisa screamed with delight and rushed over to give the old man a hug and a kiss on each cheek.

"Luisa, it wonderful to see you after so many months. Las Castillas Beverly Hills is a wondrous triumph. It is the most beautiful hotel I have ever seen," Señor Oscar said, raising his hands while he viewed his stunning surroundings.

"Oh you haven't seen anything yet, Papa. Wait until after

the party when I can show you some of the royal suites I have designed. Kings and queens from all over the world will want to stay here, Papa, I promise!" Luisa spewed like a little girl wanting to please her father.

"I am sure you are right, Luisa. However, I more interested in being introduced to your future husband," Señor Oscar smiled as he nodded his head graciously at Harry.

"Of course, Papa. Señor Oscar Mendez, this is Harry Raider, the wonderful gentleman I've been telling you about all of these months. Harry is going to be my husband," Luisa beamed, as she took Harry's hand and practically shoved him in her father's face.

"Nice to meet you, sir," Harry forced himself to say as the two men shook hands.

"Yes, Harry, it's a pleasure to meet you as well. When do you plan to become officially engaged and set the date?" Señor Oscar inquired, inspecting every inch of Harry.

"Luisa has been so busy preparing everything for tonight, I didn't want to rush her," Harry answered confidently.

"I see. How considerate of you," Señor Oscar said, not buying one word of Harry's bullshit. "I am only in town for the weekend, so tomorrow morning I'd like to invite you both to breakfast. Then, I presume you will be ready to set the date, after tonight's success," Señor Oscar said, staring Harry right in the eyes.

"A success it will be! I'm sure of it," Harry smiled devilishly. He had kept himself under control all week. Harry could taste freedom, and he had bigger things on his mind than placating the old man. "If you'll excuse me, I see some friends walking in. Wouldn't want to be rude, now would I?" Harry shook Señor Oscar's hand and headed towards the entrance, where he spotted Jessica arriving on the arm of Billie Blaine.

"I don't trust him, Luisa. Is there something about Harry that you are not telling me?" Señor Oscar asked his daughter, who was quickly becoming distracted by the celebrity entourages and the elite Beverly Hills socialites who were starting to fill up the place.

"Oh, Papa, relax, Harry is wonderful. He is just excited about this party and nervous to meet you, of course. Let's have a good time tonight and we will discuss the wedding in the morning. You will see, Papa, I have found the perfect match." Luisa kissed her father on both cheeks and rushed past him to say hello to Michael Douglas and Catherine Zeta Jones. Luisa was flying high. She so was busy hobnobbing that she didn't notice Harry fighting through the merging crowd to get to Jessica.

"Hi, Jessica, great to see you! So glad you could make it. I didn't think you guys would come," Harry said, sliding up to Jessica.

"We weren't going to," Billie said flatly, obviously not happy to be in Harry's company.

"But I was curious," Jessica added, trying to mask her excitement at seeing Harry again.

"So, I gave in," Billie said, physically positioning herself between Harry and Jessica, who were looking at each other like the long-lost lovers they were. "Maybe we should get a drink. Where's the bar?" Billie asked, trying to divert Jessica's attention.

"Right this way. Can I show you ladies around?" Harry could not take his eyes off Jessica, who looked particularly beautiful in a cream-colored Stella McCartney dress that revealed her womanly gifts.

"My God, isn't that Will Smith talking with Jamie Foxx? With all these stars here, I'm sure you don't have time to hang around with peons like us, Harry. Don't you have some bigger ass to kiss?" Billie jibed.

"Not really," Harry said to his wife, looking right past Billie. "Luisa is the supreme suck-up this evening. I can pretty much get lost in the crowd and no one would notice. Frankly, there is no one that I'd rather be talking to right now than you, Jes. I've missed you so much."

"I've missed you too, Harry," Jessica echoed, smiling a little bit.

"Jessica, can I speak to you for a moment, alone?" Harry said, reaching for her hand.

"Sure. Billie, do you mind?" Jessica answered, respectfully deferring to the woman who had been her friend and support system during this turbulent time in her life.

Billie did mind, but she didn't know what to say. She could see the look in Jessica's eyes, and it made her furious. All she wanted to do was get away before she exploded. "Oh, what the hell, go ahead, Jessica," she said as she stomped away.

Harry held on to Jessica's hand and led her to a quiet bench in the hotel garden. From the spectacular vantage point, the two had a gorgeous view of the Pacific Ocean.

"You know, Jessica, this spot reminds me of your garden back in East Hampton," Harry said wistfully, as the two sat down.

"Yeah, except you couldn't see the ocean and there was no city light show," Jessica said, taking in her surroundings.

"Well, it was still the most beautiful place on Earth to me, because that is where we first made love," Harry said, nervously pawing the ground with his foot and making circles in the grass. "Jessica, when Harry Raider makes a mistake, he makes it big. The whole thing with Luisa, jeopardizing our marriage the way I did, was definitely the dumbest thing I've ever done. And that says a lot for a guy who's done so many dumb things. I don't know if you could ever forgive me and I know that I can never make up to you for what I've done, but if you could find it in your heart to give me one more chance..." Harry mumbled.

"I love Billie, Harry," Jessica said.

"You do?" Harry said, confused. *I thought her father said that she wasn't really a lesbian,* Harry thought, as he attempted to digest Jessica's response.

"Yes. I do. I love Billie very much. She was there for me when nobody else was and if it weren't for her love and support, I don't know what I would have done." Jessica was getting a little bit teary.

"I understand completely," Harry said, putting his arm around Jessica.

"I love Billie and I owe her everything," Jessica continued. Harry looked away from Jessica, dreading what might come out of her mouth next. "But I'm not in love with her." Jessica smiled through her tears.

"You're not! That's great! That's wonderful! Incredible!" Harry screamed with delight and high-fiving the air with his hands.

"YES!" an elated Harry laughed. He wanted to kiss Jessica passionately, but found the strength to restrain himself.

"I really tried to be in love with her, but I'm just not gay, as much as I wanted to be. Believe me, my life could be so easy if I could stay with Billie, but I just can't. It wouldn't be fair to her. But I don't want to hurt her, even though I'm afraid that I'm going to let her down. So I'd appreciate it if you'd let me talk to Billie first, before anything happens between you and me," Jessica said, forcing herself to pull away from her one true love.

"But of course. That would be the only respectable thing to do!" Harry said, beaming. "Jessica, does that mean there's hope for us?" Harry said softly, once again looking down at his shoes.

"I love you, Harry. I always have. I should have been

more supportive of your desire to rebuild Sam's business. I want you to know how proud I am of you that you were finally able to raise the money back east with Milly and David. Please know that I stand by your efforts 100 percent," Jessica said, looking at her husband with a newfound admiration.

Harry was floored. "How'd you know I went back to the Hamptons?" he asked.

"Oh, a little birdie named Penny Marks told me. As soon as you left her house, she called me immediately to report on the whole scenario. You know what a professional yenta she is," Jessica giggled.

"Thank God for that!" Harry smiled.

"She also told me how you stood up to my father. Wow, Harry, I'm impressed!" Jessica said, flirtatiously.

"Yeah, well it wasn't easy, but you're worth it, Jes," Harry said, moving closer to Jessica.

"Ahem... that's enough, mister. You've got a party to tend to, and I've got to find Billie. First things first, remember?" Jessica reminded him, swiftly rising from the bench and heading back into the party.

"Absolutely," Harry said, following along behind her.

★★★

As he made his way back into the now jam-packed courtyard, Harry was practically accosted by Luisa. "There you are, Harry! I've been looking all over for you. It's the height of the evening and I have to make my welcoming speech now. I want you right there with me as I address the crowd," Luisa insisted, as she dragged Harry up towards the makeshift podium.

"Great, Luisa, let's go for it," Harry said. The moment of truth had arrived and there was no turning back.

"Ladies and gentlemen, may I have your attention,"

Luisa spoke into the microphone, oozing fake charm, quieting the buzz to get everyone to focus on her.

"Ladies and gentlemen, PUH-LEASE," Luisa bellowed at the top of her lungs, having a very ugly diva-esque moment. The crowd was so shocked that a wall of silence fell upon them.

"Thank you so much," Luisa continued, returning to schmooze control and ignoring the shocked stares on her guests' faces. "I'd like to welcome you to the opening of Las Castillas, the most elegant hotel in the universe! For those of you who do not know me, I am Luisa Mendez. My grandfather, Papa Jacky, started the Las Castillas hotel chain in Mexico and my father, Señor Oscar, who is with us tonight, has grown it into the biggest hotel chain in Latin America. In Mexico especially, my family's name is synonymous with comfort, luxury, elegance, and glorious surroundings. We are committed to upholding the gold standard of excellence in everything we do," Luisa smiled, graciously.

While Luisa posed in front of her illustrious guests, Chas and Harry knew it was time to strike. Harry looked across the crowded courtyard to give Chas the signal, but Chas was one step ahead of him. Out of the corner of his eye, Harry saw Chas making his way over to the film crewman. Chas nodded his head, indicating to Harry that it was time to start the show. Harry furtively crossed his fingers in the air, kissed them, and stuck them behind his back. Chas whispered in the film crewman's ear and instructed him to start rolling the tape. *Okay, here we go. It's all over now, baby,* Harry thought.

Within seconds, a heart-wrenching slide show of the overworked and underfed children of Bolita, slaving away in Luisa's clothing factory, filled the giant movie screens that were ideally positioned behind her and all around the

Las Castillas property. Under each upsetting picture was this caption:

Meet the workers who help build the Mendez family fortune—children, taken from their homes and forced to work by corrupt police living on the Mendez payroll. Stop the Mendez family now by boycotting Las Castillas and Luisa's Niñas kids' clothes. Don't let the children of Bolita suffer any longer! Thank you.

Gasps of horror filled the courtyard as the socialites, celebrities, and their entourages searched for the nearest exit to make a run for it. Expressions of panic could be heard rumbling through the crowd:

"Holy shit, what's going on here?"

"Fuck, I think we've been caught in a set-up."

"Will someone PUH-LEASE get my limo ASAP!"

"Oh my gawd, I'm going to totally kill my publicist!"

All of the media that had been waiting patiently for this moment descended upon the bolting A-listers like vultures. Cameras flashed and reporters yelled out names, as they caught the unsuspecting stars running for their public lives to protect their images. No one wanted to be seen at this party and be linked to what was turning into the PR disaster of the century. Celebs weren't even waiting around for their drivers or cars to be brought to them. Pampered VIPs, normally chauffeured around Hollywood, grabbed their keys off the valet board and ran down Mulholland Drive, making a mad dash for their vehicle.

It took a few minutes of sheer chaos before Luisa caught what was going on. When she finally turned around to see the children's photos on the big screens, she let out a high-pitched, unearthly shrill, enough to shatter glass for miles around. "Who has done this? Who would do this to me? When I find out who is responsible I will have them killed!" Luisa declared like a lunatic. Instead of feeling shame and embarrassment, Luisa was one big bolt of rage, shaking the podium viciously with a wild, demonic look in her eyes.

Harry was hiding under a palm tree, laying low, while Chas, the master of this well-planned disaster, was gleefully talking to reporters about what it was like to work for Luisa, and how she paid off so many people to hush up about her awful secrets. He spared none of the gory details and tried to hide the fact that he was enjoying his tirade immensely.

A big smile came across Harry's face as he watched dramatic Chas in action. It brought back fond memories of their childhood friendship and all of the shenanigans they used to get into when they were in high school. *Chas Greer, you're a classic. Don't ever change, buddy,* Harry thought to himself, as the scene in the hotel was getting more and more chaotic. Before the hotel could fully empty out, the FBI arrived with the police and two immigration officers. They immediately handcuffed Luisa and her father Señor Oscar and read them their rights. Before Luisa had a chance to spew any more venom, she and her father were whisked away in a police car. Harry wondered what was going on. He approached Chas, and tapped him on the shoulder mid-interview with a reporter from CNN. "What's this about, Chas? Why are the police here? Why are they taking Luisa and her old man away?" a delighted Harry asked.

"Well, Harry, when I saw how far you were willing to go to uncover Luisa's children's-factory scam, I just couldn't let it go at that. While Luisa was preoccupied all week preparing for the tonight's party, I did some intense snooping of my own. First of all, I found out that all of her staff is working here illegally, so of course I called the INS. Just to add a flame to the fire," Chas said, smiling confidently.

"Chas, you're a fucking genius!" Harry gave his old friend a huge hug. "I love you, man, I really do," he said, giving Chas a kiss on the cheek.

"You're going to love me even more when you see this," Chas added, pointing over towards the now disheveled bar. There was Billie Blaine heartily making out with a cute, sexy girl who was definitely not Jessica. "That's Cindy Conner, star of a new reality show about power lesbians. I introduced her to Billie when you and Jessica were having your little talk. Honestly, I think Billie understood right from the get-go that it was never really meant to be with her and Jessica. You two are soul mates and I really hope you can work it out." Chas smiled sincerely at Harry, maybe for the first time in his lying, scheming life.

"Thanks, Chas, I hope so too. Hey, where is Jessica anyway? I hope she didn't get bowled over by all of the commotion."

"I've got your back, Raider, and I'm very proud of you," Jessica said, putting her arms around Harry's waist.

"Oh, there you are! I thought you might want to get the hell out of here with all of this craziness going on." Harry turned around and took Jessica in his arms.

"I'd love to blow this pop stand," Jessica said, smiling.

"That's it, baby. We're outta here!" a jubilant Harry said, and he picked Jessica up, tossed her over his shoulder, and carried her through the fleeing crowd to her blue Bentley.

★ ★ ★

Harry lovingly placed Jessica in the car, and jumped behind the wheel. "Where to, madame?" Harry asked, suggestively placing his hand on Jessica's knee.

"I'll go anywhere with you, Harry," Jessica answered, moving his hand up her skirt.

"How 'bout home?" Harry suggested.

They pulled up to their house within minutes. "I love you, Jessica Raider," Harry whispered into her ear.

"I love you too, Harry," Jessica said quietly as she twisted his chest hair in her fingers and snuggled up closer. After a few minutes of bonding and reconnecting as lovers, Harry and Jessica got out of the car and walked hand-in-hand into the house. Peace and love had been restored to the Raider household and God was once again smiling on Beverly Hills' golden couple.

chapter thirty

When morning came, Jessica, dressed only in a skimpy nightie and her tiny satin robe, came down to the breakfast table to find Irma very disturbed. She was holding a newspaper paper in one hand, and smearing a glob of chive cream cheese on a bagel with the other. **LES-BE-ON OUR WAY! JESSICA RAIDER'S POWER GIRL LOVES HER AND LEAVES HER. AGENT BILLIE BLAINE MOVES OUT OF RAIDER PALACE TO CHECK IN WITH NEW HOT REALITY-STAR HONEY** was splashed across the headlines of the *Beverly Hills Gazette*.

"What's wrong, Mom?" Jessica said, as she poured herself a glass of freshly squeezed California orange juice and sat down on her chair that faced the outside veranda by the pool.

"I absolutely hate this garbage, but I couldn't help reading it," Irma said, throwing down the newspaper and wiping a tear from her eye.

"What does it say, Mom?" Jessica said, trying not to laugh. She couldn't wait to tell Irma that she and Harry had reunited, but right now she was going to let her mother-in-law play out this scene. Jessica thought it would heighten Irma's surprise later to learn that Harry was moving back in.

"Billie's leaving you, dear. Apparently she met someone else at a party last night. Isn't that just awful?" Irma took a bite of her breakfast for comfort. "Oh, my sweet Jessica," she said sympathetically, reaching across the table for Jessica with her bagel-free hand in a show of support. "You've been through so much and now this. You must be devastated, darling. Feel free to cry openly or to come to me for a hug," Irma offered, still chewing. After washing her mouthful down with a gulp of hot Sanka, she finally put down her bagel and opened both arms to her daughter-in-law.

"That's very kind of you, Mom, but I'm not upset," Jessica said, sipping her juice.

"You're not?" Irma replied, stabbing her fork into a platter of lox and shoving it right into her mouth without skipping a beat.

"No, I'm actually I'm really happy for Billie. She's a wonderful girl and deserves a great partner, but that's just not me," Jessica said, quickly putting some lox, cream cheese, tomatoes, and onions on her plate before Irma devoured the whole thing.

"Are you kidding? I thought you were in love with her," Irma purred, pretending not to be relieved that her daughter-in-law wasn't really a lesbian.

"I was in love with the fact that somebody was there for me, and seemed to love me so much. At the time the gender of that person didn't seem to matter. However, you can't change who you are, and as much as I wanted to be with Billie, I'm just not gay." Jessica nonchalantly took the last bagel out of the breadbasket.

"Well, I'm thrilled to hear it. I mean I'm glad to hear that you're going to be okay," Irma said, catching herself and not wanting to appear politically incorrect. "So, do you think you're going to start dating men again?" Irma asked, once again fixating on the food on her plate.

"Why, are you planning to, Irma?" Jessica giggled.

"Don't be silly, sweetie, Sam Raider may have not been an angel, but he was the only man for me. May he rest in peace, Baruch Hashem. We were married almost fifty-three years. But you, Jessica, are a young, beautiful woman with your whole life ahead of you. You really should start dating again, honey," Irma said warmly.

"No, I'm through dating," Jessica said firmly, while building herself a lox sandwich.

"Jessica, you deserve a husband and children. You shouldn't live your life alone," Irma snuffled, as she looked out the sliding glass doors, wishing that Sam would walk in, smoking his cigar and carrying the paper under his arm.

"I agree with you completely, Irma, and believe me, I don't plan to be alone," Jessica said, munching on her bagel and lox.

"But you just said…" Irma mumbled.

"Hey, I hear a lot of chewing going on down here. I hope you left a bagel for me," Harry called, bounding into the breakfast room. He ran up to his startled mother, threw his arms around her, and gave her a big kiss on the cheek.

"Harry, my goodness, don't tell me that you guys made up?" Irma squealed with delight, happy to have her family living under one roof again.

"Yup! Let's just say I finally smartened up and realized that I can't live without the two most important girls in my life." Harry pulled out the chair next to Jessica and began kissing her passionately.

"It's a miracle! My children are back together and this time it better be for good," Irma kvelled, tears running down her cheeks.

"Don't worry, Mom. I'm not going to screw things up again, you can count on that," Harry said, handing his mother a napkin to wipe her eyes.

"You better not. I'm an old lady, Harry. I can't take any-more meshugas, you hear?" Irma warned him, clearing her throat and sipping her coffee for relief.

"It's really going to be fine this time, Mom." Harry lovingly rubbed Irma's shoulder to assure her of his newfound stability.

"Besides, Harry won't have any time for fun and games when the factory opens next week." Jessica smiled encouragingly at Harry.

"What?" Irma coughed, choking on the coffee that went down the wrong way.

"Harry went back east and raised the money to reopen Sam's factory, and I have full faith that he's going to make it a huge success. We can expect big things from our boy, Irma. He's one of a kind," Jessica said, beaming at Harry.

"You don't say," Irma replied coyly, sticking her knife back into the cream cheese. The three Raiders continued eating their breakfast and talking over Harry's plans for the business. She didn't say a word, but Irma deeply wished that Sam could have been there to see Harry become the man they always wanted him to be. Although Irma knew that Sam had left this earth, she thought that she could feel his presence at the breakfast table that morning.

With Irma off to Rodeo Drive for a celebratory and long overdue shopping spree courtesy of her daughter-in-law, Jessica and Harry spent the rest of the day relaxing by the pool and making love as much as their bodies would allow. By evening they were both physically exhausted. After a candlelit dinner and a slow dance on the patio, Harry and Jessica went to bed early and blissfully collapsed into each other's arms.

When morning came, Harry popped up in bed and looked around. Practically hugging his pillow, Harry was delighted to be in bed with his wife and to be back for good in his loving home. Yet with his extreme happiness came an unfamiliar sense of dread. After his trip to Luisa's child labor factory in Mexico, Harry had grown to appreciate his own fortunate luxuries much more. Now as he lay comfortably in Jessica's beautiful bed, surrounded by Irma's exquisite interior design, Harry wondered what would happen to the children of Bolita now that the factory would be closed down.

I hope the kids' parents will be able to feed them now without that extra money coming in. I wonder what is going to happen to Javier. Where is he going to work now that there is no more factory? At least he is twenty, but still he's just a kid, really. He'll need help too. I've gotta do something to help him, especially since he was the one who helped me expose Luisa, Harry thought.

"You're up early. My, you look preoccupied. What's going on, Harry?" a sleepy Jessica asked as she rolled over and woke up to see the pensive look on her husband's face.

"I've got unfinished business, Jessica," Harry told her, fumbling with the yellow and blue Pratesi sheets.

"With Luisa? I thought that was all over."

"It is waaaaaay over, honey. Luisa's not my problem, but the kids are," Harry said.

"What kids?" Jessica asked curiously, *Oh boy, I hope he didn't get Luisa pregnant,* Jessica thought.

"The children of Bolita, from the factory. I have to know that they are going to be all right. Otherwise this whole thing wasn't entirely worth it," Harry said, taking Jessica's hand. *Thank goodness!* Jessica thought and smiled warmly.

Harry then reached over to the nightstand for the phone and dialed Chas's cell-phone number. *He stayed and talked to all of those reporters. If anyone knows what's happening now, Chas will,* Harry thought.

"Harry! I thought I'd never hear from you. I left a million messages on your cell phone. Where are you?" Chas asked, in his usual dramatic manner.

"I'm back home with Jessica," Harry replied.

"I thought as much. Isn't it like you to pull off the biggest PR stunt of the century, then leave the scene of the crime to go get laid? You dirty dog!" Chas chuckled wickedly.

"Yeah, well some things never change, buddy. So what happened? Did any of those television reporters run the story?" Harry asked.

"Harry, are you kidding? Has Jessica disconnected all of the televisions in the house? I mean, really, this is the biggest story to hit the airwaves since Michael Jackson got acquitted. It's been on every station both locally and nationally! For heaven's sake, Harry, turn on the tube!" Chas whined.

"You got it, man!" Harry said excitedly and turned on the television. True to his word, what Chas had said was now playing out before Harry's eyes. With the remote, Harry flipped through the channels to see no end to the news coverage of Luisa being hauled off to jail and the celebrities fleeing the party. Most important, Harry saw the factory in Mexico shut down by government workers and the children safely escorted back to their homes. Best of all were the shots of volunteers from several international human-rights groups feeding the children, giving them toys, blankets, and new clothes, and comforting their families. Some of the high-profile stars who had been seen at Luisa's party and who were terrified to be linked to her scandal had their people quickly establish a fund to help the families of Bolita get back on their feet. As the news coverage continued, millions of dollars poured in from the Hollywood celebs as well as donations from their fans around the country.

Harry was so amazed by all of the good that had come of his plan that he called Chas right back. "This is awesome, Chas! Thanks for helping me make it happen."

"For you, Harry, anything. See you at work next week, Boss," Chas yelled.

Harry could barely hear him. "Hey, Chas, what's all that noise in the background, man? Sounds like a storm is ragin' wherever you are," he asked.

"That's the glorious sound of airplanes landing. I'm at LAX and I'm picking up Juan. He's moving into my new apartment in West Hollywood," Chas said, as he pulled his newly purchased, used 1986 Beemer convertible into the airport parking lot. Gone was the opulent penthouse, the Rolls Royce with Rocky, the naughty chauffeur, and the rest of Luisa's luxuries that had cost Chas his dignity. Like his new boss Harry, Chas would be starting from scratch, but this time he had a real shot at building a solid future for himself, with his self-respect intact.

"Good for you, man, I know you guys are going to be really happy," Harry said, twirling the phone cord around his fingers and winking at Jessica.

"Me too, Harry, me too. Ciao, baby!" Harry hung up and flung his arms around his wife.

"Harry, you've done a marvelous thing for those kids. You should be very proud of yourself," Jessica said, pinching Harry playfully.

"Thanks, Jes," Harry replied wistfully, the smile on his face blank. Even with all the good news, something still seemed to be bothering him.

"What is it, Harry?" Jessica asked, searching his eyes for an answer.

"It's that kid, Jes. Javier. I just can't help wondering

what's going to happen to him. All the other kids in the factory were really young, so they can go to school and start their lives over. But that place was all Javier has ever known. I don't even know if he has any family. How is he going to take care of himself?" a concerned Harry said.

"I'm sure he's a smart young man. He'll find his way. He'll probably get a job doing something else," Jessica said encouragingly.

"Like what?" Harry asked, unable to let go of the memories of the young boy who helped them make a miracle occur south of the border.

"I don't know, Harry. Something," was all Jessica could say.

"Something isn't good enough for that kid. After what he did for me, I can't leave him on his own. I have to help him," Harry said, defiantly.

"How?" Jessica asked, confused.

"I'm not sure yet, but there has to be something I can do for him," Harry said.

"Well, I guess that means you have to find him first." Jessica admired her husband's compassion for this total stranger.

"You're exactly right. I think we should go to Mexico and find that kid," Harry said excitedly, getting out of bed and rapidly beginning to get dressed.

"When?" Jessica asked, happy to join her husband's project.

"How about right now? Whadda say, Jes? Let's go to Bolita!" Harry shouted, wrapping Jessica in a hug.

★ ★ ★

When Harry and Jessica finally reached the dusty, sun-baked Bolita, Harry noticed right away that much had changed drastically since his last visit. There was the obvious presence of the Red Cross and other relief workers from international human rights groups, who were on the streets passing out food, supplies, and information pamphlets to groups of children and their families. Then there was Luisa's factory, now boarded up, with government guards stationed in front. Harry could now see with his own eyes what a difference he had made in this small town. There were laughing children playing, running around freely, and eating decent meals. Most important, when Harry and Jessica parked their car and began to walk around, they sensed an air of hope in this little town, once a place filled with fear and despair.

"It's amazing what you've done here, Harry," Jessica congratulated Harry, as she proudly rubbed his shoulders.

"It wasn't all me. Chas helped too, and the media was awesome," Harry said modestly, as he picked up a ball and threw it back to a group of boys who had let it get away.

"Yeah, but you started the whole thing, Harry. If it weren't for you, none of this would have happened," Jessica smiled.

"Yeah, I guess so," Harry said nonchalantly.

"Hey, any of you boys know where I can find Javier?" The boys looked at each other and shrugged their shoulders. It was clear that none of them understood English.

"Javier? *El jefe?* Javier?" Harry asked, remembering from his fourth-grade Spanish class that *jefe* was the Spanish word for boss.

"Ah, *sí*, Javier!" one of the boys laughed, happy that he could understand the gringo in his midst. "Javier," the young boy said, pointing to a dilapidated shack just east of where they were playing.

"Thanks, guys. *Gracias!*" Harry said, waving at the group. He took Jessica's hand and rushed over. Harry knocked on the door, but after a few tries got no answer. "Do you think I should just go in there?" Harry said with fierce determination as he peeked through the dusty window.

"Go ahead, Harry, he sounds like the kind of boy who would understand," Jessica smirked, as she gently pushed the front door open.

"I guess you're right," Harry said, walking right in.

The one-room shack was empty except for a makeshift bed of cardboard boxes and some rumpled blankets on the cracked, wooden floor. Next to the bed was an old green sack stuffed with some clothes and Javier's few belongings. Carefully, Harry knelt down on the floor, opened the knapsack and began to go through Javier's things, hoping to find a clue as to what happened to his young friend. Harry pulled out some tattered socks, underwear, a pair of jeans, and faded T-shirts. As he reached into the bottom, his hands felt something that was made of metal and glass.

Emptying the whole knapsack onto the floor, Harry found a beat-up old frame with a picture of Javier as a baby in the arms of a woman. She looked like someone he had seen before.

"Do you think I was a cute baby?" Javier said, laughing, standing over his friendly intruder with his hands on hips, pretending to be upset.

"Adorable," Harry said with a guilty look on his face. All the blood was rushing out of head as he tried to steady himself, fearing that he might faint.

"Who is the woman in the picture with you? Is that your sister?" Jessica asked, taking the picture from Harry's hand.

"That's my mother," Javier said proudly, with a hint of sadness in his voice.

"My gosh, she looks so young. How old was she when we had you?" Jessica wondered, studying the picture more closely.

"Eighteen," Harry said in a wobbly, meek voice. Jessica

and Javier both turned to look at Harry, who now sat on the floor with his legs crossed, like a scared kid.

"How do you know my mother?" Javier asked.

"Her name is Consuela. She was our housekeeper when I was a teenager. After my parents found out about us, they sent her back to Mexico. I thought she had an abortion," Harry admitted, holding his head in his hands.

"Are you kidding? My mother would never do something like that," Javier said, fighting back tears.

"Where is she now?" Jessica asked, petrified of the Pandora's box from Harry's past that had just been pried open.

"She died a couple of years ago. I really miss her," Javier said, looking out the window, not being able to face Harry.

"I bet you do. Harry, I think you owe Javier a huge apology," Jessica said, sweetly putting her arm around the young man.

"Jessica is absolutely right. I am so sorry. I was young and stupid and selfish. I wouldn't blame you if you hate me," Harry told Javier, nervously rocking back and forth.

"I don't hate you, Harry, but I wish you would have given my mother a chance, that's all," Javier said.

"Believe me, I wish I could have. Consuela was wonderful. She was the most important person in my life when I was growing up. My parents were always too busy for me, but Consuela always made time for me. That's why I grew so close to her. I completely adored her and more importantly, I trusted her. That's why I was completely devastated after she left, but my parents said I'd eventually get over it. I'm so sorry about all this. I guess you will never be able to forgive me," Harry said sheepishly.

"I can forgive you, Harry. You were a kid back then and you didn't know what to do. Your parents were just trying to protect you and keep you out of trouble. I'm sure my mother would have done the same for me if I were in your position," Javier offered, staring down at Harry Raider, his biological father.

"Thanks for understanding, but that still doesn't make me feel any better," Harry said, unable to look Javier in the eye.

"Javier, you are a very mature young man. I think you and Harry have a lot to work out, so if you'll excuse me, I'll be waiting in the car." Jessica gave Javier a kiss on the cheek and walked out of his ramshackle home.

"Look, I know I can't make up for the past, but I just want you to know that Jessica and I came down here to make sure you were all right and that nothing bad happened to you," Harry said, finally finding the courage to face his son.

"I really appreciate that, Harry, and everything else you did for the children of Bolita," Javier said smiling. He bent down and held out his hand to Harry to help him stand up. Soon the two men were face to face, curiously studying each other's characteristics and physical attributes.

"You're a lot taller than I ever was," Harry said, giggling.

"I got that from my mother's side. Thank goodness! You're a shrimp," Javier laughed.

"Yeah, but when I stand on my wife's money, believe me, I'm a lot taller," Harry joked. Now that the initial shock of discovering the truth was wearing off, Javier and Harry could once again enjoy each other's company.

"You're a wild guy, you know that?" Javier said, while he began to put his clothes into his knapsack.

"I've been told that," Harry said. "So, what are you going to do now?"

"I'm going to Mexico City. I have a cousin there who works at a fancy restaurant. He said that he can get me a job parking cars."

"Oh man, you shouldn't be doing that. You've got too much experience, talent, and smarts," Harry said.

"You got a better idea?" Javier asked, hopefully. Harry's heart was racing faster than his head. He wanted so much to do something for Javier to make up for the lifetime of suffering the boy endured while he himself had enjoyed the good life in Beverly Hills. Harry reached into his wallet and pulled out a wad of hundred-dollar bills and wrote his number on an old valet stub he had from a dinner at Spago. "Here, take this. When you get to Mexico City, call me. Maybe there is something I can do to help you out," Harry said. Reluctantly, Javier took the money from Harry and stared at it like he had just robbed a bank.

"Wow. This is more money than I could ever need. Thank you, Harry." Javier put the money in his knapsack and gave Harry a huge hug. Harry trembled but leaned into the boy's heartfelt embrace. The power of it was almost too much for him. As much as he wanted to stay longer, Harry released Javier and left without saying a word.

Outside Javier's house, Harry jumped in the car where Jessica was waiting patiently. "Is everything okay, Harry?" she asked, looking curiously at Harry.

"Yup, fine. Javier is going to Mexico City. I told him to call us when he gets down there and maybe there is some-way we can help him out," Harry said uncomfortably, not entirely happy about how he was leaving the whole situation.

"Oh," Jessica said, shaking her head and looking confused.

"What's wrong, Jes? Don't you think that's a good idea?" Harry asked.

"I guess it is, but I was just thinking…Well, I just assumed that once you found out that Javier was your son, that naturally he'd be coming home to live with us," Jessica said.

"Do you mean that, Jes? You'd really let him do that?" Harry exclaimed, practically jumping out of his seat.

"Of course, Harry. He's your son, isn't he? And you know I've always wanted a child. So, I don't have a baby, so what? At least with Javier around I'll have a chance to be a real mother to your boy. I can't think of anything better than that," Jessica said, taking Harry's hand.

"Jessica Raider, you are the most spectacular human being in the whole universe!" Harry covered his wife's face with kisses.

"Well, you better go get him before he leaves. You can show me how much you love me later," Jessica said, winking.

★★★

Harry, Jessica, and Javier drove across Mexico and spent a few glorious weeks at a posh hotel in Acapulco. During that time, Harry contacted Chas and had him call in a few major favors with the Mexican government. Because Javier was Harry's biological son, Harry and Jessica were able to adopt him legally and get all the paperwork done very quickly. Soon enough, the new happy family was back in Beverly Hills.

The next few months at the Raider home were all about solidifying love, seeking forgiveness, and making new beginnings. Irma Raider got the surprise of her life when Harry and Jessica appeared with the grandson she never knew she had. Immediately ridden with enough guilt to satisfy a retirement village full of Jewish grandmas, Irma did everything she could to welcome Javier into the family. After repeatedly apologizing for sending away his mother so many years ago, Irma showed her love for Javier the only way she knew how. She shopped. Soon the young boy from Mexico was a VIP at every elite men's store on Beverly Hills' swank Rodeo Drive. Javier now had a personal shopper who arrived each day at the Raider home with bags of clothes from Ralph Lauren, Gucci, Armani, and Brooks Brothers, and shoes from Ferragamo and Bruno Magli to match every outfit. Nothing was too good for Irma Raider's grandson and she wanted to let the world know it.

When she wasn't busy with Javier's new wardrobe, Irma was helping Jessica redecorate one of the guest rooms, turning it into a room full of sports posters, computers, a stereo, and every other gadget a Beverly Hills prince living in the twenty-first century required.

Javier was completely blown away and indeed very grateful for his good fortune. But despite all the elaborate gifts and brand-new lavish lifestyle, what he treasured most was the time he was given to get to know Harry. The two boys would spend hours playing video games, hanging out by the pool, going to the boardwalk on the Santa Monica Pier, and going surfing at the beach. Harry was determined to be there for Javier. Neither Javier nor Harry had ever known such contentment and happiness before they developed the unbreakable bond that can only exist between father and son.

★ ★ ★

Quite soon there after, Milly Harrington Cohen delivered on her promise. Her moneymen were ready to help Harry get into business and open his factory doors. After many planning and strategy meetings, it was time for Harry to go to work.

Excited to venture into unchartered territory, Harry got out of bed early without waking Jessica that first morning of the workweek. Jessica slept soundly, enjoying the deep level of rest that only comes after making love into the wee hours of the morning. Harry energetically bounded down the stairs and flew into the breakfast room. He downed his bagel as fast as he could and made his way to the front door, excited for his first official day at work.

"Aren't you forgetting something?" said a voice from the top of the staircase. Standing there like a top junior executive in his tan Ralph Lauren suit, Burberry tie, and classic Gucci loafers, Javier had a firm hold on his Hermès briefcase.

"Wow, you look great, kiddo. Where are you going?" Harry asked, still amazed at Javier's transformation.

"With you, Harry," Javier smiled, as he made his way down the stairs.

"Don't be silly, kid. You don't want to go to work. You've worked enough in your young life. You should be enjoying the summer before we enroll you in school in the fall," Harry said, summoning his new paternal instincts.

"Come on, Harry, you've never worked in a kids' clothing factory, or anywhere else for that matter. I've done this practically all of my life. You could use my expertise. Besides, I really want to help out, especially after all you've done for me," Javier said, now standing face to face with Harry.

"Hey, you don't owe me anything, kiddo, let's get that straight. I brought you here because I love you," Harry said.

"I love you too, Harry, that's why I want to help you. Besides, it wouldn't hurt me to work summers at your factory. That way, when I get out of college and grad school, and you're an old man who wants to retire, I can take over the whole business!"

"Now you're thinking like a Raider. I guess I can't say no to that," Harry chuckled, proud of his son's ambition. Javier opened the front door, and the two men walked arm in arm towards Javier's new navy-blue BMW, a gift from Jessica's father.

"Please let me drive you today, Harry. You've got too

much on your mind to focus on the traffic," Javier said, escorting Harry to the passenger seat.

"I think I'm going to like having you around. You're a smart kid, you know that?" Harry said, as Javier got behind the wheel.

After a typically busy morning commute on the 101 Freeway, Harry and Javier arrived at the factory in the little town of Pasito. Harry was thrilled to see the parking lot filling up with the cars of the loyal workers he was able to rehire when Milly's money came through. Sam's old factory was once again alive with the buzz of people working and building their future. Overwhelmed with gratitude, Harry sat in the car with Javier for a minute to watch the whole scene.

"Don't worry, Harry, it's all going to work out fine, you'll see," a confident Javier said, feeling his father's nervous energy.

"I know. It's just a lot to take in at once. I don't know what's scarier, having a big dream or seeing that dream come true," Harry confessed with his heart in his throat.

"I bet once we get going, it won't be that scary at all. You're a natural salesman, Harry; no one can resist your charm. You'll schmooze orders out of every buyer from here to New York." Javier patted Harry on the back.

"I hope you're right. You know what? I'm really glad I have you with me." Harry smiled at Javier.

"Yeah, me too. Hey, have you thought about what you are going to call your new business?" Javier asked curiously.

"Gee, I hadn't really thought about it much. But hey, I got an idea. How about K.I.D.S STUFF by Raider and Son?" Harry said, winking at Javier.

"Sounds great to me, Dad. I mean, Harry," Javier replied, catching himself. He had never called Harry "Dad" before.

"Dad is just fine with me, kiddo. Just fine," Harry told his son, as he and Javier got out of the car and headed into the factory, ready to face the task that lay in front of them.

Later on that evening, after a very successful first day at the factory, Javier, Jessica, Harry, and Irma celebrated with a wonderful meal prepared by the new chef and served on the patio by the pool. It was a particularly warm night, so dining al fresco seemed like a wonderful choice. While Harry and Javier entertained Jessica and Irma with amusing stories from the day's events, Harry noticed that Jessica hadn't touched her glass of champagne. "What's wrong, sweetie? Passing up a great glass of Dom isn't like you. Isn't your bubbly bubbly enough?" Harry asked her, sticking his finger in Jessica's glass and twirling it around to stir up the fizz.

"It looks terrific, but I think I'll be laying off the champers and all alcohol for a while," Jessica said, smiling devilishly.

"Oh, I don't blame you. Too much booze makes me break out in hives. You've been looking a little flushed lately, you better lay off," Irma interjected, and picked up Jessica's champagne flute to down it in one big gulp.

"I don't have hives, Irma, but I still shouldn't be drinking," Jessica said, like she was enjoying an inside joke and hiding a big secret.

"*Ay caramba!* Am I expecting a brother or a sister?" Javier asked, lovingly patting Jessica's stomach.

"Actually, Javier, you could be expecting *both!*" Jessica burst out. "I went to the doctor today and he said that not only am I pregnant, but I'm having twins!" Jessica exclaimed, with a joy in her voice that Harry had never heard before.

Irma and Javier shared a delighted smile, while Harry's eyes lit up like firecrackers on the Fourth of July. "That's incredible, honey! I can't believe it. I'm going to be a dad again!" Harry leaned over to give Jessica a big hug and kiss.

"I'd like to propose a toast. To the birth of Raider and Son, soon to be Raider and Sons, and maybe even Raider and Sons and a Daughter! We miss you, Sammy, but life is wonderful! Baruch Hashem!" Harry raised his glass to the heavens, hoping that wherever Sam Raider was, he could share his son's good mazel today.

And from then on, life was not always perfect, but it was most definitely happier, as new challenges were met with love and support. And yet again, Harry's happiness was like a magic wand that reached out far and wide. There was happiness for all the children of Bolita, the factory workers of Pasito who Harry reemployed, for Chas and Juan who were reunited, and most of all, for Harry and the loving family he had created. Like the summer before in the Hamptons, by the simple gift of his love and charm, Harry Raider had changed the lives of the souls who were drawn into his wild and fiercely free path of wonderment. And nothing would ever be the same, since Harry hit Hollywood.

acknowledgments

Thank you to the brilliant editor Peter Lynch and the fearless entrepreneur Dominique Raccah for once again taking a chance on Mara and "Harry."

Thank you to my husband, Justin Davies, and my princess, Halle, for giving me a reason to write books.

Thank you to my mom, Roni, and my in-laws Adele and Mike and "Aunti Meryl" for their constant support.

A big thank you to Diane and Gill Glazer for their generosity, love, and support.

A big thank you to Bob MC Cabe and Charles Cartwright and everyone at Smith Barney for the wonderful cocktail party.

Thank you to Maria Cassidy and the ENTIRE Cassidy family for their friendship and support.

Thank you to Sy Presten for working miracles.

Thank you to Stacy Bereda and the Bereda family for their friendship and support.

Thank you to Cheryl Kramer for going to bat for me a million times.

Thank you to Shannon Donnelly at the *Palm Beach Daily News* for remembering her "hometown kid."

A HUGE thank you to Melanie Mannarino, Rebecca Davis, Ellis Hanican, Laura Savini, Susan Ellingsworth,

Llyod Grove, Page Six, Rush and Malloy, and everyone else who had fun covering Harry last summer.

Thank you to Katelyn O'Connell and family, Susan Zeitlan, Pam Mathe, Beth Dudan, Joelle Bova, Suzi Mareel, Mary Francis Turner, and Carolyn Noone for many years of friendship and support

Thank you to everyone at Borders Books and to all who attended the Smith Barney cocktail party for understanding why I couldn't be there and for still speaking to me.

Thank you to "Nanny" Carmela Smith, who looks after Halle while Mommy writes books.

about the author

Mara Goodman-Davies is a former stand-up comedienne turned international public relations/media placement consultant. She is the author of *When Harry Hit the Hamptons,* and is often quoted in *Redbook, Cosmopolitan,* and others. Mara splits her time between New York, the Berkshires, and her hometown of Palm Beach, Florida.